PRAISE FOR *IN THE BLEAK MIDWINTER*

"Terrific action scenes . . . what really distinguishes *In the Bleak Midwinter*, however, is the author's skillful portrayal of her protagonist's inner conflict." —*The Washington Post Book World*

"One of the most impressive 'first' crime novels I've read. A priest, a cop, a baby on the doorstep, and a lot of snow combined with suspenseful results for one great book." —Charlaine Harris, *New York Times* bestselling author of the Sookie Stackhouse series

"Atmospheric . . . [A] freshly conceived and meticulously plotted whodunit." —*The New York Times Book Review*

PRAISE FOR *A FOUNTAIN FILLED WITH BLOOD*

"Spencer-Fleming's second cozy-cum-thriller . . . is every bit as riveting as her first . . . with eloquent exposition and natural dialogue, the precisely constructed plot moves effortlessly to its dramatic conclusion." —*Publishers Weekly* (starred review)

"The plot is complicated, and the ethical issues are even thornier. Wisely, Spencer-Fleming treats them with the same delicacy she extends to Clare's forbidden love." —*The New York Times Book Review*

PRAISE FOR *OUT OF THE DEEP I CRY*

"The third and most densely textured mystery in a series by Julia Spencer-Fleming that brings new airs and graces to the traditional small-town mystery . . . [Y]es, this is a very small town, but under Spencer-Fleming's grave and tender touch it becomes a world that you want to visit and hate to leave." —*The New York Times Book Review*

"Triumphant . . . The author expertly portrays the power of grief, guilt, greed, and love, and their effect on good people in a story as chilling as the month of March in Millers Kill. A subtle sense of humor further enhances this poignant and provocative mystery."

—*Publishers Weekly* (starred review)

"This is the author's best story yet . . . presented with the flair and polish of the finest artisan. . . . The ending is enough to make the hardest heart melt."

—*Chicago Sun-Times*

PRAISE FOR *TO DARKNESS AND TO DEATH*

"Clare Fergusson and Russ Van Alstyne make a fresh and unusual detective partnership, and I always welcome Clare's impetuous but wise take on the world around her."

—Sara Paretsky, *New York Times* bestselling author of the V. I. Warshawski novels

"The friendship of these solid, down-to-earth characters moves closer to romance, and the intrigue continues to build, revealing a riveting, well-plotted criminal adventure."

—*RT Book Reviews* (starred review)

PRAISE FOR *ALL MORTAL FLESH*

"The best yet in an already amazing series."

—Lee Child, *New York Times* bestselling author

"Spencer-Fleming does it again! Taut prose, brilliant pacing, and two of the most interesting characters around make *All Mortal Flesh* all the mystery you could desire."

—Lisa Gardner, *New York Times* bestselling author

"[A] dizzying roller coaster of a ride, with one wholly unexpected plot twist after another following in rapid succession. And just when things seem sorted out at last, the author has one last surprise in store for the reader, one that raises all sorts of questions about where the series is headed."

—*The Denver Post*

OUT OF THE
DEEP I CRY

~

JULIA SPENCER-FLEMING

MINOTAUR BOOKS

A THOMAS DUNNE BOOK

NEW YORK

This is a work of fiction. All of the characters, organizations, and events portrayed in this novel are either products of the author's imagination or are used fictitiously.

A THOMAS DUNNE BOOK FOR MINOTAUR BOOKS.
An imprint of St. Martin's Publishing Group.

www.thomasdunnebooks.com
www.minotaurbooks.com

The Library of Congress has cataloged the hardcover edition as follows:

Spencer-Fleming, Julia.
    Out of the deep I cry / Julia Spencer-Fleming.—1st ed.
        p. cm.
    ISBN 978-0-312-31262-6
    1. Fergusson, Clare (Fictitious character)—Fiction.   2. Van Alstyne, Russ
(Fictitious character)—Fiction.   3. Physicians—Crimes against—Fiction.
    4. Adirondack Mountains (N.Y.)—Fiction.   5. Episcopal Church—Clergy—
Fiction.   6. New York (State)—Fiction.   7. Police chiefs—Fiction.
    8. Women clergy—Fiction.   I. Title.

PS3619.P645O97   2004
813'.6—dc22

                                                                                      2003058699

ISBN 978-1-250-01604-1 (trade paperback)
ISBN 978-1-4299-0907-5 (e-book)

First Minotaur Books Paperback Edition: October 2012

To Lois Greuling Fleming

You may have tangible wealth untold;
Caskets of jewels and coffers of gold,
Richer than I you can never be—
I had a Mother who read to me.

—STRICKLAND GILLIAN

ACKNOWLEDGMENTS

Getting a book out is like running a political campaign: One person may be in the spotlight, but it took the efforts of many to get her there. With that in mind, I'd like to thank everyone at St. Martin's Press, especially my editor, Ruth Cavin, the hardworking Rachel Ekstrom, and the sales reps who log so many miles in their cars selling my books.

Thanks also to my agent, the "brilliant and handsome"™ Jimmy Vines, and to Ross Hugo-Vidal, the greatest "husband-of-author" in history.

The Crandall Library of Glens Falls, the Nurse-Practitioner Association of New York, Timothy LaMar, and Roxanne Eflin provided expert assistance; Laura Rayfield and Norm Madsen allowed me to use their names; I thank you all.

Thanks to my parents, John and Lois Fleming, whose comments made this a better book, and to Mary and Bob Weyer, whose help keeps my family from imploding.

Susan and Peter Heldman, Tim and Margie Grein, Evonne, Daniel and Michelle McNabb gave me shelter in my travels. Thank you.

Tack vare allt, min reslig man. Jag saknar dig, min älsking.

Out of the deep I call
To Thee, O Lord, to thee.
Before Thy throne of grace I fall;
Be merciful to me.

Out of the deep I cry,
The woeful deep of sin,
Of evil done in days gone by,
Of evil now within;

Out of the deep of fear
And dread of coming shame;
All night till morning watch is near
I plead the precious name.

Lord, there is mercy now,
As ever was, with Thee.
Before Thy throne of grace I bow;
Be merciful to me.

—HENRY W. BAKER, *The Handbook to the Lutheran Hymnal*

(St. Louis: Concordia Publishing House, 1942)

OUT OF THE DEEP I CRY

CHAPTER I

THEN

FRIDAY, JUNE 26, 1970

Russ Van Alstyne had just gotten a tug on his line when he saw the old lady get up from between the headstones she had been trimming, lay down her gardening tools, and walk into the reservoir. She had been tidying up a tiny plot, four moldering grave markers tucked under the towering black pines, so close to the edge of Stewart's Pond Reservoir that a good motorboat wake could have kicked spray over the stones. She had appeared at some point after he and Shaun had launched their rowboat, and he had noted her, now and then, while they had drifted in the sunshine.

They had been fishing a couple hours already, enjoying the hot weather, and some brews, and some primo grass Shaun's older brother had scored down to Albany, but Russ had only landed a few sunnies, crap fish he threw back as soon as he had them off the hook.

So when his six-pound test tightened like a piano wire and his bobber disappeared beneath the water, he sat up, excited. He knew he had something good. Maybe a trout. He had just stowed his can of Pabst Blue Ribbon in the bottom of the boat and flicked off his safety to let the fish run some more line when he noticed the old woman. She had on a loose print dress, like one of the housecoats his mom had had forever, and it rose around her legs as she waded slowly away from the shore.

"Shaun, check this out," he said, uncertain that he was reading the situation right. "What's it look like that old lady's doing?"

Shaun turned his head, swinging his graduation tassel, which he had attached to his fishing hat. He twisted his upper body around for a better view. "Swimming?"

"In a dress?"

"Works for me, man. I don't want to see her in a swimsuit." Shaun turned back, facing away from the sight of the old woman marching into the water. His line jerked. "I got a strike!" He unlocked his reel and played out his line. "Relax, I've run the boat over that way before. The bottom slopes out a long ways."

She was up to her chest now, moving steadily forward, not stroking with her arms or ducking under the surface like people do when taking a dip. "She's not swimming," Russ said. "She's not even trying." He looked past her, to where a patchy trail led from the little cemetery, through the trees, and eventually up to the county road. There wasn't anyone there to keep an eye on her. She was alone. He thrust his rod at Shaun and tugged off his sneakers. He could reach her faster swimming than he could rowing. He stood up, violently pitching the little boat.

"Hey! Are you crazy? You're gonna swamp us!" Shaun twisted on his seat in time to see the old woman's chin sliding into the water. "Oh, shit," he said.

Russ shoved his jeans down and kicked them off, knocking over both their beers in the process. He balanced one foot on the hull's edge and launched himself into the water.

Even in mid-June the reservoir was cold, still gorged on the icy spring runoff from the Adirondacks. His whole body flinched inward, but he struck out for the shore: long, hard strokes through the water, his face dipping rhythmically in, out, in; sacrificing his view of her for the speed. He drew up to where the shadow of the somber pines split the water into light and dark. He treaded water, spinning around, looking for a sign of her. She had vanished.

"She went there!" Shaun yelled. He was struggling to get the rowboat turned around. "There, a couple yards to your left!"

Russ took a deep breath and submerged. In the deep twilight of the water, he could just see her, a pale wraith flickering at the edge of his vision. As he arrowed toward her, she emerged from the gloom like a photograph being developed. She was still walking downward, that was what was so creepy, toes brushing against the coarse-grained bottom, flowered dress billowing, white hair floating. She was still walking downward like a drowned ghost, and then, as if she could hear the pounding of his heart, she turned and looked at him, open-eyed under the water. Her eyes were black, set in a white, withered face. It was like having a dead woman stare at him.

He was an easy swimmer, confident in the water, but at her look, he panicked. He opened his mouth, lost his air, and struck up wildly for the surface, thrashing, kicking. He emerged choking and spluttering, hacking and gulping air. Shaun was rowing toward him, still a couple dozen yards away, and he knelt up on the bench when he saw Russ. "Can you find her?" he shouted. "Are you okay?" Unable to speak, Russ raised his hand. Shaun's hand froze on the oar. "Jesus! She's not dead already?"

She wasn't yet, but she would be if he didn't get his act together and haul her out of the water. Without letting himself think about it any further, Russ took a deep breath and doubled over, back into the deep. This time when she appeared in his sight he ignored her face and concentrated on wrapping his arm around her chin in the standard lifesaving position. She struggled against him, clawing at his arm and pulling his hair, which was almost a relief compared to her weird, ghostlike walking. Something normal, something he could deal with. He tightened his grip and churned upward, his free arm aching with the effort, her dress tangling his legs. Before he reached the surface, he felt her go limp. How many minutes since she walked in? Time yawned open. It felt like he had been under the lake forever. When he split the water, hauling her with him, she drifted, slack, held up by his arm beneath her chin.

Oh no you don't. He turned onto his back and stroked hard toward shore, floating her near his chest, so lost in the rhythm of pull and breath and kick that he didn't realize he was there until he reached back and hit coarse grit instead of cold water. He rolled to his knees and half dragged, half carried the old lady onto the grass. He pinched her nose, tilted her head back, and began mouth-to-mouth resuscitation. Blow. Breath. Blow. Breath.

He heard the scrape of the rowboat's keel and then Shaun was there, falling to his knees on the other side of the old lady's head. He pushed against Russ's shoulder. "Let me take a turn, man," he said. "You need to get a breath for yourself." Russ nodded. He watched as Shaun picked up his rhythm, and then Russ let himself collapse into the grass.

He heard a gargling cough and shoved himself out of the way as Shaun rolled the old lady to her side. She gasped, choked, and then vomited up a startling quantity of water. She started to cry weakly. He met Shaun's eyes over her shoulder. Shaun spread his hands and shrugged. *Now what?*

Russ staggered back onto his feet. Curled up on her side, weeping, the woman didn't look scary anymore, just old and lost. "I think we ought to get her to the hospital," Russ said. "Run up the trail and see if she parked a car beside the road."

Swinging wide around the tiny cemetery, Shaun loped to the overgrown path and disappeared from view. Russ returned to the rowboat and dragged it up onto the grass as far as he could. He retrieved his jeans—stinking of beer—and his sneakers, and had just finished getting dressed when Shaun ran back down the trail.

"'Sup there," he panted, pointing toward the road. "Keys in the ignition and all."

"Good." Russ knelt by the old woman and carefully pulled her into a sitting position. "Ma'am? Can you walk? What's your name?"

The old lady leaned against his shoulder. She wasn't exactly crying anymore, but making deep, shaky sounds like a little kid. She didn't seem to hear him. He wondered if she was senile, and if so, what she was doing driving around by herself. He looked back at Shaun. "I think we need to carry her."

"What about our stuff?" Shaun pointed to the boat. "It's not just the fishing tackle, man. I still have"—he dropped his voice, as if a narc might be hiding behind one of the headstones—"almost an ounce of grass in there."

The woman gave a rattling sigh and lapsed into a still silence that made Russ uneasy. "Bring it," he said. "Or hide it. This lady needs help. We gotta get her to a doctor."

"Oh, shit," Shaun said. "Okay." He strode to the rowboat and grabbed the backpack he used to carry his paraphernalia. "But if anything happens to the boat, you're gonna be the one who explains it to my dad."

Russ laughed, a short, sharp sound. "Fine. I'm not gonna be around long enough for him to kick my ass."

They laced their hands together and eased the woman into a seat carry. With Shaun on the other side, she didn't weigh as much as some of the sacks Russ toted for customers at Greuling's Grocery. The trail up to the county road was less than a half mile, and within ten minutes they burst out of the shade of the pines and into open air and brilliant sunshine. Shaun jerked his head toward a '59 Rambler wagon. Two-toned: baby-shit brown and tired tan. Russ pulled open the back door and shut his eyes for a moment against the wave of thick, moist heat that rolled out of the car.

"Where should we put her?" Shaun asked.

"Lay her down in the backseat." Russ looked in the rear for a blanket or a coat to lay under her, but there was nothing except more gardening equipment.

They stretched the woman out on the sticky plastic seat. She looked clammy and paler than before. Russ had a sudden image of himself and Shaun driving into town in an overheated granny car with a corpse in the back. He shuddered.

"You okay?"

"Yeah, sure. You want to drive?"

Shaun held up his hands. "No way, man. If we get stopped, I don't want the cops getting too close to me." He sniffed his shirt. "Can you smell it on me?"

Russ rolled his eyes. "You know it's good stuff if it's making you 'noid." He slid into the driver's seat and adjusted it back to fit his long frame. "Hop in."

The ride into Millers Kill passed in silence. Russ was concentrating on driving as fast as he could. Shaun was tense, hissing between his teeth whenever Russ took a corner too tightly, gripping his seat if another car went past them. And in the back was—nothing. Russ couldn't even hear the old lady breathe. As they passed from the forest down into the rolling farmland, the back of his neck began to creep. He couldn't shake the idea that if he turned around, he would see her lying there, wet, unbreathing, looking at him with her black eyes. He was grateful when they came to the town and he had to focus on navigating through the stop-and-go traffic.

He pulled into emergency parking at the Washington County Hospital and killed the engine. Shaun looked at him. "Well?" he said. "Let's get her in there."

Russ forced himself to twist in his seat and check behind him. And, of course, he saw nothing except an unconscious old lady. His shoulders twitched at the sudden release of tension. "Yeah," he said to Shaun.

If he had been less weirded out and more on top of things, he would have gone into the emergency room, fetched out a couple of nurses, and had them wheel the old lady into the place themselves. He thought of it, later, but at the time, sliding her out of the Rambler seemed like the most logical thing to do. He took her feet and Shaun took her shoulders. He was so intent on avoiding a collision while walking backward that he didn't see the commotion their entrance caused. Shaun did, though, and nearly dropped the woman on her head.

"For Chrissake, Shaun, don't just—"

"What are you boys doing?" The nurse bearing down on them had a bosom like the prow of a battleship, and the face to match. In one swift move, she caught the old woman's wrist lightly in one hand while digging her other fingers bone-deep into Russ's shoulder.

"Ow!" he said. "We're not doing anything!"

"Is this your grandmother?"

"I don't know who it is! We just found her. At Stewart's Pond. She walked into the water. She tried to drown herself."

She sized him up with a single flick of her eyelashes, and even though she barely came up to his chest, she somehow managed to speak over his head. "Skelly, McClaren, get that gurney over here." She glared at Shaun, who was looking longingly at the exit doors. "Don't even think about moving, young man."

Two nurses scarcely older than Shaun and Russ rolled a pallet over. One of them glanced sympathetically at Russ. The battleship let go of his shoulder in order to ease the old woman onto the gurney.

"Into the examination room," she said to the other nurses, who obeyed her with such speed that Russ figured she must terrorize everybody she came into contact with. She hooked her hands around his and Shaun's arms and followed the gurney, towing them past the admissions desk and through the swinging double doors into the examination room. She bulldozed through a square of limp blue curtains shielding the old woman from public view. "Get Dr. Hansvoort," she said firmly. One of the young nurses disappeared. "Well, don't just stand there," she told the remaining nurse. "Get her vitals. Ah, Dr. Hansvoort. Thank you for coming so promptly."

The young resident who had parted the curtains looked as if he wouldn't have dared take his time. "Nurse Vigue?"

She rattled Russ's and Shaun's arms. "All right, you two. Tell Dr. Hansvoort here what happened." She narrowed her eyes. "Truthfully."

Russ and Shaun fell all over themselves trying to get their story out. While they described the woman's strange actions, Russ's dive to rescue her, and the mouth-to-mouth resuscitation, Dr. Hansvoort clicked on a penlight and looked into his patient's eyes, nose, and throat.

When they had finished their recital—Shaun's last comment had been ". . . and so we'd like to go now, please"—the doctor frowned.

"Attempted suicide," he said to Nurse Vigue. "Or perhaps senile dementia. You had better put a call in to the police."

"My thoughts exactly," she said, nodding her approval at the doctor's performance. She captured Shaun and Russ again and sailed them back through the swinging doors into the waiting room. "You boys sit here. The police will have questions about this incident."

And if they don't, Russ thought, she'll make sure to tell them they ought to.

"But," Shaun began.

"Sit." She arched a thinly plucked brow at them and seemed to soften a little. "We have quite a few back issues of *Boy's Life* magazine. I'm sure you'll enjoy reading them."

"For God's sake, sit down and read," Russ muttered to Shaun, taking a chair himself and opening the first magazine at hand.

Two issues of *Popular Mechanics* later, the emergency-room doors opened and Russ looked up to see the weather-beaten face of Chief Liddle. He was neither large nor intimidating—in fact, he looked more like a farmer than a cop—but both boys sank in their seats when he glanced their way.

The chief spoke briefly with Nurse Vigue and then vanished into the examination room. "Now you're screwed," Shaun whispered. "He's had his eye on you ever since he caught us torching tires at the dump."

Russ shook his head. "I'm not scared of him," he said, and it was true. He had seen the chief a few too many times, back before his dad passed away, gently steering the incoherent and maudlin Walter Van Alstyne up the front walk and into the parlor. The chief always said the same thing: "He's had a few too many, Margy. I guess he needs to sleep it off." Then he'd look real close into Russ's mom's face and ask, "You be all right here with him while he's like this?"

And she would get all brisk and efficient and tell him they would make out fine, and then they'd help Dad to his bed and she'd press a cup of coffee—usually refused—on the chief.

It wasn't until after his dad was dead that Russ realized what the chief had really been asking his mom, and when he did, it enraged him, that anyone could think his gentle, soft-spoken father would ever harm his mother. But later, he thought about how the chief had always acted as if Walter Van Alstyne's drunkenness was a onetime thing, and how careful he was of his mom's pride. And he realized the question wasn't that far-fetched after all. Because in his own way, his dad had hurt his mom a lot.

When the chief had caught him drinking Jack Daniel's and leading a group of seniors in lighting tires on fire and rolling them downhill from the dump, he had hauled Russ behind his cruiser for a talking-to. To the rest of the guys, it must have looked as if Russ had missed getting arrested by the skin of his teeth. But in truth, Liddle hadn't threatened him with the lockup. Instead, he had looked at Russ as though he had been stealing from a church, and said, "Russell, don't you think your mother's been through enough without you grieving her with this kind of foolishness? How are you going to look her in the eye if I have to bring you home . . ." he didn't say *just like your father.* He didn't have to.

Russ didn't have the words to tell this to Shaun, so he just grunted and snapped open a year-old *Life* magazine. It showed pictures of a massive antiwar demonstration. He shut it again, leaned back against the vinyl seat, and closed his eyes. This was supposed to have been a fun day fishing, one last day when he didn't have to be anywhere or do anything. Now it was all turned to crap.

"You boys want to tell me what happened?"

Russ opened his eyes. Chief Liddle stood in front of them, his thumbs hooked into his gun belt. Russ and Shaun clambered to their feet, and Russ let Shaun rattle on about the fishing and the old woman and the rescue and the resuscitation. He wound it up by explaining how they had driven the old woman's car to the hospital, then said, "Can I please go and call my mom to come get us? Because I just now realized we need a ride back to the lake to pick up my car."

The chief looked at both of them closely. He sniffed. "You two smell like the Dew Drop Inn on a Saturday night."

Shaun's eyes got wide and white.

"It's me, sir," Russ said. "I had a couple beers. But it's not as bad as it smells—I knocked 'em over when I took my jeans off to go after the old lady. That's why I stink so bad."

The chief shook his head. "Russell—," he began.

"Russ is leaving for the army next week," Shaun blurted. "You know what they say, Chief. 'If you're old enough to fight for your country . . .'"

"You aren't going, are you?" Chief Liddle asked Shaun.

"Ah, no."

"Then I suggest you hush up and stay away from booze where I can smell you. Go on, go call your mother." Shaun didn't have to be told twice. He took off for the pay phone at the other end of the hall. Liddle looked straight at Russ, and the fact that the chief now had to look up to meet his eyes gave Russ a weird, disoriented feeling, like the time after his dad's service when Mr. Kilmer, the funeral director, had asked for "Mr. Van

Alstyne's signature" and he had realized that that was him, that he was "Mr. Van Alstyne" now.

"Is it true?" the chief said.

"Yes, sir."

"You volunteer, or did your number come up?"

Russ paused. "My number came up."

"And you're leaving next week?"

"Wednesday."

The chief bit the inside of his cheek. "How's your mom taking it?"

"About as well as you'd expect."

"I'll make sure to drop in on her now and again. To keep an eye on things."

To do Russ's job for him. "I'm sure she'll appreciate that."

The chief looked as if he were going to say something else, but he merely extended his hand. "Good luck to you, then." They shook. "I don't need you to make a statement. You can go."

"Sir?"

The chief cocked an eyebrow at him.

"Who is that old lady? And why was she going into the reservoir like that?"

The deep lines around the chief's eyes crinkled faintly. "Curious, are you?"

"Yes, sir."

Liddle glanced toward the emergency-room doors. "That's Mrs. Ketchem."

"Ketchem? Like the clinic? And the dairy?"

"That's the one."

"But she must be rich!"

The chief smiled at him. "If she is, you can't prove it by me. Rich or poor, all folks have troubles, Russell."

"Was that why she was trying to, you know, kill herself?"

The chief stopped smiling. "I'm going to call that an accident. She's an old woman, working out in the sun, getting up and down . . . it's natural she became disoriented. Her daughter and son-in-law moved back to the area recently. I'll have a talk with them. Maybe we can persuade Mrs. Ketchem that it's time to give up her house and move in with them."

"But she wasn't disoriented. She was walking into that water like you'd walk into the men's room. She knew exactly what she was doing."

Chief Liddle gave him a look that somehow made him draw closer. "Attempted suicide is a crime, Russell. It might require a competency hearing and an involuntary committal at the Infirmary. Now, as long as she has family to take charge of her, I don't think she needs to go through that, do you?"

"But what if she's . . . I don't know, sick in the head or something?"

Liddle shook his head. "She's not going off her rocker. She's just old and tired. Even her sorrows are older than most of the folks around her these days. Sometimes, the weight of all that living just presses down on a person and sort of squashes them flat."

Russ thought that if that's what old age brought, he'd rather go out young in a blaze of glory. His feelings must have shown on his face, because the chief smiled at him again. "Not that it's anything you have to worry about." He shook his hand again. "Go on with your friend there. It looks like he's done with his phone call. And keep your head down when you're over there. We want you to come home safe."

And that ended his day's adventure. At least until that night, when he woke up his mother, yelling, from the first nightmare he could remember since he was ten. And in later years, even after he had walked, awake, through nightmares of men blown to a pulp and helicopters falling out of the sky, he still sometimes remembered the sensation of sinking into the cool, dark water. The pale, withered face. The black, black eyes. And he would shiver.

CHAPTER 2

NOW

ASH WEDNESDAY, MARCH 8, A DAY OF PENANCE

The rector of St. Alban's Episcopal Church, town of Millers Kill, diocese of Albany, spread her arms in an old gesture of welcome. Her chasuble, dark purple embroidered with gold, opened like penitential wings. "I invite you, therefore, in the name of the Church, to the observance of a holy Lent," she said, "by self-examination and repentance; by prayer, fasting, and self-denial; and by reading and meditating on God's holy word." Her voice echoed off the stone walls of the church and was swallowed up in corners left dark by the antiquated lighting system and the heavy, gray day outside. "And, to make a right beginning of repentance and as a mark of our mortal nature, let us now kneel before the Lord, our maker and redeemer."

She turned toward the low altar and knelt. There was a thick woolen rustling as the twenty or so persons who had risked a late arrival at the office to attend the 7:00 A.M. Imposition of Ashes knelt behind her. A vast and somber silence settled around them as they all considered the sobering idea of their mortal nature. At least, Clare hoped they were all considering it. Undoubtedly, some were worried about the imminent storm, promising ice and freezing rain, while others were already thinking about what awaited them at work or contemplating the pain in their knees. There was a lot of kneeling in Lent. It was hard on the knees.

Clare rose. She took the silver bowl containing the ashes and turned back to the people. She cupped the bowl between her hands. "Almighty God, you have created us out of the dust of the earth; grant that these ashes may be to us a sign of our mortality and penitence, that we may remember that it is only by your gracious gift that we are given everlasting life; through Jesus Christ our Savior." They said "Amen" in unison.

She nodded to Willem Ellis, who had cheerfully agreed to act as the acolyte for the early-morning service if it got him a note excusing him from homeroom and first-period geometry at school. He hopped down the steps from the altar and drew a kneeler across the bare stone before swinging the mahogany altar rail shut. Clare waited while the penitents slid out of the pews and made their way up to the rail. As one coat-muffled form after another sank down onto the overstuffed velvet kneeler, she stepped forward. "Remember that you are dust," she said, dipping her thumb into the ashes and firmly crossing Nathan Andernach's forehead. "And to dust you shall return." She made a sooty cross beneath Judy Morrison's heavily teased bangs. Down the row, again and again. "Remember that you are dust. And to dust you shall return." The black crosses emerged beneath her thumb. "Remember that you are dust. And to dust you shall return." Finally, she turned to Willem, who helpfully scraped his bangs off his face to bare his forehead. She almost smiled. No sixteen-year-old ever remembered he was dust.

She turned back to the altar and, bowing slightly, dipped her thumb into the ashes one last time. She crossed her own forehead, feeling the grit of it pressing into her, marking her skin. "Remember that you are dust," she whispered.

The ice storm everyone was expecting had arrived by the end of the service. Clare shook hands and said farewells near the inner narthex door, in a spot strategically chosen for its relative lack of drafts. As members of the congregation opened and closed the doors, she could see glimpses of the hammered-steel sky and hear the ticks and splatters of sleet and freezing rain.

Dr. Anne Vining-Ellis paused in front of Clare to wrap a muffler around her throat. "I'm glad I insisted on bringing Will this morning," she said. "This is nasty weather for an inexperienced driver to be out in."

Clare waved to a departing parka-clad back and shivered as a cold wind speared through the doorway. "Amen to that," she said.

"I don't suppose I can suggest you stay close to home today."

"I'm never going to live down my winter driving reputation, am I?" Anne—universally called Dr. Anne—was the closest thing Clare had to a good friend among her parishioners. She was willing to let her fuss a little. "Don't worry, I'm not planning on making any home visits today. I've got two more Impositions scheduled, at noon and five-thirty. Those will keep me plenty busy."

The emergency-room doctor glanced up at the shadowy rafters. "It's Wednesday. You always go to the Kreemy Kakes Diner on Wednesdays."

Clare pressed her lips together in what she hoped was a smile. "Well, you see then? That's right in the middle of town."

"I'm not the only one who's made mention of your habit, Clare." Dr. Anne looked at her. "You know I'm not a gossip. I just think you ought to be aware that the fact you have lunch every week with a married man hasn't gone unnoticed." Clare opened her mouth. Dr. Anne cut her off. "And I know it's all perfectly innocent. You don't have to tell me that."

Clare rolled her eyes. "If having lunch once a week in a public diner is going to start stories, I can't imagine what I could do to stop them from circulating. Have the man over to my house where no one will see us together?"

Dr. Anne shook her head. "Take it as a friendly FYI." She laid a gloved hand on Clare's arm. "There are still some people in this church who aren't too keen on the idea of a female priest. Don't give them any ammunition, okay?"

"I'll try to be a credit to my gender," Clare said.

Dr. Anne laughed. "Good enough. Hey, where's that rotten kid of mine? Willem?"

The boy's voice came from the far side of the church. "Mom! Reverend Clare! Take a look at this!"

Dr. Anne looked questioningly at Clare, then set off toward her son. Clare followed, pulling her chasuble over her head as she walked. Willem was standing near the halfway point of the north wall of the church. As Clare and his mother approached, he pointed to the deeply embrasured window there, a stained-glass depiction of stately angels leading a group of children to the Throne of Glory. It had always been an odd window to Clare's thinking—it was obviously a recent addition, done in a modern mosaic style favored in the 1970s. And the inscription wasn't, as one might expect of such a scene, "Suffer the little children to come unto me" or "Unless ye be as little children." Instead, two of the angels faced the viewer, holding shields with a verse from Lamentations: "But though he cause grief, yet will he have compassion according to the multitude of his mercies. For he doth not afflict willingly, nor grieve the children of men."

It was not the singular artwork or the gloomy verse that had caught Willem Ellis's attention, though. It was water. Seeping from the top of the embrasure, running down the edges of the window, puddling at the deep sill, and making ugly brown tracks along the pale stone wall.

"Oh my Lord," Dr. Anne said.

St. Alban's had been built along traditional Gothic Revival lines, with the long walls to the north and south jutting away from the lofty-ceilinged central nave. These north and south aisles were sheltered under roofs a mere ten or twelve feet high, so that when Clare looked up, she could easily see the warmly stained pine boards, carefully lapped like ship's planking. And although the storm darkness outside leached away much of the light that normally spilled through the stained-glass windows, Clare could also see the blotches spreading along the boards' joints, giving the interior roof the brackish, mottled look of something old and unpleasantly moldy.

Clare's silence made Dr. Anne and Willem look up, too. As they watched, a fat droplet squeezed from one of the patches and fell with a splat onto the polished wooden pew below.

"This is not good," Clare said.

◆ ◆ ◆

"So what did you do?" Millers Kill's chief of police dipped a steak fry into a paper tub of ketchup and popped it into his mouth.

Clare leaned back against the crimson vinyl seat and looked out the wide window of the Kreemy Kakes Diner. Icy rain splattered the passing cars and clung to the trees, bending their branches low to the sidewalk. Across the street, the Farmers and Merchants Bank had fluorescent orange warning cones on its granite steps, which were so slick that entering to make a deposit was an exercise in ice climbing.

"What could I do? I put pails underneath the drips and roped off the area. And asked Lois to call the vestry members for an emergency meeting." She turned back to her lunch companion. "We're hauling out the last roofing engineer's report, from two years ago. They've been going round Robin's barn about fixing the thing ever since I arrived, and I suspect they'd been debating it for some years before. Probably what finished off the late, much-lamented Father Hames." She stirred a strand of melted cheese into her chili. "Now, of course, they'll *have* to make decisions. Unfortunately, they're going to be based on expediency instead of careful consideration."

Russ Van Alstyne pointed to her onion rings. "Are you going to finish those?" She waved him to help himself. "You ought to set that janitor of yours on it. I thought he was supposed to keep things running around there."

"The sexton," she stressed Mr. Hadley's title, "is unbolting the pew from the floor and putting it in storage."

"I hear a *but* coming."

"But he's in his seventies and he's not exactly in the best of health. I already have to do some fancy footwork to keep him from lugging heavy objects and climbing up the extension ladder to replace bulbs. I can just picture him clambering around an icy pitched roof trying to figure out what's wrong. He might survive, but I'd probably have a heart attack."

Russ laughed. "You young whippersnappers underestimate us geezers. I do my own roofing repairs. And my farmhouse is a good half century older than your church."

"You"—she pointed her spoon at him—"are forty-nine, not seventy-three. And I'm going to assume you aren't repairing the roof in this kind of weather." She looked back out the window and shuddered. "I can't believe it's Ash Wednesday and we're still stuck in full-blown winter. Do you know what the temperature was at my parents' when I called them last Sunday? Fifty-seven degrees."

"You're the one who thought it was a good idea to move from southern Virginia to the Adirondack Mountains. Quit your complaining, spring is coming."

"Two weeks in May. Some spring."

"This is your second March here. You ought to be prepared for it this time around."

"I was hoping last year's weather was a fluke." She ate a spoonful of chili and watched Russ as he deftly prevented a glob of ketchup from landing on his uniform sleeve. They were always in uniform during their Wednesday lunches, black clericals and brown cop gear. They always met on their lunch hours, so that they couldn't linger. They always met at the diner, smack-dab in the middle of busy South Street, and sat, whenever possible, at one of the window booths, where God and everybody could see. As she had told Dr. Anne, everything innocent and aboveboard.

Except where it counted. In her conscience. In her thoughts. In her heart.

She realized she had been looking at Russ a little too long. She dropped her eyes and dug into her chili.

"So, what's with the dirt on your forehead?" he asked.

"It's not dirt. It's penitential ashes." She looked up to see him grinning. "Which you knew very well."

"And folks say we heathens are unwashed." He swiped another of her onion rings. "Should you be calling attention to yourself like that? I mean, doesn't the Bible say something about praying and fasting in secret, and not wearing the sackcloth and ashes on the street corner?"

"'And your father who sees you in secret, shall reward you in secret.' My goodness, I'm impressed. Have you been watching those TV preachers again?"

He laughed. "Not hardly. I was a faithful, if unwilling, attendee at the Cossayuharie Methodist Church until I got too big for my mom to forcibly drag me there. I guess some of what I heard stuck." He picked up the diner's dessert menu, which was larger than the meal menu and fully illustrated with saliva-provoking photos. "What are you giving up for Lent? Chocolate? Beer?"

"I'm not giving up food," she said. "The whole giving-up-something-to-eat thing is a relic from times when we didn't have a thousand food choices in every local supermarket. When you have an abundance—a superfluity—of something, giving up a little bit of it isn't meaningful."

"Woo-hoo. Did I stumble into next Sunday's sermon?"

"Week after next," she admitted.

"So what are you doing? Anything?"

"I figure the one thing we really have a scarcity of in our society is time. So I like to volunteer mine over the course of Lent. You wouldn't believe how many not-for-profit organizations are swamped with money and assistance at Christmastime and begging for help in March."

"But you already volunteer for a ton of stuff. I know you help out at the soup kitchen, and the teen mothers' back-to-school program. And there's the outreach you do at the homeless shelter."

"Those are all sponsored by St. Alban's. Showing up for the soup kitchen and the homeless shelter is part of my job."

He suppressed a smile. "So, it doesn't count if you do a good deed while you're on salary. It only counts if it's a freebie."

"That's not quite how I'd put it." She scraped the last of the chili out of her bowl. "I'd like to help out at some place where I wouldn't normally go. Some place that's not associated with the church."

"How about the dog pound?"

"Oh, Lord, no. I couldn't. I'd wind up either adopting a bunch of strays I didn't have time to care for or breaking my heart."

"The library."

"I'd have to clear up my overdue fines first. I've been dodging their reminder notices. I think next they send a big guy out to 'talk' with me."

"Have you thought about the Millers Kill Historical Society? They always need help cataloging the collection. It's a big, boring job, stuck up in the top floor going through boxes of stuff. Hard for them to keep people interested in it."

She sat back. "That's not a bad idea." She thought of spending time with things, instead of people, for a change, up in a top floor all alone. It would be almost like going on a retreat. Monastic, even. "Where is the historical society?"

"Do you know where the free clinic is? On Barkley Avenue?"

"Yep."

"Right next door."

She crumpled her napkin and dropped it into her empty bowl. "I'll swing by there tomorrow and see what they say."

"Believe me, if you walk in and commit to a forty-day stint, they'll greet you with open arms and cries of joy."

"How do you know so much about it?"

He smiled, pleased with himself. "I'm on the board of trustees."

She laughed. "You're just full of surprises today."

"I don't want to get too boring."

"Never that."

There was a pause. Then Russ jerked around to wave their waitress over, and Clare twisted away to search for her wallet.

"It's on me," he said, plucking the slip from between the waitress's fingers.

"You paid last week. And the week before that."

"So what? I make more money than you do."

"That's not the point. We agreed to share—"

He stood up and pulled his billfold from his back pocket. "Make a donation to the historical society, then." He laid down some money next to the ketchup bottle and waited while she struggled into her expedition-weight parka, a Christmas present from her concerned southern parents. Then he stood aside to let her go first to the door. On the way, he was greeted by two aldermen, and she said hello to one of her parishioners. It was all very open. Very aboveboard. Perfectly innocent.

Remember that you are dust. Then, she had said the words. Now . . . now she really felt them.

CHAPTER 3

THEN

Norman Madsen put down the last of the legal-sized papers on his green felt blotter and looked up. He smiled tentatively across the expanse of his desk at the woman seated in the deep leather chair opposite him. She did not smile back.

"Mrs. Ketchem," he said, "I'm afraid I have to tell you, as your attorney—"

"You're not my attorney, young man," she said. "My attorney is Mr. Niels Madsen. I assume the reason I'm talking with you instead of him is that he's indisposed."

Norman propped up his smile by force of will. "I can hardly claim to be the equal of my father"—with the ink still wet on his Juris Doctor, that was certainly the truth—"but I hope I can continue to give you the excellent service you've come to expect from Madsen and Madsen." This was the whopper. Of course, his dad and his uncle wanted to keep every one of their clients, no matter how unprofitable their business or how infrequent their need for legal service. They loved to gas on about the practice during the Great Depression, when they were paid, to hear them tell, exclusively in chickens and hogs. But in the here and now, the senior partners of Madsen and Madsen couldn't afford to spend their billable hours on the steady stream of dairy farmers needing land titles or old ladies wanting to bequeath their homes to the Society for Indigent Cats. So it was left to the newest addition to the firm to handle the penny-ante clients. Norman's small office continuously smelled faintly of manure and orange-blossom water. It was not the life he had envisioned back in the stately halls of Cornell University.

"To continue: I'm sorry to say you'll be unable to deed your late in-law's property to Millers Kill. As you directed, we approached the board of aldermen quietly about your offer. Your generous offer," he added, seeing the mulish look on her face. "While they appreciated the idea of"—he glanced down at the letter he was holding—"the Jonathon Ketchem Clinic for the town's poor, they have to weigh the benefit against the likely detriments, namely, the loss to the town of the tax revenue currently generated by the house, and the cost to the town of maintenance, which, given the property's age and size, cannot be inconsiderable."

Mrs. Ketchem folded her arms over her chest. "They certainly taught you well in law school, didn't they? Never use one word when fifteen will do. You're telling me the aldermen think taking the old heap off my hands will cost them more than it's worth."

He flushed, but held himself to a mild "That's correct" in response. He reminded himself—as his father and uncle were fond of doing—that the firm had seen a sharp decline in revenues after the Howland Paper Mill closed two years ago. *Every client is a valuable client,* the old coots would say. Of course, if they would listen to some of his suggestions to lift their Dickensian practice into the atomic age, they might realize more profit.

Mrs. Ketchem was sitting silently, her gaze unfocused and her graying eyebrows bunched together as she plotted God knew what. If he was honest with himself, which he prided himself on, he had to admit she made him uncomfortable. She was decked out like all the other ladies of her age—in an out-of-date floral frock, summer gloves and hat on his desk— and she spoke with the same clipped-off drawl that identified every farm family from the hills around Cossayuharie. But she wasn't the same. He could always charm a smile out of the crankiest old lady or put a man at ease who had never worn a suit save for one borrowed for his wedding. Not Mrs. Ketchem. Meeting with her was like taking an oral exam from his stone-faced contracts professor. If his professor had been wearing a dress and sensible shoes.

Norman waited. Finally she unfolded her arms and leaned forward. "I want you to go to the board and tell them, along with the Ketchem house, I'll give them the farm in Cossayuharie. They can either run it as my in-laws did, as tenant property, or sell it outright. It's a rich farm with a good herd, productive. It'll generate more than enough money to pay for the roofing and painting and whatnot that the house in town will need year to year."

"Are you kidding?" he said. He winced as soon as the words tumbled from his mouth. The old bat would never take him seriously if he gawped like a runny-nosed schoolboy. "I mean," he tried to salvage, "that's a valuable piece of property. Shouldn't you be saving it as a nest egg for your, ah, golden years?" Which were right around the corner. She was in her mid-fifties, only a few years older than his own mother, but she looked more like one of his grandmother's generation: skinny and sharp-boned, with her coarse gray hair twisted into a bun atop her head.

She snorted. "I got enough of a nest egg already. I want that house to go for a clinic. I want for no woman to ever have to go without medical care for her children."

He pulled the manila folder containing her history with the firm out of a redwell file beside his desk. He flopped it open. "Of course, I understand. And I admire your altruism." He found the copy of the senior Ketchem's will, flipped it over to the paragraph outlining the disposition of realty, and read it. He almost smiled in relief as he laid the document on his blotter and turned it so Mrs. Ketchem could see. "Unfortunately, you aren't able to sell or deed the farm. As you can see, it's been left equally to you or your heirs and to your brother-in-law or his heirs."

"I know that." Her voice left no doubt that she thought him a fool. "David's got no interest in running a farm. I'll buy out his half."

Norman blinked. "You'll . . . buy out his half?"

"How long do you think it will take?"

"Gosh." Norman stalled. He knew the faded neighborhood where Jane Ketchem lived in her modest house; knew her thirteen-year-old car, most likely held together by spit and wire; had seen her at Greuling's Grocery, carefully counting out coins from a snap purse to pay her grocery bill. "Well, we'd have to get a commercial Realtor out there, and an auctioneer to value the livestock, and another for the personalty—that's the effects inside the house. . . ." How could he phrase this so as not to wound her pride? "I'm no expert, but I think the farm might easily be worth twenty thousand dollars. Maybe more."

He waited warily for her face to sag in disappointment or tighten in frustrated anger, but it did neither. Instead, she said in her usual snap-to-it tone, "Very well then. Can I trust you to hire the Realtor and auctioneers? I don't want to be robbed blind by a bunch of unnecessary fees."

"Mrs. Ketchem, that means buying out your brother-in-law's half interest would cost ten thousand dollars. Or more."

"I can divide twenty by two, Norman Madsen."

"But—how can you afford that?"

She leaned back into the leather chair, so that her eyes seemed sunk in shadows. "I told you I have a nest egg. I've invested well over the years."

He made one last effort to save her from her own folly. "Even so, if you deplete it to buy out David Ketchem's share in the farm and then turn around and give it away to the town, you'll be left with no other income stream but your Social Security. I have to point out that as a single woman—"

"Widow," she said. Her dark eyes beetled into his. He actually felt a narrow thread of sweat erupt on his upper lip. His father had stressed how important that title was to her. The fattest folder in the redwell contained the records of Madsen and Madsen's efforts to have the maybe not-so-late but certainly run-off Jonathon Ketchem declared legally dead.

"Of course," he said. "Without your, ah, late husband's support, you need to take even more care than usual for your old age."

She blinked her eyes slowly, as if acknowledging his rolling over and showing belly. "I don't need much. If I buy out David's half of the farm, there will still be enough to keep me until I'm a hundred. If it's the good Lord's judgment that I live so long." Her voice didn't sound as if great old age would be a blessing.

"What about the current beneficiaries of your will? Your daughter, any grandchildren you might have, your church. You risk leaving them with a substantially reduced bequest. Your estate's only assets will be your residence and your investments. There's no telling how precipitately they could decline in value over the coming years."

She rolled her eyes, and he had the feeling he'd been using too many words again. "My daughter is well married to a man who can provide for her and any children she might have. And Lord knows there are people aplenty tossing money at St. Alban's. Maybe I'll leave all my money to the clinic." She paused, frowned, and set the edges of her hands against her narrow lips. "No, I take that back. Whatever's left over when I die I'll put into trust. Let my daughter decide what to do with it. If she needs it, she can have it, and if she don't, she can give it away."

"But is this what the Ketchems would have wanted for you? An old age of counting every penny? Surely they left you the Millers Kill house and the Cossayuharie farm as a means to ensure your comfort and happiness?"

"My late husband's parents have always been good to me. But they, more than anyone else, would understand. About this clinic. About how I want Jonathon's name to be remembered." She wrapped her long fingers over the turned posts of her chair's armrests and shifted her gaze away from him, to the surface of his desk. "Does that file box of yours have anything about what happened to me and my family?"

"Yes." He swallowed. "Yes, it does."

"Let me tell you something about comfort and happiness, young man." She looked at him head-on, trapping him with her gaze. "My husband and I both came from good families, successful families, and when we wed, we were hard-set on making a success of our own farm. We got fifty acres near the Sacandaga Vlaie that was cheap because it flooded every few years, and we worked. We sweated, we scrimped, we lived for the day after the day when we'd have everything we wanted for our comfort, everything we needed for our happiness." Her face, with skin in sharp-edged folds over her bones, showed every one of her fifty-four years. But her eyes snapped with the fierce will of someone much younger. "And I never knew, that whole time we were so full of wanting, that the only happiness I would ever know in life was going on right there, on that farm with the soggy bottom acres, washing bucketloads of diapers and trying to stretch one chicken to feed a whole family for a half a week." She lifted the paper off his green felt blotter without looking at it and handed it to him. "Take my offer to the aldermen. Get me my clinic, Mr. Madsen."

CHAPTER 4

NOW

THURSDAY, MARCH 9

There was a protestor blocking the sidewalk in front of the free clinic. Clare drove slowly past the three-storied Queen Anne, a grand old lady of a house awkwardly modernized by a lumber wheelchair ramp and a rickety-looking fire escape. A large sign with MILLERS KILL FREE CLINIC and the hours had been bolted next to the entryway, fine mahogany double doors whose original windows, probably etched glass, had been replaced with scratched Plexiglas.

Blocking the sidewalk was probably an exaggeration, since the lone woman, placard over her shoulder, was striding back and forth between the edge of the walk and the foot of the clinic's stairs. Clare pulled into the parking spot she had seen on her first pass down Barkley Avenue and turned off the car's engine. She was going to have to run the gauntlet, no way around it. This was the only parking space anywhere near the historical society she could confidently get in and out of. Evidently recently vacated by a much bigger vehicle, it was practically dry. Her pretty little rebuilt Shelby Cobra, a dream car when she bought it last spring, was lousy in snow and slush. She had chosen it with her vanity, not her good sense, and she had been paying for it—literally, when its transmission gave out— all winter long. Pride's painful, her grandmother Fergusson used to say, whenever she was twisting Clare's straight hair into curlers.

The storm had blown through last night, leaving a clear, bright morning behind. The wind, when she stepped out of the car, caught her with the shock of diving into cold water. She zipped her parka up to her chin— strategically covering her clerical collar—and pulled her knit cap low over her forehead. Maybe if she was nothing more than an anonymous figure in winter woolies she could escape without a harangue.

She clambered over a rock-hard lump of brown-and-gray snow that

23

covered the curb and crunched up the salt-crusted sidewalk toward the historical society. She kept her head down and her hands jammed in her pockets to avoid having any pamphlets thrust on her.

Don't notice me, don't notice me, she chanted in her head, but as she was the only other person within two blocks of the clinic, it wasn't surprising that her incantation didn't work.

"Ma'am? Excuse me, ma'am?"

Clare lifted her eyes from the gritty walk. She couldn't help it. A lifetime of conditioned politeness kicked in, and she pasted a pleasant expression on her face.

You know what your problem is, Fergusson? MSgt. Ashley "Hardball" Wright, her air force survival school instructor, had a tendency to leap into her thoughts at times like these. *You need to have a face that says get outta my way or I'll kill you and eat your heart! Do you know what your face says, Fergusson? It says I'm a widdle bunny rabbit! Are you going to be a combat pilot or a widdle bunny rabbit, Fergusson?*

"Yes?" she said to the protestor. *Sir, a widdle bunny rabbit, sir.*

The woman looked more like a member of the PTA than a political activist. She had a hand-knit tam pulled over long, curly hair, a heavy-duty parka, and sensible snow boots. She carried her placard and a clipboard in Scandinavian-knit mittens. "Would you be willing to sign a petition asking the aldermen to remove the current head of the clinic?"

Clare raised her gloved hands. "I'm sorry, I'm not familiar with the director or what the clinic does." She realized a split second after the words had left her mouth that she had made a serious mistake. She might just as well have invited the woman to proselytize her.

"You must have health insurance," the woman said, giving Clare's expensive new coat a once-over.

"It's more because I'm fairly new to the area," Clare said. "I moved here a little over a year ago." She glanced past the woman, toward the sedate brick facade of the Millers Kill Historical Society. So near and yet so far. "I'm actually headed for the historical society over there. . . ."

"The clinic provides free health care to residents who fall in the gap between private insurance and Medicaid. In other words, the working poor. Do you think that lower-income people should have substandard health services?"

Clare blinked. "No, of course not."

"Dr. Rouse has been running the clinic for thirty years." The woman compressed her generous mouth into a flat line, as if there were a lot more she would like to say about Dr. Rouse. "I'm circulating this petition because he continues to stockpile and administer vaccines containing thimerosal to the children of Millers Kill."

"What?" Clare had braced herself for an antiabortion screed; this sudden shift into the chemical composition of vaccines left her way off in left field. "I'm sorry, I don't—what's thimerosal?"

The woman dug into her parka pocket and pulled out a brochure that looked like the product of someone's newsletter-and-greeting-card software. She handed it to Clare. MERCURY AND AUTISM—HOW TO PROTECT YOUR CHILD, it read.

"Thimerosal is a preservative that's commonly used in vaccination serums. It's almost fifty percent mercury, a poisonous metal, and exposure in children under the age of three may cause autism." She caught Clare's gaze and held it. She had big brown eyes, intense but not fanatical. "Do you have kids?"

"No. I'm not married."

The woman let out a laugh. "I wish I had been that smart." She moved closer to Clare and poked at the homemade pamphlet with a mitten. "You've probably never heard, then, that recommended schedules for vaccinations have infants going in for first shots at six to eight weeks. Can you imagine injecting a two-month-old baby with mercury?"

"No," Clare said, interested in spite of herself. "But surely we were all vaccinated with the same stuff, and most of us are perfectly healthy. I mean, isn't autism fairly rare?"

"The rate of autistic-spectrum disorders has been increasing dramatically since 1990, when two major vaccines containing thimerosal were brought to market. It's like a lot of potentially dangerous health hazards—not everyone who is exposed will be affected. There's no way to know which children will or won't develop autism or Asperger's syndrome."

Clare glanced at the brochure in her hand, then at the clinic. On the second floor, she noticed, quilted white shades had been drawn behind the original four-over-four windows. Warmth or privacy? she wondered. "What's this got to do with Dr. Rouse?"

"Many major drug companies are now producing thimerosal-free vaccines due to public and governmental pressures. But there's still a huge stockpile of the older stuff around, which drug companies can either destroy or"—she glared at the building—"sell on the cheap to clinics like ours."

"And Dr. Rouse is still using these vaccines?"

"He's not just using them. He continues to aggressively target lower-income children for vaccinations. He's threatened to report parents who refuse to immunize their kids to DSS. To say parents who are concerned about exposing their kids to thimerosal are neglecting their children."

The light dawned. "Parents? You mean, like you?"

The woman planted herself more squarely on the sidewalk. "Like me. My son developed autism when he was two, after undergoing every one of those vaccinations Dr. Rouse said he had to have. I never even questioned what they were putting into my baby. Now I've got another one, and I'll be damned if I'll expose her to any mercury-contaminated serum."

"I'm sorry," Clare said. "But isn't your quarrel more with whatever entity funds the clinic? If the doctor has to purchase older vaccines because of the cost, shouldn't you lobby the town to give him more money with which to purchase the new stuff?"

"I suspect"—here she dropped her voice—"that Dr. Rouse has personal financial reasons for continuing to buy the older serums."

Clare looked at the clinic again. One of the shades twitched. "You mean, he's getting kickbacks from the drug companies?"

"Who can say?" The woman spread her mittened hands. "I know he lives pretty cushy for a man whose salary has been paid by Millers Kill his whole life. Big house, a new car every three years, vacations in the tropics—better'n most of us are doing. I'm trying to get a referendum question to increase the clinic's funding, with citizen oversight. But even if we can get more money, the budget is dependent on the tax revenues, and there wouldn't be any change for up to a year after the referendum. In the meantime, babies are getting inoculated every day in this clinic. And parents are being intimidated into giving their consent to it. It's not just the danger for autism, you know. The bacterial toxins in many of the common vaccines can cause retardation, disabilities, death—people have no idea. The nurse hands you a sheet of paper with a lot of small print on it while your baby is lying on the exam table screaming and you're told you have to sign off. So you do." She shifted the placard from one shoulder to the other. Clare could read, DR. ROUSE A DANGER TO OUR CHILDREN. "I wish to God I had educated myself before I put Skylar in his care."

A pickup had pulled into a snow-slick space across the street, and a woman and a small girl were crossing their way. "Ma'am," the protestor called out, "are you aware that Dr. Rouse is trying to take away your right to make health care decisions about your daughter?"

The mother squinted against the sun. "What's that?"

The door to the clinic banged open. "Get the hell off my sidewalk, Debba Clow! And leave those ladies alone!"

A stocky man in his sixties stood in the doorway, his pale face mottled red, his white coat flapping as the cold air rushed past him into the heated vestibule beyond.

"Dr. Rouse, I presume," Claire said under her breath.

"This is a public sidewalk and I have every right to be here!" the protestor shouted.

"You're assaulting my patients and practicing medicine without a license!"

"I'm telling them what you won't, you quack!"

The red blotches on the doctor's face turned purple. "That's it! I'm calling the police! Then I'm calling the state! And then I'm calling my lawyer, who will sue you for defamation!" He disappeared back into the clinic, the door swinging shut behind him.

The protestor—Debba Clow—spun around. "Is that the sort of man you want treating your child?" she asked the mother, who responded by scooping the girl into her arms and hurrying up the stairs. Debba looked at Clare as if to say, *You see what I have to fight against?* "I better get out of here," she said. "I don't need any more trouble from the cops." She yanked off one mitten, fished into her parka pocket, and extracted a business card. "You seem like an intelligent, concerned woman. Here's my number. If you want to find out more, give me a call."

She tucked the placard beneath her arm and strode down the sidewalk. Clare looked at the card. It had a design of paint-saturated handprints running up one side. DEBORAH CLOW, ARTIST, it read.

The artist herself stopped halfway to the next corner. "Hey, what's your name?" she yelled.

"Clare Fergusson," Clare said loudly. Might as well come clean. She unzipped her parka so that her collar was clearly visible. "Rector of St. Alban's Church."

Debba Clow grinned and pumped her arm. "Hot diggity," she yelled. "I knew God was on my side!"

◆ ◆ ◆

Unlike the clinic, the historical society's ornate brick Italianate building had no visible concessions to the twenty-first century. "I know," Director Roxanne Lunt said, when Clare asked her about it. "We're totally out of compliance with the Americans with Disabilities Act. We're trying to get grant money for historically sensitive handicapped access. God help us if we're forced into installing some monstrosity like they have next door. We're keeping a low profile and praying we don't get sued."

Roxanne Lunt was a sleek, well-fed woman whose streaky ash-blond hair was a testament to her colorist's art. She had been excited to meet Clare, and ecstatic when Clare had committed to volunteering every Saturday afternoon through Lent. Clare was flattered to the point of embarrassment by Roxanne's enthusiasm, until Clare had a chance to observe her on their tour of the historic house, and discovered Roxanne was excited about everything. Her high heels tap-tap-tapped through the public rooms with restless energy as she spoke passionately about grant writing, cataloging, preservation, architecture, and interior design. And that was just the parlor, drawing room, and kitchen.

"I'm the only paid staff," Roxanne said as they climbed the three flights of stairs to the collection storage rooms. "That's why we so desperately need volunteers such as yourself."

"Are you full time?" Clare asked, her daydreams of solitary, monastic-like cataloging shredding before the raw energy of Hurricane Roxanne.

"Oh, no, no, no, they can't afford me full time. If I actually had to live on what they pay me, I'd be destitute. I work twenty hours a week here, that's for love, and the rest of the time, I'm a Realtor, for the money." She stopped on the landing in front of an oil of a dyspeptic-looking gentleman in black judge's robes. "Jacob DeWeese. This was his house. His daughter bequeathed it to the historical society." She tickled a mauve-lacquered fingernail beneath his painted chin. "They called him 'the Hanging Judge.'"

"He looks the part."

"It always surprises people when they hear what I do," Roxanne went on, mounting the stairs. "I'm so passionate about preservation, they can't believe I sell houses to keep body and soul together."

"I can believe it," Clare said.

Roxanne pinched a business card from her skirt pocket and gave it to Clare. This must be her day for collecting phone numbers. "Of course, you don't need my services, with that delicious Dutch revival you have. That belongs to your church, right?"

Clare nodded.

"Well, tell them if they ever want to raise money, I can take it off their hands and get a sweet price for it. I could find a nice little condo for you, not too far out of town. And it'd be a lot easier on your budget than running that big house."

Clare pictured St. Alban's leaking roof, which might as well be plugged with twenty-dollar bills for what it was going to cost to repair, and resolved to never, ever bring up to the vestry Roxanne Lunt's name or the possibility of selling the rectory.

"Here we are," Roxanne caroled, turning the handle on a paneled oak door at least twice the thickness of its modern counterpart. She pressed a button in a brass light-plate, and three sets of frosted-glass globes sprang to life, illuminating dozens upon dozens of what looked like banker's boxes stacked along the walls, butting up against a beautifully carved mantelpiece, half obscuring three tall windows running along the far wall. Clare could read descriptions in confident black marker on some of the nearest: LADIES VILLAGE IMPROVEMENT ASSOCIATION, 1916–1936 and LANGWORTHY FAMILY W/CIVIL WAR.

"This was originally the nursery," Roxanne said. "From back in the days when children were seen, not heard." She led Clare through the maze of boxes toward the back of the room, where a wooden table was pushed up to a fourth window. It held a computer, a lamp, several heaps of old books, and a plastic caddy stuffed with office supplies.

Clare leaned against the long refectory-style table to look out the windows. The ice-shrouded garden stretched out below, culminating in a green-roofed carriage house opening onto the back alley. She could see part of the clinic next door as well, shotgunning toward an identical carriage house in a series of additions that ate up any garden they might once have had.

"What you're going to do is very simple. You open a box, tag everything inside, and enter the descriptions into our electronic catalog," Roxanne said, booting up the computer. "Nothing in this room's been done. So feel free to read the notes on the outside of the boxes and start anywhere you like," she explained, pulling up a padded folding chair and seating herself in front of the monitor. "We've tried to keep donations from families or institutions physically together, although we've taken them out of whatever god-awful decaying chests and albums they came to us in and stuck them in archival boxes. When possible, we've interleaved ephemera with acid-free tissue paper."

"Ephemera?"

"Papers, letters, photos, that sort of thing. We've got three-hundred-year-old handbills touting the southern Adirondacks as the place for hardworking Scotsmen to get rich, we've got canal-era advertising calendars, we've got playbills for the Millers Kill opera house—"

"Millers Kill had an opera house?" Clare couldn't keep the disbelief out of her voice.

Roxanne laughed. "This was a very lively town before the mills closed down. We had touring grand opera in the nineteenth century. We had a luxury hotel near the train station for people traveling up to the park for the summer, quite elegant. In the twenties and thirties, after the Sacandaga was dammed and the lakes were created, we had our own airport with floatplanes. And, of course, during Prohibition this whole strip along Route 9 was known as 'Bootleggers Alley,' with rumrunners dashing between Canada and New York City and supplying speakeasies. We have a small collection of fabulous jazz recordings made in Millers Kill clubs where you had to knock three times and whisper 'Joe sent me' to get in." Roxanne's cheeks glowed with enthusiasm. "Of course, that was then, as they say. I'm afraid our big draw nowadays is peace, quiet, and affordable housing prices."

Clare thought of the confrontation between the doctor and Debba Clow. "Oh, I don't know about that. I think it's still a very lively town. You just have to know where to look."

CHAPTER 5

NOW

FRIDAY, MARCH 10

C lare's 10:30 counseling session with the Garrettsons was running over. Liz Garrettson's mother, a source of frequent conflict in the Garrettson home, had deteriorated to the point where she was going to have to be institutionalized or move in with her daughter and son-in-law. Liz and Tim circled around Liz's anger and his impatience, two people punching at a sandbag filled with guilt. It was exhausting just being in the same room with them, and Clare couldn't help glancing at her Apache helicopter clock as the minutes ticked past noon. The only thing worse than being late to a vestry meeting was being late to an emergency meeting she had scheduled herself.

Finally ushering them out of her office with a promise to put them in touch with Paul Foubert, the Infirmary's director, Clare cocked an ear for any sounds of conversation or argument drifting down the hall. Nothing. She opened the meeting-room door and stepped into the underheated splendor of a wood-paneled, Persian-carpeted gallery that appeared to have been assumed bodily from Oxford. No one was there.

"Lois," she said, sticking her head into the church office, "I've lost the vestry."

The church secretary tilted her head, allowing her razor-cut strawberry blond bob to swing just so, against her jaw. "And this is a bad thing . . . how?"

"Lois."

"They're in the church. Taking a look at the indoor waterworks."

"Everybody here?"

"Even the newbie. Let's hope they don't chew him up and spit him out."

Clare glanced over at the pink message slips accumulating on a lethally sharp spike. "Anything urgent?"

"Yes. You had a call from Hugh Parteger." Lois's British accent was devastatingly accurate. "'Lois, love, tell the vicar to give me a call sometime soon. She can't spend all her time in prayer and good works. She has to be naughty sometimes.'" Lois looked at her significantly.

Clare laughed. "He's really a very nice guy." She had met Hugh last year while he was summering in Saratoga. Since he worked for a merchant bank in New York City, they had developed a very long distance relationship, which suited her just fine. She had seen him three or four times since August, and spoke with him every other week or so.

"He's got money, manners, and he actually calls you. Of course he's a nice guy," Lois said. "Are you going to get back to him?" She nudged the phone toward Clare.

"Eventually," Clare said. "Right now, the most important man in my life is the structural engineer. Where did I leave that copy of the estimate the vestry got a few years back?"

"Here." Lois slid a folder across her desk. "Don't wait too long on Hugh. Sooner or later, you, like the roof, will start sagging and leaking. You have to nail a man down before then, if you want one."

"What a charming image. I'll be sure to think of you when I'm picking out my support bra and Depends." Clare tucked the folder under her arm and crossed to the door.

"If you were married to Hugh Parteger, you could afford to have them sent over by your personal shopper," Lois called after her.

In the church, Clare could see the vestry members gathered around what she now thought of as the Crisis Zone, a series of plastic buckets and basins set on the windowsill and spread over the floor. In the pale winter light shafting from the stained-glass window, the vestry members looked like a Vermeer painting, all well-dressed concern and solemn experience. Until she heard Robert Corlew say, "If you had just listened to me when I proposed an affordable way to fix the damn thing, we wouldn't be looking at this now!"

"Your way, which was, as I recall, to staple tarp and asphalt shingles on our historic roof!" Sterling Sumner shot back.

"Our historic wreck!"

"Hi, everyone," Clare said. "Have I missed anything important?"

There was a general chorus of greeting, and Corlew and Sumner sank back into their respective stances, glaring at each other. The former was a small-scale developer whose latest project was a drive-through mini–strip mall. The latter taught architecture at Skidmore after having retired from a firm specializing in high-end, unique houses. They were the cobra and the mongoose of her vestry.

"Sorry I'm late. Why don't we all take a seat and get started?" Clare plopped into the pew across the aisle from the Zone. She waited until all six vestry members had seated themselves near the tarp-covered pews bracketing the water-damaged space and then she said, "Let us pray.

"Heavenly Father, you have blessed us with many riches and given us stewardship over them. A beautiful house of worship, a close-knit community, and a measure of prosperity. You have raised up intelligent, passionately committed people to lead our congregation. You ask in return, Lord, that we use our resources wisely and always remember that what we do here is not to satisfy our own egos, but for the glory of your name. Amen."

There was an answering mutter of "Amen"s.

"Okay," she said, "I see everyone has gotten a clear look at the problem." There was a sound, a kind of collective unwilling groan, from the others. "I know the question of what to do about the roof has been discussed"— she paused, trying to think of a tactful way to put it—"extensively before. Gentlemen and lady"—she nodded at silver-haired Mrs. Marshall, the only woman on the board—"the time to discuss is over. We have to act on this now before the whole aisle roof caves in on us."

"I couldn't agree with you more," Robert Corlew said.

"I think we can all agree that preserving the historic nature of St. Alban's is a priority," she continued. Sterling Sumner beamed at her and tightened his English school scarf—a year-round affectation—in a way that suggested a rude gesture to Corlew. Clare soldiered on. "With the extent of the damage we can see, we're not talking about simply fixing the roof anymore. I'm sure Robert and Sterling have a much better understanding of these things than I do, but it looks as if we're going to have to replace and repair some of the interior woodwork. Lord only knows what has to be done to the window embrasure in order to make sure the stained-glass panel remains secure. Historical accuracy, in this context, is going to mean high-level finish carpentry, a window-restoration specialist, and hand-cut Vermont slate shingles for the roof."

"It's going to be pricey. Very, very pricey." Terence McKellan patted his expansive belly as if looking for spare change. The vice president for commercial loans at AllBanc, Terry was St. Alban's financial officer.

"We have a responsibility to the future generations to preserve St. Alban's heritage," Mrs. Marshall said.

"We also have a responsibility to safeguard what money we have," Robert Corlew said. He moved his hand as if he were about to jam it into his improbably thick hair, but stopped himself. Clare, who had been trying for a year to discern whether he wore a rug or not, filed the gesture away in a mental folder marked EVIDENCE FOR TOUPEE.

Norm Madsen's faded blue eyes looked thoughtfully into the middle distance. "Maybe we could knock up something quick and cheap to fix the immediate problem, and then work on raising money for the fancier roof."

"Norm, with a leak this extensive, there is no quick and cheap fix," Terry said.

Clare stood up. "Folks, this is rapidly becoming a replay of every discussion we've had about the roof since I came to this parish. I'm calling for a vote."

"A vote?" several voices echoed.

"A vote, straight up or down. Big, honkingly, expensive, historically correct blowout, or affordable ticky-tack housing stock."

"You make the alternatives sound so attractive," Sterling said.

"I vote for expensive and accurate," Clare said. "Robert Corlew."

"Affordable. And I know—"

"Just the vote, please. Mrs. Marshall."

"Historically accurate."

"Thank you. Terry McKellan."

He sighed. "I have to go with the cheaper alternative."

"Sterling Sumner."

"Historical accuracy at any cost!"

"Thank you, Sterling. Norm Madsen."

The elderly lawyer's face sank into thought. Thirty seconds passed. A minute. Finally, "The least expensive alternative. Sorry, Lacey." He smiled apologetically at Mrs. Marshall.

She leaned over the pew and rested her thin, blue-veined hand over his. "You have to vote your conscience, Norm."

Clare propped her hands on her hips. "Not too surprisingly, it's three for and three against. So . . . it looks like the tiebreaker will be our brand-new junior warden." Everyone looked toward the sixth vestry member, elected at the congregation's annual meeting only two Sundays ago.

The man of the moment nodded. "I agree with the legacy thing. I feel like I have a duty to shepherd this church, so that when my little boy is my age, he'll be able to look around him and be proud of everything we did. So I vote the full slate." Geoffrey Burns crossed his arms over his camel-hair topcoat and grinned like a lawyer tossing a winning piece of evidence in front of opposing counsel.

"Now, wait just a minute," Robert Corlew began, pointing a blunt finger at the younger man.

"No." Clare held up her hand. "Robert, I empathize with your concerns about cost. And heaven knows, as the only contractor among us, you have the best sense of what the bottom line will be. But we can't keep going round and round on this thing. If the whole board can't agree to accept the vote and move onward, I'm going to throw the question open to a vote by the congregation."

Mrs. Marshall pursed her lips. "If we present the congregation a divided face, we'll have considerably more trouble getting one hundred percent participation when it comes time to raise the money. If they think some of us don't want the project to go ahead, it will encourage those who feel wishy-washy about it to sit on their wallets."

"And while we're talking about fund-raising," Geoff Burns said, "let's consider the selling angle." He held up his hands to make a frame. "Donate generously so that American artisans can handcraft a living legacy for your grandchildren's children." He shifted in his pew and made another frame. "Or, donate generously so that Baines Roofing and Plumbing can stop the leak in the roof."

"He's got a point, Rob," Terry said. "Everybody loves giving money for a new gym. Nobody wants to pay for a boiler."

"Maybe we could have donors' names etched into the slate," Norm Madsen mused.

"Hey, I like that," Geoff agreed.

Clare was watching Corlew's face during the conversation. He looked flushed and clammy, as if he might either explode or have a coronary episode any moment. She laid her hand on his arm. "Robert," she said, her voice pitched low, "we need you on this." She dropped into the pew next to him. The others were caught up in the excitement of brainstorming suggestions for spurring on donations. "This isn't a zero-sum game, where you lose and Sterling wins. We all want the same outcome." Corlew looked up to where the water had stained the elegantly lapped pine. "Nobody else brings your kind of experience to this. You're the person we'll need to help vet the bids and the specialists. You're the one who can tell us if their costs are fair, or if they're padding the bills. And most important"—she leaned forward so he couldn't avoid looking her straight in the eye—"you're a man whose opinions and leadership are well respected in our community."

He grunted. "I'm not doing this in order to put Sterling's nose out of joint." He spoke in the same low tones as she had. "I really don't think we're in any position to take on new debt. Or to hit up the congregation for extra money when we ought to be focusing on getting more people into the pews."

"I know." She didn't argue or try to refute him. She just waited.

His broad shoulders sagged a little. "Okay. I'm in."

She squeezed his arm hard. "Good."

He squared himself up again. "But I'm going to be keeping an eye on every nail, every two-by-four, every bucket of caulk."

She grinned. "We wouldn't have it any other way." She rose. "Come on, everybody, let's adjourn to the meeting room. If we're going to talk money, we may as well make ourselves more comfortable."

CHAPTER 6

NOW

While they decamped to the meeting room, and people helped themselves to Lois's bad coffee and they settled around the massive black oak table, she congratulated herself on decisively taking the field. The glow lasted right up until Terry McKellan told her there weren't going to be any loans to actually get the work done.

"What?" she said, looking at the copy of their financial statement he had sent sailing across the table. "We have to get loans. That's the way you do it, right?" She stopped. She sounded more like a high school girl running a student council meeting than a Leader of Men. And women. She tried for a more decisive tone. "That is, my experience has been"—watching her mother run a capital campaign for their home parish near Norfolk and a single workshop on fund-raising at Virginia Episcopal Seminary, but they didn't have to know all the details, did they?—"that necessary improvements on the physical plant are started by loans from the diocese or the bank, and the capital campaign is designed to supplement them and pay them off."

"That's a good way to do it," McKellan agreed.

"So what's the catch?"

McKellan's luxurious brown mustache quirked up at each end. "You have looked at the financial statements over the past year, haven't you?"

"Of course I have."

"Did you notice the outstanding loan from the diocese? We took it out three years ago to pay for the organ restoration and the parking lot repairs."

"Sure. But we've been making regular payments on it."

His eyes flicked toward the others seated around the table. "And you noticed the monthly mortgage payment we're making?"

"Sure. The parish hall burned down nearly to the ground in '93 and the vestry took out a mortgage to cover the cost of repairs. I've looked over the records. We've never had a late payment, not once." She looked around the table. "St. Alban's must have good credit."

McKellan's mustache broadened. He was looking at her in a distinctly paternal way. She didn't like it. "Clare," he said, "have you ever taken out a loan?"

"I had a student loan. In college. I paid it off."

"I mean, a loan requiring collateral. Income flow. A debt-to-asset ratio. A mortgage. A car loan. A business loan."

"Um." She had gone from her parents' house to school and then straight into the army, which for ten years had told her where to go and given her a place to live when she got there. Then it was a group house at seminary, located for her by the housing office, and now the St. Alban's rectory. Clare realized that not only had she never purchased a house, she had never even chosen her own place to live.

The vestry members, most of whom were old enough to have paid off their mortgages when she was in diapers, were looking at her. "I, um, I've always paid cash for my cars," she said.

McKellan nodded. "We have too much debt in proportion to our income."

"Which has been falling over the past ten years," Sterling Sumner pointed out.

"You work for AllBanc," she said. "Couldn't you . . . ?"

"AllBanc holds the current mortgage." McKellan opened his hands. "If we were still doing business the old way, it wouldn't be a problem. Every officer at the bank knows this church and knows we're good for the money. But we're part of a conglomerate now. We can't make loans based on a handshake and a reputation anymore."

Clare pulled her shoulder-length hair back and twisted it. From the corner of the room, the Civil War–era grandfather clock ticked away the time. She wondered, for a moment, how much they could get for it at auction.

"Okay," she said. "We're going to need a sizable chunk of change to get repairs started while we're getting a capital campaign off the ground." She thought about the annual budget they had hashed out last month. She couldn't imagine squeezing anything else out of that stone. "Suggestions?"

"Get rid of the outreach programs," Sterling said. "If it's really important, people will take up the gap by donating their time and money."

"No!"

Clare erupted from her chair, setting it rocking unsteadily on the Persian carpet.

Sterling tugged on his scarf. "It's not as if the soup kitchen will fold without us. And I'm sure the unwed teenage mothers will continue to have babies whether we're here to 'mentor' them or not."

"Sterling," Mrs. Marshall said warningly.

"Well, they're not providing much benefit to the members of the congregation," he pointed out.

Clare braced her hands flat on the table. "Ministering to the poor, the sick, and the friendless is pretty much the whole point behind the Christianity thing, Sterling." She caught the wicked gleam in his eye and knew she had risen to his bait. "And you are being deliberately provocative." She sat down. "Next suggestion."

People looked up, down, across the room, as if thousands of dollars might materialize from the air.

"What about investments?" Geoff Burns said. "Are there any underperformers in the church's portfolio we could sell?"

McKellan shook his head. "Not without gutting our already-modest endowment."

"Ah." Burns sank back into his seat. Clare considered the leather-and-oak chair, one of twelve in the room. Maybe they wouldn't have to send anything out to auction. They could do it all on eBay. Mrs. DeWitt, St. Alban's seventy-something volunteer webmaster, had her own e-store.

"There is the possibility . . ." Mrs. Marshall's voice faded away. Clare sat up straighter. The elderly woman tended to be one of the quieter members at their meetings, but when she spoke up, she always did so strongly. Clare had never heard her sound uncertain before.

Mrs. Marshall looked down at the financial statement in front of her. "I suppose I could liquidate the Ketchem Trust."

Norm Madsen shook his head. "No, no, no no no. Out of the question."

Such clear-cut decisiveness was out of character for Mr. Madsen, the vestry's Great Equivocator. "What's the Ketchem Trust?" Clare asked. "I don't recall seeing that name in our financial statement."

"That's because it doesn't belong to St. Alban's," Mr. Madsen replied.

"But it could," Mrs. Marshall said.

"Isn't this the money—," Sterling Sumner began.

Mr. Madsen cut him off. "There's been no qualifying event to disburse the trust."

"*I'm* the one who decides what qualifies." Mrs. Marshall was sounding more like herself now, but Clare had never seen the elderly lawyer so worked up. She glanced around the table. Terry McKellan and Robert Corlew were following the exchange with baffled expressions. Geoff Burns jotted notes in his Palm Pilot, evidently keeping busy until someone filled him in. So it wasn't one of those pieces of information that everyone on the vestry knew and had forgotten to tell her.

Sterling was advising Mrs. Marshall to think of herself, and Mr. Madsen was saying something incomprehensible about "devolving" and "beneficiaries." Robert Corlew had leaned over and was whispering to Terry McKellan.

"Excuse me," Clare said. "Folks?" She might as well have been talking to herself. Geoff Burns rolled his eyes in her direction. She leaned forward. "Excuse. Me," she said, in a voice pitched to carry across the noise of helicopter rotors.

The room fell silent. "Thank you. Mrs. Marshall, some of us here need an explanation. What's the Ketchem Trust?"

Norm Madsen opened his mouth, but Mrs. Marshall said, "Let me tell it, Norm." She turned toward Clare. "It's a trust left by my mother at her death. I'm the sole trustee, and I have the power to decide if the trust ought to be ended and the principal handed over to the beneficiary."

"Who is . . . ?" Clare had a feeling where this was going.

"If—when—the trust is broken, the money goes to me, to be used entirely at my discretion. I must say, I never thought the trust would last forever, but it feels very strange now, contemplating ending it. I always thought I would leave it to St. Alban's in my will. Under the circumstances, I believe I'd better push my timetable forward." She wore coral lipstick that matched the coral scarf around her throat, and when she smiled, she looked like a banner flying in the face of defeat. "After all, I've already invested in the window. I may as well pay for the roof and the wall."

"The window? You donated that?"

"As a memorial to my mother." She frowned. "Oh, heavens. I do hope the work they did back then isn't a factor in our present problem."

Sterling shook his head. "The artisans only replaced the existing color-block window. There wasn't any structural work done."

"Kind of a grim verse there," Burns said from his chair at the far end of the table. "I thought people usually went for more uplifting resurrection theology in memorials."

"Do they?" Mrs. Marshall's polite tone implied Geoff Burns's idea of a suitable memorial would contain big-eyed children and puppy dogs frolicking about a blond-haired Jesus. "I thought Lamentations most suitable."

"Getting back on point," Clare said, "I'd like to understand more about the Ketchem Trust. What is it used for? Why haven't you broken it up to now?"

"How much money are we talking about?" Robert Corlew leaned forward on the table.

"It varies with the state of the stock market, of course," Mrs. Marshall replied, just as Norm Madsen said, "You don't have to answer that, Lacey," and Sterling Sumner chimed in, "Oh, sure, with somebody else's money you're interested."

There was a pause.

"Between one hundred and thirty and one hundred and fifty thousand dollars." Mrs. Marshall gave her defenders a quelling glance. "Roughly."

Geoff Burns whistled. "In that case, I like it rough."

Clare coughed, and McKellan and Corlew snorted, but evidently that particular phrase didn't mean anything to Mrs. Marshall. "Has it all been accumulating in there, like a savings account?" Clare asked. "Or is there money being paid out currently?" A thought struck her, and her cheeks pinked. "It's not—do you need—is it helping you out?"

"No, dear. The trust does generate a modest income, and since 1973, it's been used to help defray the expenses of the free clinic."

Clare should have been surprised, but after living over a year in a town of eight thousand, she was beginning to realize that sooner or later, everything and everybody was connected. In one way or another.

"When we were foster parents, Karen and I went to the free clinic a few times," Geoff Burns said. "Two of the moms we dealt with got treated there. Dr. Rouse does good work."

Clare noticed that when Geoff spoke of foster parenting, the veins in his neck didn't bulge out like they used to. Becoming a father—finally—had mellowed him. Of course, he was branching his practice out into criminal defense, so she supposed he hadn't softened up all that much.

"My mother founded the clinic. That is, she donated the building and money to support it. She was a deeply Christian woman. The most charitable I've ever known."

There was an expression on Norm Madsen's face that made Clare think that he, perhaps, had a different view of Mrs. Marshall's mother. "Mr. Madsen," she said, "how do you fit into all this?"

"I was the late Mrs. Ketchem's attorney. I handled the property transfers that established the clinic. I also drew up the trust documents."

"Mother wanted to make sure the clinic would be able to keep running, but she also wanted to leave a legacy to me. We discussed it before she died. Up till now, there was never any need more compelling than the clinic's. But"—she tossed up her hands—"that leak! We have to get the roof fixed and we have to do it now, before the entire north aisle becomes unusable and the rot spreads into the main roof."

"Hear, hear," Sterling Sumner said. "But I'm confident we could do the repairs with half the sum you named, Lacey. You keep the other for yourself."

She shook her head. "No. I couldn't. Besides, if I gave the whole amount, we might be able to avoid a capital campaign altogether."

"I'll drink to that," Robert Corlew said.

"There are other reasons for running a capital campaign," Geoff Burns said. "In addition to making repairs and building the endowment, it gives donors an investment in St. Alban's. They have a stake in its future, a vested interest. It's the difference between renting an apartment and buying your own house."

"I happen to agree with Geoff," Clare said, "but it's a moot point. I don't think, in good conscience, we can use the Ketchem Trust money when the clinic is struggling financially."

"Says who?" Corlew tapped his nose. "They get a fat check from the town every year. Courtesy of us, the taxpayers. Plus, they do that annual fund-raiser. Believe me, you won't be seeing sick people staggering around in the street."

Fortunately, Terry McKellan spoke up before Clare had a chance to say something unpriestly. "Besides. Even if the trust is invested in high-yield dividends, it can't be throwing off more than a few thousand a year."

Mrs. Marshall nodded. "It's usually about ten thousand."

"So eight hundred a month. It must be a welcome addition to the other funding. But it's not a make-or-break amount." He turned to Clare. "I know you'd prefer to keep that money going to the clinic. I would, too. But let's face it, we're up against the wall. Even if we started the capital campaign tomorrow and every pledging unit at St. Alban's gave, it would still be months before we actually saw any income. That roof could be down in the aisle by then."

"There must be some other way." She pushed back her chair and walked around the perimeter of the meeting room, past Gothic Revival bookcases, past diamond-paned windows, past small, thickly painted oils of biblical landscapes. "Look at all this. Look at what we have. There must be some way to raise fast cash besides taking away medical treatment from the working poor."

Mrs. Marshall surprised her by rising, too. "But then we'd be robbing Peter to pay Paul, dear. You agreed, as did I, that preserving St. Alban's unique history and beauty was worth the cost. I believe you described it as 'big, honkingly expensive.'"

Despite herself, Clare's lips twitched.

"Are you going to back out now that the price turns out to be more than you wanted to pay?"

Clare looked down at the intricate carpet. She thought she would have learned by thirty-five that saying yes to one thing meant saying no to something else.

"Before we all agree to this, I want to state my objections in the strongest terms." Clare and Mrs. Marshall both turned to Norm Madsen. "It was Mrs. Ketchem's intention that the money from the trust be used to support the clinic. Only when the trustee judges that the clinic no longer needs the funding is the principal to be disbursed. And you cannot convince me, Lacey, that you honestly think they no longer need that ten thousand a year." He shook slightly from the force of his tone. "Your mother would not have wanted this."

She sat down again. "Maybe not. But she left me to decide, Norm."

Clare never would have imagined that news of her parish getting a $150,000 gift would depress her. She sat in a funk while Corlew, who had a 1:30 appointment, wrapped the meeting up and everyone shucked on coats, hats, gloves, and mufflers. She had enough presence of mind to make her good-byes, but she was still in a blue devil, as her grandmother would have called it, when she gathered up the papers to return to her office.

She was surprised to find Mr. Madsen lingering outside the meeting-room door.

"Thanks for giving it a try," he said, sounding much more his usual evenhanded self. "Not that it helped, but I appreciate the effort."

"I feel like I did when I was a kid and found out we were moving near my grandparents. I was all excited, until I realized I was going to be leaving behind my friends. I guess this defines a mixed blessing." She looked up at him. "I was surprised at how, um, passionately you felt on the question. You must be a big supporter of the clinic."

"Not particularly, no."

"Then why were you so vehement in defending its funding?"

"Jane Mairs Ketchem, that's why. She's rolling over in her grave right now, and it wouldn't surprise me if she kicked her way out of the coffin and marched down here to defend her precious clinic." He ran his hand over his thick white brush cut. "I'll tell you something. She was the only woman who could ever scare me. And the fact that she's dead doesn't make me any less scared."

CHAPTER 7

NOW

Clare came with Mrs. Marshall to the clinic the next Monday.

"You really don't have to do this, dear," Mrs. Marshall said, pulling on her black kidskin gloves and setting her hat at an angle on the silver waves of her hair.

Clare brought her attention back from her look-around at the airy foyer of the Marshall house, one of several "executive mansions" outside Millers Kill that had been built for high-level General Electric people in the sixties. It was decorated—tastefully and expensively—at the same time and had never been changed again. Clare hadn't seen so much Danish modern and smoked glass since her last visit to an Ikea store.

"I know," she said, fishing into her pocket for her own bulky Polarplus gloves. "You don't have to tell the clinic director about your decision in person, either. But you are."

Mrs. Marshall smiled. She had on fuchsia lipstick today, and the effect against her paper white skin was startling. "I suspect we were both raised to do the right thing, whether we want to or not."

"You should have met my grandmother Fergusson." Clare opened the front door. "Do you want to take my car or yours?"

Mrs. Marshall paused on the steps to consider the Shelby Cobra, badly in need of a trip to the car wash, parked next to her Lincoln Town Car. "Mine, I think."

They didn't talk much on the ride into town. Clare watched the landscape, covered with sodden, tired snow, and tried to shake off the sick feeling in the pit of her stomach. She could handle disagreement, disapproval, even, she supposed, disdain, with equanimity. But she hated disappointing anyone. She dreaded it with the same nauseating plunge she had felt as a child, standing in front of her mother or grandmother and admitting, yes, she had lost her new shoes, yes, she had let the twins out of her sight, yes, she had brought home a report card full of low grades and slack effort.

Mrs. Marshall could evidently read minds. "It's hard to deliver bad news, isn't it?"

"It's not that, exactly," Clare said. "You can't be in the army and then the ministry without learning how to say things people don't want to hear. It's this feeling that I'm the cause of the bad news. That's hard to live with."

Mrs. Marshall slowed the car to turn onto Route 51. "You might be taking a little too much responsibility for this, don't you think? You're a wonderful priest; a little rough around the edges, of course, but experience will help with that—" Clare sat up straighter in the crushed velvet seat and surreptitiously checked her black blouse for any traces of breakfast.

"But you aren't St. Alban's, dear, and you mustn't go around confusing yourself with the institution." The scenery was more crowded now as they neared the center of town. They passed an auto repair shop, a tire store, a barren plant nursery hunkered down for the long, cold spell between Valentine's and Mother's Day. "If anyone should feel responsible, I should. It's my decision, ultimately. But even so, I came to it as part of the group, not as an individual. Neither you nor I can carry the day all by ourselves. We're part of a democracy."

"An oligarchy," Clare said under her breath.

"Perhaps." Mrs. Marshall sounded amused. "But you'll concede me my point."

Clare flipped her hand over. Mrs. Marshall turned onto Barkley Avenue.

"What the devil?" Mrs. Marshall said. From the opposite end of the avenue, two squad cars raced toward them. The elderly woman yanked the steering wheel, plowing them nose first into the nearest parking spot, but instead of racing past them, the black-and-whites skidded to a stop in front of the clinic. Clare popped open her door and jumped out in time to see the chief of police and the department's youngest officer, Kevin Flynn, pounding up the steps into the building.

Clare started forward across the street, recollected herself, and turned back to see if Mrs. Marshall needed any help. The driver's side window unrolled smoothly and Mrs. Marshall said, "I've got to do a better job of parking. You go ahead, I'll be right there. Be careful, dear."

She didn't need any more permission than that. Clare ran toward the clinic, her boots slapping through slush. One of the wide double doors had been left hanging open, and she slipped through it into a tiny foyer papered over with leaflets on AIDS prevention, domestic violence, immunization schedules, and flu shots. The inner doors—heavy, modern fireproof slabs that had undoubtedly replaced something older and more elegant—had swung firmly shut, but Clare could hear shrieking and bellowing coming from inside.

She pushed into the clinic. She was in a wood-floored hall, with pocket doors opened wide on the right revealing a waiting room. Its orange plastic chairs were knocked over and children's toys had been kicked everywhere. Immediately in front of her, a mahogany staircase swept up to a landing, where a redheaded woman in a medical jacket clutched a newel post and looked down an unseen hallway. The sounds, much louder now, came from whatever she was watching.

"Oh!" She spotted Clare and hurried down the stairs. She was a tiny thing, a head shorter than Clare, and with her sneakers, jeans, and hair braided down her back, Clare would have thought her some sort of teenage volunteer if not for the fine lines around her sharp, skeptical eyes and her white coat embroidered L. RAYFIELD, N.P.

"I'm afraid we're having a bit of trouble right now. You can—" L. Rayfield, N.P., glanced around, frowning. "You can wait in the office, back here. I'll be with you as soon as I can."

"It's okay," Clare said. "I'm a priest." Without waiting to see what effect that complete irrelevance had on the woman, Clare charged up the stairs.

"You're a what? Hey—wait! Come back here!"

The hallway off the landing ran the length of the house to a single dull gray elevator, jarringly at odds with the mahogany six-panel doors opened, two to each side, onto the hall. Above the shrieking and shouting coming from the last room on the right, Clare could hear Russ Van Alstyne's voice, hard with authority, pitched to control.

"Put the stool down! Back away from the cabinet!"

She felt a thud vibrate through her feet and turned to see the nurse headed up the stairs. Clare ran down the hall, skidding to a stop in front of the open door.

Russ and Kevin Flynn, backs to the door, were angling to box in a wild-eyed Debba Clow, who brandished a metal stool like a battering ram against a glass-fronted cabinet filled with medical supplies. "—defend myself against this monster who wants my children taken away from me!" she was saying, her words a high-pitched screech.

"And you've proven me right," roared Dr. Rouse, rearing up from his shelter behind the examination table. "You're so obsessed with revenge for nonexistent wrongs you can't even stop to think about your kids!"

Debba shrieked and raised the stool.

"Debba, stop!" Clare stepped forward into view, her hands raised. Officer Flynn twisted around to stare at her, but Russ never took his eyes from Debba.

"We're handling this, Clare," he said, his voice tight.

Clare ignored him, fumbling with her parka's zipper to yank it down like Superman revealing the *S* on his chest. "Remember me? From St. Alban's? We talked the other day." Debba stared at her, pulling the stool in tightly against her chest. Clare took another step into the room. "You don't want to do this." She could hear the sound of the nurse's shoes as she reached the doorway and stopped. "I bet you don't hit your children to discipline them, do you?"

"Of course not!"

"It wouldn't surprise me if she—"

"Not *now*, Al!" The whispered command from the woman behind Clare cut Dr. Rouse off.

Clare reached one hand out slowly. "Then you already know that violence isn't the answer."

"You don't know what he did," Debba said. "He wrote my goddamn ex-husband and told him I was endangering the children. Today I was served with papers—he's suing me for full custody! Except he doesn't want to keep Skylar, he wants to institutionalize him!" She shifted the stool in her grip as if she might throw it at the doctor. "Did you know that? Did you know that before you wrote him, you bastard?"

Clare took another step forward. She was almost shoulder to shoulder with Russ. "You're so angry and frustrated you want to hurt Dr. Rouse, don't you? But I bet you've felt that way before, haven't you? Every mother I've ever met has felt like that. Has been pushed so hard she wanted to lash out at her kids. To hit them. To hurt them."

"Clare . . ." Russ's hiss warned her to shut up.

"But you didn't give in to that feeling, did you? You didn't hurt anyone. You controlled yourself." She stepped forward. Almost close enough to touch the stool if she stretched out her arm. "You controlled yourself. *You* are in control." She deliberately looked away from Debba and laid her hand on Russ's arm. Under the slick nylon of his parka, his muscles were tensed. "Chief Van Alstyne is a good man. Why don't you let him help you? Before you get yourself into real trouble."

Debba's eyes grew larger. "I'm going to get arrested, aren't I? Oh, God." Her lower lip bowed down like a toddler's caught between anger and anguish.

"Put the stool down, Deborah," Russ said. "And we'll talk about it."

Hands shaking, Debba lowered the stool. As soon as it touched the ground, Russ stepped past Clare and took the trembling woman by her upper arms. "Okay, Deborah, listen to me." He looked directly into her eyes. "I'm going to have you sit in another room while I talk to Dr. Rouse. Officer Flynn will stay with you." He flicked a glance toward Clare. "As will Reverend Fergusson." He reached to the small of his back and unsnapped his handcuffs. "Now. I don't want you to get alarmed, but I am going to cuff you."

At the sight of the handcuffs, Debba burst into tears. She shook her head wildly, sending clouds of kinky blond hair flying everywhere. "I'm going to cuff you while you're with Officer Flynn," Russ said, his voice steady. "When I come back in to talk with you, I'll take these off."

Debba gasped out, "No, no," but obediently held out her wrists. Russ snapped the metal constraints on her. "Kevin," he said. Officer Flynn appeared and put his hands on Debba's shoulders. Russ pivoted. "Laura," he said to the nurse, "is there a place where Ms. Clow can sit down in private?"

"We've got an old-fashioned ladies' lounge with a sofa and everything." The nurse beckoned. "Follow me."

Officer Flynn guided Debba out of the examination room and down the hall, with Clare close on his heels. The nurse—Laura—opened the door closest to the stairs. It was indeed an old-fashioned ladies' lounge, with the toilets and sinks discreetly behind a second, interior door. "Come here, honey, and sit down." Laura patted the sofa, an overstuffed red velvet monstrosity that looked as if it had been taken from a whorehouse. Clare recognized it immediately as the soul mate to her own office's sagging love seat—the one piece of furniture that couldn't be auctioned off. Debba sat down shakily, still weeping. Officer Flynn perched on the edge next to her, somewhere between guarding and comforting her.

"Don't feel so bad," the nurse said. "I've been arrested plenty of times.

They'll have the bail bondsman over at the station half an hour after you get there and you'll be home in time to make supper."

Clare took a closer look at the tiny redhead. "Wait a minute—haven't I seen you before? Weren't you part of the environmental action group protesting the Adirondack Spa development last summer?"

"That was me! Laura Rayfield." She held out her hand and grinned as Clare shook it. Clare pulled her a little away from the sofa.

"So what happened?" Clare asked.

The nurse sighed. "I think Dr. Rouse overreacted to Deb's antivaccination crusade. He's been under tremendous stress lately, and everything seems to set him off. Thank God he didn't grab his gun when she came charging in here."

"You have a gun? At the clinic?"

"*Al* has a gun. In his desk." She made a face. "It makes him feel safer. We've had a few break-ins, addicts looking for Oxy, stuff like that. Me, I think you're more likely to shoot yourself than an intruder."

"Have you talked to him? About his stress?"

"I told him the best thing to do would be to schedule a couple of evening meetings where he could ease anybody's fears about vaccinations, but does he listen to me? Not hardly. He's always practiced by the 'Me doctor, you patient' model, and now he's got women coming in and questioning him about their kids' immunizations, and about flu shots, and this, that, and the other thing."

"Is that bad?"

"Hell no. But Al still thinks he's living in a world where a white coat makes you bulletproof and able to leap tall buildings in a single bound."

Clare reflexively reached back and twisted her hair more tightly into its knot. "Last summer, I saw you hauled off getting the word out about the dangers of PCBs. How come you're not helping Debba spread the alarm about this vaccination thing?"

"Because, unlike the known link between PCBs and cancer, there's not a shred of scientific evidence to back up the autism-vaccination connection." Laura looked over to the sofa, where Debba had subsided into sharp, deep breaths. "Autism can be so cruel to a family. I can't blame parents for searching for something, anything, to explain how their perfectly normal one-year-old grows into a child trapped inside his own mind. It's like the changelings in a fairy tale. You know, where the baby starts out healthy and is replaced by a sickly imposter? Except nowadays, instead of saying 'Fairies stole my son,' parents are crying that mercury-contaminated vaccines did the deed." She shook her head, thumping her braid along her back. "If I thought that were true, I'd be breaking into warehouses to destroy any stockpiles myself."

"But you don't blame Debba for what she's been doing."

"I don't. But that doesn't change the fact that she's wrong. And she's wasting her time fighting a war that doesn't need to be won." She squeezed Clare's hand. "I'd better get back there. I know he sounded in fine fettle, but Al was really shaken up when she came at him like that."

Clare lifted a hand in parting and turned back to the sofa. She shucked off her heavy parka and draped it over the back of one of a pair of orange plastic chairs appropriated from the waiting room. She dragged the chair over to Debba and plopped down, flashing a smile at Kevin Flynn, who was looking even younger than his twenty-one years this morning. Then she touched Debba's hands, twisting together beneath the steel shine of the handcuffs.

"Debba, tell me about your kids." The woman looked up. "How old are they? What are their names?"

"Um, I have two. Skylar, he's my son, he's six. And Whitley's my little girl. She's three and a half."

"Where are they right now?"

"At my mother's house. We all live there. I moved in a few years ago when Jeremy left us." Debba drew a deep breath. "We've never had any problems before. He made his support payments, he got his visits with Whitley, and other than that he left us alone."

"No visits with Skylar?"

Debba shook her head. "No. Jeremy couldn't handle being a father to an autistic kid. He divorced me when Whitley was a baby. He was dead sure that she'd turn out to be like her brother."

"That's terrible!" Kevin Flynn's outburst made both women look over at him. He reddened. "I mean, a guy turning his back on his handicapped kid and his baby."

Debba nodded. "Your preaching to the choir here."

"So why is he suddenly set on taking full custody of both the children?" Clare asked.

Debba clenched her fists. The handcuffs clicked. "He always wanted to institutionalize Skylar. After it was obvious that Whitley was . . . normal, he used to bring it up every now and again. Said it would give me more time for her. The implication being, of course, that time spent on Skylar was wasted. But he never said anything about taking her himself." She pulled her arms apart, watching as the handcuffs dug into her flesh.

Clare laid her hands over Debba's. "Stop it. Hurting yourself isn't going to help your kids, any more than hurting Dr. Rouse will."

"I just don't know how I'm going to fight him. It's not like I've got the money to hire a decent attorney. Or any attorney. God. My mom said I ought to give up my art and get a real job."

Clare's mouth quirked up in a one-sided smile. "My mom said I ought to give up flying helicopters and get a real job. Then I became a priest. Now she wishes I had the army job back."

Debba smiled a ghostly version of the smile Clare had seen on her last Thursday.

Clare interlaced her fingers and pressed her hands against her chin. "I know a good lawyer who could help you. She works part time from her home."

"You don't understand. When I say I don't have the money, I mean I don't have any money. At least if I'm charged with assault, the state will get me a lawyer for free."

Kevin Flynn nodded. "That's right."

"I think she'll waive her usual fee. She owes me a favor."

"What did you do? Forgive her all her sins?"

Clare thought of Karen Burns's face as she held Cody after the month-old baby had been rescued from drowning. "I helped her when she and her husband were trying to adopt their baby boy. If you'll let me, I'll set up a meeting."

There was a knock on the door, and Russ entered. He reached behind his back and unsnapped the handcuff key from his belt. "Deborah Clow," he said, kneeling down to unlock her, "you're free to go."

"What?" Kevin and Debba spoke at the same time.

"You talked to Dr. Rouse," Clare said. She tried not to sound like a teacher whose protégé has done something terribly clever.

"I talked to Dr. Rouse," he agreed.

"And he's not pressing any charges? I threatened to kill him, for God's sake. I nearly smashed up his examination room."

Russ put a hand on his knee and levered himself up. "I'm glad to hear you can appreciate the seriousness of what you did today." He hitched his thumbs in his gun belt. "Dr. Rouse has been extremely generous in not pressing charges. Seeing as how he's willing to let the assault and criminal threatening go, I'm willing to take a pass on resisting arrest. But." He stabbed toward Debba with one finger. "I've told Dr. Rouse that if he wants to swear out a restraining order against you I'll support his motion before the judge."

Debba was very still. Clare suspected she had never considered herself as the sort of woman another person needed a restraining order against.

"And restraining order or no, I don't want to see you within two blocks of the clinic or anywhere near Dr. Rouse. In fact, if you so much as jay-walk in the next few months, I'll haul you in and see if some jail time will help you to think before you act." He hooked his thumbs in his pants pockets. "Are you going to be okay to drive yourself home? If you're feel-ing too shaky, Officer Flynn here will be glad to give you a ride."

"I . . . I . . ." Looking back and forth from Russ to Kevin to Clare, Debba started to cry again.

"Yeah, I thought so. Kevin, take this lady home, make sure she gets in safe, and come back to fetch me."

"Yes sir."

Clare grabbed her parka and made to follow Kevin and Debba out the ladies' lounge door. Russ snagged her by the arm. "Reverend? A word?"

"Busted," she said under her breath.

He crossed his arms. "Not that I don't have the greatest respect for your people skills, but next time you see me talking a potentially danger-ous person down, stay the hell out of it. Okay?"

"Debba Clow was not potentially dangerous."

"Yes. She was. And you're just going to have to yield to my more exten-sive experience on this." He pulled his glasses off and rubbed them against his uniform shirt. "There's a certain look. Don't ask me to describe it. I just know it when I see it. Someone goes over the line and is willing—is going to do something scary." He replaced his glasses. "What are you do-ing here, anyway?"

"Oh! Mrs. Marshall!" She whirled and banged through the door. Russ followed. "I completely forgot about her." She rattled down the stairs. "Mrs. Marshall? Are you—"

"Here I am, dear." The elderly woman came out of the office, still in her Republican cloth coat and velvet beret. "I didn't know what was going on, but I thought I had best stay out of the way."

Clare ignored Russ's pointed look.

"Is everyone okay? There was a young woman crying as she left."

"Everyone's fine," Russ answered. "There was a little excitement, but no one was hurt."

"Mrs. Marshall, this is Chief Van Alstyne. Russ, this is Mrs. Henry Marshall, one of my vestry."

Russ nodded. "I believe you're on our drive-by list, Mrs. Marshall."

"Yes, I am." She looked at Clare. "The police department comes around to check up on us old ladies during the winter months."

"I like to think of you as women of a certain age." He smiled at Mrs. Marshall. He had a breathtakingly charming smile when he used it. "And we also have a few gentlemen on our list as well. Folks who live by themselves. Did you come by for a checkup?" His voice sounded doubtful.

"No, Clare and I came to deliver some bad news to Allan Rouse in person." There was a noise from the second floor and they all looked up. "Although perhaps this isn't the best time."

"Mrs. Marshall runs a trust that's been giving money to the clinic for years," Clare explained. "She's decided to dissolve it and sink the principal into the repairs at St. Alban's."

"I'd have to agree with you then, Mrs. Marshall. I don't think now is the time to tell Dr. Rouse his funding is getting cut."

There was another noise upstairs. It sounded like someone stomping back and forth. Mrs. Marshall pinched her fuchsia-colored lips together. "Tomorrow, then. Clare, I think I'll just powder my nose and then we can go."

Clare nodded. She and Russ stood silent while Mrs. Marshall made her way around the corner of the back hall, where an arrow under the universal male and female symbols pointed visitors to the bathrooms.

"So you found a way to get the money to fix your leaky roof," he said when they were alone. His voice was neutral.

"It's more than a leaky roof," she said. She knew she sounded defensive, but she couldn't help it. "It's the roof, the stained-glass-window setting, there's damage to the exterior wall, and we need new guttering to redirect the water away from the foundations. It's the most expensive work St. Alban's has undertaken since the '93 parish hall restoration."

"Don't churches usually raise money from their members for this sort of thing?"

"It wasn't my idea," she burst out. "I wanted to apply for a couple of loans. But it turns out St. Alban's is in hock too deep to take on any more debt. And it'll take months and months to raise sufficient monies from a capital campaign. Maybe a year. We don't have that kind of time. The repair work needs to begin now."

He looked down at her, carefully, as if he was trying to understand her. "So you're taking money away from the free clinic."

She wanted to explain, to tell him all about Mrs. Marshall's trust, and her family history, and the architectural heritage of St. Alban's. But when it came down to it, those were all just excuses, meant to make her look better. "Yes," she said. "Yes, I am."

The *thunk-thunk* of Mrs. Marshall's old-fashioned rubber-heeled snow boots interrupted anything he might have said. "Ready to go, dear?" the old woman said.

"Yes." Clare fished in her pockets for her gloves.

Mrs. Marshall took her arm. "It looks like I've wasted your morning, dragging you down here for nothing."

Clare met Russ's bright blue eyes, then let her gaze slide away. "It wasn't for nothing," she said. "There's always time to deliver bad news."

CHAPTER 8

NOW

WEDNESDAY, MARCH 15

Clare had installed one of those large read-it-from-inside-your-house thermometers on the high fence separating her rectory drive from the tiny parking lot behind the church. She didn't know why she had done it, really. To torment herself about the miserable weather in this miserable, godforsaken part of the world. She read the dial face now, as she stood in her kitchen, waiting for the AAA guy to show up and jump-start her car. Fifteen degrees Fahrenheit. That was, of course, without the windchill.

The phone rang. She lunged for it, hoping that it was the AAA dispatch, calling her back to say the road-service truck was on its way.

"Hello?"

"Hello, dear. It's Mrs. Marshall. You're still at home."

Clare steadied the coat tree beside the door, rocking from her dash for the phone. "My car won't start. I've called AAA, but they told me there were cars stalled all over the area and it would be forty-five minutes to an hour. I'm sorry, I should have rung you first thing. . . ."

"Don't worry. I'll tell you what, I'll head over to Allan Rouse's house, and if you still want to come, you can meet me there."

"Absolutely. Tell me how to find it." Clare grabbed a pen out of her junk drawer and jotted down Mrs. Marshall's directions on the back of a Niagara Mohawk power bill. After assuring Mrs. Marshall that she would drive carefully and watch out for black ice, she hung up. The phone hung on the wall between her kitchen door and window, beneath an ecclesiastical calendar with all the saints' feasts and commemorations delineated in bold black print. The first day of spring, bright in red lettering, was only a week away. She glanced out the window again at the heaps of ice-crusted snow threatening to close off her narrow drive completely. It was never going to be spring. The sooner she reconciled herself to that fact, the calmer she'd be.

The phone rang. She snagged it, a bit less hopeful than last time.

"Hello?"

"Hi, it's Karen Burns. I called over at the church, but Lois said you were still at home."

"I'm waiting for AAA to come and start my car."

"My sympathies. You really ought to think about getting a winter rat with a monster battery." Karen and her husband, Geoffrey, owned a Land Rover, a Saab, and a beat-up little Honda for tooling around in the slush and salt. Clare refrained from pointing out that she could barely afford one car, let alone two. Karen went on, "The reason I'm calling is that I've made an appointment to see Debba Clow, and I wondered if you wanted to sit in, since you're counseling her."

"I'm not—" Clare paused. Of course she was counseling Debba. "Sure. When is it?"

"Noon. It's trickier for her to haul her kids around, so we're meeting over at her house. I'm going to bring Cody. Sort of a legal strategy session slash play date."

Crud. There went her lunch with Russ. "Sure, I'll be there. Did she give you any details about what happened at the clinic?"

"Not as many as you did when you asked me to represent her. I got the impression she's still pretty pissed off at the old guy, but doesn't want to admit it."

"I'm going over to Dr. Rouse's house this morning, as soon as my car's resurrected."

"Boy, you do get around, don't you?"

"Mrs. Marshall is going to tell him about using her trust for St. Alban's building fund. Geoff told you about that, right?"

"Oh, yes."

"Well, I thought that as the official representative of the church, I ought to be there when he got the bad news. Anyway, I'll try to sound him out as to whether he's going to go ahead with a restraining order against Debba."

"Great. We'll see you later, then."

"Karen?"

"Yes?"

"Will the squeaky toy be there?"

Karen laughed. "Of course. Wherever Cody is, there also is Squeaky the Squirrel."

Clare replaced the phone on the hook. She was going to spend her lunch hour trapped in a house with three kids, a lawyer, and the most obnoxious baby toy ever created. Instead of sharing chili and conversation with Russ. *And when did lunch with Russ Van Alstyne become the highlight of your week, missy?* Her grandmother Fergusson would most definitely disapprove.

The phone rang. Clare eyed it. She didn't get this many calls in her office.

"Hello?"

"Hello, Father."

"Mr. Hadley." Glenn Hadley, St. Alban's sexton, was the only person on the planet who called her Father. Not Father Fergusson, just Father. He never referred to her predecessor by his last name, either. He was simply "the late Father" or "the last Father." She figured Mr. Hadley had totally embraced the concept of "It's the office, not the officeholder."

"I'm afraid I've got some more bad news."

"Now what?" The boiler leaped to mind, followed by the furnace, the pipes, a chimney fire, and mice infesting the undercroft.

"You know the spot where the water's been leaking out of the aisle ceiling?"

"Yeah..."

"It looks as if it's froze up solid. There's an ice dam up there must be three inches thick. It's forcing the ceiling boards out of joint."

Clare closed her eyes.

"Father? You there?"

"Yes," she said. "I don't know, what's the best thing to do about it?"

"Ain't nothing we can do about the hole right now. I'll make sure there's a big bucket underneath it. Soon as it gets warm enough to melt up on top of the roof, it's gonna come gushing through. If we don't get it fixed up before it starts heating up and the rains come, it'll be like a shower over there."

"Anything else you can suggest?"

"Well, I could try to unbolt the other two pews from the floor and drag 'em out of the way."

"That's a great idea," she said, trying to force some enthusiasm into her voice. "I'll let the vestry and the roofing company know about this latest development. Thanks for getting on it so quickly."

"You want me to get on the roof, see if I can fix a tarp up there?"

"No! That is, let's see what the roofing guy says before we start messing around with anything."

There was a long pause. "Okay." Another pause. To give her time to change her mind. "Talk to you later."

He hung up. She sighed. Now she had to think of a way to ease his hurt feelings over not being allowed to clamber all over the ice-covered roof.

She replaced the receiver and considered the tall green thermos of coffee sitting on the pine kitchen table. She always brewed more than she could drink in the morning and carried the rest with her to the office, since Lois evidently put used industrial waste in the church's Mr. Coffee. She could really, really use another cup right now.

The phone rang. She pulled a teaspoon and a FORT RUCKER—HOME OF ARMY AVIATION mug from the dish drainer and unscrewed the thermos top. The phone rang. She poured the coffee in, breathing in the steam and smell of it. She reached for her oversized sugar bowl and began spooning in sugar. The phone rang. She stirred her sugar into the hot coffee, first clockwise, then counterclockwise. The phone rang. She picked it up.

"Hello?"

"Hey, I'm glad I caught you. Your secretary said you were still at home, but I thought I must have missed you."

"Russ." She smiled into her coffee. "What's up?"

"I have to cancel out on lunch."

She felt a ridiculous dip in her stomach. "What's happened? Is everything okay?"

"Yeah. Lyle MacAuley and Noble Entwhistle have both called in sick. Lyle's illness might be the dreaded 'last-chance-to-snowmobile fever,' but Noble never bags work unless he's on death's door. I'm going to have to spend all day in the car. I'm calling from there right now. I'm afraid my lunch'll have to be a heart attack in a sack."

"Ah. It's just as well. I just made a date to sit in with Karen Burns and Debba Clow while they go over Debba's custody case."

"You know that woman is a fruitcake, don't you?"

She grinned. "Now, Russ, I know you don't like lawyers. . . ."

"I use words other than *fruitcake* to describe the Burnses. Seriously, try not to get too sucked into Deborah Clow's problems. I've dealt with her before."

"You mean because of her protesting at the clinic?"

"That's been an issue. But not what I was thinking of. I used to come out to her place when she and her husband were first married. They got rowdy with each other all the time."

"My God. She was an abused wife?"

She could hear him sigh over the phone. "It's not always as clear-cut as that. They both used to go at each other. I'd come out there, she'd have a purpling eye and he'd have a busted lip and his forehead cut open. And then neither one of them would press charges. Nowadays, I'd run 'em both in, but this was before we had a mandatory-charge law. So I'd warn them both and hand them the counseling brochure and leave 'em until next time. Things quieted down when they had their first kid. Or maybe they just fought quieter." He sighed again. "She says she's an artist. I don't know if she's any good, but she sure has the artist's temperament. Wacky."

"Thanks for tipping me off."

He groaned. "I shouldn't have told you that, should I? It's like showing a dog raw meat. You'll take her under your wing, give her anger-management counseling, get up a committee to send her to art school, and do her picketing for her while she's in class." She laughed. He went on, his voice more serious. "Just try to cool it a bit and get a sense of what's going on before you leap into someone else's life, okay?"

"Okay," she said.

"Okay, then." There was a pause. "I suppose I ought to go."

She sat down in one of the kitchen chairs and propped her chin in her hand. "I suppose so."

"You gonna be okay with that idiot car of yours? Your secretary said it wouldn't start."

"I've got AAA. They'll be here. Eventually."

He snorted. "If you had a decent late-model four-wheel drive instead of a thirty-something-year-old sports car that weighs about as much as one of my snow tires—"

"Yeah, but if I got one, you'd just have to find something else to complain about."

He laughed. She stirred her coffee slowly. The silence stretched out.

"Well, if they don't show, give the station a call and I'll drive over and jump you." There was a sort of strangled non-noise. "Jump your car. Jump-start it. The cruisers have incredible batteries."

She started laughing. "Is that a Freudian slip, or are you just happy to see me?"

"Oh, Christ. Okay, now that I've made a complete ass of myself, I will get rolling."

She smiled.

"You're grinning at me, aren't you? I can tell."

She laughed. "Go on. Go keep the streets safe from the breakdown of traditional values." She smiled again, and wondered if he could hear this one, too. "And keep yourself safe, too."

"Always." There was a pause, as if he were going to say something more, but then he said, "Bye."

"Bye."

She let the receiver slip out of her hand and dangle by its cord. Finally she stood to rehang it. There was a beep from her drive. She opened the kitchen door to see the AAA road-service truck. A skinny young guy bulked up like the Michelin tire man in insulated overalls climbed out of the cab.

"You called, lady?"

"You're here sooner than I expected," she said. Her voice carried through the bitter air.

"Yeah, well, the office tried to call you, but your line was busy."

◆ ◆ ◆

Allan Rouse, as it happened, lived several blocks down on the same street as Geoff and Karen Burns, in a brick Italianate not much different from theirs. Elm Street had been laid out for lawyers and doctors, mill owners and land speculators, from a time when those worthies had families of a half dozen children, and servants slept in low-eaved fourth-story bedrooms. The land speculators developed vacation condominiums instead of railroads now, and the mill owners had been replaced by two-career couples who commuted down to Albany, but the serenity of place and position remained. Clare was frequently exasperated by people who lived cocooned from the harshness of life in their various Elm Streets, but as she parked her Shelby and walked to the Rouse's front door, she couldn't help but admire the beauty of a neighborhood where every window gleamed, every historically accurate piece of door hardware shone, and the potholes were always filled in immediately.

The door opened. "Hello. You must be Reverend Fergusson." The woman welcoming Clare was somewhere around sixty and holding, her body running to plumpness but not there yet, her hair still a determined glossy brown. "I'm Renee Rouse."

Clare shook her hand and let the doctor's wife take her coat. "I was admiring your house," she said. "It's lovely."

"Thanks," Mrs. Rouse said, opening a hall closet and hanging Clare's coat inside. "It's far too big for us now the children are grown, but we love it too much to leave. And the location is great. In nice weather, Allan likes to bike to work."

He wasn't biking anywhere today. In fact, when Clare caught sight of him after being ushered into the parlor, she wondered if he was ever biking anywhere again. He was sitting in a well-worn recliner that looked as if it had been his favorite chair for the past three decades. His whole body was clenched, furling in on itself, like that of an animal trying to enfold its soft underbelly within its tough outer hide.

Mrs. Marshall was perched on the edge of a sofa, leaning forward slightly. She glanced up when Renee Rouse led Clare into the living room, her relief and discomfort plain on her face.

"Oh, here you are, here's Clare now, Allan." Mrs. Marshall's tone was the same one used by relatives at the bedside of a dying person—a kind of forced obliviousness to the graying reality beside them.

Mrs. Rouse crossed the plush carpet and knelt down by her husband's side. "Sweetie?" she said. "Can I get you anything? How about some home-made hot chocolate? You know you love hot chocolate."

Dr. Rouse closed his eyes for a moment. "Sure," he said. "That'll be fine." He opened his eyes again. "Reverend Fergusson. Of course. You were the one who leaped in front of that Clow woman."

There was a pause. Clare stood fixed to the carpet, wondering how she should respond. His greeting was hardly enthusiastic. She settled on a "Pleased to meet you," and a wave.

"So, Clare," Mrs. Marshall said, in a voice as bright as her fuchsia lipstick, "I've been telling Allan about the terrible situation with the roof, and how I'm going to be using the trust principal to help out the church."

Clare looked for a seat that would require the least amount of movement from here to there. She picked a striped barrel chair kitty-corner to the sofa and balanced herself on its edge. *If you're feeling twitchy about a situation,* "Hardball" Wright said, *it's because it's a bad situation to be in.* Unfortunately, she couldn't just flop to her belly and elbow-crawl to the door, as her former survival school instructor would probably have advised. She had asked to be here. Furthermore, she was, if not directly culpable, at least one of the people responsible for Dr. Rouse's ravaged expression.

They sat in a silence more full than speech. Mrs. Marshall glanced at Clare, then at Dr. Rouse. "Allan, since Reverend Fergusson is here, are there any questions you'd like to ask her?"

His eyes peered at her from a long way away. "Yes, I would," he said, his voice rough and creaky. "I'd like to know how a priest gets to value bricks and mortar over human lives."

"Oh, now, Allan, let's not be melodramatic," Mrs. Marshall said. "The ten thousand the clinic gets from the Ketchem Trust isn't going to mean the difference between life and death. And I promise you, I'll do everything I can to make sure the board of aldermen increases the town's funding to the clinic to compensate."

Clare thought Mrs. Marshall's persuasiveness as an advocate for the clinic would take a hit, given the fact that she had withdrawn her own support. But she kept her mouth shut.

Mrs. Rouse returned with a tray bearing three brown-glazed mugs, the tall, slope-sided style unique to university gift shops and German beer halls. "I made some for everyone," she said brightly. She gingerly set a mug on the table next to her husband's chair, patted his shoulder several times, and then deposited the tray on the coffee table, within easy reach of her guests. "Honestly, Lacey, I don't think we're going to have to worry about replacing your contribution." Renee Rouse dropped into a comfortable velveteen chair that sat kitty-corner to her husband's. Books, magazines, and word-search puzzles were stacked on a broad stool at its side, and Clare could picture the Rouses, on long winter evenings, sharing the space together, reading. The *Journal of the American Medical Association* on his lap and the *Ladies' Home Journal* on hers.

"The last two times there were changes in one of the revenue sources for the clinic, the town adjusted their share to compensate," Mrs. Rouse went on. "As I recall, when that grant from the state ran out, they didn't even wait for a regular session. They passed an amended budget at a special town meeting."

Clare could feel the stone of guilt rolling away. "Really? That's good to know."

"If they do it again," Dr. Rouse said. "If." He lurched forward, his hands tightening on the arms of the recliner. "These are hard times! The board has been making noises about cutting down library hours and firing the high school art teacher to save money. Do you honestly think they'll just hand it over to me and say, 'Oh, here's your ten thousand, Allan, and thanks so much for asking'?"

Mrs. Rouse recoiled.

The high color in Allan Rouse's cheeks drained away. He shook his head. "I'm sorry, sweetheart. That was uncalled for." He scooted to the edge of his chair and reached out a hand to her. "Please forgive me."

Renee Rouse took his hand, squeezed it in hers. She nodded. "I shouldn't have snapped at you. I'm just . . ."

She nodded again, then stitched a smile on her drawn face. "Why don't you have some of that hot chocolate, lovey." She stood. "I'm going to tidy up in the kitchen."

Dr. Rouse took his mug off the table and sank back in on himself, as if his reserves of indignation had been spent. Did all that relentless consideration for your spouse help or hurt? Clare had really only seen one marriage up close and personal—her parents'—but she couldn't recall her dad apologizing over a snapped remark like Dr. Rouse's. Of course, she also couldn't envision her mother bringing Dad hot cocoa on a tray or working to smooth his ruffled feathers.

Clare took her drink off the coffee table with a murmur of thanks. Mrs. Rouse gave her husband another look—checking his emotional temperature—and whisked out of the room. Mug in hand, Clare read COLUMBIA UNIVERSITY COLLEGE OF PHYSICIANS AND SURGEONS in Gothic gold lettering. "Did you attend Columbia?" she asked, trying for some semblance of conversation.

Dr. Rouse gestured toward Mrs. Marshall with his mug. "Her mother sent me. Paid my way through medical school and my residency. That's how I wound up at the clinic, you know." He sat up straighter, speaking directly to Mrs. Marshall. "It's not as if it was my dream to sink my life into that two-bit practice, you know. I was going to do my time and get the hell out."

Mrs. Marshall sat stiffly, knees together, and sipped her cocoa. Clare waited for her to respond to Dr. Rouse. When she didn't, Clare ventured, "Why did you stay on?"

"Mrs. Ketchem died right around the time my obligation was up. I had agreed to head up the clinic for as many years as she supported my medical training, you see. Seven years. But when it was time for me to go, I could see there wasn't anyone competent willing to take on such a thankless, underpaid job. And by that time, I had become sort of—infected by Mrs. Ketchem's passion for the clinic."

"*And* you had a life here," Mrs. Marshall said, "*and* Renee didn't want to move away from her family. . . ."

He shot a fierce look at Mrs. Marshall. "That's true. But mostly, it was the clinic. You have no idea what that place meant to your mother. None at all. If I told you—" He cut himself off.

Clare thought it sounded a bit theatrical. Evidently, Mrs. Marshall did, too. "Allan," she said, her voice gentle, "I'm sure you have insights into my mother that are different from my own. But I'm the person she left as trustee, and I can only act according to my judgment about her wishes." She put her mug down on the coffee table. "I think our presence here is just causing you more distress right now. Why don't we leave and give you a chance to absorb what we've talked about. You have my number, and if you want to speak further after you've . . . adjusted to the news, please give me a call."

She stood, and Clare hastily followed suit. Mrs. Rouse met them at the door as they retrieved their coats from the hall closet. "Leaving so soon?" she asked.

Mrs. Marshall laid her hand on the woman's arm. "Renee, I'm sorry to have had to bring bad news. Please let me know that he's doing okay."

For a moment, Mrs. Rouse's chirpy facade fell away, and she looked older, tired, scared. "He's just so unpredictable lately," she whispered. "Sometimes he'll sit for hours in that old chair, not reading, not watching television. Just sitting. Then other times he'll come home ranting and raving and ready to take on the world. I wish I knew how to help him."

"Have you thought about taking him to a psychiatrist?" Clare said. "Maybe he's depressed."

"He can't be!" Mrs. Rouse's expression went flat. "He's the most stable person I know." She reattached the cheery look on her face. "He probably just needs a break. We're going away this Friday to a medical conference in Phoenix. We've planned to take a few extra days afterward, to lie by the pool and order room service."

"That sounds wonderful, dear. I'm sure it will cheer him up," Mrs. Marshall said. "Do keep in touch, won't you?"

The two women exchanged hugs and Clare shook Mrs. Rouse's hand.

Outside, on the top of the steps, they paused to pull on gloves. "You ought to encourage her to get him to see a doctor," Clare said. "Stable people suffer from depression, too. And he was acting very oddly in there, you have to admit. Like he couldn't decide if he wanted to curl up and die or come out fighting."

Mrs. Marshall clutched Clare's arm against icy slips as they descended the steps. "Maybe," she said.

"You sound doubtful."

At the walk, Mrs. Marshall let go of Clare and snapped open her clutch to retrieve her keys. "We're from another generation, dear. We don't go popping off to get mood-altering pills whenever life hands us a setback."

Clare rolled her eyes.

"I will check in with Renee when they get back from Phoenix."

"Thanks." Clare fished her keys from her parka pocket. "Let's hope it starts."

"Oh, I think it's warmed up."

"Yeah. It's twenty degrees instead of fifteen." Clare walked Mrs. Marshall around the snow piled against the curb to her Lincoln and held the door open as the elderly woman got behind the wheel. "What was that remark about you not knowing your mother?" she asked.

Mrs. Marshall pursed her lips. "My mother, because of several tragic events over which she had no control, was the subject of all sorts of gossip over the years. I've already heard every variation of her supposed secrets. I don't need to sit around and have Allan Rouse repeat old stories." She started up her car. "I'll see you on Sunday."

"I'll be there." Clare shut the Lincoln's door and walked to her Shelby. Thankfully, it started.

On the drive back to St. Alban's, she passed the clinic. It looked vaguely accusing to her in the hard-edged morning light. For the first time, she noticed the carving in the granite lintel over the door giving its original name: THE JONATHON KETCHEM CLINIC. She wished Mrs. Marshall hadn't interrupted Allan Rouse. Maybe the older woman had already heard it all, but for her own peace of mind, Clare very much wanted to know what the clinic had meant to Jane Ketchem.

CHAPTER 9

NOW

Clare didn't have cause to drive into Cossayuharie much, so she was worried she'd go right by Debba Clow's place. Narrow roads ran like cow paths around rolling hills and pastures in Cossayuharie, most of them unmarked and all of them passing clapboarded houses and dairy barns, until all at once the driver ran out of fields and was in the sharp switchbacks of the mountains.

"Don't worry," Debba had said over the phone. "It's impossible to miss our house. We have purple shutters."

Cresting a large hill, the written directions pinched between her hand and the wheel, Clare saw the Clow residence where Debba had promised it would be, straddling the road at the bottom of a narrow valley. Debba had underreported the impossibility of missing it.

It was shaped like the typical Cossayuharie farmhouse, an overlarge, undermaintained structure that had started life as an 1850s four-up-four-down and had shotgunned backward through an 1870s parlor, an 1890s kitchen, and a 1920s extra bedroom. However, the Clow farmhouse also had the less typical 1960s addition of a rotting psychedelic bus in the side yard, multiple 1970s solar panels, something that looked like a steppe-dweller's tent, and a paint job that defied categorization. The purple shutters were the least of it. As Clare shifted into neutral and let the Shelby roll downhill—her personal gas-saving technique—she could see yellow-and-black checkerboards over the chimney bricks, door lintels encrusted with D-I-Y mosaics, and painted jungle vines flowering up the front porch posts. The porch stairs were colored like Easter eggs and embellished with stencils of what proved to be, as Clare pulled into the dooryard, farm animals. She could make out pink pigs on the lavender step, brown cows on the yellow.

Clare got out of her car, crunching and slipping in the poorly plowed

drive. Across the road from the house, an enormous barn had been partially gutted, its old doors widened into something resembling a munici-
pal garage. There were two purple buses parked inside. She shook her
head. She couldn't wait to see what Karen Burns, whose brick town house
was straight out of *Traditional Homes* magazine, would make of the Clow
place.

She slipped and slid past Karen's Saab and climbed the stairs to the front
door, which was painted to resemble an underwater scene. She pressed the
bell—a turtle—and stared at an octopus waltzing with a mermaid while
she waited.

"Hi! You must be Reverend Fergusson." The door was opened by a
woman in her late forties or early fifties, with the lean, weather-beaten
face of someone who spends most of her time outdoors and active. "I'm
Lilly Clow, Deb's mother." She took Clare's hand and combined shaking
it with pulling her inside. "It's colder than a Norwegian well digger's you-
know-what out there," Lilly said. Deb's mother looked vaguely Norwegian herself, dressed in an embroidered sweater with her gray hair hanging
in long braids. "Thanks for coming out."

"Thanks for having me," Clare said, shucking her coat. "It's quite some
place you have here."

"Yeah, it's wild, isn't it? The kids love it. The paint fumes are probably
destroying whatever brain cells I have left, but what the heck. C'mon back
to the kitchen, it's warmer. Deb and the lawyer are meeting there while
I ride herd over the kids in the playroom." Lilly led the way through a
room that was either a living room or an artist's studio, and another that
was either a dining room or a craft shop.

"Reverend Fergusson's here," Lilly announced as they entered the
kitchen. Karen and Debba looked up from their seats at a scrubbed pine
table and greeted her distractedly.

"We've got some nice herbal tea already made up," Lilly said. "Or I
could offer you some juice, or some bottled water." The table was set with
three mugs and a honey jar that had all the earmarks of someone's first
pottery project. A more professionally made teapot sat on a woven mat in
the center of the round table.

"Coffee?" Clare asked.

"Sorry, no coffee. We have some chai tea in the fridge if you want caffeine."

"Ah. Thanks, I'll just help myself to what's here."

"Okeydokey. Me and Raffi will be entertaining the kids if anyone needs us." Lilly opened a door in the back of the kitchen. Clare caught a blast of "Baa, Baa, Black Sheep" before it latched shut.

She pulled out a chair—mercifully unpainted—and sat down. Karen had a yellow legal pad in front of her and had been jotting notes. "Have I missed much?"

Karen shook her head. "No, we were just going over the terms of Debba's divorce decree." The lawyer picked up her mug and took a drink. When she put it down, Clare noticed that, despite the mug's lumpy and uneven edge, Karen's lipstick was unsmudged. There were women who always looked perfect, Clare reflected, and then there were the rest, who had mystery stains on their blouses and unevenly-bitten-off fingernails. Being in the same room as Karen Burns always reminded Clare that she was one of "the rest."

"So he's been paying his support on time, and using his visitation schedule," Karen was saying.

"Yep," Debba said. "Although only with Whitley. When we went through mediation, he said he didn't feel competent to meet Skylar's special needs." Her voice made it clear what she thought of this excuse.

Karen pulled a document toward her. "That fits in with the motion his lawyer's filed. He states"—she riffled through the pages until she reached a spot marked with a sticky—"'The minor Skylar has been diagnosed with autism and requires highly specialized care and teaching which Ms. Clow is unable and unwilling to provide. Petitioner would enroll his minor son in a residential educational facility in order to maximize the child's emotional, physical, and intellectual development.'" She squared the document and placed it next to her legal pad. "He's obviously going to make an argument that you're retarding your son's development by keeping him at home."

"That's not true! Mom and I both work with Skylar all the time! Plus, he gets all sorts of services through early-childhood intervention. He has occupational therapy and speech therapy twice weekly. His therapists will say I've been providing a rich educational environment for him to develop in."

"Are they specialists in autism?"

"No, but—"

Karen raised her hands. "I'm not trying to argue with you, Debba, I just have to let you know what we're facing here. I've dealt with some of the people in the early-childhood intervention program, mostly through my volunteer work at our church." She nodded toward Clare. "We sponsor a mentoring program that hooks up teen mothers with older women. I'm sure everyone who's a part of your son's team is caring and competent. But now he's six, and it's almost time for him to be enrolled in school."

"I'm home schooling him."

"Which is a perfectly valid choice. But look at it from a judge's perspective. You're going to provide at-home schooling, which many people still see as inferior to 'professional' schooling. You don't have an educational degree, do you?" Her voice raised hopefully.

"I never went to college."

"Hmm. Not good. So you'll have Skylar at home, and he'll be eligible for special-education services, but you'll be hauling him back and forth to the school for those. The judge will be comparing that to the glossy, professional gleam of a special school."

"An institution!"

Karen took another drink. "We can't afford to put special-ed institutions on trial, Debba."

"So what should I do?"

"One thing would be to find out what your ex really wants. Lower support payments? Different visitation? Maybe he's tired of paying his half of Skylar's noncovered medical expenses."

"Maybe he's sincere," Clare said.

Debba and Karen looked at her.

"Maybe he really believes that Skylar needs something different now that he's reached school age. Maybe he's worried about Whitley not having been vaccinated."

"Hah," Debba said.

"Regardless, unless Debba wants to give up custody, she needs to figure out a way to counter his position. I think the first thing will be to find another M.D. who's willing to state that the kids are in excellent health and that Skylar's doing well under the current program." Karen jotted a note on her legal pad. "Are you sure Dr. Rouse will back your husband instead of you?"

"It's that son of a bitch's fault I'm in this mess," Debba said.

"I'll take that as a yes. Would you consider changing your position and getting Whitley immunized?"

"No."

"What about at a different venue?" Clare asked. "Someplace where you could feel sure that the vaccinations were mercury-free?"

"No." Debba thumped the table. "It's not just the mercury, you know. We've been letting the medical establishment put living viruses in our bodies for years now. Look at the unexplained rise in autoimmune diseases and asthma. Were you aware that while the flu vaccination rate went from thirty-five to sixty-five percent, the mortality rate from flu has increased a hundredfold?"

Clare lifted the teapot. "Couldn't that reflect the fact that there's a lot more old people around than there used to be?"

"Let's stay on point, people." Karen tapped her mug handle with her pen, a risky move in Clare's mind. "Debba, I need a list of everyone involved in Skylar's care."

Clare breathed in a cloud of fruity steam as Debba gave Karen the names of therapists, counselors, special-ed techs, and relief caregivers. She thought about her conversation with Laura Rayfield, the clinic's nurse practitioner. It was one thing for Debba to risk everything to protect her children from harm. But if there was no real harm? Should she be counseling Debba to give up her crusade against vaccinations? And what could she say to persuade her? Debba's beliefs about the evils of immunizations had the strength and conviction of religious faith. How would I react, Clare wondered, if someone tried to persuade me that God was a figment of my imagination, and that I should stop wasting my time with all those silly rituals?

"Clare?"

She jerked her attention away from the mug of tea. "Hmm? I'm sorry, what?"

"Would you be willing to testify about the incident at the clinic?" Karen asked.

"Testify?"

"As to how Debba was distraught but not violent."

I used to come out to her place when she and her husband were married. They got rowdy with each other all the time. She could hear Russ's words as if he were sitting in the kitchen next to her.

"I can certainly testify that she put the stool down and didn't offer any violence toward anyone after I got there," Clare said carefully. She looked at Debba. "I can't say what's happened in the past. I don't know if you've had any other incidents."

Debba shook her head, sending her spiraling curls bouncing. "No. I've picketed the clinic lots, and I admit Rouse and I have had some shouting matches, but never—no. I was just pushed over the edge that day when I got the letter from Jeremy."

Clare's heart sank. Debba wasn't going to rise to the bait and spill all about her history of marital violence. She reached for the honey bowl and unenthusiastically spooned some of the drippy stuff into her tea. Now what? She had always kept whatever Russ had told her in strictest confidence.

No, that wasn't true. She had blabbed private information to a reporter, on camera. In her defense, it was because she thought lives were at stake. But she had been wrong, and she had regretted it.

She sipped the tea, wrinkling her nose at the taste. It would have been greatly improved with a shot of bourbon. Better still, go straight to the bourbon and skip the tea. Karen was going on about financial and medical records, and Debba was taking down what the lawyer recommended. Considering the emphasis Karen was placing on past behavior, how important would those fights loom? They must have taken place over six years ago, if Russ was right, and they had stopped brawling when Skylar arrived. Clare took another sip. The tea didn't improve with familiarity. Would Debba's ex-husband even dare to bring up the matter? It would reflect as badly on him as on her. More.

"Mamamamamama," a small voice wailed from its playroom exile.

The door at the back of the kitchen opened. Lilly poked her head in. "Sorry, Karen, but your little one is getting pretty fretful. Do you have—"

Cody Burns broke through the line and pelted across the kitchen floor for his mother, who scooped him up onto her lap. He turned his face into her shoulder and clutched at her with the arm that wasn't holding Squeaky the Squirrel.

"Hey, little boy. What's the matter? Are you a sleepy baby?" Karen looked up at them. "I think we may be running into nap time. Can we continue this another time?" She sniffed. "Whoo. We need a diaper change before beddy-bye. Lilly, where's the bathroom?"

Clare put the lumpy mug down. She couldn't tell Karen what she, in confidence, had been told by Russ. Nor could she let Debba know she had some private police information about the artist's past. "Debba," she said, after Karen had slung her baby bag over her shoulder and followed Lilly down the hall. "I'd love it if we could take some time, just the two of us, to talk about how this is affecting you. I can see you have a terrific support person in your mother, but sometimes it helps to let your feelings out with another person."

Debba pushed her cloud of hair back with both hands. "Funny you should mention that. I've just been thinking, lately, how stressed I'm feeling. And I think part of it is, I'm trying to be real strong and upbeat for my mom. She has enough to deal with without worrying about me. I have to tell you though, I'm not particularly religious."

Clare laughed. "If the only people I talked with were particularly religious ones, I'd have a lot of free time on my hands." She stood up and dug into her skirt pocket. "Here's one of my cards, to trade for yours. It's got all my numbers on it, although you'll take your chances if you try to reach me by cell phone." She made a face. "I got one last winter after I was in an accident, but I didn't realize that all these mountains mean I can only get a signal if I'm headed down the Northway toward Saratoga."

Karen toted Cody back into the kitchen. "Oh, cell phones are useless around here. You should do what Geoff and I did, get a satellite phone. It's a little more expensive, but it's worthwhile. So reliable."

Clare caught Debba's eye. They both bit back grins.

"Clare, will you hold Cody while I get my stuff together?" Karen thrust the baby into Clare's arms. Cody drew back, eyeballed her, recognized a face he knew, and promptly butted his head against her shoulder. Karen and Debba had put their heads together over their calendars and were trying out different dates and times for their next meeting. Cody stuck his thumb into his mouth and began to rhythmically squeak the squirrel.

The weight of him always surprised Clare, the solidity and size of him. Somehow, she always expected the fragile, kitten-sized bundle she had first seen, the awe-inspiring, panicky thought she had first had: This baby's life is in my hands. She wondered if this was what motherhood felt like. She wondered if she would ever know.

There was a tug on her skirt. She looked down to see a tiny girl, with kinky blond hair identical to Debba's, staring at her. "Hi," the girl said. "What's your name? My name is Whitley. I have a rat. Do you want to see?"

"Whits, Reverend Fergusson doesn't want to see your rat," Lilly said from the playroom door. "Be polite and say hello."

"I did," Whitley said. "What's that thing around your neck? It's not a turtleneck shirt. I have turtleneck shirts and they're soft and squishy. Sometimes they have flowers on them."

"You're right," Clare said. "This is called a clerical collar. I wear it so people can see that I'm a priest. Kind of like a police officer wearing a badge. If I weren't holding Cody, I could show you where it fastens and unfastens in the back. It's not even really attached to my shirt."

"Neat," Whitley said. "Put the baby down and show me."

"Whitley!" her mother said, reaching for her.

"You have quite a conversationalist there," Clare said.

"Yeah, it's a shame she's so shy and retiring." Debba's face softened. "And here's my boy."

The child who followed Lilly into the kitchen was clearly Whitley's brother. They had the same fair skin and finely etched features. But where the little girl's brown eyes were direct and penetrating, her brother's wandered, sliding away from faces, seeming to track dust motes in the air. He walked hesitantly, moving his arms back and forth like a child trying to feel its way through a dark and featureless landscape. Debba knelt down and circled her arms around the boy, holding him loosely, anchoring him in space. "Sky, this is Reverend Fergusson. Can you say 'hello'?"

He was a beautiful boy. He fastened his eyes on the table, not like a kid disobeying his mom, or like a shy child. It was as if, Clare thought, he didn't even see her.

"When we meet somebody new, we say 'hello,'" Debba went on. "Can you say 'hello'?"

His gaze was still on the table. "H'lo," he said, still ignoring Clare. He tapped the fingers of one hand in the palm of the other and circled them around.

"Sure, you can draw. Get up on your chair."

Skylar headed for where Clare had been sitting, and she jumped out of his way. He climbed into the seat while his mother laid a stack of blank papers and a pencil in front of him.

With fierce concentration he bent over the paper. "Whatcha drawing, Scoot?" his mother asked, although it was obvious. Under Skylar's pencil a bus was emerging, startlingly accurate and in perfect perspective.

"Grammy's bus," he said. "The tires, the windows, the door, the lights . . ."

"Mmmm. I like your busses." Debba stroked his hair while the boy finished one picture, thrust the sheet away, and started another. The second bus was identical to the first. Clare watched Debba's hand, rising and falling, like a benediction said over and over. What was it like to love that fiercely? How much would you be willing to pay to make your child healthy, wealthy, happy, wise? What would you do to protect your child? As she watched Debba reach over and slide a box of crayons toward Skylar, tempting him with color, she knew the answer: *anything*.

CHAPTER 10

THEN

FRIDAY, APRIL 9, 1937

Dead and gone. Niels Madsen contemplated the phrase as he turned the pages of the Ketchem file. It implied first the one, then the other. Turning that natural order around was going to be difficult. He squared the papers within the green baize folder and pressed the yellow button on his intercom.

"Miss McDonald, will you send in Mrs. Ketchem now?"

A moment later, he heard the tack-tack-tack of heels on wood, and his office door opened. He stood up, came around his desk, and crossed to greet her.

"Mrs. Ketchem." He shook her hand, gesturing to one of two leather chairs positioned in front of his desk. "Make yourself comfortable." He studied her from beneath half-closed eyes as she sat down and smoothed her dress over her knees. His awareness of fashion didn't extend much beyond an approving nod at his wife's purchases and an occasional groan of pain when he got her bills, but even he could tell Jane Ketchem's brown wool dress was several years out-of-date. Her shoes, polished to a shine and neat below her crossed ankles, were worn at the heels.

"Can I have Miss McDonald get you some coffee?" he asked, seating himself behind his desk.

She shook her head. "No, thank you." Beneath her hat, he could see the gray threading through her glossy brown hair. They had met a few times over the years—he had drawn up the papers when she and Jonathon bought their farm and had advised them when the Conklingville Dam project was buying them out. Jane had had a fresh farm-girl sort of beauty in her younger days, the kind that should have aged into plump cheeks and soft jowls by now. But the events of her life had laid waste to that softness, and the forty-one-year-old woman looking calmly at him from across his desk was drawn, sharp. Someone he didn't recognize.

He folded his hands. "What can I do for you today?" he asked, redundantly, because he knew what she must be here for, had known it as soon as his secretary had shown him the name in his appointment calendar.

"I want you to have Jonathon declared legally dead."

"It's been seven years now, has it?"

"It has." Her face was still calm, but he could see her hands tightening over her purse, the leather also polished but worn, like her shoes.

He leaned forward. "I don't want to offend you, Mrs. Ketchem, but if we're going to pursue this, we're going to have to touch on some personal matters, so I'm just going to jump in with both feet." He softened his voice. "Are you in financial straits? Because—"

"The life insurance company went under. Yes, I know. I got your letter, and another one from them, and I certainly haven't forgotten either. No, I'm not facing the poor farm." She glanced down at her out-of-date dress. "Though I suppose that's another thing folks in this town like to speculate about. Truth is, I'm keeping a Scotsman's grip on whatever comes in. I want my daughter to go to college."

He raised his eyebrows. "A laudable ambition." He touched the file on his desk. "You do realize that if we petition the court of probate to rule Jonathon dead, it won't be cheap. My retainer alone is one hundred dollars, and there may well be expenses and fees beyond that, depending on how long it takes."

She nodded. "I know. I asked your secretary what your price was when I asked to see you."

"Are Mr. and Mrs. Ephraim Ketchem going to join in the petition? To help you with the cost?"

"No." Her face softened a fraction. "They'd just as soon go on hoping he'll turn up one day. The good Lord knows I can understand their feelings. There's nothing hurts as bad as the death of your child, and if they can keep on pretending he's alive . . ." She shrugged. "It's a comfort to them."

A hard, cold comfort, Niels thought. "Do you worry that you'll be taking that away from them if we succeed in having Jonathon declared dead?"

She closed her eyes for a moment. He could see the beginnings of fine lines, the slight extra droop where her eyelid would someday sag onto it-self. She startled him by opening her eyes and staring directly into his. "I love Mother and Father Ketchem dearly, and I wouldn't hurt them for the world. But I've been saying that my husband is dead for seven years. It's what I told Chief McNeil the day after Jonathon disappeared, and I knew it was true then as I know it's true now. They choose to believe otherwise. I don't think anything I do will change their minds."

"What about your daughter?"

"Her father disappeared when she was barely six. She missed him some-thing fierce at first, but seven years in a child's life is forever. I can't even re-call when she last mentioned him. And now she's getting to an age where she can hear the gossip, and be hurt by it, and I don't want her to go through what I've had to go through." She let her purse drop flat on her lap and leaned forward, her hands curling over the edge of his desk. "For seven years I've been not fish nor fowl nor good red meat. Not a widow and not a wife. Every soul in Millers Kill either pitying me because they think my husband abandoned us or wondering what I did to drive him away. I can't have a cup of coffee with my brother-in-law or have Father Wallace pay a call without setting tongues clacking all over town. My friend Nain once overheard Tilda Van Krueger saying in the beauty shop that it was mighty convenient having an absent husband, because if I turned up in a family way, I could just claim he stopped back in for a visit." She took a deep breath. "I want my respectability back, Mr. Madsen. I want to be able to set up a memorial stone for my husband and put him to rest once and for all."

◆ ◆ ◆

Niels Madsen thought about his client while he strolled home for a 12:30 dinner with his family. He paused at the walkway to his home, square and roomy and comfortable, and thought about her keeping her own roof over her head instead of moving back in with her parents or in-laws, as so many other women would have done. And when Marion, his oldest, danced past him with the suggestion of a kiss and an "Off to Helen's house" tossed over her shoulder, he thought about the difficulties facing a single mother of a growing girl.

In the dining room, after a heartfelt thanks over a good lamb stew and quizzing the younger children on how their mornings went at school, he asked his wife if she had ever heard any gossip about Jane Ketchem.

"I heard Mrs. Ketchem took an ax to her husband and buried him under her cellar floor," ten-year-old Pauline said. "When there's a full moon, you can hear him moaning, 'Give me back my head! Give meee back my heeeead!'"

Doris, who was eight and still slept with a night-light, shrieked.

"Girls!" Ruth Madsen said. "Quiet down this instant or you'll both have bread and water in your room. What nonsense."

The girls giggled, but resumed eating. Mrs. Madsen turned to her husband. "One does hear a few things around town," she said. She glanced at Normie, who was clearly bristling with something to say but too intent on showing up his sisters with his good manners to just blurt it out. "What is it, Normie?"

"Lacey Ketchem's in my class," he said.

"I know that, dear."

"Well, she says that her father was away on a trip and that he was set upon by desperate men. Probably murderous hoboes who didn't have a thing to lose. She says that there would have had to be a lot of them, because her father was a big, strong man, and that they killed him and stuffed his body in a tree and set it on fire."

"Good heavens!" Mrs. Madsen looked at her husband.

He shrugged. "You're the one who insisted we buy the radio. It's no wonder all our children sound like announcers for next week's episode of *The Clutching Hand.*"

"Can we get down, Mother?"

"Can we get down?"

"May we," Mrs. Madsen corrected automatically. "Normie, are you finished? I want you to walk your sisters back to school."

Normie excused himself and pushed his chair away from the table. Niels reached one hand out and took his son's arm. He looked directly into the boy's face. "What I was discussing with your mother had to do with the practice. And anything concerning the practice—"

"—is not to be repeated outside this house. I know, Father."

"Good boy. You can come by the office after school if you like."

There was a clatter of shoes and a general banging of the door, three, four, five times. Niels had never been able to figure out how three children could sound like a horde of Huns ransacking a town.

Satisfied that their offspring had well and truly departed, he turned to Ruth. "So, what sort of things does one hear around?"

"I'm curious. Why the sudden interest in Jane Ketchem?"

"She's asked me to petition the court of probate to have her husband declared legally dead."

Ruth arched her brows. "Interesting." She broke open a roll and buttered it. "The general consensus among the gossips—not that I'm one of that number, mind."

"Of course not."

"Is that Jonathon Ketchem ran off on her. The disagreement is whether he took off because he couldn't find work, because he had a girl waiting, or because she drove him away."

"Huh. I hadn't heard the story about there being another woman involved."

"Oh, people say he was paying a lot of attention to one of those Henderson girls whose father worked on Ephraim Ketchem's farm. I forget which one. Evidently, she did leave shortly after he disappeared. Supposedly headed out west to seek her fame and fortune."

"That makes sense." He helped himself to another serving of butter beans. "I never could believe it was poverty that made him take off for a shoe-leather divorce. Things were starting to get tight around here in '30, but the younger Ketchems got a reasonable price for their farm when the dam was being raised. Certainly no worse than anyone else caught up in the shuffle. There should have been enough to buy new land elsewhere or start himself in a business."

"Maybe he ran off with the money, too."

"Maybe." He thought about Jane Ketchem's shoes and outdated dress. "What's this about her driving him away?"

His wife looked at him speakingly. "Consider that the Ketchem girl was six when her father disappeared. Same age as Normie."

"So."

"So, in the six years after we had Normie, I had two more babies and lost a third. Maybe it was just that God chose not to bless the Ketchems with any more children. . . ."

"Or maybe there wasn't any chance for any more. I see your point." He folded his napkin and stretched. "I'll see what I can do for her, poor lady. If she did damp the fire down until he left for good, she's paid dearly for it."

Ruth stood and began to stack the dishes. "Can you really argue for Jonathon Ketchem to be declared legally dead? When no one except Jane and her daughter believe it? What on earth are you going to say to the judge?"

"Oh, no problem with that." He grinned up at her. "I'll just bring in Normie and have him testify as to how Ketchem was set upon by murderous hoboes."

CHAPTER 11

NOW

SUNDAY, MARCH 19, THE SECOND SUNDAY IN LENT

Russ hung up his parka in the mudroom, pried off his boots, and walked into his darkened kitchen on stockinged feet. Lord, he was tired. He had pulled two shifts a day since Friday, and his body was letting him know he was too old for that schedule. Contrary to his less-than-charitable thoughts, Lyle, like Noble, really had been knocked out by a nasty stomach flu. His deputy chief had told him over the phone that he hadn't been more than five feet from the bathroom since the thing started.

He flicked on the light and went to the refrigerator to see if there was anything to eat. Linda was gone again—off for a week to visit her sister in Florida. Her girlfriend Meg had driven her down to Albany to catch the plane, because covering one-fourth of his department hadn't left Russ with enough time to do it himself. That rankled. He hated not being there for her when she needed him.

He pulled a Coke out of the fridge, nudged the door shut, and wandered into the pantry, hoping there would be some Tuna Helper or something. Although he normally enjoyed cooking, tonight he wasn't up for anything more than opening a box and a can. Thank God he had had the sense to assign his two part-time officers to night duty. If he'd had the patrol tonight, with its homeward-bound tourists getting lost and running into each other, or its domestic calls, which were always worse on Sunday nights, after a weekend of togetherness with another crappy Monday morning staring people in the face . . . he'd probably have driven off the Route 100 bridge into the river.

No Tuna Helper. He slid a box of macaroni and cheese off the shelf and got a pan from under the counter. He should have just told his mom he was coming over for dinner tonight, but the price for a hot meal would have been listening to her razor-thin slices at Linda for abandoning her hardworking husband for sun and fun with a divorcée. He had pointed out that he was welcome to join Linda on her annual sisterfest. The last time he had gone had been two years ago, and the pleasure of escaping from the cold March weather hadn't made up for the boredom of hanging around a Fort Lauderdale condo while the two women shopped and got their nails done. Plus, he called the station house so many times to see how they were doing without him that Linda claimed flying back home would be cheaper than the phone bill.

He put water on to boil and collapsed into one of the kitchen chairs with his Coke. Linda had done something different with a St. Patrick's theme. There was a new tablecloth on the table, new place mats and napkins, and curtains festooning the windows. All green-and-white fabrics, tweed and tiny gold-edged shamrocks and presumably Irish shepherds helping Irish shepherdesses over a stile. Their house was a laboratory for Linda's burgeoning drapery business, which meant they were more or less in a state of constant redecoration. At least she had farmed out some of the work—three neighboring women stitched away at ruffles and blinds and whatnot, so Linda could meet her orders without sewing eighteen hours out of twenty-four.

The rattle of the lid on the pot told him the water had come to a boil. He heaved himself out of his chair and poured the macaroni in, stirring it with a big wooden spoon. Maybe he should have just said the hell with it and gone to Florida. Maybe he would. Just fly down there, surprise her. They could go out to dinner together, take a long walk, rent a boat and get out on the ocean. Well, no, she didn't really care for long walks and she didn't do too well on the water unless she was in something pretty big. Okay, he could swallow his dislike of sunbathing and lie around on the beach with her. He could make the ultimate sacrifice and take her shopping. Anything. They just needed to spend some time together and talk about something other than who bought the groceries and who was going to the bank.

He drained the pot, went upstairs, and changed out of his uniform into sweats. Back downstairs he ate his mac and cheese in front of the TV, flicking from one lousy show to another, wondering why the networks couldn't schedule one of the NCAA finals on a night when he was at home. He rinsed out his bowl and loaded the dishwasher. He wandered down to his cellar workroom, but the thought of putting in time on one of his projects made him feel as if a lead blanket had been placed on his shoulders, so he went back upstairs. He thought about calling a few airlines to see how much it would cost for a last-minute ticket to Florida. He thought about calling his sister Janet, catching up with what his nieces were doing. He thought about calling his mom.

He picked up the phone and dialed Clare's number.

She answered on the second ring. "Hello?"

"Hi, it's me."

"Russ." He could hear her smile. "I knew it was you."

"How did you manage that? I didn't know I was going to call until I had finished dialing."

"I'm your Psychic Friend."

He laughed. "Does that mean I'm being charged by the minute for my call?"

"Yeah, but think about it. Isn't a dollar ninety-nine a minute a small price to pay to have all your secrets revealed?"

"God, I hope not. I don't think I could live with all my secrets revealed."

"Mmm." There was something—an audible quality to Clare's listening. He couldn't ever put a finger on what it was, just that he could hear the force of her attentiveness. "What's the matter?"

"Oh, nothing. I'm beat to the ground from working double shifts for the past few days, and Linda's left for Florida, and there's nothing on TV, and I guess I'm feeling pretty sorry for myself."

"Why don't you invite yourself to stay at your mother's? She'd love to fuss over you."

"I don't need fussing over. I just need . . ." He wasn't sure how to finish the sentence.

"A little human connection."

"Yeah." He pulled another Coke from the fridge and strolled into the living room. "What have you been up to lately?"

"Let's see. Robert Corlew and I met with the roofing guys. It's going to be a big job. The engineer says the chances are good that water has been spreading through the roof laterally, so there may be additional structural damage they'll have to replace and more framing before they actually get to the reshingling and gutters. He quoted us some material costs. My Lord, you wouldn't believe how expensive this waterproof-barrier stuff we're getting is."

He sat in his favorite chair. "I've checked it out myself. I believe it."

"I have to confess, I've been feeling guilty as sin over taking Mrs. Marshall's trust fund money and stiffing the clinic, but I walked away from the meeting so grateful that we at least have that option. I got the impression that the whole north aisle was ripe for a cave-in."

"Well . . . ," he said, his skepticism showing through.

"I know, I know. But even if the damage is only half what they're predicting, it's still going to be a costly job." She sighed. "When I became a priest, I surely didn't think I was going to be spending so much time worrying about leaking roofs and the price of oil and water heaters."

He laughed a little. "Every job has its boring scut work. It's one of the great universal truths." He drank from his can.

"What are you drinking?"

"Decaffeinated Coke."

"I'm having a Saranac Winter Ale. Ha ha ha."

He laughed. "Do you normally taunt recovering alcoholics with your beer drinking?"

"Just you. You're special."

They were silent for a beat. Then he said, "What else did you do?"

"I had a couple counseling session on Friday. Spent the afternoon in Glens Falls Saturday with one of my parishioners who's undergoing surgery. So I missed my stint at the historical society."

Russ clucked disapproval.

"It's okay. I told Roxanne I'd be in Monday. Then, we had a nice Eucharist this morning. Practically a full house. I think everyone wanted to see the roof before it fell in."

"Huh." There was a clunking sound over the line. "What are you doing now?"

She laughed. "Putting another log on the fire. I've got a good one going to take the edge off the chill. This old house is drafty, and if I have to buy another tankful of oil, I'll be eating mac and cheese for the next month."

"You should have your church get it weatherproofed."

"I don't want to draw the vestry's attention to the fact that they own a desirable property that's wasted with one single woman rattling around in it. I'm afraid they'd sell it out from under me and I'd have to move to one of Corlew's awful town houses."

"One of those places with the fake names where they spell *town* with two *n*s and an *e*? God, that would be a fate worse than death." He shook his head. "What are you wearing?"

She laughed. "Is this that kind of phone call?"

"Oh, Christ, you know what I mean. Sometimes people who aren't used to the climate take a while to remember to put on another layer instead of turning up the thermostat."

She was still laughing. Then she coughed, and in a heavy southern accent dripping with honey, she said, "I'm wearing nothing except some very high heels and a teeny-weeny—"

"No, no, no, no."

She laughed some more. "I'll bet the women who do those phone calls are dressed pretty much like I am now. Turtleneck, my brother Brian's old Virginia sweatshirt, and these really warm leggings my folks sent me for Christmas. Woolly socks and ratty old Passamaquoddy slippers."

"Oh, baby," he said.

She giggled. "It's the slippers, isn't it? They drive men wild."

"Up here in the North Country, you have to learn to appreciate warmth."

"And my thermostat is set to sixty-two."

"Jeez, that is cold. Maybe this spring I'll check out your windows and walls, see if there are some simple things we can do to tighten the house up."

"As long as I don't have to go to the vestry for maintenance money, that would be—" She fell silent.

"What?" he said.

"Someone's pulling into my driveway."

He glanced at the anniversary clock on the mantel. It was almost 8:30.

"Hang on a sec," Clare said, and he heard the clunk of the phone being put down.

He rolled out of his chair and paced into the kitchen, the phone still pressed to his ear. Who the hell would be dropping by unannounced at this hour? He envisioned a gang of rowdy teens who liked to make noise and scare single women. Then he thought of a sexual predator, who knew she lived all alone. Some serial rapist, just out of Clinton, looking for easy pickings—

She came back on the line. "It's Debba Clow."

"Debba Clow? Does she have her kids with her? She's not trying to skip out on her ex, is she?"

"No, she's alone. She seems really upset. I have to go. Sorry . . ."

She hung up on him, leaving only a wistful echo behind. He held the phone for a moment, listening to the dial tone. Debba Clow. At Clare's. At 8:30 on a Sunday night.

He dialed the station house. Weeknights, all calls to the station were routed through to the Glens Falls dispatch, since Millers Kill didn't have the need or the resources to keep a dispatcher on 24/7. But weekends, the busiest time of their week, they had live coverage with Harlene. Harlene had been working for the police department back when Russ was still spitting out sand during the first Gulf War, and he had no doubt she would still be there when he was retired to Arizona.

"Millers Kill Police Department."

"Hey, Harlene."

"What are you on the horn for? You're supposed to be at home, getting some R and R."

"Look, there hasn't been any trouble at the free clinic, has there?"

She whistled in his ear. "You're scary sometimes, you know that? I think this is a clear sign that you're spending way too much time at work. No, there hasn't been anything at the clinic, but just after you left this evening, Allan Rouse's wife called in. He's the clinic doctor."

"I know who he is."

"Bet you don't know why she called, though."

"I'm waiting with bated breath for you to tell me."

"He's gone missing."

"What's that mean, exactly? He's a grown man, and it's eight-thirty on a Sunday night. He's probably hoisting a few at a sports bar, where they have something on worth watching."

"You'd think, wouldn't you? But it turns out they were due to leave for Albany late this afternoon. They're flying out to a medical conference in Phoenix, Arizona. Or at least they were. She had already missed the flight when she called."

"Maybe he had some sort of medical emergency? Had to make a house call, or go to the hospital?"

"Mrs. Rouse said he's always checked in with her before. She was calling their friends all this afternoon looking for him. She checked Washington County and Glens Falls Hospitals, thought he might be with a patient someplace. But no luck. She also called Laura Rayfield—that's the clinic nurse practitioner."

"I know who she is."

"Well, she hadn't seen him. Anyway, according to Mrs. Rouse, the doc seemed kind of restless and distracted, but she put it down to his upcoming trip. She says he left home around eleven o'clock this morning to run a few errands. He told her he was going to the clinic to deal with the mail and dictate notes for files. They were planning to be gone for a week. She reminded him he had to be home by four for them to make their flight in good season. Then he drove off. When he didn't show up on time, she went over to the clinic, but he was gone. She hasn't seen him since."

He thought for a moment. "Did she check to see if he'd been admitted to one of the hospitals as a John Doe?"

"I dunno. Though you'd think someone would recognize him even if he had no ID. The man's been practicing medicine in this town for thirty years."

"What about a girlfriend?"

"I certainly haven't heard anybody gossiping about one at my hairdresser's. It wasn't a question I wanted to put to his wife."

"No, I suppose not." He trailed across the kitchen floor slowly, letting his feet follow his thinking. "What did you tell Mrs. Rouse?"

"I told her that unless there's evidence of something funny going on, we don't declare adults officially missing for forty-eight hours. But it's a slow night, so I asked Duane and Tim to stop into any bars that they pass and see if anyone's seen the doc."

"Good."

"And since the man is sixty-five years old, I circulated a description of his car and plates to the staties. I told 'em it was a possible medical. For all we know, he had a heart attack behind the wheel while he was running those errands."

"Good call." There were a lot of stretches of road in and around Millers Kill where a car could roll off into the brush and not be noticed. "I don't know why I bother to come in, Harlene. You go ahead and do my job for me."

She snorted. "Someday this department will finally get a female officer, and then you'll see it's not that I'm so great, it's that women are naturally smarter than men."

"I never doubted that for a second. I have a hunch about the doctor, and I'm going to look into it. I'll be back in touch ASAP."

"Gotcha. I'll call if one of the guys turns him up in the meantime."

He said good-bye and rang off. He stood for a moment, the phone's stubby antenna just touching his forehead, like a meditative finger. There wasn't any reason to suspect that Debba Clow's unexpected appearance at Clare's house was connected to Allan Rouse's equally unexpected disappearance. But he had been a cop, military and civilian, for a quarter century now, and he had learned to trust the little nudges that occasionally bubbled up from the bottom of his brain. He dialed Clare's number again.

This time, her machine answered. He listened to her mechanically flattened voice advise him of her office and cell numbers, and when invited to leave a message, he said, "Clare, it's Russ. Please pick up. I need to—"

"Hi, it's me. What's up?"

"Is Debba Clow still there?"

"Yes, and we're having a pretty intense discussion, so I really can't—"

"I'm not calling to chitchat, I promise. I'd like to speak to Debba."

Clare's voice was more guarded. "Why?"

"Just tell her I'd like to speak to her. Please."

"Okay . . ."

He walked upstairs to his bedroom while he waited for someone to come back on the line. He pulled his jeans out of a pile of clothing on a chair. After a second's thought, he also retrieved the uniform shirt he had worn earlier that day. He hoped he wasn't going to have to put them on.

"She would rather not speak to you right now." Clare was trying to sound neutral, professional, but he could hear the undercurrent of distress in her voice. "Can you tell me what's going on?"

"Can you tell me why she needed to talk to you so bad she couldn't wait until tomorrow?"

There was an exasperated burst of air. "You know I can't disclose what I'm told in priestly confidence."

"She's not one of your congregation."

"Russ, I'm not a priest just for card-carrying, pledging Episcopalians. I'm a priest for anybody who needs one. My obligations remain the same."

He almost smiled. "I know." The thought of telling her about Allan Rouse went through his mind. Followed by the thought of her telling Debba, and Debba splitting before he or anyone else had a chance to ask her what she knew about the doctor's whereabouts. "It's okay. I'm sorry I interrupted your conversation."

"Russ." Her voice was pitched halfway between exasperation and concern. Concern won out. "What's going on? Can I help you?"

He did smile. "Not at the moment. But I'll let you know. Later."

"Okay." She trailed off. "Later."

He dropped the phone on his bed and shucked off his sweatshirt. He had been right. He was going to have to get dressed again after all.

CHAPTER 12

NOW

When Russ rolled his pickup to a stop in front of Clare's house, Debba Clow's Toyota Camry was still parked in her drive. He got out, shrugging into his parka and tugging a wool cap over his head. The night sky was clear, with a full moon and winter-bright stars, and the temperature, which had risen a few degrees above freezing during the day's sunshine, had plummeted back into the low teens.

There was barely enough space for him to edge between the cars and the icy snowbanks crowding the drive. The heavy, compacted snowbanks, tossed up over four months of shoveling the drive, were slipping forward, like glaciers riding on their own melting remains. Clare's front door, sheltered by a graceful Dutch revival porch, was inaccessible to anyone without an industrial-strength snowblower. He clumped up the back steps to her kitchen.

The door opened before he had the chance to knock.

"Chief Van Alstyne. What a surprise." Clare stood blocking his way, one hand cocked on her hip. She didn't look happy to see him.

"I'd like to speak to Debba Clow."

"Have you got a warrant?"

"Do I need one? For Chrissakes, Clare, it's colder than the monkey's brass balls out here. Lemme in."

He could see in her eyes the exact moment when she calculated it wasn't worth it. "Come in, then," she said with ill grace, stepping back from the door.

He kicked the ice off his boots and entered. He hadn't been in this room in over a year. It was still a bland white box, straight from the lowest-grade aisle of kitchen fittings in HQ, but she had cluttered it into warmth with a braided rug and splashy seat cushions and a surprising number of glossy green houseplants that hadn't been there a year ago.

He stuffed his hat into his pocket and hung his parka on her coatrack. "Where's Debba?" he asked.

She pointed to the swinging doors that led to the living room. "What are you looking for, Russ? Why do you need to question her?"

"You've been talking with her for an hour or so. I figure you probably have a better idea than I do."

She shook her head. "She hasn't told me anything"—she paused to choose her words carefully— "of a criminal nature."

"Good. I hope she doesn't have anything of a criminal nature to tell me, either." He pushed through the doors into the living room. This, at least, was exactly the same as it had been last winter. A few more books in the bookcases flanking the fireplace, a few more pillows on the overstuffed couch and chairs. A few more pictures standing on the wooden console and a few less bottles on the drinks table in front of the window. Where Debba Clow sat, perched on one of a pair of tiny caned chairs.

She looked at him warily, and nodded.

"Ms. Clow," he said. "I have a few questions I need to ask you. Mind if we sit in front of the fireplace? I'm afraid I'd break one of those chairs if I tried to sit down on it."

He matched his actions to his words, sinking into one of the armchairs, consciously relaxing himself into a friendly, unthreatening posture. He waited while she detached herself from her chair and walked reluctantly to the sofa. She sat as far away from him as she could.

"Nice fire," he said to Clare, who stood behind the sofa table, her arms crossed over her chest. "Takes the edge off of this cold." He turned to Debba Clow. "It must have been pretty urgent business for you to leave your kids at home and come see Reverend Fergusson this late."

She glanced up at Clare.

"You can tell Chief Van Alstyne whatever you feel comfortable with," Clare said. "I've already told you, I won't talk to him about anything you've said to me." Her glance flickered away from Debba, toward Russ. "However, it's been my experience that he's a fair-minded man. And a good listener."

He dropped his eyes to his lap so he could concentrate on not smiling. When he had his cop face on again, he said, "How 'bout it, Debba? Want to tell me what's on your mind?"

She glanced up at Clare again, then at him. "Nothing. I'm just . . . going though a hard time emotionally with this . . . with everything going on right now. I wanted to try to sort things out with Clare's help, instead of dumping on my mother."

Time to play one of his cards. "How about seeing Dr. Rouse today? Was that hard, emotionally?"

Her eyes went wide, showing white like a spooked calf's. For a moment, all she did was blink at him. He held her gaze. "He was the one who called me," she said, her voice loud. "He wanted to see me, not the other way around. I knew I wasn't supposed to go near him. I told him so."

He half closed his eyes to shield his satisfaction. "So why did you agree to get together?"

She sat up, away from the sheltering corner of the couch. "Because he said he had some important information about the vaccinations. I asked him to just tell me over the phone, I did! He was the one who insisted he had to show me in person."

"Where did you meet him?"

She looked down at the floor. "This place. Out by Stewart's Pond. He called it the Ketchem cemetery."

He had one of those unpleasant moments when the inside of his head tilted and everything he had assumed he knew changed. "The Ketchem cemetery? Where is that?"

Debba seemed more exasperated than upset at this point. "I can give you exact directions, 'cause he gave them to me. Take Old Route 100 north. Turn off on the Old Sacandaga Road, cross the Hudson, and go another mile and a half until you see County Road 57 on the left. Follow that past—"

"A boat launch site," he interrupted.

"Yeah," she said.

"You go up a short hill, then at the top you pull off."

She was looking at him oddly. "Yeah. You know the place."

He thought of the gravestones clustering beneath the black pines. Cold, dark water. An old woman with her hair like a shroud of seaweed, staring at him. Staring at him.

"Yeah," he said. "I know the place." He dragged himself back to the moment. "You two met there. Was he driving his own car?"

"Of course he was." She suddenly clamped her hand over her mouth. "There hasn't been an accident, has there? I didn't know—" She twisted in her seat, looking up at Clare. "He hurt himself, after we talked, I didn't tell you. He slipped in the snow and smacked his head against one of the headstones." She twisted back, facing Russ. "I tried to help him. Really. But he wouldn't let me drive him. He said he had a first-aid kit in his own car." She twisted again, the very picture of concern. "I shouldn't have left him there all alone." Back toward Russ. "Has there been an accident? Is he okay?"

"That's what we're trying to find out," he said, his voice mild. "He seems to have gone missing." He rose from the oversized chair. "Can I use your phone?" he asked Clare.

She nodded, still gazing distractedly at the woman on her couch.

"Maybe you can show me where it is?" He had hung up his coat less than a foot away from where the phone hung.

Her eyes sharpened. "Certainly," she said. "Follow me."

Once through the swinging doors at the end of the living room, she turned to him. "What's going on?" Her voice was pitched low.

He kept his at the same level. "Dr. Rouse's wife reported him missing. Last time anyone's seen him was two o'clock. She really didn't say anything to you about this alleged slip and fall?"

She frowned up at him.

"C'mon, Clare, you can't claim priestly confidence if she's just told both of us."

She worried her lower lip. "No. This is the first I heard of it."

"But she did tell you about meeting with the doctor?"

She nodded.

"Funny detail to leave out, don't you think?"

She looked miserably toward the swinging door. "I'd better get back."

"Go 'head. I'm going to call in that location, get one of the patrol cars over there." He caught her arm as she stepped toward the door. "You might want to encourage Ms. Clow to dredge up any other details she forgot to mention to you."

He reached Harlene, gave her the directions, and was relieved to hear that Mark Durkee was already up on Old Route 100, probably on his way to the nightly swing past Russ's mother's house. Russ told Harlene to patch Mark through to Clare's if and when he turned up anything.

"I'd love to know how you managed to work Reverend Fergusson into this one," Harlene said.

"Reverend Fergusson manages to work herself into these things all on her own," he said. "She doesn't need any pushing from me."

"So you're going to be staying over there."

"Since Debba Clow, the last person known to have seen the doctor alive, is here, yeah. I am."

He heard a snort over the phone. "Isn't this Linda's week to be visiting in Florida?"

He exhaled slowly, counting to—well, he didn't make it to ten. "Don't you have any police business you could be attending to? As I am doing, right now, keeping tabs on this witness?"

There was another snort. He gave up. "Make sure Mark calls me ASAP. Fifteen fifty-seven over." He hung up.

Clare looked up as he came through the doors. She was sitting in the other armchair, kitty-corner to Debba Clow. She tilted her head slightly. *Any information?*

He shook his head. Aloud he said, "Is there any coffee?"

Clare rose. "I'll make some up. I could use a cup, too. Debba?"

Debba nodded. Clare vanished through the swinging doors, giving Russ a look as she passed him.

He sat in the armchair. "An officer is headed for the Ketchem cemetery right now. He was up in the area, so we should hear back from him shortly."

Debba pushed her cloud of kinky hair back from her face. "I didn't think about the possibility that he could really have been hurt. Are you sure he's not . . ." Her voice trailed off.

"We don't know what's going on at this point," he said. "We're trying to eliminate possibilities. What did you do after Dr. Rouse hit his head?"

"We went back to the cars. He was bleeding, but he didn't want any help. He pointed out that he was the doctor, not me." She raised her eyes, as if to say, *What can you do?* "He got in his car, I got in mine, and then I took off."

His next question was cut off by the faint sound of the phone ringing in the kitchen. He had half raised himself out of his chair when Clare pushed through the door. "It's for you. Officer Durkee."

In the kitchen, he took the phone from Clare and waited until she removed herself to the living room. "Mark? Russ. What have you got?"

"I've been tramping around the area. Freezing my butt off. I haven't seen any sight of the doctor, but I found his car. It's a good ten yards off the road, smashed into a tree. Abandoned."

CHAPTER 13

NOW

Russ faced toward Clare's wall and pitched his voice low. "Have you called the state crime scene folks yet?"

"I had Harlene send for them and notify the mountain rescue squad. I told 'em it's still officially a missing person. I mean, he was a pretty old guy, after all." Russ reflected that Dr. Rouse was—or had been—maybe fifteen years older than he was. Mark went on, "But if he wandered away in a confused state when the dark came on, he's a corpsicle by now."

"I agree. On the other hand, maybe he didn't wander off. Maybe he was removed from the scene." He pressed his forehead against Clare's calendar, right over a florid picture of an angel and the Virgin Mary. THE ANNUNCIA-TION OF OUR LORD JESUS CHRIST TO THE BLESSED VIRGIN MARY, the tag read. He was eyeball to eyeball with the Virgin, who didn't look all that pleased that she was about to become an unwed mother. He thought about Allan Rouse. Confused and elderly? No way. But calling Debba Clow and ask-ing her to meet him at some old cemetery was way out of character. If that's what he did. Maybe she confronted him, whacked him over the head, and drove him out there in his own car to dispose of the body. No, that didn't work. She would have had to walk at least two hours to her house to retrieve her car before driving into town to see Clare, and he would lay money that Debba Clow wasn't the sort to go on long walks along dark, icy mountain roads. No matter what the provocation.

"Chief?"

"Sorry, Mark. I was thinking. I don't know what to make of this. There's too much unexplained stuff, and I hate unexplained stuff." He pushed away from the wall, setting his thoughts in order. "We have to act as if this is a missing-person case, because if Rouse did somehow wander off, we have a chance of finding him alive if we move fast. So I'll call out the volunteer fire department search team as well. They'll get there faster than the mountain rescue team."

"Okay."

"On the other hand, when the statie gets there with the CSU kit, I want every print that can be lifted off Rouse's car. We've already got Debba Clow's prints on record, so we won't need to get a warrant to check for a match."

"Hang on a sec." There were sounds over the line, someone talking, muffled. Mark came back on. "We're in luck. The crime scene guys are here."

"That's a land speed record."

"They were taking the shortcut along the Old Lake George Road, coming back from a demo at the Troop C barracks."

"Look, what I said about Debba Clow's fingerprints? Don't mention we've already got a suspect. I can think of some scenarios where somebody else might have whacked the doctor, and I don't want those guys taking shortcuts because they think we've got it all sewn up."

"You mean, like the unknown girlfriend idea?"

"Or the fact that he had access to major amounts of prescription drugs."

"I don't know." Mark sounded doubtful. "Seeing as how Clow admitted she was here with the guy . . ."

"I know, I know. But I don't want to miss anything just because it's less likely than Debba doing it."

"Debba does doctor," Mark said, sniggering. "Has a ring to it. So what are you going to do with her?"

Russ glanced over his shoulder and made a snap decision. "I'm bringing her out there with me."

"Why?"

"If he's gone missing, she might be able to remember a detail that she's overlooked."

"Or she might be able to invent something that jibes with the physical evidence once she's back out here."

"I'm aware of that. Mostly, I want to keep her out of her car until the staties have a chance to sweep it."

"Why not just impound it?"

"I intend to. But I'd like her permission to search it. I have a feeling if we go to Judge Ryswick with what we've got—most notably, what we haven't got, a body—he'll laugh at a warrant request. That man's enough to make me yearn for the good old days, when we could just look for whatever we wanted."

"Chief, the Miranda rules went into effect before you became a cop."

"I know. But I can dream." He brought himself back to the subject. "If she's out at Stewart's Pond and her car's back here, it'll be easier to get her to say yes. Her attention will be split, and she'll be thinking more about what we might find out there, not about trace evidence in her vehicle."

"If she just dumped him out here, there might not be anything in her car anyway."

"That's right. And in that case, bringing her back to the scene might just sweat something out of her."

"Okay. I'll see you when you get here. Make sure you got your boots on. It's colder'n a witch's tit out here."

Russ laughed as he hung up. He skipped Harlene and called John Huggins, the volunteer fire department chief, directly. He explained the situation and asked John to turn out his men in their cold-weather gear for a search.

"I'll call Glens Falls and tell them to take any calls we might get," Huggins said. "This'll be good for my boys. We been practicing turning out for lost hikers and whatnot. Nighttime work'll be a challenge. See ya there in twenty."

"Drive carefully—," Russ said, but Huggins had already hung up. Sometimes Russ suspected the main reason John Huggins had devoted years of his life to the squad was because it gave him a legal excuse to drive like a bat out of hell.

He hung up the phone and walked back into the living room. Clare was down on one knee in front of the fireplace, nudging a log into place with an iron poker. Debba was sitting where he had left her, tucked into the corner of the sofa, arms wrapped around her knees. "Dr. Rouse's car is still there, but he's nowhere to be found. The fire department search team and the mountain rescue folks are on their way, and I'd like you to come back there with me, Debba."

"Me?"

"You're the last person known to have spoken to the doctor. You may be able to help the searchers in some way." Clare rose, looking at him suspiciously. He was willing to bet that the next words out of her mouth would cut right though that bit of tissue paper he had just hung up, so he went right for her weak spot. "If he got confused and wandered off, there's a chance we can still save him. But we don't have much time. The mountains are a bad place to be lost on a bitter cold night."

As Clare knew firsthand, having narrowly escaped hypothermia and frostbite last winter. He could see the unpleasant memories flicker behind her eyes, erasing, at least for the moment, her doubts about Russ's motives in bringing Debba along. He felt a twinge of guilt, but absolved himself with the thought that it might, after all, be true.

Debba uncurled from her protective position and stood up.

"Do you want me to make you a thermos of hot coffee?" Clare asked her. "To take in your car?"

"We'll take my truck," Russ said. Both women looked at him. This time, it was Debba who frowned.

"It'll be a lot simpler for me to go home from the reservoir," she said. "Unless you don't think I'll be going home?" Her voice held a challenge.

He tucked his thumbs into his belt. "Your tire tracks are already part of the scene. No need to add confusion by having another set around."

Clare frowned, too. No wonder. That sounded lame, even to him.

"I don't feel comfortable with that," Debba said.

"I'm sorry about that. But I need your car to stay here, away from the scene." He kept his tone even, glossing over the fact that he had almost said "the crime scene."

Debba looked at Clare. "I'll drive you," Clare said.

"Wait a minute—" Russ began.

"Are you sure?"

"It's no problem."

"*I* have a problem with—"

"Okay, I'll hit the bathroom and then we can go." Debba vanished upstairs.

"You can't—," he tried again.

"I don't know what you're up to," Clare said, rounding on him, "but I don't entirely trust you."

"This is police business, Clare—"

"This is human business, Russ," she said, mimicking his tone. Her voice softened. A little. "I know you'll stay meticulously within the law. But you wouldn't see anything wrong with manipulating that woman into getting whatever you need out of her."

"A life may be at stake."

She jerked her chin up. "Tell me you think Dr. Rouse is still alive. And make me believe it."

He was silent.

"If he is alive, another pair of eyes won't hurt. And if he's dead, and you're planning on pinning it on Debba, well, then she'll need a friend."

He felt his hands clenching and forced them to relax. "God save me from do-gooders."

She grinned. "Not a chance. God has plans for you."

He shook his head. "Keep out of the way. Do not talk to anyone at the scene. And for God's sake, put something warm on."

CHAPTER 14

NOW

W ell, she thought, two out of three's not bad. She might not have been prepared for her first North Country winter, but she was a fast learner, and thanks to last spring's sales and this year's Christmas presents, she was as well protected from the cold as any of the men clumped around the hood of the volunteer fire chief's Jeep Cherokee.

The chief, who had introduced himself as "Huggins—John Huggins," was scoping out her qualifications. "You ever done anything like this before?" He was a short, well-braced two-by-four of a man, wearing a hat with flaps that fell to his chin and a suspicious expression. He reminded her of a crew chief she had met on her first posting, a lifer who had called her "girly." One of the guys handing out equipment from the Jeep looked over at her, and she felt uncomfortably like the shaky second lieutenant she had been back then.

"I was a helicopter pilot in the army for nine years," she said. "I've been trained in search and rescue." Admittedly, that was searching and rescuing from the air. Who would waste a pilot by having her walk grids on the ground? But there wasn't any air support for this operation, and if she couldn't persuade Huggins—John Huggins to let her join in the search party, she'd be stuck sitting in her car, going crazy.

She had driven to this spot in the middle of County Road nowhere, parked obediently where Officer Durkee directed her, and sat patiently in her Shelby while Russ escorted Debba past the halogen-light poles shoved upright in the snowbanks on the opposite side of the road and the two of them disappeared into the shadows leading toward the reservoir.

But when the cars and pickups and SUVs started to arrive, stringing along the edge of the narrow roadside and disgorging members of the volunteer fire department, it suddenly struck her: Maybe Allan Rouse really was alive, injured, disoriented, slowly freezing to death in the snowy woods. And here she was, sitting on her tail in her comfy car while other people prepared to turn out and look for him. It wasn't so much that she decided to volunteer, but that she was out of the car, pulling on her hat, before she decided not to.

"You. Were in the army." Huggins squinted at her. He unsnapped a kangaroo pouch on his anorak and pulled out a topographical map, similar to the ones his men were spreading out over the hood of his truck. He folded it open and handed it to her. "Can you locate us on this map?"

The moon was near full, spotlighting down on them all when it wasn't covered by fast-skimming stratocumulus clouds promising more snow. Of course, the search and rescue boys all had flashlights trained on their maps. She glanced over at them, then squatted down, her back to the warm artificial lights, and let her eyes adjust to the moon's hard brightness. She scanned the map, flipped it over, unfolded it, and located the road and the reservoir. "Here," she said, rising and holding the map out to Huggins.

"Okay," he said, slowly. "Can you show me the inside and outside search boundaries?"

This guy wasn't as much of an amateur as she had taken him for. "What's the average walking speed in snow?" she asked. At his expression, she said, "I trained for warm-weather operations. Desert Storm. The Philippines."

"Say two miles an hour."

"Do you have a grease pencil?"

Huggins fished inside his big pocket and handed her one. She knelt in the crushed and dirty snow and spared a moment to thank her brother Brian, who had sent her the ripstop snow pants she wore. Then she did the math in her head, read the contour lines of the map, and drew in two circles, smoothly rounded over the reservoir, jagged where they followed the lines of the hills around them.

She got to her feet and handed the map to Huggins. He studied it. He looked at her. "Why'd you include the reservoir?" he said.

"It's not fifty feet from the road right here. Dr. Rouse could have walked out, thinking he was getting clear of the trees, and—" Huggins was shaking his head. "No?"

"Well, yeah, he may have wandered out there, if he was disoriented. But we're not going out there."

"Isn't it still frozen over? I heard the ice doesn't leave most of these lakes until mid-April." Clare surreptitiously flexed her toes inside her boots to help ward off the chill. *Next time, wool socks.*

"Parts of it may still be a few feet thick," Huggins said. "But the temperature's gone above freezing more'n once over the past week. And we've had rain. There'll be rotten spots all over the surface. Too much risk of . . ." He made an expressive gesture indicating someone falling through ice.

"Oh."

"Tell you what. You say you came out with Chief Van Alstyne?"

"I drove the woman who was out here with Dr. Rouse." Huggins's eyebrows went up, and she realized how that sounded. "I mean, she was the last person to have seen him. They were, um, visiting the cemetery."

"Don't worry," Huggins said, "I've been doing this job for twenty-five years now and I've seen it all. Doesn't matter to me what folks do. I only come in if they get lost after doing it." He spread the map open again. "I'll give you this section, along the reservoir edge. It'll be easy viewing and less chance of you stepping into a woodchuck hole and breaking your leg. Seeing as how you trained for warm-weather operations. Hey, Duane!"

A mustachioed man in a Day-Glo orange parka detached himself from the rest of the team. "Duane, this is Clare Fergusson. She's been trained for search and rescue by the *army.*"

She forcibly squashed her irritation and reminded herself that Huggins was doing her a favor by letting her help. Calling him a Neanderthal wasn't going to get her anywhere. Besides, he probably thought it meant a brand of German beer.

Duane nodded at her, then looked at her more closely, interested. "Are you *Reverend* Clare Fergusson? The priest?"

"She's a priest?" The disbelief in Huggins's voice would have been priceless if she hadn't been worried he was going to turn her down for sure now. "I been a Catholic my whole life. There aren't any women priests."

"Ah, I guess you haven't been to mass lately, have you?" She let the shot hit home as she turned to Duane. "Have we met?"

"No, no, but I work part-time as a patrol officer. In Millers Kill. I've heard a lot about you at the station house."

Huggins was now looking uncertainly at her, as if wondering what other surprises were forthcoming. "You don't have a record, do you?" He looked up at Duane. "Has she been in trouble?"

"She hasn't been arrested or anything." Clare thought that answer artfully sidestepped the question. "She's a good friend of Chief Van Al-styne."

Oh, crud. She could see on Huggins's face the same expression he had shown when she stumbled over her description of Dr. Rouse and Debba. "Ah," he said. "You know Russ from his army days?" Evidently he had just decided to ignore the whole priest thing. Too much to try to fit in.

"Nope," she said. She was saved from further explanation by a pair of headlights coming toward them. Huggins stepped into the road and waved his light back and forth. The vehicle, a Chevy Suburban with skis racked on top, slowed to a halt. The driver unrolled the window. "What's up?" he said. Clare could see a woman and a couple of teens in the car.

"A man's gone missing along this stretch," Huggins said. "Mid-sixties, about my height, gray hair. You haven't seen anyone, have you?"

The driver shook his head. "Sorry. We're heading home from Hidden Valley." He pointed toward the roof. "Last ski trip of the season."

"Where's home for you folks?"

"New York City."

"Okay, drive safe."

"Thanks." The Suburban's window scrolled up and the car resumed its trip down the mountain.

"Flatlanders," Huggins said. "That's the third group so far tonight. Nine times out of ten, when we're called for search and rescue, it's one of them. I don't go down to the city and get lost and make them come looking for me. I don't see why they can't return the favor." He looked at Clare. "You're from away, too, aren't you?"

Hardball Wright had been a big believer in retreating to a ground of your own choosing. She decided now was the time, before she got lumped in with all the other incompetent flatlanders. "Do you want me to take that waterfront stretch now, or do I need to wait until you've organized the rest of the team?" She gestured toward the Jeep, where the map meeting had evidently ended.

He followed her hand, saw the men waiting for him to be done with her. "The waterfront. Yeah." He marked off a section rounding the edge of the reservoir and handed her the map. "Duane, give her a walkie-talkie and a flashlight." Duane handed over the goods. She shoved the walkie-talkie in her parka pocket and switched on the flashlight, testing it. "Walk slowly," Huggins went on, thankfully sounding less interested in her relationship with the police chief and more like a man delivering a well-rehearsed spiel. "Better to cover less ground thoroughly than more ground and miss something. You see anything, give a squawk. You get into trouble, give a squawk. We're on—what channel are we on, Duane?"

"Two."

"We're on channel two. Do not step onto any surface if you don't know where it bottoms out. In fact, Duane, grab her one of the poles." Duane ambled over to the Jeep and pulled something that resembled a long ski pole out of the back. He returned and handed it to her. "Use that to test for objects beneath the snow," Huggins went on. "Return to the base, that's here at the truck, after you've finished your section. And don't take any risks. We're here to rescue someone else, not you. Got it?"

"Got it."

He waved her off, and she broke for the other side of the road before he could think of one of the many good reasons why she should be back in her car instead of joining in the search. She glanced back and saw Huggins pulling Duane in by the shoulder, as if to get the confidential on her "friendship" with the police chief. Double crud.

She paused at the edge of the road. If she plunged straight ahead toward the reservoir, she was likely to run into Debba and Russ, who wouldn't pass on her search and rescue experience no matter how many topo maps she plotted. Instead, she headed down the road, walking around the Millers Kill cruisers and the state crime scene investigation van toward where a loudly huffing tow truck was maneuvering into place to ratchet Dr. Rouse's Buick out of the woods. As she got closer, she could hear the clank of heavy chains as the tow truck operator went to work hitching up the ditched vehicle.

In the yellow-white glare from the various headlights, she could see deep ruts in the crusty snow where the car had gone off the road. She glanced behind her. There was a definite downward slope from the area where the doctor and Debba would have emerged after their visit to the cemetery. She could easily imagine a dizzy, possibly concussed man getting behind the wheel of his big old boat of a car, shifting it into drive, and then passing out, letting the car steer itself off the pavement, through the scrub brush at the side of the road, and finally into the tall pines, where it had hit nose first, crumpling the hood back to the engine block. She could also imagine someone—a voice inside her head supplied *Debba Clow*—opening the driver's door, shifting the car into neutral, and running it down the road until it tore away toward the trees.

"Hey! You!" The bulky figure of a man hailed her out of the near-darkness just beyond the lights. She squinted to see who it was as he came closer. She could make out the brown police parka and winter hat, but his features were obscured beneath the balaclava protecting his face from the cold.

"Reverend Fergusson?"

The voice she recognized. "Officer Durkee?"

"What are you doing wandering around out here?"

She spread her arms open, displaying her pole, flashlight, and map. "I'm volunteering for the search and rescue team." Before he could point out that she had no prior connection with the team or anyone on it, she added, "I was trained in search and rescue in the army." Mark Durkee was young enough for references to a higher authority to carry some weight.

"Huh," he said. He pushed the balaclava up, revealing his face. "I was just headed over there to talk with Jim."

"About the search?" She glanced at the tow truck, shuddering and chuffing as it wrenched the Buick out of the trees. "Was there any sign that he walked away from the crash?"

Durkee nodded. "There were some boot prints around the car. Pretty indistinct. With the crust on the snow, every step just caves it in, leaves a big jagged hole."

"Can you tell which way he went?" She looked at his expressionless face and thought, Don't ever get in a poker game with this guy. "Let me rephrase that. Can you tell which way the footsteps went?"

"They intersect with the trail from the tires. Crunched flat."

"So you can't trace them from there?"

He shook his head.

"So maybe he made his way back to the road and was picked up . . ." She trailed off. "But if that happened, he'd be home by now, wouldn't he?"

"I'd think so."

"Did the crime scene investigation team find anything?"

"They always find something."

"You're a very closemouthed man, Officer Durkee."

"Thank you, ma'am." He smiled at her.

She looked around her, to where the unfathomable darkness of the Adirondack wood was held back by a few headlights and the whirling amber flashers of the tow truck. Even though she hadn't started yet, her search of the reservoir frontage seemed suddenly futile, an exercise designed to soothe them into thinking they had some control over this great and terrible beast all around them. "Russ doesn't think Dr. Rouse is going to be found alive," she said. "Do you?"

He shook his head. "No. But I think the effort is worth it. Whatever we do to find out what happened, to find him, it'll be a comfort to his family. There's something to that."

"Yes. There is." She gestured with her pole. "I better get to it." He lifted his hand in a salute that also pulled his balaclava back over his face, and headed up the road to deliver his news to the rest of the search and rescue team.

Clare waded into the snow. She discovered right away what Officer Durkee had been talking about. The stuff was covered with a frozen sludge of snow and ice, pitted with pinecones and broken bits of branches. It was just strong enough to hold her body weight for a second or two before breaking, so that each step jarred up her spine. When she lifted her foot for another step, the powdery snow hidden beneath the crust seeped in between the top edge of her boot and her ripstop pants, so that within minutes, she felt cold rivulets running down her socks.

She would have thought that the clear, cold air would carry the sounds from the road aloft, that she would still be able to hear the truck axle grinding and voices talking, but the tall pines swallowed everything in a fine-needled screen. The light, too, disappeared shade by shade, which surprised her, since this was a mature forest, no scrub trees or opportunistic bushes to push through. Just northern white pines, one after another after another until, when she looked back to where she had come from, there was no sign of lights or movement, no indication that there had ever been any artifacts of civilization.

She plowed on, trying to ignore her wet socks and the quiet, trying to ignore the narrow thread of panic that fluttered beneath her breastbone, chanting *Cold and snow and the woods and you're out here all alone,* because it was ridiculous. She had a map, a light, a walkie-talkie, and probably twenty cops and firefighters within a half-mile radius. It was just a leftover fear from an older and colder encounter with the Adirondack woods in winter. She paused for a moment, braced her mittened hands against a tree, told herself she had never had a panic attack in her life and she wasn't having one now, and pressed forward, sloping downward.

She could see the reservoir through the trees now, white and shining, and she hurried to break through into the clear air and was astonished when she did. Up on the road, all the lights casting the rest of the world into darkness had dimmed the effect of the almost-full moon. And beneath the pines, neither the moon nor the sun ever reached the ground. But here—she turned her flashlight off and blinked at the dazzle. The frozen surface of the water was neither white nor black, but glinted like layers of mica. And the size of it! When she had heard the term *reservoir,* she had created a picture in her mind of a squared-off city-block-sized container, like a giant bathtub waiting to be drained. This thing was a lake, vanishing into the curve of the forest at either end, far enough across so that it would be a challenge to swim the round-trip.

She could make out more details of the surface now that her eyes were light adapted, and she could see grayer spots and pockmarks where the ice had melted, broken, re-formed, and refrozen. But even with Huggins's warning playing in her head, the urge to step out onto that dazzling openness was strong. The Gospel writers had had it right when they described Jesus walking on water. What could feel more godlike than standing in the middle of a lake, water stretching away from you on all sides, the night turned to day by the light of the moon?

The walkie-talkie in her pocket crackled. She tugged her mitten off, retrieved it, and keyed the mike. "Fergusson here," she said.

"Where are you, Reverend? Over."

O-kay. So much for being one of the boys. She glanced at her map to remind herself of her distances. "I'm at the reservoir shore, about a quarter mile west of the cemetery site. Over."

"Head east until you hit the cemetery and then come back up the hill to the road. Over."

"Why? That'll be the world's shortest search."

"Chief Van Alstyne wants you to drive Debba Clow back to her home. Over." Additional emphasis on the "Over" to point out how she had forgotten that detail in her last message.

She was tempted to ask exactly how long it had been between the time Chief Van Alstyne found out she was here looking around and his decision Debba could be released. However, considering that every man on the search and rescue team could hear the conversation, she resisted the urge. "Will do. I'm headed that way now. Fergusson out."

She turned her eyes away from the frozen water and began slogging east, driving her pole through the crusted snow, scanning left, right, left, looking for any sign that someone had come this way before her. They could pull her off this duty assignment, but she by God would do it to the best of her abilities until the end.

Unfortunately, no broken branches, conveniently torn-away bits of clothing, or telltale footprints appeared for her to triumphantly report. From the edge of the reservoir as far into the woods as she could see, the icy snow lay unbroken.

She forgot to check her progress against the map, and was startled when a flashlight beam splashed across her face. For a moment, she was back on a logging road, hearing a cold voice slithering out of the darkness, the snick of a gun's safety releasing. Her heart tried to squeeze up through her throat.

"It's me." Russ's voice came out of the shadows. "I came back down to make sure you—are you all right?" He crunched into the moonlight and wrapped his hand around her upper arm, bunching his fingers in the insulated fabric as if to keep her from falling.

She nodded, pressed her free hand against her mouth, breathed against the mitten. "Yeah, I'm fine," she said when she could. "Your flashlight . . . it startled me, that's all."

He looked at her closely, his eyes washed colorless in the moonlight. When had he developed that look, like he was seeing right through her, right into her? She made herself busy with stuffing her map back into her pocket. "I'm fine," she repeated, although he hadn't asked. "Let's go."

"It's real slippery through here," he said. "Take my hand." He reached toward her. She stared at his glove for a moment, knowing that if Mark Durkee had been there, offering to help her keep her balance, she wouldn't have hesitated; hating that voice inside her that wondered, *Is this okay? Is this safe?*

She put her mittened hand in his and squeezed. He pointed the flashlight past a shadowy, cleared area—the cemetery—through the pines. "That's where we're headed," he said. "Don't want you falling and cracking your head open, too."

"Is that what happened to Dr. Rouse?"

He flashed his light on the gravestones. They were crumbling at the edges, their carving blurred by decades of acid rain. "It looks as if there's been a lot of thawing and freezing around the stones. They soak up the heat from the sun during the day. The snow melts, then when night falls, everything ices over again."

She tightened her grip on his hand as she struggled for footing. "You didn't answer my question."

"We found smears of blood on the corner of one of the stones consistent with Debba's story."

"Can I see?"

He pointed with his light, and she could just make it out, dark blackish spots along the rounded edge of the stone. She would have taken them for moss if she hadn't known. "So do you believe her version of events now?" She could pick out the name on the marker in the wash of the flashlight beam. JACK KETCHEM. JULY 21, 1920.

"At this point, I don't know what happened here." Russ played his beam over the ground. "This was all churned up even before the CIS guys started tromping around."

Clare let go of his hand and removed her own flashlight from her pocket.

"What?" he said.

"I want to see," she started, then turned her light directly on the blood-marked gravestone. JACK KETCHEM. JULY 21, 1920–MARCH 14, 1924. OUR ANGEL.

"He was just a baby," she said. She redirected her light to another stone. LUCY KETCHEM. JANUARY 8, 1918–MARCH 14, 1924. BELOVED DAUGHTER OF J. A. AND J. N. KETCHEM.

Clare stepped closer. "This was what Dr. Rouse wanted her to see? This?" She turned her light on another stone. PETER KETCHEM. JUNE 3, 1916–MARCH 18, 1924. BELOVED SON OF J. A. AND J. N. KETCHEM.

She turned back to Russ. "My God."

He nodded. "I know. There's one more of them." He flashed his light onto a fourth stone. A lump of ice half obscured a bas-relief carving of a lamb near the bottom. Above it, Clare read, MARY KETCHEM. NOVEMBER 5, 1921–MARCH 15, 1924. OUR LITTLE LAMB.

Two and a half years old. She reached back, and Russ took her hand again, holding hard. "Children," she said. "Just babies." She looked at the dates again. "They all died within a week of each other."

"Yes," he said.

"Jane Ketchem was their mother, wasn't she?"

"Yes," he said. "I met her here, when I was still a kid myself. I didn't know at the time. Later, I heard the story."

The money for the clinic, for Allan Rouse's medical training, it all fell into place. This is where it sprang from. This was what Jane Ketchem had been thinking of. And Clare was taking it, using it for roofing. Inside her mittens, the palms of her hands crawled. She turned her face toward Russ. "Let's go, please."

He nodded, and tugged her away, his arm helping her find her footing over the icy patches. Long after they had disappeared into the pines behind her, she could feel their stone faces watching her. Peter. Lucy. Jack. Mary. *Our Little Lamb.*

CHAPTER 15

THEN

TUESDAY, APRIL 1, 1930

Harry McNeil heard the commotion as soon as he pushed through the doors of the police station. Some woman gabbling upstairs for Sergeant Tibbet to *do* something, to *help* her. Not knowing that "doing something" was no longer in the vocabulary of Sam Tibbet, who had been slated to retire this spring but who was staying on because his son had recently lost his mill job and the whole extended family was eating off one police salary. Harry had pulled Sam off foot patrol two years ago when he had discovered the old guy was mostly working the seat instead of the beat. He wasn't a praying man, but the Millers Kill chief of police devoutly hoped that Tibbet junior would find good employment. Soon.

Stevenson and Inman came in behind him, both officers looking as tired as he felt. "You boys sign in your hours and then head on home. Get some sleep," Harry said.

Ralph McPhair, spiffed up with fresh-shined shoes and his gloves on, descended the stairs, heading out for morning traffic duty. "You three look like you got dragged through the bush backward. I hope the rum-runners came off the worse."

Roll Stevenson rubbed his face. "We thought we had one of 'em leaving that old barn behind McAlistair's place. Chased him almost to the gee-dee county line. Turns out it was Roscoe Yarter's kid, up all night sparking McAlistair's girl."

Pete Inman laughed, a short, sharp gasp of a sound. "We could have plugged the kid, and he woulda thanked us, just so long as we didn't turn him in to McAlistair."

"You going out again tonight, Chief?" McPhair asked.

"Maybe. I'll get on the phone to Glens Falls, see if they had more luck than we did last night." Harry tried not to let the complete lack of hope show in his voice. Attempting to plug the constant flow of illegal liquor running from Canada down to New York City was a mug's game. The bootleggers had as many men and more money than any of the police departments coming up against them, and appeals to citizens' civic virtue couldn't compete with hard cash in your pocket for leaving your barn unlocked and looking the other way. Harry knew, like he knew his kids' names, that within ten miles of where he was standing there were at least two or three delivery vans stashed out of sight in some farmers' hay barns, their drivers and gunmen snoring safely in the lofts. He knew, and he couldn't do a thing about it. He forced a smile, grinned at his men. "You see any bootleggers passing through town, Ralph, you be sure to stop 'em, you hear?"

McPhair threw them a jaunty salute as he tossed open the doors, and Harry, Stevenson, and Inman trudged up the marble stairs to the accompaniment of the unseen woman's voice, now demanding to see the police chief. Which was usually how it worked out when anyone with a problem came through the doors and encountered Sergeant Tibbet.

The long reception hall stretched away from Harry, with doors along both sides. The hall was guarded by Sergeant Tibbet, who seemed as oaken and massive as the desk he sat behind. A slim brown-haired woman stood there, taut as fishing line snagged on a snapping turtle. When she caught sight of him, she said, "Chief McNeil?" and in her voice he could hear she was right on the edge of breaking down.

He gestured the two officers to continue on to the patrol room before taking the woman's hand. "I'm Harry McNeil," he said. "How can I help you?" He hoped she was here to complain about a neighbor leaving her panties out on the line or kids stuffing her mailbox with fire crackers. He was tired to the bone.

"It's my husband. He's missing."

He sighed. That could mean something as simple as a broken-down automobile or as messy as a raided bank account and another woman. "To tell the truth, I was on my way home, Mrs. . . . ?"

"Ketchem. Mrs. Jonathon Ketchem. Please, you've got to listen to me. He's never done this before. I don't know who to turn to."

He rubbed his eyes with the palms of his hands. "Where do you live, Mrs. Ketchem?"

"Number 14, Ferry Street."

Not a bad neighborhood. Hardworking, churchgoing folks who paid their bills and went to bed early. "How'd you get here this morning?"

"I walked."

He nodded. "Well, Mrs. Ketchem, Ferry Street is on my way home." Sergeant Tibbet raised his shaggy eyebrows at that whopper. "How 'bout I drop you off on my way, and you can fill me in on all the details."

"How will you be able to start the search for Jon if you're at home?"

There's not likely to be a search, he thought, but said, "I can telephone the station and get someone working on it right away."

Mrs. Ketchem glanced at Sergeant Tibbet, who yawned. "All right," she said. "You can drive me home."

In his car, she perched on the edge of the seat, twitchy, as if she were ready to bolt as soon as he slowed down. Maybe she was more used to a buggy. She had a country look to her. "You and your husband have an automobile?" he asked.

She stilled. "Yes," she said. "Jonathon took it. He always drove it, not me." Her skittishness reminded him of the last carriage horse he had had before buying the Studebaker. Half-Thoroughbred mare, wide-eyed and spooky as all get-out. Good wind, though, once you got her in harness. He wanted to settle her some before he got her story.

"Are you folks related to the Ketchems up to Lick Spring?"

"They're my in-laws."

He turned down Elm Street. "They've got a pretty good-sized farm," he said.

"Yes." She was pale, visibly controlling herself. He swung down Burgoyne Street and turned onto Ferry. "This is us," she said. The Ketchem house was small, but neat, with a barn big enough to house a stall and a buggy attached to the rear of the house by a breezeway. He parked by the curb, got out, and opened the door for his passenger. She walked stiffly up the front steps. It looked to Harry as if she were bracing herself to reenter her home, and for a moment he wondered if her missing husband had been in the habit of knocking her around.

He wiped his boots on the mat before stepping inside. The tiny entry hall opened straight onto the parlor. A heap of painted blocks were tumbled next to the radio. "You have kids?" he said.

She paused in the middle of taking off her coat. "A little girl."

"She in school?"

"She's playing at a neighbor's." He followed her into the parlor. "She's been asking where her father is. I just don't know what to tell her."

She paused in the middle of the parlor, her glance darting from davenport to easy chair to rocker, as if she had never seen the place before. He had seen other folks acting the same way when calamity had visited their houses. People came unstuck, got lost in the familiar. He made it easier for her by sitting in the rocker and gesturing for her to take the other one.

"So what is it your husband does?"

She looked at him. Her eyes were red-rimmed. "He's . . . been trying out this and that . . ."

Drink, Harry thought. Or he's lost his job and is bluffing out finding a new one.

"We used to farm in the Sacandaga Valley until the Conklingville Dam project bought us out the year before last. My husband put some of the money into his parents' farm and some into his brother's business. David has a gasoline and service station in Lake George."

"David's your brother-in-law?" Speaking of her relations made him realize what seemed out of kilter in the room. There were no family photographs. Not one.

"Yes."

Harry nodded. "There wasn't enough for your husband to buy himself a new farm?" He knew some of the folks who had owned property in the way of the dam got pretty well rooked by land speculators before the official condemnation notices went out.

"I don't know. I suppose there was." She cut her eyes away. "Jonathon didn't know if he wanted to go back to being a farmer. It's a hard life, you know. He thought maybe things would be better if we stayed in town."

"Things?"

A faint suggestion of color came over her high cheekbones. "He did some work for the electrical company, but he was last hired and first fired when they started cutting jobs. Since then, he's picked up work here and there, but nothing permanent. He also helps out at Father Ketchem's farm."

He decided to ignore the fact that she had skipped over his question. He was forming a picture of a man cut loose from his familiar roles as farmer, and landowner, and provider, relying on make-do work from his old man to keep him and his pride afloat. "Tell me about the last time you saw him," he said.

She squared her shoulders beneath the blocky cardigan she wore and frowned, distantly, as if looking backward for the exact moment when it all started. "He had been home all day. His stomach was bothering him— it's been bothering him a lot lately. He was feeling right irritable. . . . I remember trying to keep our girl out of his way." Her eyes dropped to the blocks on the rug, and the strained look on her face eased for a moment. "Anyways, after she was in bed, we got into a fight. It was one of those silly things, you know, first you say something, and then he says something, and next thing you're going at it hammer and tongs without really seeing how you got there." She let out a breath. "He went off in the car that night and I haven't seen him since."

Harry reached into his blouse pocket for his notebook. "How long ago was this?"

"Saturday night. The twenty-ninth."

He paused in the act of reaching for a pencil. "He's been gone two days?"

"That's right. I could tell myself he had gone somewhere to settle himself down, but when he didn't come home last night, either . . . I know something terrible's happened to him."

Harry relaxed back into the polished curve of the rocker. "Mrs. Ketchem, we can't say a grown man's missing when he's only been away from home for a few nights. Have you checked with his family?"

"I used a neighbor's phone last evening, when he didn't show up for supper. Mother and Father Ketchem aren't home, but I spoke to their herd foreman at his house. He hasn't seen Jonathon."

"How about his brother up in Lake George?"

"David said he wasn't there."

Harry wondered how truthful the brother might be. He could easily imagine the husband pulling in in the wee hours, spending the next day bellyaching about the little woman, and telling his brother to lie through his teeth when she called. Especially if he was going on a toot. "Mrs. Ketchem," he said, "does your husband drink?"

She blanched. "No! We're good Christians. My husband has never indulged."

That had struck a nerve. He'd bet a dollar against a plugged nickel that if he were to go into the cellar right now, he'd find a couple mason jars of 100 proof. Behind the coal bin, or at the back of the husband's workbench, never where she'd find it, but enough there so she'd wonder about the husband's long trips downstairs and the smell of Sen-Sen on his breath when he came up again.

"Has he ever gone off before? After you've fought? You know, to cool off some?"

She shook her head, absolute in her denial. "No."

"Any money missing?"

"He has his wallet, of course, but nothing's been taken from the household money. I didn't think to ask about our account at the bank." She looked worried. "The checkbook is still on Jonathon's desk. He usually takes care of all that."

"It might be a good idea to stop in at the Farmers and Merchants and see if he made any withdrawals in the past few days. Yours wouldn't be the first husband to take off in a huff, find an extra few bills in his wallet, and decide to spend them on himself before coming home."

"But Jonathon isn't like that," she said, her voice rising. "That's why I know something bad's happened to him. He would never be gone so long without letting me know where he was." To Harry's discomfort, her eyes filled with tears. "I just don't know what to do. Please. Please, find my husband." The tears overflowed.

Harry leaned up out of the chair, yanking at his handkerchief. "Aw, now, don't—don't cry." He thrust the white fabric at her and prayed she wouldn't fall apart completely. Growing up the one son amid five sisters had left Harry with a lifelong horror of bawling females. "I'll tell you what. I can't put out the alert on him as a missing person. It's at least five days too early." Mrs. Ketchem started to cry even harder. "But!" he said. "If you can calm down and write me out a list of your husband's friends and the places where he's found work recently, I'll begin asking around for him."

Mrs. Ketchem lifted her face, red-eyed and blotchy, from his handkerchief. "Would you?"

"Yes, ma'am, I would. And I want you to try to stop worrying. In all likelihood, he's holed up with some buddy of his, trying to think of a way to come back and apologize without bruising his pride too much." He thought it was more likely that the missing man was either on a bender or shacked up with some sympathetic floozy, but Harry wasn't about to suggest that to a jumpy, frightened wife. Either way, ol' Jonathon would be back as soon as his funds ran out.

She went upstairs for some writing paper, which gave him a chance to poke around some. The place was small, just the parlor, a dining room, a tiny sitting room that looked to be used as a playroom, and the kitchen out back. The furniture was quality, but old. He guessed most of it had come down from a grandparent or two. Mrs. Ketchem was a good housewife— the china in the cupboard shone, the little girl's toys were all stacked away, and the kitchen was scrubbed. A closet-sized room off the kitchen held a washing machine and a heap of dirty clothes, which he picked through quickly and efficiently. No signs of foul play, drunkenness, or any other type of disorder, except that of an orderly housewife neglecting her Monday wash. Which, if she feared the worst, he could understand. Nothing could bring back a person's smell once it had been laundered away.

He was peeking out the back door, which led onto an enclosed porch, when she strode into the kitchen. She handed him a sheet of paper with a list of names and addresses written out in neat Palmer penmanship. "Here you are," she said. Doing something, anything, had helped. She looked around the kitchen with more energy than he had seen so far. "Can I offer you a cup of coffee?" she asked.

Coffee. Oh, yes. "That's kind of you," he said. "Yes."

"Can you fetch me some wood from the bin on the porch back there? It's right beside the door."

Like the rest of the house, the woodbin was just as it ought to be, tidy and well-stocked. There was a hatchet hanging over a chopping block, and he casually picked it up and examined it for signs that it had been used on something other than wood. But the fine wood dust caked in the joints between hatchet head and handle would never have survived a thorough cleaning.

Inside, Mrs. Ketchem had set the dripolater on and was reshelving a Chock full o'Nuts bag. He loaded the stove's fire box and asked her where the necessary was. She pointed him back out through the porch, and by the time he had done his business and washed up in the kitchen sink, Mrs. Ketchem was ready with a white crockery mug in each hand. She sat at the kitchen table and he joined her.

"I ought to get my daughter soon. At least now I'll have something positive to tell her. That the police are going to try to find her father. Maybe . . ." She faltered, and Harry could see her forward momentum die away. She reached into her sweater pocket, withdrew his handkerchief, and wiped her eyes again. She began to hand the damp cloth back to him and then started, as if she had really seen it for the first time. She jerked her arm back and balled it in her fist. "I'll launder this for you."

"You don't need to—"

"Oh, it's the least I could do." She stood up, looking frail inside the large sweater, which, Harry realized, was probably her husband's. "I'm sorry for falling apart like that." She offered him a rendition of a smile. "I know men hate to have a woman go off on them like that."

Harry waved his hands in denial. "Not at all. You were upset."

She smiled a bit more genuinely. "You're very patient. Thank you." She took the handkerchief into the laundry closet and then resettled herself in the kitchen chair. "Is there anything else I can do?"

"Let me get the inquiries in motion. Then we'll talk again, if he hasn't turned up."

"When can I expect to hear from you?"

"I'll follow up on these this morning," he said, consigning his nap to the realm of impossibly beautiful dreams. "I wouldn't be surprised if we have your husband back home in time for supper."

Her face fell blank and still. Only her eyes seemed alive, like dark water cast into shade by a cloud. "No," she said finally. "I don't think so." She blinked, and the illusion was broken. She looked at him. "Have you ever had a feeling, Chief McNeil? That something bad has happened? That's how I feel. I don't think my husband's coming home for supper. Not to-night. Not any night."

CHAPTER 16

NOW

C lare woke up late. Most days, the alarm hauled her out of bed early so she could get her run in before morning prayer or the 7:00 A.M. Eucharist. Mondays, she left the alarm off, but she usually woke up at the same time anyway through force of habit. She rolled to one side to look at the clock. Nine A.M. Good Lord.

She flipped the covers off and was instantly all over goose bumps. Holy crow, had she left a window open overnight? She grabbed her robe, which had been tossed over the foot of her bed, and belted it tightly. She tiptoed to the upstairs bathroom, trying for the least amount of contact with the cold floorboards. The little window over the toilet was shut tight.

She tiptoed back to her bedroom, spent a few minutes in a vain search for her slippers, and pulled on a pair of thick sweat socks instead, before going hunting for the window that was letting her expensive oil-fired heat escape.

She couldn't remember opening anything last night when she got in, but she had been asleep on her feet. After her encounter with the dead Ketchem children—*don't go there*—she had driven Debba Clow back to the house Debba shared with her mother. It had been a nonstop stream of speculation on Debba's part; what might have happened to Dr. Rouse, what the police suspected, how her ex would react, how this would affect the custody case.

After Clare had finally delivered the anxious woman to her front door, she had turned homeward, only to be blocked out of her own drive by a tow truck, chaining Debba's car in preparation for hauling it away. Clare had gotten out of her car and demanded to know what was happening, but the answer was a laconic "Impounded. Police." The tow truck driver, a man as broad and walleyed as a trout, had actually wound yellow sticky tape around the entire car before levering it up onto his flatbed and rumbling away down Elm Street. Despite the hour, or maybe because of it, Clare had seen lights on and curtains fluttering at most of her neighbors' houses. Yessir, just another dull night at the rectory.

She reached her thermostat in the dining room and discovered why her house was slowly sinking into a deep freeze. The temperature was set for sixty degrees, but it was only registering fifty. She turned the thermostat up, expecting to hear the soft roar of her furnace firing, and instead heard only silence.

"Oh, wonderful," she said to the wall.

In the kitchen, she turned on the oven to four hundred and cracked open the door. Then she called her oil company and begged them to send a repairman as soon as possible. She was pretty good with engines—she could tinker with cars and do basic repairs to light aircraft—but there was no way she was going to try to fix her own furnace. The oil company's burner tech was out on call, but he would get to the rectory when he finished with his morning appointments—no later than two o'clock. Three at the most.

"Tell him I'm leaving the door unlocked and a check on the kitchen table," she said. Okay. She could have tried for a parish in southern Florida and missed out on the experience of her house turning into a giant meat locker, but on the other hand, she wouldn't have been able to leave the house open and a blank check on the table in Miami. She consoled herself with that thought while wriggling into her clothes with her nightgown tented around her for warmth. She briefly considered lighting a fire in her living room, but the thought of what might happen if she wasn't around to keep an eye on things dissuaded her.

Instead, she grabbed her parka and her car keys. She was headed for Mrs. Henry Marshall's house with a whole boatload of questions. On the drive over, she ricocheted between frustration that she had been kept in the dark about Jane Ketchem, sympathy for Mrs. Marshall's silence about her family's grievous loss, and a deep bafflement as to Dr. Rouse's role in all this.

Mrs. Marshall's doorbell was set flush in an angular chrome-and-Lucite plate: the best the sixties had to offer. Clare caught a faint "Come in!" when she rang the chime and opened the door.

"Mrs. Marshall? It's me, Clare Fergusson."

"I'm back here, in the kitchen," Mrs. Marshall called out. She emerged in a doorway at the end of the hall, wiping her hands on an apron tied over her wool pants. Her lipstick was a marigold orange, almost the same shade as her turtleneck sweater, and from the distance down the hallway, her face softened in the shadows, Clare could almost see the slim and fashionable matron who had come to this house in the 1960s. "I'm making a meal to take to Renee Rouse, poor thing. Ham-and-cheese strata. It's wonderful, because you half bake it ahead of time, and then when you want to eat it you pop it in the oven and out it comes, hot and ready."

Clare hung up her parka in the hall closet while Mrs. Marshall extolled the virtues of her dish. "How did you hear about Mrs. Rouse?" she said, advancing toward the kitchen.

"She was calling everyone she knew yesterday. Frantic, poor thing. I telephoned her this morning, and she told me the police found Allan's car, but not Allan." She ushered Clare into her kitchen. "Can I get you some coffee?"

"No, thanks." Clare looked around. Unlike the rooms she had seen before, the kitchen had been thoroughly remodeled, and recently. Everything was creamy walnut, glossy dark granite, and brushed steel. As up-to-the-minute as the rest of the house had once been. Clare wondered how old she would be before the flush-to-the-cabinets Sub-Zero would be considered as hopelessly unfashionable as an avocado Kenmore.

"If it's all right with you, dear, I'm going to put you to work." Mrs. Marshall withdrew an apron from a drawer and handed it to Clare. "Will you chop up the ham and the broccoli for me? The knife's on the cutting board."

Clare obediently fastened the apron around her waist and went to the thick butcher's board next to the sink. She found a head of broccoli waiting to be rinsed and turned on the water, considering how to get into the topic that was foremost in her mind. "So Mrs. Rouse told you about how they found Dr. Rouse's car," she said, turning the broccoli beneath the spray. "Did she mention where it was?"

Mrs. Marshall pulled a metal mixing bowl from a cupboard and put it on the counter across the sink from Clare. "Off the road, up into the mountains, she said." She shook her head, her silver-white hair catching the light. "Bad news. Not what a wife wants to hear."

"It was by a place called Stewart's Pond Reservoir."

Mrs. Marshall crossed the room toward the refrigerator.

"Do you remember that woman who was so upset the day we went to see him? Debba Clow? He asked her to meet him out there. He showed her a little cemetery at the edge of the reservoir."

Mrs. Marshall faced the open refrigerator, her back to Clare. "Stewart's Pond," she said. "We used to call it the lake." She bent down, pulled a box of eggs from a lower shelf. "So that was where he went missing. I didn't know." She straightened, returned to the side of the sink with her egg carton in hand.

"I was there last night. Debba had come to the rectory to talk with me after . . . after she had met with Dr. Rouse. Chief Van Alstyne wanted her back up there to see if she could help them figure out where Dr. Rouse had gone."

Mrs. Marshall looked out the window over the sink. "Why on earth would he take anyone there?" she said. Clare didn't think the old woman was talking to her.

"That's the question, isn't it?" Clare steadied the broccoli on the cutting board and watched her hands as she cut off the thick stalk. "I saw the headstones. Sons and daughters of J. N. and J. A. Ketchem."

There was silence for a moment. "My brothers and sisters." Mrs. Marshall blinked, then looked at the egg carton. She picked up an egg and cracked it over the edge of the bowl.

"Would it disturb you to tell me about it?"

Mrs. Marshall turned to her, her expression almost surprised, as if she had lost track of the fact that her priest was in the kitchen with her, sleeves pushed up, chopping broccoli. "Disturb me? No." Then she smiled a little, the smile of a woman who has lived long enough to appreciate human nature. "Besides, if another man's gone missing it won't take too long for all the old stories to resurrect themselves. That's the trouble with living in your own hometown. Long memories."

Clare dropped her eyes to the cutting board and began slicing off the florets, halving the larger ones and peeling away the woodiest part of the stems. "What happened?"

"Diphtheria." Mrs. Marshall bent down and pulled a waxed cardboard milk carton from beneath the sink. "Compost garbage in there." She tossed in her eggshell and reached for another egg. "They called it the black diphtheria back then. It took all four of them within a matter of a week or so."

"But not you."

"I wasn't born until five months after."

Clare slid the cut broccoli to one side of the butcher's block board. She thought about her own mother and dad, heartsick after her sister Grace's death, their lives narrowed to a long, dark tunnel of mourning. "I can't imagine how parents could live with a grief that huge."

"My mother never talked about them. Ever. Everything I know, I found out from my grandparents." Mrs. Marshall cracked another egg, tossed the shell. "But the loss was with her always. Every day." She looked directly at Clare. "She loved me ferociously, I never doubted that, but at the same time, I know I was a constant reminder of my brothers and sisters. The pain of it just hollowed her out eventually." She shook her head. "After I was grown and married and gone, there were a few accidents that weren't accidents. She always got stopped in time, but it became obvious to me that she was trying to do herself harm. That's when Henry put in for a transfer so we could move back here. To look after Mother."

Clare reached out and rested her hand on Mrs. Marshall's thin arm. It felt like bird bones wound in wool. "I'm so sorry. Is that how she died?"

"No, surprisingly; she lived to be seventy-four years old. She was finally taken by pneumonia. Allan Rouse was her doctor, at the end." She smiled again, that small, sad smile. "He was her protégé."

And now he had gone missing, after a last visit to the graves of Jane Ketchem's long-lost children. "Can you think of any reason why he would have taken Debba Clow to see your brothers' and sisters' grave site?"

"She's the woman who's been protesting against vaccinations, isn't she?"

"Yes."

"Then I suspect he was hoping what happened to my family would be an object lesson to her. According to my grandma, the children died because my parents wouldn't have them vaccinated."

"You're kidding me." Clare touched her mouth. "Excuse me, that sounded flippant, and I didn't mean to be. I guess I meant, it's hard to imagine."

"Well, the diphtheria vaccination was quite new then, and not widely used. My grandma never blamed my parents. She said lots of folks in those days worried that the vaccinations themselves were the cause of a growing list of ills, everything from mental retardation to social diseases." She cracked another egg and tossed the shell. "And, too, folks living a clean, healthy life out on a farm didn't think they were likely to have to face the diphtheria. It was supposed to be a disease of the slums, passed around by poor unwashed immigrants." Mrs. Marshall gave Clare a dry look. "You'll recognize that line of reasoning. It seems human nature doesn't change, just the name of the disease."

"Do you think your parents blamed themselves?"

"I'm sure of it. They made what they must have thought was a good decision, in the best interests of their children, and they lost everything." Mrs. Marshall rested her hands on either side of the metal mixing bowl, cupping it abstractedly as she looked out the window again. "I believe that's the real reason I never had children."

Clare must have made some involuntary gesture, because Mrs. Marshall turned to her.

"Oh, yes, it was a choice. People assumed Henry and I simply weren't fortunate, but we knew before we got married that neither of us intended to have children. In fact, I turned down two men who asked me first, because I knew they wanted their own families one day. But thinking about it"—she paused, worrying her lip so that a tiny smudge of marigold appeared on one of her front teeth—"I see that it wasn't the fear of what losing a child would do to me. I mean, that was always there, but . . . I think it was a fear of the responsibility. My parents took on that responsibility, and in the end, it destroyed them."

"What happened to your father?"

"Well, you see, that's why people are going to start repeating the old stories. Now that Allan Rouse has suddenly gone missing. My father walked out of our house the night of March twenty-ninth, 1930, after having a fight with my mother. He climbed into his car, drove away"—Mrs. Marshall sighed and turned to Clare—"and was never seen again."

CHAPTER 17

THEN

By the time he headed out to Lake George to talk with Jonathon Ketchem's brother, Harry McNeil was beginning to think that Mrs. Ketchem was right about not seeing her husband again.

He had started with Ketchem's buddies, four names on the top of the list. His first call was pretty much a bust. He had scarcely descended from the Ford when Hutch Shaw's wife, washing the windows at the front of their narrow row house, yelled, "He's not here!" What followed was mostly a waterfall of complaints about how the economy had forced her husband into working for a road crew building up past Warrensburg, and now every day he had to travel all the way to Warrensburg, for heaven's sake, and what kind of life was that for a man with children?

The two useful pieces of information Harry winkled out of Mrs. Shaw before escaping were that neither she nor her husband had spoken with Jonathon Ketchem since Friday before last, and that all the men Mrs. Ketchem had listed were members of the Grange and the VFW.

"So you two were in the Great War together?" he asked Arent De Grave, a blocky blond whose good-sized farm seemed unthreatened by the hard times that had sent poor Hutch Shaw up to Warrensburg.

"Ayup," Arent said, pitching a forkful of rotted manure onto his spreader. They were standing in the cobbled yard between De Grave's two barns, and except for the pile of crumbling manure that had been composting over the winter, everything was clean enough to eat off of, in that particularly Dutch way Harry always admired but could never achieve.

Arent continued, "That is, we were both in it. I was in Dordogne. Jon sat the whole thing out in Fort Knox, running their motor pool."

"So you knew him before the war?"

De Grave tossed another forkful into the already heavily loaded spreader and then swept his hand past his tidy white house, past the firepond, to a notch between two hills where a many-gabled roof could be seen. "That's the Ketchem place. My family's been farming next door since my dad moved us from North Cossayuharie in aught-six."

"They there? Mr. and Mrs. Ketchem?"

De Grave shook his head. "They've got hired hands running the place over winter. Mr. Ketchem's been having a bad time of it with his lungs, so they went out west for the winter. I imagine they'll be coming back right soon, but they ain't home yet."

"Is anyone living in the house?"

"Nope. The hands that ain't married have their own place, back along the crick." He paused for a moment. "You're thinking Jon might have gone to his parents' house. I would have seen a light there if anyone had been inside the last two nights. Besides, I can't imagine Jon running back to his mom and pop. That's the last thing he'd do."

"So you know him pretty well."

"As well as anyone, I reckon."

Harry kicked a clump of hay-studded manure out of his way. "Tell me true now. Is he likely to be off on a bender?"

Arent De Grave rested his pitchfork against the cobbled stones and looked at Harry. "Now where would he be getting booze around here, Chief?"

Harry sighed. "I'm not asking where anybody's getting anything. But your friend walked out on his wife in a temper and hasn't been seen since. Most men, that means they're either drinking or whoring."

De Grave raised his barely there blond eyebrows.

"Or they're bivouacking with a friend. So how 'bout it? Which category would you place Jonathon Ketchem in?"

"He's not here." De Grave dug his pitchfork into the manure pile and tossed another twenty pounds into the spreader. "Who-all's on that list you got?"

Harry pulled the creased paper from his back pocket. "You, Hutch Shaw, Leslie Bain, and Garry MacEacheron."

"We're all of us married men. With kids. I can't imagine any of those men's wives not picking up the phone and letting Jane know that Jonathon was there." He smiled, almost shyly. "I know for sure my missus would."

"Could he be holed up in a speakeasy someplace? Maybe gone to Glens Falls, taken a room there?"

De Grave clanged the pitchfork tines against the cobbles to loosen the muck and kicked what remained off with the edge of his boot. "Help me get the team hitched up," he said, walking into the barn. Harry followed him. For a moment, his vision shut down in the difference between the bright, chill sunshine outside and the warm animal gloom inside. Two enormous geldings, half-Percheron by the looks of them, stood patiently, and Harry was relieved to see that they were already in tack. It had been a long time since he had harnessed up his own dad's team, and he didn't want to look a citified fool fumbling around in front of De Grave. "This is Ned"—De Grave indicated the horse at the left-hand block—"and that one is Nick."

Harry took Nick by the bit strap, scratched his neck, and stroked the outside of his nostrils with a light finger. From between black leather blinders, Nick looked down on him with clever brown eyes that seemed to say, *This is all nice and good; but I'm supposed to be to work.*

Harry led Nick out of the barn, blinking again as they emerged into the light. "Nick is the far horse," De Grave called over his shoulder, and Harry led his charge to the right side of the rig. The gelding was so well behaved that the slightest pressure of Harry's hand on his bit rein caused him to back neatly into his place beside the spreader's wagon tongue. Harry and De Grave lifted the crossbar, and Harry held it steady while the farmer clipped Ned's straps to the bar's left ring and adjusted their tension. Then Harry did the same for Nick while De Grave returned to the tack room to retrieve the heel chains, which would attach the horses' tack to the spreader itself.

De Grave came about the front of the team and handed Harry a three-foot chain, thick and heavy enough to break a skull open with one blow. "So how 'bout it?" Harry asked as he smoothed a hand over Nick's broad flank. "Is Jonathon the type of man to have poured himself into a bottle? Does he have a girl somewhere who might have taken him in?"

He bent down to clip on the chain, and through the stolid stacks of the horses' hind legs, he could catch glimpses of De Grave: muck boots and faded pants and hands that looked older than his thirty-some years, meticulously attaching chain to ring, checking the latch, checking the straps.

"Jonathon liked his whiskey as much as the next man in his younger days," he said, his words slow and thoughtful. "He never was a temperance man, that I heard. But I haven't seen him near liquor for . . . well . . ."

He stood, resting one hand on Ned's muscular croup. "Well, not since his children passed."

Harry stood up, the heel chain still dangling from his hands. "What?" He could just see De Grave's head over the horses' rumps. "What do you mean, after his children passed? I thought he and his wife had the one daughter."

De Grave nodded. "She was born after. They had four youngsters before. All of 'em died of the black diphtheria in '24."

"Good God."

"Sometimes His will is hard. Hard to bear." De Grave's hand traced the leather lines of the straps crisscrossing Ned's hip and rump. "Jonathon was different after that."

"Different how?"

De Grave tilted his head up and squinted at the pale blue sky of early spring. "He had always been real certain about where he was going, what he wanted. He was going to make a big success of his farm, buy more land, do better than his father. After the children passed, he just sort of . . . spun free."

"You mean he started acting up? Getting wild?"

"No, no, just the opposite. He didn't have any more spark for fun in him, I think. He was more like . . ." Harry waited while the farmer chose his words with care. "Like a working barge that's been set adrift on the river. You see it traveling downstream, it may look like it's doing what it's always done, but there's no purpose there. No hand on the tiller."

"Sooner or later, an unmanned boat will wreck."

De Grave looked at Harry. "I know."

"But not on a bottle."

De Grave shook his head. "I don't think on other women, either, although I can't say for sure, one way or tother. It's hard to imagine a man with a pretty, sweet wife like Janie looking elsewhere."

Harry didn't find it hard to imagine at all. He could picture it, long nights lying next to the woman, and every time you looked at her seeing your lost children in her eyes, her mouth, the color of her hair. Never touching each other without the chains of grief weighing your limbs down, making your flesh cold. He glanced at the heel chain, heavy in his hands. Easy to imagine wanting to hide yourself in someone else's hot, blank, forgettable body.

He squatted down and attached the chain to Nick's trace strap, tugging on it to make sure the latch was secure. He fastened the other end to the big steel ring bolted to the corner of the spreader. When everything was neat, he stood again, looked across the horses' backs at De Grave. "What's your guess, then?" he said. "You know the man. What would you think he'd done, disappearing from his home and not coming back?"

De Grave weighed the question with the same deliberate concentration he gave to everything. "My guess would be," he said after a minute, "that he'd finally drifted downstream out of sight."

◆ ◆ ◆

When Mrs. Ketchem had described her husband investing in his brother's gas station, Harry had envisioned one of those ramshackle affairs that were popping up in the wake of the new road construction up north, converted livery stables or smiths with a pump out front and bales of hay still stacked in the rear. He was surprised, then, when he spotted a brilliantly enameled brand-spanking-new sign emblazoned KETCHEM'S GAS AND MOTOR SERVICE. The low, wide building on the intersection of Route 9 and Tenant Mountain Road was whitewashed within an inch of its life, stuccoed into rounded edges and smooth curved arches through which three service bays beckoned to distressed motorists. There were no fewer than three pumps outside, protected from the elements by a bright red roof supported by more stuccoed pillars. It looked as if it had been lifted up bodily from Hollywood, California, and transplanted to Lake George.

Harry pulled alongside the far edge of the building, out of the way of the pumps. As he got out of his Ford, a tall, gangly youngster in coveralls popped out of the first service bay. "Help you, sir?" he said, his voice cracking halfway through the greeting. He coughed and blushed.

"I'm not here for service, son, but thank you. I'm looking for David Ketchem. Might he be around?"

The kid tucked his chin in an attempt to keep his Adam's apple in place. "My dad's in the office," he said, pointing to a red door sandwiched between the service bays and a gleaming expanse of plate-glass window.

The door didn't tinkle when Harry opened it. Instead, it set off a musical *bing!* that sounded like an hour tone on the radio. He began to suspect that, had life turned out a little differently, Jonathon Ketchem's brother would have gone into show business instead of being a pump jockey.

"Can I help you?" The man behind the counter was about Harry's age, mid-thirties, with thinning blond hair and a face that fell easily into smiling. Harry didn't need the DAVE badge sewn over his right breast pocket to identify him as the skinny kid's father.

"David Ketchem?" Harry smiled himself, a salve against the sting of his next words. "I'm Chief Harry McNeil, Millers Kill police."

Ketchem's smile faltered, and he darted a glance toward the door separating the office from the service bays. Then he reached his hand over the counter. "How d'ye do. I hope there isn't any trouble." His voice, which had been as smooth and accentless as a soap salesman's before, took on a strong up-country Cossayuharie accent, so that "isn't" came out "in't."

"I'm here because of your brother, Mr. Ketchem. Seems Jonathon Ketchem had a fight with his wife this past Saturday night. He stormed off in his car and hasn't been home since. Mrs. Ketchem is mighty upset about it, and I told her I'd make some inquiries. I'm hoping you can help me locate him."

"Yeah. Janie called me yesterday. Said he'd taken himself away and she didn't know where he was." Ketchem's body relaxed, and the storm cloud that had been brewing in his eyes dissipated into amused surprise. "I can see why Janie'd go on about it to you. He's never done that before, that I know of."

"He hasn't come here? To cool off or to keep his head down for a few days? Give her a scare?"

"Nope. He's welcome to stay anytime, but I haven't seen him for a couple, three weeks at least."

"You sure? Maybe he drove through here on his way up north, and your boy saw him?" Harry figured if this guy was protecting his brother, it would be a good idea to give him a graceful way out. He leaned forward on the counter, confidential, man-to-man. "Obviously, we don't get involved in a quarrel between a man and his wife, but now that we're out looking for him"—skipping over the fact that Harry wasn't wasting any of his men's time on this—"I'd hate to keep on spending the department's money looking for him if someone knows where he's gone."

David Ketchem shook his head. "Honest, I don't know. And Lewis, my boy, he'd 'a told me. Janie's a good girl, and she's been a good wife to him. I wouldn't help to scare her."

"You ever know your brother to drink?"

"We used to sneak a bottle here and there when we were younger, but no, not for some while. Our dad is an elder of the Presbyterian church in Cossayuharie, so you can imagine how our folks feel about liquor. I just figured Jon followed their example."

"What about women? Any chance he might have a girlfriend on the sly who'd take him in?"

Ketchem laughed. "Jon? Not a chance. Farm and family, that's all that interests him."

Harry polished an imaginary spot on the gleaming white counter. "That's not the impression I've gotten from speaking to a few people. His wife says he's been moody and out of sorts since they lost their farm to the Conklingville Dam project. Hasn't figured out what to do with himself. A friend of his agrees." He glanced up at Ketchem. "What's your take?"

David Ketchem rested his forearms on the counter, bringing himself down to Harry's eye level. He frowned, and gazed out the plate-glass window at the stubby pasturage across Tenant Mountain Road. "I guess that's true. Having to sell the farm, that was hard on Jon. Only thing he ever wanted to do, really. Be a farmer, just like Dad." He looked at Harry. "I told him he ought to get into a business. Farming." He shook his head. "You bust your hump three hundred sixty-five days a year doing the same work your great-great-grandfather did. And never get any further along in life than he did." He glanced around his movie-star-bungalow garage. "You have to look to the future, that's what I told him. He got a bundle from selling his land to those development folks. It's worth more under-water than it was growing corn and feeding cows. That's a sign, don't you think? The mountains are changing, and a smart man changes along with them." The satisfaction in his eyes as he surveyed his red-and-white kingdom left no doubt as to which path David Ketchem had chosen.

"Mrs. Ketchem said your brother invested in your business here."

"He did, and it was a smart thing, too. I'm going to get him a good return on his money. It's quiet now, 'cause it's spring, but you should see this place during the summer. From June through September, the pumps never stop ringing and we have cars parked around the building waiting for garage service." He came around the counter and opened the red door. "You see that lot across the way?" He stepped out onto the macadam and Harry followed. The sun was sliding fast toward the mountains, and a cold breeze had sprung up, reminding Harry that they were still just a few weeks past the rawest nights of the year. He hunched his shoulders inside his wool jacket as Ketchem pointed across the road, where a tired-looking farm stand leaned in on itself, empty except for a few bunches of rhubarb propped in buckets and a tin can for customers to put their money into. "You know what oughtta be there?" Ketchem said. "A restaurant. Doesn't have to be fancy, just someplace clean and fast where folks driving to the lake or up into the mountains can pull over and eat. I got my eye on the property. I tried to get Jon to think about it, buying the land and building a place." He shook his head again, this time with the frustration of a man navigating by a map that everyone else ignores. "I told him, you'll get more for cooking and selling food to tourists than by growing it. He's not interested."

"What is he interested in?"

David Ketchem frowned at Harry, as if he had lost track of the purpose of their talk. "Huh?"

"Your brother doesn't seem to drink. No one can place him with a girlfriend. And he's never gone off and left his wife and kid with no word. But he's been missing two days now. Where do you think he is?"

Harry could see the exact moment when Ketchem realized he had no answer for the question that his brother might really, truly be gone, in one of the ways that have no relieved reunion, no happy ending. A thought had been swimming around in Harry's mind, hard to catch, like a fish in a shady brook. Just glimpses, as it darted into the sun-clear water. *It was one of those silly things, you know, first you say something, and then he says something, and next thing you're going at it hammer and tongs.*

After the children passed, he just sort of spun free.

Having to sell the farm, that was hard on Jon.

He leaned in closer to Ketchem, dropped his voice. "How blue do you think your brother really was?"

David Ketchem's mouth sagged open. Then he snapped it shut. "No."

"Dad?"

Both men turned to see the boy, framed in the archway of the first service bay.

"Is Uncle Jon missing?"

Ketchem looked at Harry, an edge of panic sharpening his features, his question as clear as if he'd spoken it. *What do I say?*

"Your dad says your name is Lewis," Harry said.

"Yessir."

"Did you overhear us talking in the office, Lewis?"

The kid ducked his head. His cheeks pinked up, but he managed to look Harry in the eye. "Yessir. I'm sorry, Dad. It's just, without a car running in the garage, it's easy to hear through the door—"

"And you were curious what a cop had to say to your father?"

"Yessir." The kid ducked again, then looked at his father. "Dad, what if Uncle Jon was out at night and ran into some bootleggers?"

This, his father seemed to know the answer to. "That's not very likely, Lew. And even if Uncle Jon happened to be on the same road as a bootlegger, they wouldn't be bothering with him. They want to get their liquor to where it's going as fast as they can, not have shoot-outs with folks driving by."

"But you wouldn't let me go out last Saturday with Boyd and Morrie in his jalopy 'cause of the rumrunners. You said we might wind up in serious trouble."

Harry had used enough spurious reasons to say no to his kids to recognize one when he heard it. Any serious trouble Ketchem expected came from the idea of three half-bearded kids gallivanting around the countryside on a Saturday night. "Your dad's right. Bootleggers aren't likely to pick on a grown man, but kids could be an easy target. But that's still an idea worth looking into. If your uncle doesn't show up in a few more days, I'll send a wire to the other police stations all along Route 9, and have 'em keep an eye out for your uncle's car." He turned to Ketchem. "Any hunting cabins, fishing shacks, someplace he might have gone to"—*put an end to it*—"be alone?"

Ketchem shook his head. "No."

Harry glanced over at the future restaurant site. He kind of favored the old farm stand himself. He looked back to David Ketchem, held out his hand. "Thanks for your help. If you think of anything, give me a call. Millers Kill six-four-five."

Ketchem gripped his hand a little too tightly. "Do you really think—," he said, his voice shrunken, then shook himself and released Harry's hand. "I'm sure he'll turn up soon," he said, in a normal tone. "And when he does, I'll be first in line to kick his keister for making us worry."

"I'm sure you're right," Harry said.

Pulling out of the gas station and turning onto the road back to Millers Kill, Harry could see David Ketchem had gone to his son's side. He watched them in his rearview mirror, watching him, until they disappeared in the distance, Ketchem's arm wrapped tight around his son's shoulders. Keeping him safe at home.

CHAPTER 18

NOW

Did you ever find out what happened to your father?" Clare shifted in the passenger seat of Mrs. Marshall's Town Car, taking pains not to move the dish towels shielding her thighs from the hot casserole dish balanced on her lap. She had wheedled her way onto the delivery, in part because she had a guilty need to extend her sympathy and support to Allan Rouse's wife, and in part because she didn't know, if she cut off the tale in its telling, if Mrs. Marshall would ever open up this way about her family again.

"No. Although there was no lack of theories. My mother was convinced he was dead, though she never speculated whether it was by accident or some misadventure." She glanced away from the road briefly, smiling an old smile. "I suspect it was easier for her for him to be dead than for him to be alive somewhere, making a new life without us."

"How about you?"

"When I was a girl, I was definitely in my mother's camp. I was sure he had been set upon by brigands and murdered after fighting like a lion to escape. Later, as an adult . . ." She flicked on her turn signal and swung the car majestically onto Main Street. "I came to believe he ran away. He certainly wasn't the only man to take that way out during the depression. I didn't notice it much as a little girl, but those were hard times. The year he disappeared, two of the four banks in town closed. I remember the Ladies Auxiliary started coming by my school with box lunches because some children had nothing but a hard roll or an apple to eat. I found out later, from my grandmother, that by the time my father had been ruled dead, his life insurance was gone. The company went bankrupt. That happened far too often in the thirties." The light turned red a block ahead of them, and Mrs. Marshall braked, reducing the speed of the boat-sized car from thirty-five miles an hour, to twenty-five, to something Clare could have matched during a good run. Clare tried not to twitch.

"How did you and your mother get on without your father? Did she have a job?"

They were still slowing down when the light turned green again. "No, Mother never worked. Of course, few women did, even in those days. There was so much more work to do at home than there is now, you know. It was hard for her, but she always managed to pinch by. She had investments. She and my father helped Uncle David start his garage, and that certainly did well over time. We never had luxuries, but I never wanted for anything important. And when the time came, I was able to attend college. I was the only girl in my high school class to do so. That was before the GI Bill and student loans and all that."

"Where did you go?" Clare asked, imagining one of the state universities or subsidized colleges.

"Smith. Class of '47."

Clare blinked. "Good school. Were you a work-study student?"

"No, Mother paid for it all." She risked another glance at Clare before returning her attention to the road. "She never spent anything on herself. Everything she had she spent on me, and then on the clinic, and then it went into the trust at her death."

Clare opened her mouth to point out that Jane Ketchem hadn't done too badly for a woman with no job and no visible means of support, but her grandmother Fergusson hissed in her ear, *Nothing's more vulgar than talking about money!* So she snapped her jaw shut and watched as they turned with great deliberation onto Elm Street.

Several cars were parked along the street in front of the Rouses' house, including, Clare noted with no surprise, the chief of police's pickup truck. Mrs. Marshall pulled in as close as she could, and Clare juggled the casserole dish out of the car while Mrs. Marshall retrieved a cherry pie—"Store bought, I'm afraid"—from the backseat.

This time, Clare didn't have a chance to admire the deep moldings and polished brass on the Rouses' door. The minute Mrs. Marshall set foot on the steps, it whisked open, revealing a little pear-shaped woman with a face like a homemade dumpling. "Lacey Marshall, you be careful on those steps," she said, reaching for the pie. "Give me that. Come on in. Oh, is that a casserole? How nice. Renee will be set for a few days at this rate. Which'll be a help. Although you know, sometimes puttering around in the kitchen can be a relief from thinking about your problems. Oh! Who is this?"

During the course of the monologue, Clare had followed Mrs. Marshall into the foyer, set the casserole dish on a marble-topped commode that had probably stashed mittens and hats in the Rouses' child-rearing days, and unwound her scarf from around her neck.

"Yvonne, I'd like you to meet the Reverend Clare Fergusson, our priest at St. Alban's. Clare, this is Yvonne Story. Yvonne was our librarian at the Millers Kill Public Library until she retired, much to our loss."

"Oh, I had to retire in order to fit in all the other things I was doing at the time. Not that I didn't love being librarian. Everyone always said it was a natural fit, a librarian named Story." She snorted at her own joke. "So nice to meet you. I'd heard the Episcopalians had a new minister. I used to be a Methodist myself. But when Dr. Gannet left, it all went straight downhill. That new fellow couldn't preach his way out of a paper sack. So I abandoned ship. Now I watch this nice television preacher. So much easier than getting up and dressed on a Sunday morning!"

Clare tried to squeeze in a how-do-you-do while Yvonne Story pumped her hand, but it was futile. She settled for smiling and nodding.

"Isn't this terrible about poor Allan? I mean, I hate to assume the worst. But there's not much of a way you can put a good face on this, is there? Poor Renee. I hope he left her well set up. She's never had to work, like me. What will she do without him? That's the downside of having a husband. That's why I never got married."

Clare felt her smile glazing over. *Deliver me, O Lord,* she prayed.

"Yvonne." Renee Rouse appeared in the doorway between the front hall and the living room. "Would you be a dear and go make some more coffee? And a pot of tea. I'm sure everyone would like something warm on such a cold day."

"Oop. Of course, Renee. And I'll put this pie in the kitchen for you, Lacey. Did you get it from the IGA? They do nice pies. Not as good as homemade, mind you, but good."

"Thank you so much, Yvonne," Mrs. Rouse interrupted.

"Oh, you're right. To the kitchen for me. Ta-ta. See you later. Nice meeting you, Reverend." She continued to talk as the door to the kitchen shut behind her. Clare took off her coat and hung it in the hall closet. *The librarian?*

Renee Rouse closed her eyes. She was holding the edge of the archway, her knuckles white.

"How long has she been here?" Mrs. Marshall asked.

"Since nine." Mrs. Rouse tried to smile.

Mrs. Marshall picked up her casserole. "I'll pop into the kitchen and keep her occupied for a bit."

"Bless you, Lacey." Renee Rouse squeezed one of Mrs. Marshall's slender arms. She was dressed much the same as the older woman in a simple sweater and warm slacks. Classics. Her grandmother Fergusson would have approved. But unlike Mrs. Marshall, who radiated warmth in her marigold sweater and lipstick, Renee Rouse looked cold. The wall that had held life's problems at bay had crumbled in the space of an evening, and now she was drowning in reality.

"Reverend Fergusson." She blinked, as if she had just noticed Clare. "Thank you for coming by." Her smile was a bad copy of the smooth social face Clare had seen on her last visit.

She took Mrs. Rouse's hands. "How are you doing?"

"Okay. It seems to vary from minute to minute. Last night, when the officer called to tell me about Allan's car, that was very bad." She bit her tongue, and for a moment, it looked as if she was going to cry. "But Chief Van Alstyne is here, and from the things he's been asking me, I know he's still holding out hope Allan is . . . all right."

Clare squeezed her before letting go. "No one will do more to get your husband back than the chief." Then, because even hopeful speculation about the future would likely be painful, she said, "Tell me about Allan. You two seem very close. How did you meet?"

This time, Mrs. Rouse smiled the genuine smile of happy recollection. "It was the oldest cliché in the book. I was his secretary." She linked her arm in Clare's and led her through the living-room archway. "He was fresh from his residency in New York and had just started working at the clinic. The old secretary couldn't spell and refused to take dictation from a machine, so he fired her."

Clare could see three women in the living room, grouped together on the sofa, and another pair at the gleaming dining-room table, visible from the doorway separating the two rooms. Someone had evidently brought a Bundt cake, and the tables were littered with porcelain dessert plates and straight-edged coffee cups in saucers, as if the gathering were a morning bridge game that had taken on an unexpectedly somber cast.

"I had been working for the Glens Falls Insurance Company, but I wasn't terribly happy there, so when my mother told me about the handsome, young, single doctor who was looking for a secretary, I jumped ship."

"And it was obviously a good career move."

Renee Rouse laughed. The three women around the sofa glanced at her, as if checking to make sure it wasn't the opening salvo of a hysteric fit, and then returned to their conversation. Mrs. Rouse led Clare to a love seat tucked between two bookcases and sat down. "It was the best thing I ever did. Allan had been in New York for several years, in medical school and afterward, and he was the most cosmopolitan and sophisticated man I had ever met. He had been dating a woman in New York but wasn't seeing anyone here, and he was always complaining at the clinic about how his life was all work and he never had any fun. One day I screwed up my nerve and said to him, 'Why don't you come to Lake George Saturday night with me and some friends?' I was sure he'd think the carny rides and boardwalk would be stupid, compared to what he was used to in New York. But we had a wonderful time, and we went the next weekend, and the next, and one thing led to another, and we were married the next summer."

"That's so romantic." And it was true. Every story of "how we met" was romantic because every one had the magical element of blissful chance—if he had kept on the old secretary, if her mother hadn't told her about the job—and the sense of divine providence. They were meant to meet. They were destined to fall in love.

Russ Van Alstyne walked through the living-room door.

He was jacketless, in jeans and a uniform shirt, which meant he was probably not officially on duty. He was carrying a cardboard box big enough to hold the contents of a file cabinet drawer, and as he turned, scanning the room for Mrs. Rouse, Clare had just enough time to register that he was overdue for a haircut, before his eyes settled on hers.

He covered the space between the door and the love seat in three steps and was lowering the box to the floor before he shifted his gaze from Clare to the woman sitting next to her. "Mrs. Rouse," he said, "I want to take a minute to go over what I'm bringing with me, but first"—he smiled a little—"can you point me toward a bathroom?"

"Through the dining room, into the kitchen, on your right," she said.

"Thanks." His eyes returned to Clare. "Reverend."

"Chief." She twisted toward Mrs. Rouse, quite deliberately not watching him walk away, and picked up the first thread she could find leading back to their conversation. "So you've been married since . . . ?"

"Nineteen sixty-four."

"And have you lived in this house since then?" Clare glanced around the room, safe now that Russ had disappeared through the dining-room doorway. "It has a wonderful feel to it. Very welcoming, as if it's been sheltering a family for a long time."

Mrs. Rouse smiled. "Thank you! But no, we didn't move here until we'd been married about ten years. When we started out, we were the proverbial church mice. We had Kerry right away, which was what everyone did in those days, start your family before the ink had dried on the wedding certificate." She leaned forward and patted Clare's knee. "Your generation is much more sensible. Wait until you've established yourselves before having children." Clare had a flash of self-consciousness—*is* that *what I'm doing?*—before returning her attention to Mrs. Rouse. "Of course, Allan was working for the clinic, so it wasn't as if he was earning what he could have in private practice."

"Did he ever consider leaving the clinic?"

"All the time. At least during those early years. He had a plan all worked up for after he had fulfilled his obligation to Mrs. Ketchem. She had paid his way though medical school and his residency, you know, so that he could come back and serve in her clinic."

"Like the military."

"Yes. He was going to go back to New York once his seven years were up and join in a partnership with some of his friends from medical school. Then life would be grand, we wouldn't have to eat beans, etcetera. I used to tease him about it, call him Jacob. Laboring seven years to win his bride."

"But you didn't leave."

"No. He became very close to Mrs. Ketchem in her final illness. He was with her when she died, you know. I think he became caught up in her vision of what the clinic could mean for the town. He knew darn well the board of aldermen would never find anyone as dedicated to the job as he was." Her smile tipped up on one side. "And it didn't hurt that they revisited his salary after Mrs. Ketchem died. It's funny," she said, her eyes easing into nostalgia. "During the years when you're living on macaroni and cheese and falling into bed exhausted each day from taking care of little kids, you long so for the future. And it isn't until the future arrives that you realize how wonderful it all was."

Clare reached for Mrs. Rouse's hand at the same moment Russ reentered the dining room. Without turning to look, she knew he was there, circling around the shining walnut table, coming through the archway, crossing the floor. "Mind if I interrupt you two?" he said. Mrs. Rouse's relaxed expression tightened into taut lines of reined-in panic.

He squatted next to the love seat, resting one hand on the cover of the cardboard box. "The first thing I want you to know is that we'll be calling the friends that you said you were calling the night your husband disappeared. We're not checking up on you—"

Oh yeah? Clare thought.

"—but maybe talking with the police will jar some memories loose." He smiled, an I'm-on-the-job-so-everything-will-be-all-right smile that seemed to ease Mrs. Rouse's tension.

"I've got a lot of your husband's financial information here," he said. "Bank account statements, credit card bills, things related to your expenses. There were also a lot of miscellaneous papers in the middle drawer of his desk; I've packed them up, too."

"I can't imagine what use all that will be, except for you to see I spend too much on clothes." Renee Rouse laughed, a brittle sound that died away almost before it had begun. "What do you think you're going to find?"

"I don't know yet. But if we go on the assumption your husband is alive, then either he's taken himself off deliberately, or he is, for some reason, unable to come home to you. I'm going to look for something that might give us a push in one direction or another." Clare watched Mrs. Rouse's face as she came to the realization that there could be explanations behind her husband's disappearance almost as painful as his death.

"One thing we know is that he had his wallet and his checkbook with him. You two keep your accounts at Key Bank, right?"

"Yes."

"Then I'd like to contact the manager and have them place an alert notice on your accounts. They'll notify us if a check is written on the account or if he uses his ATM. Obviously, this'll be a lot easier if you aren't writing checks and using your card—"

Mrs. Rouse held up one hand. "I have a separate account that I use most of the time. Allan's checkbook and ATM card are to our big joint account, and I hardly ever draw on that. He was—" She caught herself, her eyes terrified by the way she had put him into the past tense. "He is," she began again, "the bill payer in our house."

At that moment, a single voice in a one-woman conversation flowed out of the kitchen, cascaded through the dining room, and began to swirl around the living room. "Here comes the coffee! And Lacey has the tea. Nancy, you go back and bring out the tray with the sugar and cream on it, will you? I hope everyone is okay with leaded. I couldn't find the decaf. But nowadays they say it's not the caffeine that's bad for you, but the stuff they use to take it out. So we're probably all better off."

Renee Rouse stood. "Yvonne's finished in the kitchen."

"Now, Renee, you sit right down and rest! That's what we're here for, to make things easier for you. Who wants a cup? And there's another crumb cake in the kitchen I'm going to bring out."

Russ, who had evidently already met Yvonne, squared the box of documents under his arm and thrust his hand toward Mrs. Rouse. "I'll let you know the minute we have any news," he said, his voice pitched low. "You have my card. Call me at any time, day or night, if you need to."

"Thank you, Chief."

"It looks like a homemade crumb cake. You can always tell because the store doesn't use enough butter to hold things together. Of course, enough butter, you might as well just call ahead and book your bypass surgery. So who made the crumb cake? Fess up!"

Russ glanced at Clare, as if he might say something, then settled for nodding and disappearing through the living-room door as fast as he could.

"Reverend? How about you? Coffee? Crumb cake? You don't look like you have to watch what you eat, like some of us. Of course, all black is very slimming, isn't it? Maybe I should join the clergy, too. Ha!" Yvonne tipped her head back and hooted.

Clare turned to Mrs. Rouse. "I have to catch Chief Van Alstyne. I have a question for him."

Renee Rouse nodded. Clare ducked through the door, snatched her parka out of the coat closet, and was through the front door before Yvonne's voice could pick up again. She spotted Russ next to his truck, the cardboard box wedged awkwardly between his hip and the driver's-side door as he fished in his jeans pocket for his keys.

She tumbled down the steps. "Russ?"

He turned. "Hey." He drew the keys from his pocket and unlocked the door. "You leaving so soon?"

"I can't. I rode here in Mrs. Marshall's car. I'd be willing to walk home to avoid that Story woman, but then I'd still have to get over to Mrs. Marshall's house to pick up my car."

He tilted his seat forward and shifted the box onto the narrow back bench. "Gee," he said. "I've got a truck right here. Drives and everything."

Her grandmother Fergusson said, *Only a tacky person would drop a cake and run on a condolence call. A lady stays as long as she can be helpful.* MSgt. Ashley "Hardball" Wright bawled, *Retreat is not dishonorable when you're facing superior forces. He that fights and runs away, lives to fight another day!* Her grandmother Fergusson replied, *On the other hand, a lady never outwears her welcome.*

"Let me see if Mrs. Rouse or Mrs. Marshall need me," she said to Russ. "If not, you've got yourself a passenger."

CHAPTER 19

NOW

Russ was sitting in the cab, idling the engine and scanning the radio for music performed by someone free of piercings or tattoos. Nowadays everything on the air seemed to be by so-called artists who were younger than his favorite pair of jeans or by groups he had first listened to on 45s and AM radio. He could live happily without ever hearing "My Generation" again. He pressed the play button on the CD, taking his chance with whatever he had left in there last. The voice of Bonnie Raitt poured out of the speakers like a long, tall branch-and-bourbon.

Clare popped the passenger door open, and he turned the music down a notch while she swung up into the seat. She grinned at him. "It was okay. One of the other ladies had corralled Yvonne Story, and Mrs. Rouse's sister is on her way over. They didn't need me." She buckled up, worrying her lower lip. "I'm bad. I shouldn't feel this relieved to escape."

He shifted the truck into gear and pulled away from the curb. "What, you mean Yvonne? Don't be. My mom used to volunteer at the library when she was there. Had to quit. Said she was going to commit homicide if she didn't."

She laughed. "How is your mom?"

"Happy as a clam. She's decided coal-fired electrical plants in the Midwest are responsible for our acid rain problem, so she and her cronies are busing to Illinois in April for a big protest rally."

"Uh-oh. What if she gets into trouble again?"

"If she does, at least it won't be me arresting her, thank God. Janet and I will stand by with bail money and Western Union."

Clare twisted sideways in her seat and looked at him. "You look tired."

"I am. I was up at the Stewart's Pond site until one o'clock." Talking about it made him feel the fatigue, and he pushed up his glasses and rubbed his eyes. "It would have been nice to sleep in, but we're short staffed as it is, with Lyle and Noble knocked out by this stomach thing going around."

She glanced over the seat, to the evidence box in the back. "Can you leave this stuff at the station and go home for a quick nap?"

"Nah. I'm headed back to Stewart's Pond after I drop you at your car." As soon as the words were out of his mouth, he regretted them. Clare got that look in her eyes—the unholy light, he was coming to think of it.

"Take me with you," she said.

"No." He downshifted to slow for a red light up ahead.

"Take me with you."

"No. Why do you want to go, anyway?" He knew starting to argue with her was a mistake, but he couldn't resist it.

"Probably the same reason you do. To see it in daylight. To try to get a feel for the place. To imagine what happened there."

"Before you get on your high horse about Debba Clow, I want to assure you that the Millers Kill Police Department does not officially consider her a suspect."

"At this time."

"At this time," he agreed. "I'm still open to the idea that Rouse is alive somewhere, although since we've contacted every hospital within a fifty-mile radius, I'm not holding out much hope. But who knows? Maybe the Amish took him in, and he's mending up in a beautiful widow's bed-room, like in that movie."

"Are they going to continue searching the area?"

"Mountain rescue got there right as I was leaving, with two dogs. When I checked in at seven this morning, they hadn't found any sign of the doctor." He turned up Main Street. "I'm driving you back to your car."

"Take me with you," she said. "I want to get a better look at those gravestones. I spoke with Mrs. Marshall this morning." She reached up and touched her neck where her collar would be if she were wearing cleri-cals instead of a sweater. "She said all of her brothers and sisters died of diphtheria while her mother was pregnant with her. The parents chose not to use the vaccine, and they died. Can you imagine anything so awful?"

His mind slid to Stuttgart, and the Dumpster, and opening the gar-bage bag, slick and rancid from a splash of rotted fruit, and the baby inside. One of his fellow MPs had started to cry. Something must have shown on his face, because she leaned over and laid her hand on his shoul-der. "Of course you can. I'm sorry. That was a thoughtless question."

"No," he said. "Seeing terrible things shouldn't make any other terrible thing less . . ." He couldn't find the right word.

"Hurtful?"

"Yeah." He flicked on his turn signal and swung the truck onto the Mill Road. They drove past the old mills, ornate brick mausoleums for the town's prosperity, headed for Old Route 100, which would take them into the mountains.

"How many years have you been a cop?" she asked.

"Over twenty-five, now. Most of it as an MP, of course."

"But you don't feel . . . I don't know, jaded by everything you've seen? Inured to tragedy?"

He wasn't sure what *inured* meant, but he could guess. "For a while I was. Toward the end of my army career, some days I felt like I was encased in clear plastic. Like I could see and hear everything around me, but nothing touched me. No feelings about anything. Of course, I was drinking real heavily, but I never felt drunk. You know, happy and loose and uninhibited. All I ever was was numb." He glanced out his side window at the Millers Kill, the river that gave his town its name, running low and slow in these last winter days before the snowpack melted and the ice-clotted water came roaring out of the mountains.

"What happened?"

"Linda," he said. "She had been going to these Al-Anon meetings, for families of alcoholics? She gave me an ultimatum. Booze or her. Then she flew to her sister's. She had been gone three days when I realized she meant it. I spent two of the worst weeks of my life, missing her like crazy and hating her for what she was putting me through. Man, I had it all drying out—shakes, sweats, cravings, nausea—I looked like Ray Milland in *The Lost Weekend*. Then she came home, and I went back to work, and I sort of fell apart."

"Fell apart?"

"I started—I couldn't—I had to come home from the office. I started crying and I couldn't stop. Linda thought I was dying or something. I had what I guess you could kind of describe as a sort of nervous breakdown. So that's when I retired."

Her hand was still on his shoulder. "You're lucky to have Linda."

"Don't I know it. I wouldn't be alive today if it weren't for her." It was an old thought, and a well-worn one, like a stone he carried in his pocket, reaching in to rub it every now and then.

They drove in silence for a few minutes, which was okay, because silence with Clare never felt like you had to quickly start filling it up with words. Bonnie Raitt was singing about cool, clear water, and wanting to go under, and he could get that, for sure. He eased to a stop before the Veterans Bridge and turned right, away from the river.

"This isn't the way to Mrs. Marshall's house," she said.

"I know."

"I've bent you to the awesome force of my will again, haven't I?"

He laughed. "If I don't take you, you'll just drive up there yourself in that idiot car of yours and get stuck in the snow. At least this way, I know I can get you in and out safely." He could see her out of the corner of his eye, smiling to herself in a satisfied way.

They wound up into the mountains, quiet again, so that they were really listening to the music, and when Bonnie sang "I sho do . . . want you," he wanted to mash the button and eject the CD so it wouldn't be there, hanging in the air between them. But he didn't.

Both sides of the road along the trail to the little cemetery were churned to slush, the ground-in tire tracks and foot-flattened snow looking as if an army had been encamped there. "Wow," Clare said, after they had parked and gotten out of the truck.

He paused, listening for any sounds of the mountain rescue team or the search dogs nearby, but the only thing he heard was the thin, cold air moving through the pines. He started to tell Clare to bundle up, but she was already wrapping her scarf around her neck and pulling her mittens out of her pocket. "This way," he said, gesturing toward the trees.

The legion of footsteps that had compacted the snow along the trail didn't make the walking any easier. The hard, dense surface had slicked up under the midday sun, and he found he had to keep his arms outstretched to counter the unpredictable terrain beneath his boots. "Careful," he warned Clare.

"Uh-huh," she said, her eyes and attention focused on the path. They crept down the trail like toddlers learning to walk, lacking only the all-enveloping snowsuits to complete the picture.

A crack echoed through the air. "Oh my God," she said. "Was that a gunshot?"

"Ice breaking up." He pointed ahead, to where portions of the reservoir gleamed through the trees, gray ice slicked over with pale green water. "It makes all kinds of noises. Loud bangs, groaning, creaking. Very dangerous this time of year."

"I hope Dr. Rouse knew that," she said, and then, "There they are." The headstones looked smaller, softer, sadder today than they had last night; more like the memorials connected to real human beings, less like objects at a crime scene. Clare picked her way through the few snow-covered lumps representing the older graves and sank to her knees in front of the Ketchem children's stones, sitting back on her heels, Japanese style.

She was silent while he stepped closer, getting a better look at the smear of blood that might or might not have been the last trace of Allan Rouse. He envisioned Debba Clow and the doctor, arguing in the darkness with the dead all around them. When he had questioned her here late last night, she had been upset but had kept herself reined in, uncomfortable but cooperative. Earlier, though, out here with the older man haranguing her, worried about her own kids and exasperated with him driveling on about the Ketchems . . . what had she been like then? He couldn't imagine her planning a murder, but he could see her fed up, blaming Rouse for her troubles—in his experience people like Debba always blamed someone else for their troubles—maybe yelling at him to just shut up and then a good hard shove to get him out of her face. . . .

When Clare crossed herself, he realized she had been praying. "This makes me think of Debba Clow," she said.

"Me, too."

She looked up at him. "I mean about the children. About the weight of responsibility parents take on. Mrs. Marshall told me her parents chose not to inoculate their children with the diphtheria vaccine. They did what they thought was best, and this was what they got." She spread her hands, encompassing the stones. "Her mother spent the rest of her life grieving, and her father skipped town." She dropped her hands to her thighs. "Debba's the same. She tried to do everything right, and she's got an autistic son and an ex-husband trying to take away her kids."

"I'd be a lot more sympathetic to her plight if I hadn't seen her trying to brain the doctor with a stool." He held out a hand to help her to her feet.

"Do you really think she dragged him away somewhere, unconscious?"

"That's a thought. Maybe he's in her basement, chained to the wall until he agrees to sign a statement declaring she's the best mom ever and he's a quack for vaccinating kids."

She ignored his flippant remark. "If she hit him here, or he fell, and then she left him to die, where's his body?"

They both looked through the pines toward the reservoir. "I wish I had a few weights I could chuck out there, see if there are any thin spots that break right through," he said. His fingers shaped a large imaginary rock.

"Like those stones they slide for curling," she said.

"Yeah." He faced her. "Okay, you're Debba and I'm Rouse. I slip and fall, hitting my head on this gravestone. I'm bleeding." He knelt at an angle to Peter Ketchem's stone. "What do you do?"

"I try to help you up," she said. She reached down and wrapped her hands around his upper arm.

"But I'm heavier than you, and disoriented." He stood up. "Plus I'm a cranky old bastard and I don't want your help."

"So I'm reaching for you, trying to grab you to take a look at your head." She thrust her arms out toward him.

"And I step backward." He did.

"Be careful," she said.

"What do you do next?"

"I'm still trying to get ahold of you." She put her mittened hand against her mouth, frowning in thought. "I'm scared and probably getting ticked off. So maybe I'm yelling at you to stay put." She advanced a step toward him.

"I'm backing away," he said, "because you're looking crazy, backing away and—" He was moving as he did so, not looking back because, of course, Rouse hadn't been looking back, he had been wiping blood out of his eyes, and when Clare shouted, "Look out!" he started to turn to see where he was going but it was too late, his heel stepped down into nothingness and he tilted crazily, his whole boot sliding into the frozen maw of a woodchuck hole, and he was going over, arms careening, Clare yelling something, and then there was a split second where it felt as if a mallet smashed against his leg, pain, agonizing pain above his ankle, and then he hit the frozen snow with a thud that snapped his skull and threw his glasses off.

CHAPTER 20

NOW

O h, fuck!" he said.
   Clare smashed down onto her knees beside him, gabbling something, reaching for him, and he was bellowing about his glasses, don't step on his glasses, as if the goddamn glasses mattered with his goddamn leg in a goddamn hole, except that they had cost three hundred bucks and weren't covered by his insurance.

"Ssh! Ssh!" Clare was saying. "I've got them, Russ, they're right here. Right here." And she slipped his glasses on, her hands stroking his face, rubbing his chest. He shut his eyes for a second while chills swept through him, surging like snowmelt waters, shaking his whole body. The pain in his leg was so bad he wanted to weep and howl. He opened his eyes. Clare filled his whole range of vision, hanging over him, her hazel eyes wide and bright with fear. Her voice was steady, though. "I want you to move your head slowly if you can."

"I broke my leg," he said.

"I know." She brushed a shock of his hair off his forehead. "But before I try to move you, I want to make sure you didn't injure your spine as well."

That sent another icy wave washing through him, leaving him trembling. He lifted his head from the ground and stared down the length of his body to where his left foot was half in, half out of a snow-rimmed hole. His shin above his boot top was bent backward, and the sight of it, the wrongness of it, made his stomach lurch with nausea.

Clare leaned back, giving him more space. "Can you sit up?"

"I think so." He tightened his gut and curled up, working hard because he was lying downslope, his head lower than his feet. He got high enough to prop himself on his elbows, then stopped, exhausted. The effort of it made him sweat, and another chill, weaker than the last, shook him. The pain in his leg was receding, replaced by an intense heat. He was panting for breath. Everything his eye fell on was supernaturally sharp, the glint of sunlight on the ice, the rough crumbled edge of a gravestone, the reddened tip of Clare's nose. "Okay," he said. "I think I'm going into shock."

She reached behind his neck and pulled his parka hood over his head, tugging on the strings to keep it close. "Lie back down," she said, taking him by the shoulders and guiding him back onto the snow. She slapped her parka until she felt whatever she was looking for. She unsnapped her coat, dug into an inside pocket, and pulled out a cell phone. "We're going to get you some help fast," she said, jamming her thumbnail against the power button.

He rolled his head away from her and stared at the pine boughs over-head. Their color, a green so dark it was almost black, reminded him of his friend Shaun, of Shaun's dad's boat, of hours rocking on the surface of the reservoir when he was a kid, the pines and the dark water and the mountains rising around them.

"You're probably not going to get a—," he said, just as Clare snarled, "God damn!"

"—signal," he concluded. "Because of the mountains." He closed his eyes again. "I don't think I've ever heard you say that before."

"I've never been stuck in a snowbank with you and a broken leg before," she said. She looked at her cell phone with loathing. "Useless machine! I can never get a signal when I need one. Why do I even have this?"

His leg still felt hot, but the pain was coming back, not sharp, like be-fore, but a deep ache, like a tooth gone bad. He could feel it all the way up to his groin. "Forget about it," he said. "You're gonna walk me out of here. You can drive me to the hospital."

Her face was a mixture of anger and frustration. "I can't carry you out of here, Russ, don't you get it? You must weigh close to two hundred pounds. Maybe on a dry, flat surface I could get you in a fireman's carry and stagger a dozen steps with you, but there's no way I can make it all the way up that trail with you, not with all that slippery snow and ice. I can't do it."

She looked close to tears. "Hey," he said. He caught her bare hand in his gloved one and squeezed hard. He focused on making his voice as close to normal as possible. "It's just a broken leg. It's broad daylight and I got a perfectly good truck less than a half mile away. If you can't get me all the way there, you can drag me over underneath a tree and I'll wait while you go get help. It wouldn't be more than"—he calculated the walk, the drive, scrambling the EMTs, the time it would take an ambulance to get here—"an hour and a half. Two hours, tops."

"But it's freezing out here! And your jeans aren't going to keep you warm."

"Yeah, well, I'll survive."

She worried her lower lip. She was still gripping his gloved hand. "Is that what you want me to do? Leave you here and go get help?"

"Hell, no. I'm not going to freeze my ass off for two hours when it'll take us twenty minutes to walk back to the road."

She let out a choked-up laugh, shook her head. "I—," she started, her voice liquid and warm, like maple syrup fresh from the boiler. She cut herself off and pressed her lips together in a smile.

Love you. He could hear it as clearly as if she'd spoken it. She dropped his hand, stuffed her mittens in her pocket, and stood up. "Let's do it," she said.

It took them forty-five minutes, not twenty. They leaned into each other, her arm as far around his back as it would go, his arm over her neck and shoulders, their hands clutching each other's parkas. She would take a small step, he would hop. He kept his teeth gritted against the throbbing ache in his leg, but every fourth or fifth hop his useless left foot would hit the hard, packed snow and he'd swear loudly. He kept apologizing for his language until Clare snapped that if he didn't stop she'd rip his tongue out and beat him with it. They didn't talk, except for exchanges like "Do you want me to take your boot off?"

"No."

"It might make it easier to keep your leg up."

"I don't want you to take my goddamn boot off."

They fell down twice. The first time, he could feel Clare lose her footing and he wrenched his arm away from her. She let go of his parka and he was able to twist sideways, tumbling onto his good right side. The force of the impact vibrated through his broken leg like a dental drill, and he had to lie there for a few minutes, gasping for control, while Clare apologized over and over. The second time, he hopped, landed wrong, and toppled backward, dragging Clare by her neck. When he could speak, he asked her if she was okay.

"I hate snow," she said. "I really, really hate it. Ice, too."

He couldn't help it. He laughed. His whole body hurt, and he laughed and laughed while she rolled over, got to her feet, and hauled him upright. He laughed until he ran out of air and he stood there, dizzy and panting, clinging to her shoulders.

"Slow. Slow," she said. "Take a few deep breaths." He did. "Better?" she asked. "We're almost there."

And they were. Although the last few yards, with the truck in sight, were an agony, as what had been a twenty-second stroll along the shoulder of the road stretched into five minutes of step-hop-step-hop-step.

"Almost there," she said, relief lightening her voice.

"I know we're almost there," he snarled.

When they reached the truck, he leaned against the side of the cab while Clare wiggled the keys out of his pocket and unlocked the doors. She slid the passenger seat as far back as it would go and then, while he sat on the floor of the cab, interlaced her fingers into a stirrup. He planted his good boot in her hands and shoved up, humping himself into the seat.

"Is there anything we can use to brace your leg?" She winced as he bumped his left foot against the floor mat and swore again.

"Let's just get out of here." He leaned back and closed his eyes while she got in and started the truck. He felt as if he had just staggered past the finish line of a ten-mile race, slick with sweat and trembling with fatigue. He concentrated on breathing, steady and deep. Inhale. Exhale. Inhale. Exhale. The truck jounced through a pothole and he hissed.

"Sorry," Clare said. He didn't answer. Just went back to his breathing, keeping the pain not at bay, because it sloshed up against him like waves slapping at the side of a boat, but riding it, staying inside the hull, not letting it swamp him.

Clare didn't ask him how he was or try to distract him with chatter, and the part of him that was thinking about anything was grateful to her for her silence. He kept his eyes closed. He could hear the rumble of the county road give way to the whoosh and crunch of traffic. They stopped, waited, rolled, stopped, waited, rolled. They eased over a speed bump and sloped upward. "We're here," she said quietly, and he opened his eyes to see her nosing the truck into the emergency-room portico. "I'll go get someone," she said, and he closed his eyes again as her door opened and shut. He had time for four more slow breaths before his door opened and a familiar voice said, "Well, what have you done to yourself this time?"

He opened his eyes. "Hey, Alta." He reached for the edge of the doorway and the outstretched hand of the nurse who had ruled the emergency department since before he had returned home to become chief of police.

"Easy now," she said, and Clare was on the other side, reaching for him as well, and there was a gurney, set nice and low and easy for him to sit on, fall back on, stretch out on. An orderly helped him settle his leg and then raised the gurney to table height. Russ stared at the sky, bright and cold.

"You'll have to move that pickup," Alta was saying to Clare. "Back out of this drive, down the street, next hospital entrance is visitor parking."

Clare leaned over so that her face was hanging above him, just like she had done in the moments after he had fallen. "I'll be back as soon as I can," she said.

"Call the station for me," he said. "They're shorthanded already with Noble and Lyle out. Tell Harlene to call in the part-time guys. Tell her to let the staties know we may need backup. Call Bob Mongue, the zone sergeant at Troop B, he's got like a dozen kids and he always needs over-time. Tell her—"

"Russ." She rested one hand on his chest, her mouth quirked in a smile that was half exasperation, half amusement. "Harlene's been the dis-patcher for what, twenty years? She'll know what to do."

Her face was replaced by Alta's. "Let's get you inside and give you something to take the pain away, hmm?" She grabbed the side of the gur-ney and they began rolling. "I thought for sure when the reverend ran in here that you musta been shot or something. The ice got you, hmm? I was hoping for something more exciting than a slip and fall. We get three-four cases a day this time of year."

He wondered, as they shouldered their way through the double doors into the steamy, moist heat of the emergency room, if Debba had been telling the truth. If Allan Rouse had slipped and fallen just like he had? And if so, then where the hell was he?

CHAPTER 21

NOW

Now, her cell phone worked. She pocketed it as she crossed the parking lot toward the sidewalk that ran along the front of the hospital. She knew if she used the main entrance, there would be a lot of meaningless red tape about signing in and checking if Russ had been admitted yet. She was going back to the emergency room.

She had had a short conversation with Harlene, who became all brisk and efficient as soon as Clare had reassured her that Russ was safe and unlikely to need anything more than a cast. "Fell down at a crime scene and broke his leg, huh? The guys are never going to let him forget this." She had promised to notify everyone in the department and directed Clare to not let Russ fret. "No fretting. Got it," Clare said as she rang off.

She pushed through the entrance of the emergency department, the old-fashioned swinging doors whump-whumping around her, and spotted Alta manning the admissions desk at the end of the drab green hall.

"He's already inside, getting his prelim workup done," Alta said as Clare neared. "They're getting him changed and starting an IV. I'll let you know when you can go in."

Clare thanked her and took a seat in the waiting room. Someone had thumbtacked glossy cardboard hearts and doilies onto the institutional green walls and forgotten to take them down after Valentine's Day. Maybe they kept them up until they could be replaced by jolly cartoon bunnies and two-foot-high chicks for Easter. Rather than cheering the place up, they emphasized the vinyl sadness of the brown-and-chrome chairs, which looked as if they had been bought secondhand from a modernistic jetport lounge in 1964. Clare settled into the slightly curved back of hers and tried to resist picking at the peeling piping. Across from her, a woman with the look of a farmer's wife from up Cossayuharie way was resolutely leafing through a *Woman's Day* magazine, ignoring the waiting room's other inhabitant, a man dressed in the contents of a Goodwill donation bin. He smelled powerfully of alcohol and was mumbling to himself.

Clare glanced at the contents of the table at the end of her row of chairs. Three *Sports Illustrated*s, a *Fly Rod and Reel,* two *Travel + Leisure*s. None of them less than two years old. She crossed her arms over her chest and sat. She could hear the drunk mumbling, not angry or threatening, but more like he was holding up both ends of a conversation. She glanced back at him. He looked worn down and used up.

She leaned over the back of her chair so she could see him better. "Excuse me," she said. The farmer's wife lowered her magazine and stared. "Excuse me," Clare said again. "Do you have a place to stay?"

The man stopped talking and looked at her, like one party to a tête-à-tête examining an interloper.

"Because if you don't, I know a shelter. You can't drink there, though."

He blinked at her, dropped his head, and resumed mumbling to himself.

"Don't worry about him, Reverend." Clare whipped around to see Alta standing there, a clipboard in her hand. "He comes in every once in a while. He'll be here overnight, drying out." She spoke a little louder to the man. "Doctor will see you in just a few minutes, Mr. Arbot. You hang in there." The man gave no sign he had heard the nurse.

"Can I go in?" Clare asked her.

"Yep. He's had some pretty powerful narcotics, so don't be surprised if he seems out of it. We're waiting on radiology to clear out, and then he'll go in for his X rays."

"Did the doctor say anything?" Clare knew that under the privacy laws, Alta really had no business telling her anything. She wasn't a relative, nor was she visiting in her official capacity. But the nurses had gotten used to seeing her around as she and the town's other clergy rotated through the unpaid post of hospital chaplain. Alta responded exactly as she would if Clare had been going in to pray with or counsel a patient who had requested her.

"Looks like a simple fracture, although of course we won't know for sure until radiology. It's a bad break, though, and Dr. Stillman will want to put him under to set it. So I suspect the chief will be our guest at least until tomorrow." As she spoke, she led Clare to the brushed-metal doors separating reception and waiting from the actual emergency room. She whacked a fist-sized button set in the wall, and the doors hissed open. "Right through there," she said. "He's in the third bed down."

Clare, following the nurse's directions, parted the third pair of limp blue curtains. "Hey," she said.

Russ was reclining on an angled hospital bed, begowned in a johnny, his broken leg elevated on a pair of poofy pillows. As Alta had said, there was an IV in his arm, and whatever was in it must have been pretty good stuff, because the lines of pain and fatigue that had been chiseled into his face were gone. In fact, Clare had never seen him looking so relaxed.

"Hey," he said, waving her in.

"How are you feeling?"

"Stoned." He laughed. It was different from his usual laugh, lighter, younger.

Clare smiled. She nodded toward his leg. The break was hidden by a twill-covered ice pack the size of a small sandbag. "I meant that."

"I'm not feeling much pain, but Jesus, it looks awful. Take a look." He sat upright and flipped the ice pack off. He was right. It did look awful, swollen and spectacularly bruised. He resettled the bag over the break and leaned back again.

"I called Harlene," Clare said. "She's taking care of everything. I'm supposed to tell you not to fret."

"No fretting, yes ma'am." He grinned.

Clare bit her lip to keep from laughing. "I called your mother, but she wasn't at home. I left her a message. I told her you'd broken your leg, but that you were going to be fine, and I left her my cell phone number in case she wants to reach me. I figured that way, I can let her know what's going on if she calls when you're getting it set or something."

He sobered fast. "Before you tell her anything, make sure she knows I didn't break my leg while on duty."

"But you were examining a crime scene."

"I was walking in the woods." His face took on a stubborn cast. "If my mom thinks I was injured in the line of duty, she'll freak out. Her biggest fear is that something's going to happen to me because of my job." He took her hand in his and looked up at her, confiding, "She's not really wild about me being a cop."

"I had gotten that," Clare said. "Okay, I'll tell her we were taking a walk." She pulled her hand out of his and looked around for a chair, but there was nothing in the drapery-enclosed space except a rolling cart full of medical supplies and Russ's IV pole.

He stroked the side of the bed. "You can sit here."

"I'll stand, thanks."

"Come on. Keep an injured man company." He gave her a smile she had never seen before: wheedling, charming.

"I'm getting a look at a whole other side of you," she said, compromising by leaning her hip against the edge of the bed where he had indicated.

"If I get up in this damn hospital gown, you'll get a look at every side of me." He laughed again.

She glanced back at the wilted blue curtain. Maybe she ought to open that. It wasn't as if they were alone; she could hear one of the nurses cracking a joke and a doctor quizzing a blood technician. And it wasn't as if she were being inappropriate; when she visited patients they almost always talked in private, behind a drawn curtain or a closed door. But she was uncomfortable with this version of Russ, this sloe-eyed, uninhibited Russ. She liked his inhibitions. She relied on them.

She jumped up and pulled the drapery aside, just in time to whack a doctor standing opposite her who had obviously been reaching for the curtain himself. "Oh!" she said. "I'm so sorry."

He gave her a hesitant smile. "I'm Dr. Stillman," he said. His glance flickered to either side of her, as if he were checking to make sure no one else was going to leap out at him. "I'm the orthopedic surgeon. Are you Mrs. Van Alstyne?"

She swallowed her first response, and said, "I'm Reverend Clare Fergusson. I brought Chief Van Alstyne in."

Russ sat up straighter. "Dr. Stillman?" he said. He peered at the man. "You can't be Dr. Stillman."

Clare looked, too, but the doctor seemed authentic enough. White coat, stethoscope, a short stack of medical-record jackets under his arm.

"You must have been one of my dad's patients," he said, moving to Russ's side and peeling the ice pack off his leg. "What did he have you for?"

Russ was still looking suspiciously at him. "Broken collarbone."

"Your father practiced here?" Clare said. "In Millers Kill?"

Stillman looked up from where he was delicately touching Russ's leg. "I'm the third-generation Dr. Stillman in these parts. My dad was an orthopedist, too, so I get this reaction a lot from people who had their bones set by him when they were kids." He grinned. "They can't figure out how Dr. Stillman's stayed so well preserved." He stood up. "Okay, Chief, I'm going to deliver you to the tender mercies of radiology. I've already scheduled an operating room for you, so we'll be able to get this taken care of right away."

"Operating room!"

"Trust me, you're not going to want to be awake for this one." Stillman unlocked the bed's wheels, rehung Russ's IV on a stubby hook at the head of the bed, and rolled through the open curtains.

"Clare?" Russ sounded disoriented, like someone calling for a light in a suddenly dark room.

It took her several long strides to catch up. "I'll be here when you get out," she said.

They exited the emergency room through a side hall. "It'll be a few more hours before he'll be able to see anybody," Dr. Stillman said. He brought the bed to a stop in front of a pair of elevators. "I'm not sure what room he's being admitted to."

The elevator doors opened. Russ caught at her hand, squeezed it tightly, let go. Stillman trundled him into the freight-sized elevator.

"I'll be here," she said again.

Russ reached toward her, his arm stretching, his hand outflung as if he could pull her through the elevator doors and take her with him. His eyes were dilated black with the painkillers pumping through him, and even though she knew it was just the drugs, she had to stand for a long time, staring into her scratched and blurry reflection, after the stainless-steel doors closed on his final words: "I'm still holding on. Not letting go."

CHAPTER 22

THEN

FRIDAY, APRIL 16, 1937

Harry McNeil was just picking up his lunch at the Rexall's soda counter when he felt a tap on his shoulder. He turned, and was surprised to see Niels Madsen.

"I've been looking for you," the attorney said.

Harry held out his hand. "And you found me." They shook. He turned back to the counter, where the jerk was wrapping his ham-and-swiss. "You could have just called my office."

"You're never in your office," Niels said, in a faintly accusing voice.

The jerk stuffed a small container of cole slaw and a paper napkin into the bag. "You want a pickle with that?" he asked. Harry shook his head. "Two bits," the jerk said. Harry fished the coins out of his pocket and handed them over.

"I'm never there because very little crime happens in my office," Harry said, picking up the conversation. "It's good for the citizens of the town to see their police chief out and about." He grinned. "And I get antsy if I'm cooped up too long." He glanced at the lunch counter, its row of seats fully occupied. "Let's go across the street and sit in the park."

"It's too cold to sit in the park," Niels said, although he followed Harry out of the store. Harry didn't see what the lawyer had to complain about—his long woolen coat looked far more substantial than Harry's own police-issue jacket, which hadn't been replaced in over eight years. He paused at the curb, looked both ways, and then jaywalked across Church Street toward the park.

Despite the early-April chill, Harry wasn't the only person to have thought of an open-air lunch. The benches were filled with people eating, talking, sitting with their faces turned up, starved for the spring sun after the long winter. "How 'bout over there?" he said, pointing to a bench beneath an enormous old elm. It faced St. Alban's, the age of the tree gently reproaching the church's fake-medieval front. "Nobody's sitting there."

"That's because it's in the shade," Niels said.

Harry ignored him and sat down. He took the paper napkin out of the sack and spread it over his knees. Niels grunted as he joined him. Harry removed the sandwich and unwrapped it, careful to not let any of the lettuce fall out. "So what's up?" he asked.

Niels shifted on the bench. "How are your kids?" he said.

"Fine," Harry said. "And yours?"

"Fine," Niels said. "How're things at the station?"

"Great," Harry said. "And at the law firm?" He bit into his sandwich, closing his eyes for a second at the harsh tang of the mustard.

"Oh, great," Niels said. He seemed fascinated by St. Alban's red doors.

"Niels," Harry said around a mouthful of cheese, "what were you looking for me for?"

Niels kept studying the church front. "Jane Ketchem came to see me last week." Harry felt the twinge at the base of his skull he always got when he heard the Ketchem name. Like a bell ringing out over a defeated fighter, telling him he was out of the ring, his time was up. He waited for Niels to continue.

"She wants me to petition the court of probate to have her husband declared legally dead."

Harry managed to swallow his bite. "Don't you need to have some sort of reasonable belief that he's actually dead?"

"I could get her a divorce based on abandonment easily enough." Niels seemed to be speaking more to himself than to Harry. "But no, she wants to be a widow." He turned to Harry. "You investigated his disappearance. What conclusion did you come to?"

Harry dropped his sandwich onto his napkin. "I never came to a conclusion. It's still an open case. Every few years I send the description of Jonathon Ketchem out on the wires. Nothing ever comes back."

"You're joking," Niels said.

"I wish I was." Harry picked his sandwich back up. "I interviewed everyone who knew the man. I sent wires out all over the state, describing him and his car. I even had the police department of Santa Barbara, California, go out and talk to one Darlene Henderson, whose father worked at

Ketchem's dairy and who left town around the time Jonathon disappeared. Nothing." He eyed the sandwich. His appetite was suddenly off. "I even checked out Jane Ketchem."

Niels's eyebrows shot up to where his hairline had been a decade before.

"Don't look at me like that. Wives have been known to kill their husbands before. Of course, they don't usually come running to the police the next day, asking for help in finding the body."

"And?" A barely repressed quiver of interest ran through Niels's voice.

"And her story checked out. The neighbor across the way was taking out his trash can and heard them arguing around the time she said. Not too much later that evening, the lady next door spoke to Mrs. Ketchem in person and then saw her return to her house." He looked up to where the gnarled limbs of the elms wrote patterns in the sky. He could just make out the fuzzy gray buds studding the branches. Hard to imagine now, with the chill air pushing against his less-than-adequate coat, that they could swell and burst into voluptuous, intemperate green. Other people thought February or March were the worst, the time you got so sick of winter you wanted to take an ax to your wall and chop your way out. But for him, this was the longest stretch, these cool, ascetic days of early spring, when he most wanted the hot sun on his skin and the smell of new-mown hay making him dizzy with desire.

"So that was the end of it?" Niels's question brought him back into himself.

"If there had been some reason for her to want him dead—if he had a girlfriend, or she had another man on the side. Or maybe a big insurance haul. But there wasn't. That was the problem. No one had a reason to want Jonathon Ketchem dead."

"What do you think happened to him?"

"I finally boiled any evidence I got—not that there was much of it— down to two theories. The one thing everyone I spoke with agreed is that Jonathon Ketchem had had a hard few years. He had lost four kids and his farm, he was blue and distracted, he didn't know what to do with himself next." He took another bite and let Niels wait while he chewed and swallowed. "First theory. He walked. He left behind everything bad that'd ever happened to him and he took off for a new life somewhere out west." He bit off another piece and ate it. "Second theory. He killed himself. Of course, there's a problem with that one." He took another bite to give Niels time to find it.

"If he committed suicide, where's his car?"

"Right. Now maybe he left the car on the side of the road with the keys in it for someone to steal and he hiked into the mountains so deep no one has run across his body. But I wouldn't put money on it."

Niels nodded. "My son Norman says the kids at school have a theory. The Ketchem girl is in his class, you know. Anyway, he says Ketchem was set upon by desperate men."

"Yeah, that's the prevailing Ketchem theory. Except for his parents, they're all convinced he was iced by bootleggers." He balled up the paper the sandwich had come in.

"Isn't that possible? From what I read in the paper, there were some pretty desperate characters back in those days. Judge DeWeese was handing out eight-year sentences and ten-thousand-dollar fines back in the twenties, for heaven's sake. I'm sure there must have been some who were willing to kill to keep their money and their freedom."

"Yes. There were." Harry breathed in through gritted teeth, damming up the rage that washed through him whenever he thought of those days, good men's lives poured out in defense of an idiot law that the government later turned around and repealed. Already, not five years on, people were starting to talk about the bootleggers as if they were Robin Hood and his Merry Men, as if they were some sort of gentlemen bandits instead of goddamn killers and thieves. He worked his jaw, trying to relax so he wouldn't look as if he were glaring at Niels. "Yeah, there were." He sighed, letting go of some of the heat in his head. "But even if he had stumbled across some gang unloading their cache, you have the same questions. Where's the body? Where's the car?" He shook his head. "He walked. Away from his wife and his kid. He's a different person now, and maybe that helps him sleep nights, the selfish bastard."

Niels sat silent for a moment. "So," he said finally, "I guess I can't count on your testimony as to his status as a decedent."

Harry snorted a laugh.

"How about this," Niels said. "You let me use those records detailing all the steps you've taken to find him. You don't need to draw any conclusions. We'll let the court do that. The fact that you haven't closed the case after seven years and there's still no sign of him may work in our favor."

"And then what happens?"

"And then Mrs. Ketchem gets to become a widow. We can give her her life back."

Harry thought about the woman he had first seen on the marble steps of the police station. Over the years they had met, at first frequently, then at longer and longer intervals, and each time, Harry felt the weight of letting her down, of failing to live up to his first ignorant promise to bring her husband back to her.

"I'll do what I can," he said. "But I don't think anyone can give Jane Ketchem her life back."

CHAPTER 23

NOW

Clare was debating whether to grab some lunch from the hospital cafeteria or make the trek to the Kreemy Kakes diner, grateful it was her day off and she didn't have any appointments eating up her time, when it suddenly struck her that she had promised to volunteer Monday at the historical society after missing last Saturday. Her first thought was to call Roxanne and beg off again. She'd understand that waiting for a friend to get out of surgery took precedence over sorting out one-hundred-year-old advertising circulars. Except she heard Roxanne's voice, when she had shown Clare the boxes and boxes of uncataloged donations. *I'm afraid everyone who tackles this job gets bored too quickly to do much good.*

Then, of course, her conscience took her by the chin and forced her to look at whether she would hang around the hospital for hours waiting for anyone else to get out of surgery. She had sat with family members before, anticipating good or bad news, but never just for herself. And she had to admit a broken leg wasn't in the same league as a triple bypass or a bone-marrow transplant. If Mr. Hadley, for instance, ever took one of those tumbles off a ladder she feared would happen eventually, she knew she would go to the historical society, and simply call in periodically to find out how he was.

Which is how she found herself driving the chief of police's pickup through town. She prayed no one would take a good look at who was behind the wheel, and she parked in the first spot she could find on the street, envious, with the part of her brain that wasn't worried about her reputation, at the ease with which the truck crunched over the snow and ice to muscle its way into the parking space.

She trotted up the sidewalk, too late not to make an effort but also too late to think an outright dash from door to door would make any

difference. She looked at the clinic as she went by, noting the legend THE
JONATHON KETCHEM CLINIC carved in the granite door lintel. The sign
bolted next to the door, the way everyone in town referred to it as the free
clinic—it was as if Jonathon Ketchem were disappearing in his memorial, just as he had disappeared in life. Even though the sign indicated it
was open, the clinic somehow looked abandoned, bereft without the man
who had been its driving force for the past three decades. Clare thought
about dropping in to find out how Laura Rayfield was doing manning
the ship all alone, but her guilty conscience spurred her on to the historical society.

Another volunteer let her in, let her know that Roxanne wasn't working today, and then sank back into a chair by the door with an open book.
As she climbed the stairs, Clare could hear the voice of a docent leading a
tour through the public rooms and the soft thud of a researcher taking
down one of the massive tax-enrollment books in the second-floor library.
She reached the third floor and went into the former nursery, closing the
door behind her to discourage any of the other volunteers from drifting in
and chatting. She switched on the lights, dumped her coat and scarf in
the extra chair, and turned on the computer, all with a weird sense of
disconnection from her surroundings—a few hours ago she had been
listening to Russ grinding his teeth against the pain as she hobbled him
up the trail, freezing, sweating, and here she was now, in a clean, well-lit
room, surrounded by white boxes and history.

She logged on to the catalog and scrolled down to her entries from
last Saturday. She had been going through the records of the long-
defunct Fonda-Johnston-Gloversville Railroad, whose primary claim to
fame seemed to be hauling passengers to the Sacandaga Amusement Park,
which had apparently closed down about 1930. She reached into the
acid-free storage box and pulled out another set of folders stuffed with
ads, timetables, newspaper clippings, and photographs.

She grouped a small stack of ads together—one of them, which promised "a gay holiday," made her smile—and entered them as one item. The
clippings, brown and brittle as dead leaves, had to be layered between sheets
of archival tissue paper. Most of them were so dull—notices of stockholder
meetings, appointments to the board—Clare found it hard to believe anyone, before or after her, would read them, but then she saw a lengthy story
that made her stop. DAM PROJECT APPROVED: MAN-MADE RESERVOIR TO BE
STATE'S LARGEST. She skimmed over it to see what it had to do with the

railroad. The Conklingville Dam to be built . . . flooding the Sacandaga River valley . . . preventing flooding of Hudson downstream . . . over forty square miles to be submerged . . . ha, here it was, "including large sections of the F,J&G line." So that was why they folded. There was a map, too, taking up two columns' worth of space between the story and a Sears Roebuck ad, and after comparing it to the landmarks in her head, she realized that the reservoir in the story was the Great Sacandaga Lake. Huh. She hadn't known it was a man-made lake. She examined the tiny dot-towns on the map and had another realization. Stewart's Pond had also been created by the flooding of the Sacandaga.

She wasn't aware she had been hunched over the table until she tipped back into her chair. She had known it was a reservoir. Someone had described it that way to her. But she had assumed, somehow, that the Ketchem graves were there because of a connection to the man-made lake. Maybe a summer camp there, or a sentimental attachment to the spot. But those children had been buried five years before there was a reservoir. What had it been then? A shady spot beneath the trees growing at the edge of a farm? Jonathon and Jane Ketchem's farm?

She folded the clipping in a sheet of tissue paper and left the nursery. Down one flight of stairs, she found the library, two rooms that had once been bedrooms, fitted out with oddments of shelving: everything from utilitarian gunship gray steel to glass-encased mahogany. A gaunt man whose brown sweater looked as if it had fit him thirty pounds ago was bending over one of the reading tables.

"Excuse me." Clare glanced at the stack of leather-bound books at his side. "Are you the librarian?"

"Yes," he said. He stood up, like a heron righting itself. He inspected her over his reading glasses. "You're not one of our regulars."

"I'm Clare Fergusson," she said. "I'm a new volunteer. Logging in the collections upstairs." He continued to stare at her, as if he couldn't imagine what she might want with him. She got the impression that the historical society's library was underutilized. "I ran across this newspaper article"—she unfolded the tissue paper and laid it on the table—"and I was wondering if you knew anything about it."

He bent over again to study the clipping. "Yes, of course," he said. He sat up. She waited for something else, an explanation, but he continued to look at her.

Okay, then. He evidently didn't feel compelled to share information like most reference librarians. She was good at asking questions. "From the look of that map"—she pointed to the clipping—"several towns were flooded. What happened to them? To the farms?"

"The Hudson River Regulating Board bought out the landholders in the late twenties and either tore or burned everything down. Houses, towns . . . chopped down all the trees, too." He glanced around the room. "We've got a nice collection of original photographs. . . . Where is that archive?"

"Where did the owners go?"

"Most of the residents who were displaced relocated nearby."

"Like to Millers Kill."

"That's correct."

"Wow." She tried to imagine what it must have been like for the Ketchems, leaving their home, knowing it was going to be razed to the ground and drowned. Did Mrs. Marshall remember it? She would have to ask. If she wasn't hunting with the wrong dog over the Ketchem burying ground. "What about cemeteries?" she said. "There must have been a lot of them inside that forty-square-mile line."

"Bodies were dug up and reburied. There are quite a few transburial cemeteries around these parts."

She didn't want to imagine what that job must have been like. "I've been to a tiny family plot right on the banks of Stewart's Pond. Could that be a relocated cemetery?"

"Stewart's Pond Reservoir," the man said, frowning. He stood up abruptly and circled the table, one hand held out as if to grasp the spine of a book. He circled again, closer to the bookshelves along the perimeter of the room, and with a grunt he darted forward and drew a three-ring binder from a high shelf.

"What's that?" she asked.

"Copies of the land-grant information. Deeds, parcels, all that. We don't have the originals. Have to go to Saratoga for those." He sounded distinctly put out about that. He flipped rapidly through the pages. "Where is it?"

"Uh . . . you drive up Old Route 100 and get on a county road . . . um, and then you go a few miles. . . ."

He looked up from the binder with an expression that said *Spare me.* "See that cord hanging down from that bookcase there?" He pointed.

"Sure do."

"It's a map of the area. Pull it down."

Moving next to the shelves, Clare could see the long black tube fastened to the bookcase's uppermost molding. She pulled the cord, and a large map unrolled, smoothly as a window shade. "We had these in my classroom when I was in grade school," she said.

"Show me the place you were talking about."

Maps were much easier than remembering the names of roads. She found the location of the Ketchem children's burial ground and stabbed it with her finger.

"Ah," the man said. He flipped some more. "Yes, yes, yes yes. Here it is." Clare looked over his shoulder. He was turning back and forth between a page showing a line drawing of what appeared to be property boundary lines and a reduced-sized, badly photocopied legal document. "Your cemetery is on its original ground. See here?" He pointed to the drawing. "It would have been at the back end of the property. That county road didn't exist back in the twenties. The road ran down here"—he pointed to another spot—"along the Sacandaga River."

"Was this the Ketchems' land? Jonathon and Jane Ketchem?"

He flipped to the legal document. "Jonathon Ketchem is the last landholder." He looked up at her. "It wasn't customary to include the wife on land grants in those days." He dropped his attention back down to the binder. "Bought it in 1916. They probably sold it to a land speculator in the twenties. If they didn't, it would have been condemned in 1929."

"Condemned?"

"Some of the small landowners turned down the river regulating board's offer and tried to stay put. Didn't do them any good, of course. The HRRB wasn't a governmental agency, but it had plenty of political muscle behind it. Anyone who didn't sell voluntarily at the board's asking price found their land condemned by the state. Evicted."

"Did they get any money for it?"

"Of course they did. The government can't take land without compensation, that's unconstitutional." He looked up at her. "Of course, once it was condemned, it was the state that decided what would be a fair price. And how much do you think land that's going to be at the bottom of a lake is worth?"

"So the Ketchems wouldn't have made much money from the deal?"

"Probably not."

"Then where did—" She stopped herself. The historical society's librarian wasn't going to know where Jane Ketchem got the money to send her daughter to college and pay for Allan Rouse's medical education. Besides, that was years after she had been forced off her farm. And Mrs. Marshall had said her mother was good at investing. Maybe she bought into IBM when it was fifty cents a share. "Why did the Hudson River Regulating Board decide to dam the Sacandaga, anyway?"

"To control flooding. The Sacandaga is part of the Hudson's watershed. It's a natural floodplain, that's one of the reasons it was such fertile soil." He pulled the clipping toward him with two fingers, keeping it flat. "See the course of the river before the dams went in? All along here was the Sacandaga Vlaie."

"The Sacandaga Fly?" Clare said.

"Vlaie. It's an old Dutch word meaning a swamp or lowland meadow. Ours was a huge marshland, teeming with wildlife. If they tried to build this dam nowadays, the DEC would be all over them. But in those days, wetlands were something to get rid of, not something to protect." He traced the course of the river as it meandered east toward the Hudson. "The floodwaters would overflow the Sacandaga, fill up the Hudson, and next thing you knew, you'd have people rowboating through the streets of Albany. Caused some bad breakouts of disease in towns along the way, too, with the floodwaters washing sewage out into the open. Typhoid, cholera."

"Diphtheria?"

"I suppose so. Businesses were the moving force behind . . ." He was on a roll now, recounting the movement to dam the river and the formation of the regulating board, but his words flowed past Clare like the river itself. She felt the awful weight of it, the rushing of her own blood the sound of the water. The river had run through Jane and Jonathon Ketchem's life, bringing them good rich soil and cool summer days and the disease that destroyed their family. And then it had washed them away and cast them up in the village of Millers Kill, where Jane had lived out her days, pouring her grief into her remaining child until the mother Mrs. Marshall might have been sank beneath the depth of it, ensuring no more children to be carried away, ever. And Jonathon? Clare had a sudden, piercing conviction she knew where he had gone. Not to start over again, as his daughter had grown to believe. Clare could see him, as clearly as if she had been there, driving his car far away from the town, back toward his burned, wrecked farm, back toward the road that ran by the river that had sluiced through his life. When was it Mrs. Marshall had said her father disappeared? March 29, 1930.

"When was the dam completed?" she said, cutting off the librarian's discourse on the railroad's suit for compensation. "When did the valley start flooding?"

"Nineteen thirty."

"But when? What date?"

"Ah," he said, his eyebrows knitting together. He got up again, reaching his hand out, as if the book he needed could fly off the shelves into his grasp. He pulled a narrow paperback off a shelf, flopped it open, and flicked through a few pages. "March 27, 1930."

Two days before Mrs. Marshall's father disappeared. He probably couldn't have made it to that road by then. He would have known which way to head, though. He must have made the trip dozens of times in the past, between the town and the farm, so that his hands on the wheel would have known the way, even at night. Even with every landmark cut down, torn away, burned. He would have kept on driving, the water rising around his wheels, until his engine submerged and he could no longer drive. Then he would have gotten out, wading through the pitch-black, icy water, rising as he pressed on into the valley, rising as the snowmelt-swollen mass of it piled up behind the new dam, rising until he couldn't feel his legs or his arms or his chest for the cold of it. And still she could see him walking, walking farther and farther, until he disappeared from sight forever. Heading home.

CHAPTER 24

NOW

Clare rested the box of one dozen of Kreemy Kakes' finest on the counter of the nurses' station and smiled at the woman typing away at a computer behind it. "I'm looking for Russ Van Alstyne's room?"

"Mr. Van Alstyne." The nurse glanced at a clipboard stretched to its limit with a sheaf of papers. "Oh, yes. The broken leg. He's in 403."

"Thank you." Clare settled the box beneath her arm and made her way down the hall. The door to room 403 was closed. She knocked.

"Come in," Russ yelled.

She sidled through the door. He was alone in the two-bed room, propped up at an angle, his injured leg slung between a pair of struts assembled at the end of the bed. His cast ran from the ball of his foot to below his knee, and was highway-department orange. It reminded Clare of one of the Tonka cranes her brothers had played with back when they were kids. He was talking on the bedside phone.

"I'm sorry, go on." He beckoned Clare into the room. "No. No, it's not my mom." He glanced at Clare, and his eyes fell on the box she was holding. "It's just someone dropping off some food," he said.

She raised her eyebrows.

"How much extra?" he asked. He held out his hand for the doughnuts. "Six hundred bucks? For a one-way flight? That's ridiculous! I thought it was like a fifty-dollar fee to change your departure date."

Clare handed him the box, which he dropped in his lap. He flashed her a distracted smile, then frowned.

"Why do you have to buy a whole new ticket? That's three times what you paid to get down there."

Clare glanced around and spotted a boxy little chair of blond wood and fake leather in the corner. It looked as if it had been designed to discourage long bedside chats. She pulled it away from the wall.

"See, that's why I hate the idea of those Internet specials. If you'd have paid a little more to start out with, you'd have more flexibility now."

Clare paused before sitting down. Maybe getting a soda would be a good idea at this point. The newspaper. A magazine.

"Maybe you shouldn't." She glanced over toward Russ, but his face was turned toward the room's other, empty bed. "I mean, you just got down there yesterday. You only get to see your sister once a year. I don't want to ruin it for you." Clare watched as he twisted the phone cord back and forth in one hand. "I could ask Mom to come stay with me until you get home." He tilted his head back and squinted at the ceiling tiles. "I don't know. I might be able to drive one of the squad cars. They're automatic. There's nothing wrong with my right foot." He glanced over at Clare, then looked away. "I know you do. And I want you home, too. I'm just thinking six hundred dollars is a lot to pay for the privilege of playing my nursemaid." He flicked at the hospital-issue blanket covering him from knees to stomach, brushed it as if something unclean were stuck to it. He smiled a little and pushed a laugh out. "Not until my leg's healed up some more, we're not."

Enough eavesdropping. Way more than enough. Clare pasted a social smile on her face and waved bye-bye. Russ shook his head sharply. "All right, honey, if you feel that strongly about it, sure. Yep, you're right, it's not like we don't have the money. But don't try to get a flight tonight. I'm going to be here at least till tomorrow afternoon." There was a long pause. "Do you think you can get your friend Meg to do it? Okay, that'll be fine." Clare took one step, then another, toward the door. Russ held up one hand. "Honey? I think I need to get off now. Yeah, there's someone waiting for me." His eyes cut away from Clare. "Yes. I will." There was a final pause. "I love you, too. Bye." He twisted away from Clare and hung up the phone.

"Linda," he said.

"I gathered."

He looked down at the box of doughnuts as if he had forgotten putting them on his lap. "Thanks."

"I figured you'd like them more than flowers."

He smiled to himself, still not looking at her. She wondered how much he remembered about his behavior while he was pumped full of painkillers and whether she ought to mention anything. Set his mind at ease.

He popped open the top and took out a French cruller. "You want one?"

She got just close enough to take a peanut-covered doughnut while still maintaining the maximum degree of personal space. Okay, she thought, now I'll tell him he was stoned and being silly and it gave me a good laugh on the way to the historical society. And I'll ask him all about how Linda's doing and how soon she's getting home. She opened her mouth, but what came out was, "Did you know that the Ketchem graveyard was part of a property that was flooded when the Sacandaga was dammed?"

He stopped, a bite of cruller half in, half out of his mouth. His expression spoke even though he couldn't: a polite *So what?*

"Jane Ketchem and her husband lived there. The couple that lost the children. She's the one who went on to found the free clinic. It was named after her late husband. He disappeared in 1930. Mrs. Marshall, who's on our vestry, is her daughter." She knew she was babbling, but once she got going, she couldn't seem to stop it. "She thinks her father took off for a new life, but I've been thinking, and I think he killed himself. He drove off one night two days after the dam was finished. I think he went back to their old farm and drowned himself."

Russ swallowed his cruller. "Great. As soon as I get out of here and back to the station, I'll close the case."

"There's a case?" Her info dump had been as much protective camouflage as a genuine desire to share what she had found out, but his remark caught her. "What sort of case?"

He tore another piece of the cruller off. "You may be surprised to know that you're not the first person to look into Jonathon Ketchem's disappearance. The department spent a lot of time trying to track him down back when he disappeared. They couldn't find him, but the chief at the time refused to close the case. It's been handed down through the generations." He popped the bite into his mouth and chewed with relish. "It's probably our oldest cold case. I wouldn't have been aware of it, but I saw the name when I was going through the files when I first came on board. I had had a"—he paused, as if choosing the right word—"very weird run-in with Mrs. Ketchem back when I was a kid. I saw the name and was curious."

She dragged the chair next to his bed. "What sort of run-in?"

"She tried to drown herself in Stewart's Pond. I was fishing that day, and spotted her. I jumped in and pulled her out."

She sat in the chair, but found she was irritatingly low, like a prisoner in the docket. She stepped onto the seat and perched on the back of the chair. "That place, that reservoir—it's a bad place."

He laughed. "Oh, come off it. It's just a graveyard. I may not be all up on my Christian theology, but I'm pretty sure being afraid of the dead goes counter to some of the basic tenets."

"Not like that. I mean . . ." She broke her doughnut apart, trying to put into words how she had felt at the historical society. The sensation of cold water in the middle of old books and three-ring binders. "There's a specific gravity to the place. The drowned farm and the dead children. It's dragging people down."

He raised one eyebrow. "Well, now we know why I broke my leg."

"Think about it. Ketchem disappears, his wife tries to kill herself there, and now Dr. Rouse has disappeared." She cat-cradled her fingers. "And they're all connected to one another."

"Three bad things happening over a spread of what—seventy years?— does not a bad place make." He finished off his cruller and flipped the box open again, considering his choices. "You forget what a small town this is. Between Millers Kill, and Fort Henry, and Cossayuharie, we have maybe ten or eleven thousand people. Three quarters of us are related if you go back far enough. Of course there are going to be connections." He eased a chocolate-frosted doughnut out without breaking its glossy surface.

She took a different tack. "Why was Jonathon Ketchem's case never closed?"

"Because there's no statute of limitation on murder."

"Was that what they thought had happened? Back in 1930?"

"It was one theory. I guess the chief at the time didn't want to close out any possibilities."

"Like you, with Dr. Rouse's disappearance."

"Like me," he agreed. He bit into his doughnut.

She stuffed part of her peanut doughnut into her mouth and thought while she chewed. Have you considered," she said, after she had swallowed, "that Allan Rouse might have committed suicide? His wife told me he was acting erratically recently—sometimes manic, sometimes depressed. He's had this protest thing with Debba Clow going on. Then Mrs. Marshall and I came along and told him the clinic was losing the funding from Mrs. Ketchem's trust." She felt an acid twinge in her stomach at that one, but went on. "So he takes Debba Clow to the grave site, tries to convince her one last time how important vaccinations are. She doesn't listen, he falls and cracks open his head, then he gets into his car and drives into a tree—maybe it was all too much for him at the moment."

Russ swallowed another piece of his doughnut. "So he walked back to the grave site and down to the reservoir," he said. "And kept walking until he found a spot where the ice gave way underneath him."

"Huggins, the rescue guy, warned me not to go onto the ice. He said there would be plenty of rotten spots with the shifts in daytime and nighttime temperatures."

"Yeah, I've thought about it. If he went into the water, the hole he went through could have been totally invisible from the shore last night. When you fall in through a weak spot, the ice that was there bobs right back up. It doesn't fit together like a manhole cover or anything, but unless it was real close to the shore, it would have just looked like a rough patch on the surface." He licked the chocolate icing off his fingers.

"Are you going to send a dive team down there to look for him?"

He shook his head. "Not yet. There are still too many other possibilities. We don't have any forensics back on Debba Clow's car yet, for one thing."

"Do you seriously consider her a suspect?"

"She's the only one we've got at this point."

"I just can't see it. Admittedly, she thinks he's responsible for her son's autism. And she was all fired up about her ex's custody suit, and what Dr. Rouse might say against her. . . ." She let herself trail off. The problem with Debba was, the more you thought about it, the more likely she seemed.

"You keep on thinking that people commit murder because of this reason or that reason." Russ tore a tissue from the bedside box and wiped his hands. "But most homicides occur for one reason only. Someone becomes stupid angry and strikes out as hard as he can, with whatever he has at hand that will hurt the most." He crumpled the tissue and pitched it toward a plastic basket beneath the window. "The thought doesn't go into the killing. It comes, if there's any thought at all, afterward, when it's time to cover up the mess. And if you're going to ask me if I think Deborah Clow could get angry and go nuts, the answer is yes. I do."

"I have a confession to make." Clare propped her boots on the wooden arms of the chair so she could rest her elbows on her knees. "I'd almost rather he was murdered than killed himself. Because if he committed suicide, St. Alban's roof is going to be repaired with blood money."

"Oh, come off it. Okay, the clinic's lost a few thousand a year."

"Ten thousand."

"Nobody offs himself because of a cut in funding. Except—" His eyes focused inwardly. "No, forget it."

"What?"

"I was thinking, except in cases where someone's been cooking the books. But the clinic's not a business, where there's a profit to fiddle with or shareholders to scam. The board of aldermen go over the clinic's budget every year as part of the annual meeting." He looked at her. "At any rate, it's not St. Alban's fault. Maybe it's not your finest hour, and maybe you'd have liked to keep funding for the clinic as well as save your roof. But you make decisions like this all the time."

"I do not," she protested.

"Sure you do. Every time you choose to spend the church's money and time on one thing, you're choosing not to spend it on another. You've got a group of volunteers working with teenage mothers, helping them get through school, find jobs, baby-sitting, right?" She nodded. He went on, "That means that you're not helping divorced single moms of older kids with education, child care, and getting back into the workplace."

"That's not the same."

"Sure it is. Your parishioners give money to the church, right? Put it in the basket every Sunday."

"They make pledges and then pay on them. Sort of like public television."

"Except you don't give them *Masterpiece Theatre* video sets in exchange."

She couldn't help smiling, even though she knew which way he was going and it still didn't feel convincing.

"There's no difference between what they do and what Mrs. Marshall did," he continued.

"But it feels different."

"Why?" He crossed his arms over his blanket-covered chest and looked steadily at her.

She opened her mouth to respond only to realize that she hadn't thought out the answer to that question. She sat up straighter and pulled back her hair, knotting it at the back of her skull. Russ lay there, propped up in the hospital bed, giving her all the time she needed.

"Because," she finally said, "if it had really been up to me, I would have given the money to the clinic and stuck a tarp over the roof." She ducked her head. "That doesn't make me a very good steward of my church, does it?"

"No, you would have been a bad steward of your church if you had actually turned the money down in favor of the tarp. It just makes you someone whose duty conflicts with your own interest. It happens."

The tone in his voice made her raise her head, and she found him looking at her as if he were touching her face. Their eyes met, and she remembered an afternoon years ago, flying along the coast of Panama, her helo low over the impossibly blue waters, the smell of the sea everywhere and the rush of the sky and feeling as if the whole world were out there for her taking.

Then he dropped his gaze to the doughnut box and smiled. "I bet you always vote for universal health-care coverage, don't you?"

She tipped her head back and laughed, and that was how Margy Van Alstyne found them.

"Well! Looks like I'm missing the party." She bustled in, a short, rotund fireplug of a woman, dropping her car coat on the other bed. "Hello, Clare." Clare scrambled off the chair and barely got out a greeting before Margy swept to the head of the bed. "Hello, sweetie." She leaned up on tiptoe and kissed her son. "How are you feeling? Is it a bad break? Is it in the same spot where your old break happened?" She glanced at Clare. "Russ fell into a foxhole and busted his leg back when he was in Vietnam," she explained.

It had been both legs, and he broke them jumping to escape a helicopter that had been blown out of the sky. Russ gave Clare a warning look. She nodded.

"Breaking a bone at eighteen is a lot different from breaking it when you're fifty," Margy went on. She smoothed his hair back from where it had flopped over his forehead.

"I'm not fifty yet, Mom."

"Close enough as makes no difference. What did they do? What did the doctor say?"

"He put in two pins. I have to be in the cast six weeks."

Margy Van Alstyne turned to Clare and they shared a moment of total communion over the ability of men to turn the most dramatic, complex subjects into two sentences. Short sentences. With one-syllable words.

"And how did this happen?" Margy asked her.

"Ah." Clare recalled the script. "Russ and I were taking a walk. In the woods."

"Really?" Margy turned again and pinned Russ with a skeptical eye. "When I called the station, Harlene told me you had been tramping around a crime scene, looking for someone who disappeared last night."

"Busted," Russ said.

"It was in the woods," Clare said. "We were walking."

"You see what can happen?" Margy said to her son. "And this was after the fact, not right there, confronting some criminal. Sweetie, you've been at this too long. Sooner or later the odds are going to go against you and you're going to wind up at the wrong end of some maniac's gun." Her voice was tight. In all of Russ's exasperation over his mother's protectiveness, Clare had never thought what it was like from Margy's point of view, to be afraid that one day your son would stop a car or enter an apartment and never walk away.

"Mom, it was just a stupid accident. It could have happened anywhere." Russ had a tone in his voice, half pleading, half jollying. "It's Allan Rouse who's gone missing," he said. "The doctor who runs the free clinic. He was last seen up by Stewart's Pond. We found his car, but no sign of him."

Margy's expression clearly said she wasn't fooled by this transparent attempt to change the subject. But she went along with it anyway. "What did he do, jump in?"

"We don't know," Russ said. "There was a woman with him right before he disappeared. We're going to be questioning her further."

Margy's eyes rounded out. "Why, that old dog," she said.

"No, Mom, not like that." He frowned at her. "I'll tell you, but you have to promise not to repeat a word. It was this woman who's been picketing the clinic. Deborah Clow."

"I know her!" Clare and Russ both blinked. "She came to one of our meetings once," Margy went on. "Wanted us to get behind her crusade to stop vaccinations. Said they caused autism." She rolled her eyes. "My first reaction was to send her packing outright. I remember when polio was around, when they closed down public pools and shipped kids off to the country to escape it. But I thought, I'll look into it. See if there's anything to what she says."

"And?" Clare said.

"It's all hooey. No reputable scientific study has ever shown a relationship between vaccinations and autism. I told her we couldn't support her. There are too darn many real scary things out there for us to be wasting our time on imaginary monsters." She crossed her arms over her low-slung bosom and burrowed her hands up under her sweatshirt sleeves. "Everybody wants something or someone to blame when bad things happen. You have to learn how to figure out if there was a fault or not, that's what I think. Otherwise, it'll drive you crazy. Nobody can live with thinking that right out there, just out of reach, is the person who hurt you. It'll drive you crazy."

CHAPTER 25

NOW

SUNDAY, MARCH 26, THE THIRD SUNDAY IN LENT

And in the prayers of the people, we continue to pray for the recovery of Lauraine Johnson after her recent surgery; for Roger Andernach, who has been admitted to a nursing home; for David Reid and Beth Reid, on bed rest with twins; for Renee Rouse and for Dr. Allan Rouse, still missing; for Russ Van Alstyne, recovering from a broken leg. Please add your own prayers and petitions." Nathan Andernach, St. Alban's deacon, paused. There were some semiaudible mumblings from the congregation. Names. The suggestion of a petition. Someone said firmly, "For all the men and women serving in our country's armed forces."

Clare smiled to herself, but her mind was on Allan Rouse. He had been missing for nine days now. There had been an initial flurry of articles in the *Post-Star,* short because of the lack of information, and getting shorter each succeeding day until they had disappeared. The consensus at Thursday's Stewardship Committee meeting was that he had, as Dr. Anne baldly stated, "snuffed it." "It just builds on you over the years," she had told the rest of the committee members, who had left the capital campaign prospectuses unread on the table in favor of dissecting the town's most newsworthy event. "Especially solo practitioners. There's no one to confer with, no one to help you. Every bad decision, every shortcut you've taken, every patient you sent away, wondering if you've done any good—it can just drag you under sometimes. Some doctors get hooked on their own prescription pads. Some of 'em retire to fish in Florida. And some of 'em . . ." She had drawn a finger across her throat.

"Lord, let your loving kindness be upon them," Nathan said.

"Who put their trust in you," the congregation answered.

"We pray to you also for the forgiveness of our sins," Nathan said. He bowed his head and stepped away from the lectern.

Clare flew back into the present moment, her hands resting on the smooth white linen of the altar cloth, the sound—rumbling, creaking, sighing—as a hundred people got to their knees. "Have mercy on us, most merciful Father," they began. The corporate confession of sin went on, smooth and untroubled, not like the halting sentences and tearful interruptions she heard in the privacy of her office, when people wrestled one at a time with failings, with ugliness and nasty truths inside them.

There was an "Amen," and the church fell silent. Heads bowed or faces covered with a splayed hand or tilted up, eyes closed. Waiting for her to forgive their sins. She reached for the cord of compassion inside her, plucked it, let it resonate until she felt herself a small reflection of the Great Compassion. "May our God who always tempers justice with mercy pour out forgiveness over you," she said, "washing clean all your sins, strengthening you to do all good things, bringing you day by day and hour by hour into eternal life." She held back the long, loose sleeve of her alb so that it couldn't knock over the elements on the altar before her, and sketched a huge cross in the air. "In the name of the Creator, the Redeemer, and the Sustainer, amen."

"Amen," they replied. The sound of a hundred people getting to their feet before the Peace and the announcements—parents hissing, bulletins flapping open, hymnals thumping to the floor—was louder than any other part of the service.

"The peace of the Lord be always with you," Clare said cheerfully, but as she turned to embrace Nathan her eyes fell on Mrs. Marshall, collected and composed in her usual place, and Clare's mind flashed to what she had found out about Jonathon Ketchem. And suddenly she didn't feel so peaceful.

◆ ◆ ◆

After the service, after the coffee hour, after speaking with a hundred people, making appointments, promising phone calls, asking after ailments, sharing news from the committee meetings, commiserating about troubles and laughing at jokes, after all that, Clare liked to take a turn around the church alone.

She didn't have to. All that needed to be done after everyone had finally left was to lock and bolt the great outer doors. Up the main aisle, down the aisle, three minutes, tops. The rest of the locking up—the parish hall and kitchen doors, setting the alarm—all of that happened outside the sanctuary. She always flew through those steps, eager to get out of the place by then, to get back home and change out of her cassock into jeans and a sweater, ready for the rest of Sunday afternoon. She frequently had an invitation to one of her parishioners' houses, or she would go running, or curl up with the Sunday paper and then try out a new recipe for dinner. She looked forward to her afternoon away from the church. But before she left, she visited her sanctuary. Alone.

She locked the doors and closed the inner narthex doors behind her. The church was darkened. The sun was bright outside, but the light shafting through the stained-glass windows was filtered, softened, different from workaday light meant to illuminate. This light was meant to teach, and as she walked toward Jane Ketchem's window, she was ready to learn.

Mr. Hadley had been mopping down this area regularly, but the slowly warming temperatures continued to send water streaming and dribbling around the casement and splattering against the glass. The shield-bearing angels appeared to be wading through water toward her, presenting to her their message of cool comfort. *For he doth not afflict willingly nor grieve the children of men.*

She had always registered the figures climbing into the radiant light as a group of children, but now she saw they were two girls and two boys. *Peter. Lucy. Jack. Mary.* Mrs. Marshall had said her mother never spoke of them. Clare wondered if, as a girl, their surviving sister had ever gone to their graves. With her grandmother, perhaps. Their short lives and long deaths had cast a shadow over so many people. If they had lived, Mrs. Marshall might now have children and grandchildren and great-grandchildren filling up her life, instead of an empty, outdated house and vestry meetings. There would be no Jonathon Ketchem Clinic, because his memorial would be a stone in the town cemetery, next to his wife's. Allan Rouse would have found some other way to pay for medical school, and settled far from Millers Kill. Clare would be looking at a far different window. She glanced up to where the roofers were disassembling the ceiling to expose the rotten beams. And she would be going from door to door with her begging bowl, looking for enough money to cover the bare minimum of the repair.

All that because four children weren't inoculated with the diphtheria vaccine. No wonder Dr. Rouse had taken Debba Clow out there. The thought of Debba turned her away from the window. Whatever Allan Rouse had told her that night, it hadn't persuaded her to go ahead and have her little girl vaccinated. If, as everyone assumed, Dr. Rouse had committed suicide, Debba would be off the hook as far as police suspicions of her involvement went. But she would still be facing a custody battle with her ex and, more significantly, an ongoing struggle with her children's father about what was best for them. Clare couldn't do anything to budge Debba off Russ Van Alstyne's very short list of suspects in Rouse's disappearance, but she could give the artist the support she needed to help make decent decisions about the future. And the first step, Clare decided, would be to find out more about the past.

◆ ◆ ◆

"Hi, Mrs. Marshall," Clare said as the older woman opened her front door. Mrs. Marshall rearranged her look of obvious surprise into a more polite welcoming smile. "Can I come in for a sec?" Clare stepped into the foyer. "I'm sorry I didn't call first, this idea popped into my head and I—oh! Hello, Mr. Madsen." Norm Madsen smiled from the door to the dining room. *We don't invite ourselves over to other people's houses, young lady,* her grandmother Fergusson said. "Oh." Clare could feel her cheeks pinking. "I'm afraid I'm intruding."

"Nonsense," Mrs. Marshall said. "We've just finished lunch. You can join us for coffee. Did you get your furnace repaired? You were having a problem with it earlier this week, weren't you? You know, you should save your bill and bring it to the vestry. We would recompense you."

If they ever want to raise money, I can take it off their hands and get a sweet price for it! "It didn't cost enough to make it worthwhile getting the vestry involved," Clare lied. "Hi, Mr. Madsen."

"Great sermon this morning," Mr. Madsen said, walking her to the round-edged table. "Lacey and I were just talking about it. We agreed you hit it spot on when you said that thing about abundance and scarcity."

"How difficult it is to make a meaningful sacrifice when you have everything in abundance," Mrs. Marshall clarified. The luncheon plates had been cleared away, and a tray holding a coffee service was stationed next to Mrs. Marshall's seat. It was silver, the pieces buffed and curved like the fenders on a '50 Cadillac. Wedding present, Clare thought. Mrs. Marshall gestured to a chair across the table from her. "Please, sit down. Coffee?"

For a moment, Clare was tempted to ask if she had any leftovers. The smell of pot roast emanating from the kitchen was making her mouth water. "Yes, please," she said, thereby proving that there were still meaningful sacrifices to be made.

"It was a different world when we were growing up," Mr. Madsen said, holding out his cup to be filled. "I remember when Christmas meant three toys—one from my parents and one from each set of grandparents. Plus socks or mittens and some candy."

"And you were one of the rich kids in town," Mrs. Marshall said. "Milk?" She passed him the pitcher.

"I guess I was, at that." He poured a generous amount into his coffee. "The point is, when I had to give something up, it hurt. And when I got something, I really appreciated it. Every one of my toys fit into a box the size of a small suitcase when I was a boy. You should see my great-grandchildren's rooms. They look like FAO Schwarz."

"Milk?" Mrs. Marshall asked Clare.

"No thanks," she said, reaching for the sugar bowl. She looked across the table to Mrs. Marshall, who was pouring her own cup. "It's funny you should have been talking about your childhoods, because I have a question for you. If you don't mind."

"What is it?"

It felt wrong to start by firing a salvo into a sensitive subject, so Clare said, "I'm doing some counseling work with a woman who has doubts about vaccinating her youngest child. I wanted a better feel for what might go into that decision, and I was hoping, I wondered . . ."

"Whether I could tell you more about my parents' decision?" Mrs. Marshall said.

"I'll understand if you don't want to talk about it."

"I just don't know if I have any useful information. My grandma Ketchem told me back then, they didn't get children immunized ahead of time. If you fell sick, you'd get the serum. You have to remember, it was brand-new. Antidiphtheria serum wasn't even available in this country when my brother Peter and sister Lucy were born."

"People were slower to run to the doctor then, I think," Mr. Madsen said. "Nowadays, we're at the doctor's office every time we feel a twinge. Back in those days, you had to be some hurting for your parents to get the doctor out to the house."

"That's true," Mrs. Marshall said. "I hadn't really thought about that. There was no telephone out at the old farm. No electricity. My parents didn't own a car until 1929. My father would have had to drive his buggy into town and find Stillman any time they needed any medical treatment."

Clare lowered her coffee cup. "I just met a Dr. Stillman at the Washington County Hospital. He said he was the third generation of his family to practice medicine here in Millers Kill. He's an orthopedic surgeon."

Mr. Madsen snorted. "Well, the old Dr. Stillman was a country doctor. Which meant he did everything from setting bones to delivering babies to performing surgery—"

"—on kitchen tables. With the patients' butter knives." Mrs. Marshall arched an almost invisible eyebrow at her old friend. "You think everything was better back then."

"Maybe the old Dr. Stillman didn't push the vaccine back then," Clare said. "Since it was so new."

Mrs. Marshall tilted her head for a moment. "No, I don't think that was the case. As I remember him, Dr. Stillman was always after you with a needle."

"You were immunized?"

Mrs. Marshall smiled a humorless smile. "Against everything."

"Me, too," Mr. Madsen said, apparently oblivious of the expression on his hostess's face. "I think you're right. I think he was a bug about inoculations. No pun intended."

"Would your parents have gone to Dr. Stillman for their other children?"

"I suppose so," Mrs. Marshall said.

"Dr. Rouse was your mother's physician in her last years, right?"

Mrs. Marshall smiled wryly. "Allan Rouse was my mother's physician from the moment he proposed serving in the clinic in exchange for the money for his medical degree. Not that he treated her. That didn't come about until she was in her seventies. But he was hers. As much her creation as the clinic itself."

"Do you know if she ever spoke to him about what happened to your older brothers and sisters?"

"I don't know." Mrs. Marshall sipped her coffee. "She so rarely spoke of anything to do with those times. If it weren't for my own memories of the farm and my father, I might believe that my life started at age six, in the little house on Ferry Street." She replaced the cup precisely on its saucer. She left a faint imprint of today's lipstick on the rim. Scarlet. "I must have been a poor substitute for what she had lost, one child instead of four. And, of course, I was alive, and so could make mistakes and speak rudely and come home with disappointing grades and smoke cigarettes behind the garage. It must have been too painful to compare me to those perfect, dead children."

"Perfect?" Clare said.

"Haven't you noticed? Every dead thing is perfect." She glanced at Mr. Madsen, who was gawking at her over the rim of his cup. "Like Norm's yesterdays. Unchangeable, and so unable to disillusion you."

Clare looked into her coffee. "Have you considered that maybe your mother didn't bring up your brothers and sisters because she didn't want you to feel as if you had to live their lives for them?"

"What do you mean?"

"It's easy, when you're the surviving child, to feel as if you have to carry all the expectations your parents had for your dead sibling." She was speaking from raw personal experience at this point, with knowledge gained from countless conversations when her mother would sigh over her sister Grace's name or point out when friends' daughters joined Junior League or got married or had babies. All the things Grace was supposed to have done. "Maybe your mother wanted you to know that she loved you for who you were, complete. That you didn't have to try to be Peter or Jack or Lucy or Mary. That they were her past, but you were her future."

"You know, she may have something there." Norm Madsen reached across the corner of the table and patted Mrs. Marshall's delicate arm. "That would certainly jibe with the name she gave you."

Clare raised her eyebrows. "Your name?"

Mrs. Marshall smiled, the first wholehearted smile she had given Clare since they began their conversation. "You don't know my Christian name, do you?"

"I've heard Mr. Madsen and Sterling Sumner call you Lacey."

"That's my nickname. My pet name, I suppose you'd call it." Her smile wisped away into something softer and sadder. "I don't think there's anyone left alive who calls me by my real name."

Clare opened her hands in question.

"Solace. That's what my mother named me. Her Solace."

CHAPTER 26

NOW

MONDAY, MARCH 27

R uss came out of the handicapped elevator to thunderous applause.
"Elvis is in the building, repeat, Elvis is in the building," Deputy
Chief Lyle MacAuley megaphoned the announcement with his hands.

"Yeah, thanks, I missed you all, too," Russ said, swinging forward on
his crutches. "Now stuff it."

"I bet Linda forced him to come back to work," Lyle said. "One week
of him stuck at home and she threw his ass out of there. You can tell he's
a bad patient."

"All men are bad patients." Harlene Lendrum adjusted her headset over
her springy gray curls. "You should see my husband Harold. What a
whiner. The last time he got the flu, I told him I was sending him to the
Quality Inn out on the Northway. I was perfectly willing to pay so long as it
meant someone else fluffing his pillows and fetching him room service."

"Welcome back, Chief!" Kevin Flynn had gotten a regulation haircut
while Russ had been on sick leave. Now the kid looked even more like
Opie from *The Andy Griffith Show*. How was he going to do credible traffic stops when he didn't look old enough to have a learner's permit? Clearly,
a week away was too long.

Russ thumped up the corridor toward the squad room, an overblown,
big-city name for the station's central work area. "How 'bout you guys show
me what you've gotten done on the Rouse case while I've been at home
making life difficult for my wife?"

Noble Entwhistle, bless his plodding, methodical soul, followed Russ
through the squad-room door and went straight to his desk. "We've just
gotten the CIS results back on the Clow woman's car." He swept up several papers that had been scattered over the desk's metal surface and held
them up for inspection.

"In one week's time?" Russ said. "It's a miracle."

"You must have a special in with the Almighty," Lyle said, hiking himself up onto his desktop. Russ shot him a look. Lyle grinned.

"What'd they find?" Russ asked, turning his back on MacAuley's amusement.

"Rouse was in the car." Noble couldn't have looked more pleased if they had found the doctor's body stuffed in the trunk. "They got hairs and a blood sample from the passenger-side headrest."

"Shee-it." Russ whistled. "Any prints?"

"A couple of partials along the outside edge of the roof, just above the door. It's not anything that'll hold up in court, but it looks like he propped against the car with the door open or maybe reached up while he was inside, sitting down."

"Now that's more like it." Russ tilted toward Noble. "I want Debba Clow in here for questioning like, five minutes ago. Lyle." He pivoted on one crutch to catch his deputy. "Get the paperwork together and fax it over to the DA's office. I want a warrant for her house and I want us out there looking before she leaves the station."

Lyle slid off his desk and took the CIS results from Noble. "This is what I live for," he said, strolling toward the file cabinet where the application forms were stored. "Pulse-pounding action."

Forty minutes later, Russ gimped up to Harlene's operations board for his fifth check-in of the morning. "Anything yet?"

She swiveled her chair around to face him. "Aren't you supposed to be keeping that leg up? Go to your office! Sit down! I will let you know when Noble calls in."

"My office is a pain in the ass to navigate," he said. "There's not enough room around my desk and the damn chairs get in my way. Last time I went in, I knocked over a pile of *Law Enforcement Quarterlies.*"

"Serves you right for not ever picking up in there." Harlene swiveled back toward her board.

"What the hell's keeping him so long?"

She swiveled toward him again. "Deborah Clow has little kids, remember? Maybe she has to arrange for someone to sit with them."

"Oh." He knew he sounded like he needed someone to sit with him. "I thought her mother—"

Harlene held a hand up, cutting him off. She clipped the microphone back in place in front of her mouth. "Go ahead, fifteen forty-six."

Russ propped one crutch under his arm and leaned forward to snap on the intercom button. Harlene swatted his hand away and flicked the switch herself. "—with an ETA of twenty minutes," Noble was saying. "Ms. Clow has agreed to accompany me for questioning. Sus LU'd prior so expect a suit shortly. Fifteen forty-six over."

Suspect lawyered up before leaving, so expect her attorney shortly. Damn. That was not what he wanted to hear.

"Who do you think she called?" Harlene asked.

"We'll know soon enough," Russ said.

As it turned out, Debba Clow's mouthpiece arrived before she did; not such a surprise, considering his office was a five-minute walk away on Main Street. Russ could hear him before he saw him, badgering Ed at the reception desk. "I want to see my client *before* she's processed, and I want a copy of any and all warrants extending to her arrest and any searches of her property."

Russ thumped down the hall toward reception. "Your client's not under arrest, Mr. Burns. She's coming in of her own accord to help us locate a missing person."

Geoffrey Burns looked Russ up and down. Mostly up. He was a little guy, maybe five and a half feet, and Russ figured "little" described him in more ways than one. It would go a long way toward explaining his bantamcock attitude toward the world. Compensatory something, it was called.

"I'd heard you broke a leg. Reverend Fergusson included you in the prayers yesterday."

"She did? Huh." He'd lay good money Geoff Burns hadn't been praying for his quick recovery.

"Where's Ms. Clow?"

Evidently they had met the minimum daily requirement of chitchat. "She's not here yet. Officer Entwhistle is driving her in."

"What's the basis of your warrant?"

"I told you, we're not arresting her. She was the last person to see Dr. Allan Rouse alive." Or dead, he thought.

"She told me you impounded her car last week and had it searched. What did you find?"

Russ smiled pleasantly. "Let's wait until we're all together before we discuss that, shall we?"

"Are you planning on a search of her home?"

He had to give it to Burns, he knew how to stick you like a butterfly on a pin with his questions. "If necessary." He was saved from further disclosures by the sound of footsteps echoing up the marble stairs in front of them. Noble Entwhistle and Debba Clow appeared, the latter with an angry pink flush high on her cheeks and her kinky hair flying every which way. It was not shaping up to be a promising questioning.

"Deb, thanks for showing up," Russ said. "Let's all go back to the interview room." Aka the interrogation room, but that didn't sound so friendly. He gestured down the hallway with his head. The department's small briefing room was where they usually interviewed friendly witnesses or victims. It had windows, tissue boxes, a plug-in coffeemaker. The interrogation room had audio- and videotaping feeds. He knew which one he wanted when talking with Debba Clow. "Noble," he said as they reached the interrogation room, "will you see if Ms. Clow or her attorney needs anything? Coffee, water . . ."

"Let's get down to business," Burns said. "First order is, I need a minute in which to confer privately with my client." He cast a glance at the interrogation room's reinforced door. "Not there."

Russ smiled, a bit less pleasantly. "We don't eavesdrop on attorney-client discussions, Mr. Burns." Burns simply stared at him. Russ breathed in on a slow three-count and turned his head toward Noble. "Officer Entwhistle, will you please escort Mr. Burns and Ms. Clow to my office? You can wait outside to make sure they don't get lost on their way back." He bared his teeth at Burns, who bared his in return.

"Thank you. That will do nicely."

Russ crutched up to the squad room as Burns and Debba Clow disappeared into his office. "Lyle?" he said.

Lyle rounded the corner from the other end of the room. "Sorry. I was in the can."

"You got anything on that warrant?"

"Amy Nguyen from the DA's office is in with Judge Ryswick right now. As soon as she's got it signed, she'll hand it off to Kevin and me and we'll split for Clow's house."

"Remember, Clow lives with her mother and she has two little kids. One of 'em autistic. So use your good manners and play nice."

"I always play nice. I'm like the real-life version of that Jerry Orbach guy on *Law & Order*." Lyle stroked his bushy gray eyebrows.

"Except that Jerry Orbach is a lot better looking than you." Russ stumped back down the hall to the interrogation room. Balancing on one crutch, he unlatched the door and pushed it open. He wanted to be sitting when Debba Clow and Burns came in. He figured the sight of him balancing precariously as he lowered himself into a chair wouldn't do much good for his image as the Guy in Charge.

He had just stowed his crutches under his chair when Noble escorted Debba and Burns in. Russ watched her as she took in the room's window-less, institutional green walls and the steel case furniture bolted to the floor. Her eyes widened and she turned to Burns. That's right, honey, this is the real deal, Russ thought. Scary, isn't it?

Burns looked at him coolly. "Don't be intimidated, Debba. You're here doing them a favor." He took the chair across the table from Russ. Debba checked the seat beside Burns before settling in it, as if there might be something waiting to bite her.

"Just to avoid misunderstandings, we like to run tape when we're asking questions." Russ smiled in what he hoped was an easy, nonthreatening way. "It's easy to forget who says what, and this way there's a record for us all to refer to. So, Debba. Do we have your permission to tape you?"

She looked at Burns, who nodded. "Okay," she said.

"And we will want a copy within twenty-four hours," Burns added.

Russ nodded at Noble, who had taken up his position by the door. Ent-whistle pressed the recording button set in the wall. "Okay, then," Russ said. "For the record, this is Russ Van Alstyne, and I'm interviewing Debo-rah Clow—"

"I prefer Debba," she said.

"We need your legal name on the record," he said.

"Deborah Clow. Today is Monday, March twenty-seventh, and it's"—he glanced at his watch—"nine-forty A.M. Deb, we have your consent to tape this, right?"

"Yeah. Yes, you do."

"Deborah Clow is accompanied by her attorney, Geoffrey Burns." *Prick.* "Debba, I want you to think back a week ago to Sunday night, March nineteenth. You met with Dr. Allan Rouse. Did he call you, or did you call him?"

She looked at Burns, who nodded. "Dr. Rouse called me," she said.

"Were you surprised? Since you two had a run-in just a week before?"

She looked at Burns, who nodded. "Yeah. I was. Surprised."

"What was the subject of his phone call?"

"Pardon?"

"What did Dr. Rouse want to talk about?"

She looked at Burns. Christ, this was going to take forever if she had to get his okay for every word out of her mouth. "Mr. Burns, you're pretty quick on the uptake," Russ said. "Maybe you could tell your client that you'll interrupt if there's anything you don't think she should answer. Otherwise, I'm afraid we'll be here for a very long time."

Burns nodded to Debba. "It's okay. Rest assured, I'll jump in if he goes over the line."

Sentence by sentence, Russ led her through the events of that evening. Her language was stilted, the way some people got when they knew they were being recorded, but her account was substantially the same as the one she had given him that Sunday in Clare's living room. She had agreed to meet him because he had kept insisting he was going to show her the truth about vaccines, and she thought anything he said to justify himself might be ammunition in her custody fight. No, she didn't think her lawyer for the custody dispute would approve. No, she didn't know where the directions he gave her would lead to. No, she didn't see him until she arrived at the spot along the county road. Yes, they were each alone. Dr. Rouse had led the way through the trail to the tiny cemetery. He had a flashlight. She didn't. No, she hadn't been afraid of him. "I'm at least as big as he is," she said. "I figured if he got weird on me, I could take care of myself."

"Were you contemplating having to use force to defend yourself?" Burns asked before Russ could get his next question in.

"No," Debba said. "I believe in nonviolent resolutions. Discussion, not disruption."

Russ thought he remembered seeing the same sentiment on a bumper sticker on her car. It hadn't impressed him then, either. "How does that jibe with your breaking into Dr. Rouse's clinic and trashing one of his examining rooms two weeks ago?"

Burns's arm shot in front of Debba like a parent holding a kid back at a stoplight. "That's irrelevant to Dr. Rouse's whereabouts," he said. "You don't need to address that, Debba."

Russ waited a beat, and when it became apparent she was going to follow counsel's advice, he went on. "What did Dr. Rouse say to you when you reached the graves?"

She looked at Burns. He nodded. "It's hard to remember," she said. "It was cold and dark, and I was thinking that I had made a major mistake, because obviously, he wasn't going to tell me anything about the vaccines *he* had been using on the children of Millers Kill." She caught a strand of her long, curly hair and wrapped it around one finger. "He told me to look at the dates on the headstones. He wanted me to understand how deadly and contagious some of the epidemic diseases were. Please. Like I hadn't already spent two years reading up on them."

Burns laid his hand on her arm. "Just stick to the question."

"Oh. Okay. He had this idea that the epidemic wasn't just the disease, but the effects of the disease. He said the parents of those four children died when their kids did."

"What?" Those kids died in 1924, and he knew that whatever had happened to Jonathon Ketchem, he had been alive and kicking until 1930.

"I think he was speaking metaphorically. You know, they died inside. For a supposed scientist, he used a lot of metaphors. He was going on about links in the chain, about how each death sent ripples across the water, until more and more lives were swamped." Russ must have been giving something away in his expression, because she nodded to him, her long corkscrew hair bouncing up and down. "Yeah, I didn't know what to make of it, either. You can see what I meant when I said it was hard to tell what he was talking about." She pushed some of her hair away from her face. "Then he said that if anything happened to my children, I would never forgive myself. Now, up to that point, I was feeling a little sorry for him, because I could tell he *meant* well, and he seemed to be in total denial about the role his vaccinations have played in screwing up kids' health. But when he said that, I got mad."

Geoff Burns was on her statement before she had time to draw breath. "When you say you got mad, Debba, do you mean you attacked the doctor?"

"Of course not."

"You shouted at him? Threatened him in some way?"

"No. I got mad. I told him I thought between the two of us, he was the one who needed help, not me. Then I told him he should either give me the flashlight or escort me back to the road, because I was going home."

"What did he do then, Deborah?" Russ leaned forward slightly. This would be the meat of it.

"I turned to go, and I took a few steps, and he must have tried to follow me, because I heard him kind of yell—you know, that noise people make when they're falling on ice?"

He nodded. Oh yeah, he knew that noise.

"When I turned back toward him, he was laid out in front of one of the stones. I grabbed his flashlight and I could see that he had whacked himself pretty hard, he was bleeding and all." She glanced over at Burns, as if to check if she could use the word *blood*.

"What did you do?"

"I helped him up the trail, back to where we had parked the cars. I took a better look at his gash, and I offered to drive him into town, but he turned me down." She spread her hands in appeal. "How was I to know? He was the doctor, not me. Besides, if you're a parent, you see plenty of head cuts over the years. They always bleed like crazy, but they don't amount to anything."

"So what happened next?"

"I watched him get into his car and turn it on. It was running, I saw the exhaust. Then I took off. That's the last I saw of him."

"Where did you drive to, once you left?"

"I needed gas, so I drove over to the Quik-Fill that's by the Kmart. I was seriously shaken up by the weird stuff that had happened. I didn't want to go straight home. So I went to Clare's house."

"Why Reverend Fergusson?"

Debba tilted her head, twisting another strand of hair around her finger. "She had told me, when we . . . during that thing at the clinic"—she glanced over at Burns, checking to see if she was on dangerous ground—"that I should come talk to her anytime. I thought . . . I had a lot of stuff in my head, and I thought she could help me sort it out and make sense of things."

Russ nodded. "When you say that's the last you saw of Dr. Rouse, do you mean alive? Have you seen his body at any time after you left him Sunday?"

"Ugh. No."

"Have you seen him alive any time after you left him Sunday?"

"I told you, no."

Burns tapped the table. "Don't badger my client, Chief Van Alstyne."

Russ ignored him. "You say after you reached the trailhead, you took a closer look at Dr. Rouse's injury. How did you do that? With his flashlight?"

"Yeah. He sat in my car and I turned on the lights and took a look. He had a handkerchief, a real cloth one, and he kept it pressed against his cut."

Crap. "How long was he in your car?"

"A few minutes, maybe. He seemed really exhausted. That's when I tried to get him to let me take him home, or to the hospital or something."

This was not what he wanted to hear. Rouse taking a breather in the car was totally plausible. There wasn't any other sign of him in the car—no indication that she had stuffed him in the trunk or laid him out in the backseat. If Lyle and Kevin didn't find anything in her house, there was no way they were going to connect Clow with Rouse's disappearance. The DA wouldn't even bother with their paperwork—it would go straight into the circular file. "What time was it when you left Dr. Rouse?" he asked.

"I'm not sure. Maybe seven-thirty or so?"

"And it took you an hour to get gas and reach Reverend Fergusson's house?"

"I guess. I wasn't in any hurry."

"Did you make any other stops?"

"Nope."

"What time did Dr. Rouse contact you?"

"It was after dinner, so . . . between six and six-thirty."

"Which?"

She looked at Burns before answering. "Closer to six, I guess."

Burns placed both hands on the table. "I think that just about covers it, don't you, Chief?" He stood up. "Ms. Clow has covered all the events of that night in which she played any part. She's been nothing but cooperative, both today and during the night Dr. Rouse disappeared. I trust there won't be any need for further questioning."

Debba glanced at Russ, then at Burns, checking to see if she really could just get up and leave.

"I'm sure Debba here understands that we need to do everything that we can to find Allan Rouse," Russ said.

Burns hooked a hand under Debba's arm and levered her out of her seat. "Then I suggest, Chief, that you stop hounding my client, get off your butts, and start tracking the man down."

CHAPTER 27

THEN

TUESDAY, MARCH 29, 1955

Allan checked the address on the mailbox against the one scrawled on the paper in his hand. This was it? This cruddy little house on Ferry Street was where his last hope for med school lived? If he didn't know that Dr. Farnsworth had no sense of humor, he'd think the old guy had been jerking him around. But he was the one who had set up this meeting between Allan and the founder of the new clinic. There must be more to Mrs. Jane Ketchem than met the eye. Allan looked at the peeling green paint on the door of the tiny barn and the front room's sun-bleached curtains, whose barely discernible pattern was distorted through the ripples in the window glass. There certainly couldn't be less.

He took the granite block steps in one stride and knocked on the door. It jerked open, startling him so he nearly tumbled backward off the top step. The woman standing there stared at him. "You must be Allan Rouse," she said.

He recovered his balance. "Yes, ma'am."

"I'm Mrs. Ketchem. You're late."

He saw she was buttoned into a navy coat, with a knit hat tied beneath her chin. Oh, Christ, had he blown it without ever getting a chance to present his case? "I'm sorry," he began, "I was—"

"I'm due to volunteer at the clinic. You can walk with me." She reached behind her and snatched a purse and gloves from a hall stand. He jumped out of her way as she swung out the door, shutting and locking it in one efficient movement. She tugged on her gloves and narrowed her eyes as she gave him the once-over. "Is that all you're wearing?"

"Uh . . ." he gestured toward his mom's Chevrolet. "My coat's in the car. Can I drive you?"

"I'd rather walk. It keeps your joints young." She nodded toward the car. "Well? Better get it if you're coming along. It's raw out today."

Allan stumbled down the steps and loped across her bath mat–sized lawn. He retrieved his coat, a long, heavy thing that had been his brother Elliot's, and slipped into it while following Mrs. Ketchem down the sidewalk. Evidently, she didn't wait for stragglers. He fell into step beside her, and studied her in quick glimpses that could be passed off as checking out the ways home owners had tried to individualize this row of identical houses. If Mrs. Ketchem's joints were young, they were the only part; she was gaunt and rawboned, with deep grooves running from her nose to her chin and tomahawk-slashed creases radiating out from her eyes.

"Dr. Farnsworth tells me that you want to become a doctor."

"Yes, ma'am, I do."

"Why?"

Because I've always been the smartest one in my class and I don't want my brains to shrivel up behind a desk. Because I don't ever want my fate to be decided by some faceless, cigar-puffing board in Cincinnati. Because I don't want to work for thirty years with nothing to show for it but a paid-up mortgage on a house nobody wants to buy. Because I want respect, and money, and to travel on jet planes to places where no one has ever heard of Millers Kill.

None of which was what financial-aid boards and admissions officers wanted to hear. "Because I want to use my gifts—my facility with science, my curiosity, my empathy—to help people. Not in a lab, but hands on. One-on-one."

"Have you thought about alternate careers? Medicine should be a calling, you know, not something you pursue because you can't think of anything better."

"I've always wanted to be a doctor, ma'am. Since I was a kid. I was the one who was always collecting hurt pets and trying to treat them."

"But you don't want to be a vet?"

He risked a grin. "People don't bite you."

"Don't be so sure of that." The reached the corner and crossed the street, to where the new cemetery lay behind a squared-off granite wall. That was another thing he wanted to put behind him, a place where something "new" had been built a hundred years ago.

"Tell me why it is you're looking for funding," Mrs. Ketchem said as they rounded the corner onto Burgoyne Street.

"My folks can't afford to send me," he said. It was embarrassing, but at this point, he had rehearsed the details on so many applications and forms that it was almost as if he were talking about some other Allan Rouse. "I'm going to Albany on a scholarship, and working for my room and board. I've applied for scholarships and loans for medical school, but I haven't been able to pull together nearly enough money to cover all the expenses. Plus, they only go through school. I'd be left looking for money to live on all over again when it was time for my residency."

"Couldn't you work while going to school?"

"Not if I wanted to learn anything." He looked at her, willing her to understand. "Medical schools only accept the best of the best. You have to be there, giving one hundred percent every day, if you hope to keep up. I don't want to just keep up. I want to excel."

She cocked a graying eyebrow. "Why not sign on with the military? They'll pay for everything. One year of service for each year of schooling, isn't it?"

His fingers closed around the edges of Elliot's coat. "I had an older brother who was in the marines. He died in Korea three years ago. It would just kill my parents if another of us joined up."

"I'm sorry," she said. They reached the corner of Pine Street, and she paused, the toes of her shoes hanging off the edge of the curb, while a dump truck chuffed past. "It's hard to lose a child. Real hard. I can understand your parents' point of view." She stepped across the street and he followed, dodging the mucky gutters still wet with melted snow and the earliest spring rains. "Your parents used to live here, didn't they?"

"Yes, ma'am. I graduated from Millers Kill High." He tilted his head back to look at the sky, heavy with scudding gray clouds. "My dad worked at the mill until it closed down. They moved to Johnstown a couple years ago."

"This town's been going through some hard times. I don't mind telling you, that's one of the reasons I told Dr. Farnsworth I'd be willing to speak to you. I gave them the building for the clinic—practically had to ram it down their throats—and I gave them my in-laws' farm that had come to me, so there'd be money to support the thing. But I can't make the aldermen pony up enough money so's to keep a steady doctor around. If it weren't for the hospital staff doing volunteer shifts, we'd have to close it down."

She fell silent. Should he leap into the gap? Tell her he was dying to come back to town as Dr. Rouse and take care of her clinic? She looked as if she was thinking about something. Maybe he ought to just keep his mouth shut.

They reached Elm Street. "Down this way," she said. She continued on, saying nothing, as they strode down Elm. He loved this street, loved the deep, wide lawns and the shiny new cars he could see peeping from inside old carriage houses or parked beneath porte cocheres. The enormous elms that had astonished him as a boy were all dead now, and the immature saplings that had taken their place looked imbalanced against the three- and four-story houses. Still, this place had the same certainty that he had seen in a few of the kids at SUNY Albany, the ones who never had to stop and think about whether they could afford a pizza pie or walk back from an evening out because a taxi was too expensive. The certainty he wanted for himself. He wondered if any of the homes here belonged to doctors.

"Did Dr. Farnsworth tell you what I was thinking of?" Mrs. Ketchem's voice snapped him back to attention, and his gut jerked, as if she had seen the thoughts inside his head and could tell he was no lily-pure altruist. "All expenses paid, room, board, tuition, books, what have you. During the school year and for three years of residency, which is what he tells me it takes to make a man into a doctor fit to look after the needs of a town."

"Yes, ma'am. He and I talked about it after I got in touch with him."

"And a year serving as the clinic's full-time physician for each year of support. Same as with the military, although I can promise you you won't get shot at here."

They turned down a short two-house street and emerged onto Barkley Avenue. "There it is," she said, pointing with her chin. He followed her gaze two houses down and saw . . . a house. It resembled several other houses on Barkley and Elm Streets, tall, narrow, made of brick and fancy wood trim. He had known Mrs. Ketchem donated her in-laws' house to get the clinic started, but somehow, he had drawn a mental picture of something more . . . modern. Something that looked more like a medical facility and less like a place where someone's rich grandmother lived. "It looks great," he said.

"It's pretty plain inside. I sold all the furniture and whatnots that my brother-in-law and his family didn't want to keep. Used that money to fit out the waiting room and the offices. Got some local doctors to help out with medical equipment and stuff for the examination rooms, and what

I couldn't wrangle, the town bought cheap off the hospital when they did their renovation two years back."

She escorted him up the walk. "Up there's the only change I made that didn't go directly into treating the patients." She pointed to the granite lintel above the etched-glass-and-oak door. THE JONATHON KETCHEM CLINIC.

He was still digesting the news about their flea-market approach to equipping the place. "That was your husband? Jonathon Ketchem?"

"Yes." The hard edges of her face softened. "This is his monument. I never did put one up in the cemetery. Some folks talked about that, you know. Said it just went to prove how cheap I was. But this . . ." She nodded approvingly. "No one in town has as big a memorial stone as this."

He wished he knew the dividing line between being an eccentric and being a fruitcake.

"Well, let's not hang around. Come on in," she said, all business again. He opened the door for her and they went inside into a narrow front hall. He lunged for the interior door and managed to jerk it open a second before her hand fell on the doorknob.

Straight ahead of him was a staircase, sweeping up to a second-floor landing. The stained-glass windows and the gleaming woodwork looked as if they ought to be in a church, but the noise would certainly have been out of place. He pulled his eyes away from the stairs' perfection and saw what was making all the hubbub. To his right, in what would have been the drawing room, at least a dozen people were sitting in sturdy wooden chairs that he swore must have come from the high school. One woman with a baby perched on her hip was trying to chase down a bratty little kid without actually breaking into a run and grabbing him. "You come right here this minute, Russell!" she hissed. Two old men who had evidently turned off their hearing aids were having a loud discussion about the benefits of red wheat versus winter clover. A teenage girl sitting next to an older woman kept popping her gum until the woman shrieked, "Will you stop that!"

Thumbtacked onto the walls behind them were simpleminded posters extolling the benefits of vaccinations, dental hygiene, and eating the five food groups every day. The only thing missing was the magic-bullet ad: Use a condom, prevent the clap. A wide wooden desk blocked most of the squared-off archway that would once have divided the front room from the family parlor, separating the two areas into waiting room and office.

An old lady of the sweet and little variety manned the desk, a blue-and-white-striped apron over her street clothes.

"This way," Mrs. Ketchem said, and he followed her down the hall, past the parlor lined with metal filing cabinets, and into a small room just the right size to have been a butler's pantry. "This is the doctor's office," she said. It had no personal touches, no family photographs or diplomas on the wall. The desk and chair were cheap metal castoffs that looked like Army-Navy surplus. The single window, behind the desk, was half covered with an old-fashioned green roller shade, complete with thick silk cord and pull.

The enormity of what it would mean, seven years of his life in this place, broke over him like a massive wave. He would be thirty-five years old before he was released from his self-imposed bondage. One-fifth of his life would be spent coming here every day, walking past those idiot posters, saying hello to a succession of little old ladies in striped aprons, seeing patients with ingrown toenails and conjunctivitis and the flu.

He closed his hand tightly over the edge of one of the shelves that ran along each side of the office. Pantry shelves, he realized, once used for the family china and pots and pans. Now they were filled with anatomy books, medical texts, journals in grosgrain boxes. The books. Filled with things he wanted to know. He breathed in again, forced himself to relax, to look around with apparent approval. There were medical students who earned out their educations serving in big-city ghettos, or in Appalachian hamlets where all their patients had bare feet and married their cousins. Compared to that, coming back to Millers Kill would be a cakewalk.

"It's great," he said. "I admire what you've done here."

"Come on upstairs. If they aren't all in use, you can see some of the examining rooms."

He followed her up the grand staircase and down the second-floor hall. "Here's where we've put in a ladies' room," she said, pointing to the first door on the left. "Ran the piping up from the kitchen belowstairs. Men's room is the old second-floor toilet. I figured they didn't need the space the women did. This one's taken, this one." She pointed to the closed doors as they walked past. "Here," she said, entering through the last door in the corridor. It was an examining room. Plain, but with everything he'd expect to see. The wooden floor had been replaced with linoleum. She saw him looking at it. "The doctors said you can't keep wood sterile. This stuff can be scrubbed down with hospital-strength disinfectant."

For a moment he wondered if the clinic's doctor would be responsible for that job, too.

Mrs. Ketchem crossed her arms and looked out one of the room's two windows. "This house belonged to my husband's grandparents before it came to my in-laws and then to me. Grandmother Ketchem was some house proud. Sometimes I can't help but imagine those old folks rolling in their graves at some of the things I've done to this place."

"Why?" Allan couldn't restrain the question that had been swelling inside him since he had first seen her dumpy house on Ferry Street. "I mean, I know it's great to give away money and all, but most folks who do it are rich. Didn't you want to keep this house for yourself? Live, you know, in style?"

She didn't answer him right away, and he wondered if he had just blown it, by showing that he was not the sort of person who would give away riches as soon as they fell into his hands. "I gave birth to my first child in this room," she finally said. She let her gaze roam over the walls and windows, as if she were looking through time, to the way it used to be. "We had a farm out in the Sacandaga River valley, a good half day's ride by horse and cart, which was all we had. So when my time came near, my husband brought me here, into town, to stay with his grandparents. It was in here I had my son Peter." Her voice had gone all thin, as if it were coming from a long way away.

She looked straight at Allan. "I'm going to tell you something I don't speak of, because I want you to understand what this clinic means. What it's for."

He nodded, desperately curious and afraid of what he might hear, both together.

"I had four children once, in that farm. It's all gone now, children, farm, everything. But back then, it was my life. I never thought it wouldn't all go on like it had, each day following the one before."

He nodded again, feeling that he ought to make some acknowledgment.

"It was March, in '24. It had been a cold March, like this one, after a cold winter. Jonathon had taken our two oldest to a party, one of our neighbors who lived upriver. I figured they must have gotten it there. Some of the older kids came down with it, but they recovered after a bad croup. It works that way, you know. Once they're eight, nine, ten, it mostly sickens them. But younger, it kills. My Lucy and Peter were the youngest there that day."

Allan wanted to sit down, but his legs seemed nailed to that spot on the linoleum floor.

"About two days later, they both came down sick. It could have been most anything. They were feeling poorly, with a cough and a fever. Their coughs got worse and worse, and I could see how bad their throats looked, all white and red, and them pulling for breath and spitting out nasty mucus. I stayed up all night for two nights running with both of them, steaming 'em, making potash gargle, giving them saltwater drops to keep their noses clear. Then the next day, they seemed to be on the mend. Both of them terrible weak, but their throats clearing up and their breath coming easier. I had kept the two younger ones away. . . ." She looked out the window again. "Three days after Peter and Lucy got over the worst of the coughing, Mary and Jack came down with it. But it was worse, so much worse. It went through them like wildfire. High fevers, and their little throats all swollen and choked. They couldn't hardly breathe. It was when I saw their throats and tongues all dark that I couldn't deny anymore that they had the black diphtheria. You know what they used to call the diphtheria, don't you?"

Allan tried to nod. "The Strangler," he said.

"That's right. Jack died by the next morning, died hard, fighting it with everything in him. And then that evening, my little Lucy. Her heart stopped. That's what it does, you know. If it doesn't choke off the breath and blood, it paralyzes the heart."

Allan felt as if his throat were closing up. At that moment, he would have promised Mrs. Ketchem another seven years' service if she would only stop talking about it.

"That night, Jonathon went for the doctor. Mary . . ." She sighed. "I rocked her and rocked her all night. When Dr. Stillman came back with Jonathon in the small hours, he gave Peter the serum. He told us Mary was . . . She died just before the sun came up. I remember praying, praying harder than I ever did, that the angel of death would pass us by, and leave us our firstborn. But the poison had gotten too far, and Peter's heart and kidneys were damaged too bad. He died three days later."

Allan stood there. What could he say? His experience with sorrow was losing a grandparent. The death of a pet. He shifted from foot to foot, intensely uncomfortable and ashamed of himself for feeling that way.

"I had worried plenty, over the years, about the German measles, and mumps, and scarlet fever. But I never thought about the diphtheria. It had always seemed a faraway thing to me. Something you read about in the papers, happening in the cities. Places where folks lived all crowded together and didn't know how to be clean. Whooping cough and influenza, that was something you had to worry about, living on a farm. Not the Strangler." She moved then, stepping toward Allan, making him start backward as he had on her front steps. "That's what this clinic is for. I want you to understand it, not like book understanding, but living-it understanding. You're hardly more than a boy yet, but someday you'll have children, and when you do, you'll think of my children, and you'll picture in your heart what it feels like to lay all four of your babies into the ground. You'll know what it is to spend the rest of your life wishing you had done different things."

Allan backed into a cabinet by the examination table, jarred it hard, and lurched forward as a glass container filled with cotton swabs tipped over. His hands closed on empty air and the container smashed against the floor, spraying glass shards and swabs across the linoleum, over his shoes, into the cuffs of his pants.

"Hold still," Mrs. Ketchem said, in an entirely different voice than the one she had used when recounting her spooky history. "There's a closet over this way." He stood stock-still as she retrieved a broom and swept up the mess in short, efficient strokes. "Shake off your pants," she directed, and he did as he was told. She bent over and squinted at his shoes. "You're fine," she said. "Go fetch me the dustpan." He picked his way over to the closet and found it. He held it to the floor while she swept the glass and wood into a sparkling pile, and then he carried it, at her direction, to the waste bin.

"I sure hope you won't be as careless as that when you're working here." She stepped out into the hall and beckoned him to follow. "We don't have much of a budget and we have to stretch the supplies as far as we can."

"Yes," he said, trailing after her. "I mean, no, I'm usually not that clumsy. I was—" *Scared.*

"Jane?" On the stairs below the landing, he could see the old lady who had been working the reception desk. "Are you ready?" She was untying her striped apron. "I'd stay longer, but I promised my daughter I'd watch her girls this afternoon."

"Sorry, Ruth," Mrs. Ketchem said. The other woman passed her the apron, and Mrs. Ketchem tied it on over her dress. The starched sweetness of the blue and white stripes seemed to cast Mrs. Ketchem in a deeper darkness, like a witch wearing an angel's robe. "I didn't mean to keep you over," she was saying as they all three descended the stairs.

Allan looked with longing at the door as the morning's volunteer receptionist let herself out, but Mrs. Ketchem had cast a spell over his shoes—or perhaps they, more than his head, knew how much he wanted to become a doctor—and he found himself following her into the parlor turned office.

"It'll be up to you to see you get accepted into medical school and that you keep your grades up. If you drop out or flunk out, I'll be after you to repay the money I've spent. You or some other, I'm going to find someone to help me establish this clinic so that it can't get knocked down." Mrs. Ketchem enthroned herself on the desk chair and swiveled toward him. Across the desk, he could see the patients waiting for their turn with today's doctor. These people would become his responsibility. This clinic would become his responsibility. For seven *years*. "I don't mind telling you, I'm hoping that if you take the job on, you'll want to stay even after your term is over." A hint of the woman upstairs, the woman of the terrible story, rose in her eyes. "I need someone who believes in this place like I do. To keep it going in perpetuity after I've died. That's the word my lawyer used when I gave over my in-laws' dairy farm to the town. 'To be used in perpetuity for the benefit of the clinic.' I like that."

The language reminded Allan of the way Roman Catholics paid to have masses sung for the souls of the dead. In perpetuity.

"Well?"

"What?" he asked, feeling that she had caught out his secret thoughts again.

"Do we have a deal?"

He thought of the upstairs room, the glass shattering, the rising and falling of her voice. He thought of his dad's face when he came home and told them the mill was closing down. For good. He thought of his own name, Allan G. Rouse. M.D. Then the bratty boy in the waiting room coughed, hard, whining his misery, and he thought suddenly of four small coffins.

"Yes," he said. "We have a deal."

CHAPTER 28

NOW

R uss couldn't settle on the worst part of having a broken leg. Was it being driven around town like a kid too young for a permit? Or struggling along sidewalks slick with muddy water and the last remnants of crumbling ice, praying he wasn't going to fall on his ass? He had plenty of time to contemplate both while humping himself up the South Street sidewalk toward the free clinic.

He hadn't started out the day in the best of moods, and the rapidly falling barometer didn't help. His leg registered every change in the pressure with a new ache or twinge. The search at Debba Clow's home yesterday had turned up a big fat nothing, and he was getting that feeling, the one he hated, of chasing his own tail.

"Isn't this a great day, Chief?" Officer Kevin Flynn feinted side to side across the walk and up and down the stairs, dribbling and shooting an imaginary basketball. He had been detached to squire Russ around, on the grounds that shadowing the chief might be considered advancing his education in law enforcement. "I heard it's gonna get over fifty!"

Russ paused for a moment to flex his aching hands. He looked up at the gray clouds coursing across the sky, the shafts of sunlight sweeping down the mountains and away to the east. "Forty-five degrees tops," he said. "And it's going to rain." If there was one thing worse than hobbling around on crutches, it was hobbling around on crutches in the rain. He creaked his way up the walk and squared the crutches' rubber tips on the lowest step.

"Hey, Chief, don't you want to use the wheelchair ramp?" Kevin paused in front of the door, the imaginary basketball still held between his hands.

"No, I do not want to use the wheelchair ramp." Russ gritted his teeth and teetered his way to the clinic entrance, where he was forced to let Kevin open the door for him.

The noise, even in the tiny foyer, was confounding. They pushed through the inner doors to a waiting room overflowing with kids, moms, babies, old folks—everyone except the family pet. "What the hell's going on?" Russ asked.

"Maybe these are all the people who didn't like to see Dr. Rouse," Kevin said. "I think he could be kind of intimidating."

A kid of maybe four broke from the room and dashed across the hall, nearly knocking into Russ. "You come right here this minute, Max!" his harried mother hissed.

Russ beckoned to Kevin with his head. "C'mon, let's see if we can find Laura Rayfield."

A strained-looking volunteer behind the reception desk let out a weak "Ha" when Russ told her he wanted to speak to Ms. Rayfield. "Sign the list," she said. "But I warn you, your wait will likely be well over an hour and a half at this point."

Of course. He looked like a civilian in his Dockers slit up to the knee and his bomber jacket zipped up over his uniform blouse. "I don't think you understand," Russ said. "This is official police business. I'm Chief Van Alstyne. . . ." He forgot he couldn't just unzip his jacket pocket and haul out his ID. One crutch clattered to the ground. He swore under his breath. "Kevin—," he started, but the officer had already scooped it up and was holding it out to Russ, beaming like a Boy Scout.

"Thank. You." Russ lifted his elbow and allowed Kevin to slide the crutch back home. He had retrieved his ID, but it was moot now that the receptionist had seen Kevin's uniform.

"Oh!" She glanced back and forth between Russ and Kevin. "Is this about"—her voice dropped to a barely audible whisper—"Dr. Rouse's disappearance?"

"That's right," Russ said.

"Oh. Well. That's a different story, isn't it?"

Russ allowed as how it was, and let her escort him and Kevin into the conference room, a square space whose elegant moldings and central chandelier gave evidence of its past as a dining room. "You wait right here, and I'll send Laura to you as soon as she's done with her current patient," the receptionist said.

Kevin obediently sat down at the conference table and stared out the windows. Russ stumped around, examining the space. The door opposite the hallway turned out to be the old house's kitchen, modernized with a cast-off green refrigerator, a microwave, and a coffeemaker. The door between the kitchen and the hallway opened onto the doctor's office.

It was the size of a roomy closet, but comfortable, with a leather desk chair and a desk that would have been handsome if it hadn't been covered with heaps and piles of papers. Interspersed among the medical books lining the walls were framed photos of Rouse and his family. There was one of the five of them in what looked like Cape Cod, and another, with the children much younger, taken in Disney World. There was one of a tanner and slimmer Allan with his arm around his tanner and happier wife. They were on the deck of a cruise ship, and the silver frame was engraved with the words OUR 30TH ANNIVERSARY.

"I'm sorry about the mess." Laura Rayfield stood in the doorway, clipboard in hand, sections of her red hair escaping from her braid. "Your officer was searching for something that might provide a lead to what happened to Al, and I haven't had time to put everything back to rights."

"I apologize," Russ said. "Officer Entwhistle should have done that for you."

"No, no, I'd rather handle it myself. Doesn't matter, really, unless and until Allan reemerges or we get a new doctor in here." She tilted her head toward the conference room. "Mind if we sit down while we talk? I'm beat."

She eyed him as he crutched out of the narrow office and lowered himself into a chair. "Your officer said you'd broken your leg. What happened?"

"Slipped on the ice. Greenstick fracture."

"Any pins?"

"Two. I'm supposed to be out of this in another five weeks."

"Who was your orthopedic surgeon?"

"Dr. Stillman."

She collapsed into the chair opposite him. "He's good." She tossed the clipboard on the table. "What can I tell you, Chief? I already gave a statement to Officer Entwhistle last week."

"I know. I read his report." He matched up the crutches and laid them on the floor. "It looks like you've got half the population of Millers Kill back there in the waiting room. Are we in the middle of an epidemic I haven't heard about?"

Her mouth twisted. "Yeah. It's called the no-health-insurance epidemic. These folks are here because the volunteers and I have been calling all our current patients and letting them know we're about to close up shop. Everyone's coming out of the woodwork to get their prescriptions or to take care of problems they've been putting off. As of April first, their only recourse is going to be the ER."

"Wow," Kevin Flynn said. "That really sucks."

"How come?" Russ asked.

"I'm a nurse practitioner. Do you know anything about nurse practitioners?"

"I know you can examine and treat patients. And write prescriptions."

"That's right." She tucked a loose strand of red hair behind one ear. "We practice in collaboration with a physician. Every NP works under a particular practice agreement that's filed with the state board. Mine states that I will practice under the direct supervision of Dr. Allan Rouse or such physicians as he may appoint—that's in case we hand off one of our patients to a specialist—with Dr. Rouse reviewing my patient records no less than every fifteenth day. That covers his two-week vacations."

"Okay," Russ said.

"Don't you see? Without Al here, I'm effectively barred from practicing fifteen days after his disappearance."

"Can't you call up whoever is in charge of these things and explain the situation? Get an extension or something?"

"No. In order to resume practicing here at the clinic, I'm going to need to find another M.D. willing to serve as my collaborating physician. Then we'll have to draw up a practice agreement and a practice protocol and file it with the office of Professions at the Education Department. Then we have to wait until the agreement and protocol are approved."

"Sounds time consuming."

"It can be."

Kevin leaned in. Russ noticed that he and Laura Rayfield had identical coloring. He wondered whom they might have in common on their family trees. "Can't you apply for the new agreement now?" Kevin asked. "That way, you might not have to wait so long to reopen the clinic."

She shook her head. "Doctors can be very protective of each other's turf. Until we know for sure that Al's"—she flipped her hands: *Who knows?*— "not coming back, it's an uphill battle to get another M.D. to sign on as my collaborating physician." She turned to Russ. "I really hope you find something soon. Not just for Al's family's sake, but for the clinic. He's been carrying this place for thirty years, and it would kill him if he knew we were closing down."

If something or someone else hadn't already killed him. Russ pulled his glasses off and polished them on his blouse. "Was he happy here? With his work?"

Laura blew out a puff of air. "That's hard to say. He was dedicated. Conscientious. He had the kind of emotional control a lot of doctors do, in my experience, good at showing you his calm, controlled side, good at hiding the other stuff."

"What other stuff?"

"Like I told Officer Entwhistle, he was under a lot of stress in the weeks before he disappeared. That thing with Debba Clow really ate at him. The fact that it was about vaccinations, which he sort of held as the holy grail, made it worse. He had to field a lot of questions from mothers, and justifying his medical decisions wasn't something Al was good at." She grinned one-sidedly. "Justifying himself at all wasn't something he was good at."

Russ resettled his glasses on his face. "Was anything else bothering him?"

"He was very down about Mrs. Marshall yanking her funding. We all were. Finding out you're going to lose ten grand a year isn't any fun. Although she did notify the board of aldermen about the change in funding, which is supposed to trigger some sort of review of our money situation. She sent them a letter the day after she told Al. We got our copy of it the same day he disappeared." She sighed. "I bet he didn't even have the chance to read it."

"How's this review supposed to work with the aldermen?"

"I don't know. The letter said something about the provisions of the gift and reviewing the funding." She shrugged. "The only financial document I'm familiar with around here is my paycheck."

"Do you have the letter around?"

"It's in there. It may still be in his in-box. I don't know."

"See if you can find that, Kevin." He indicated the doctor's office, and the young officer bounced out of his seat and disappeared though the still-open door.

"Any other issues bothering him that you know of? Anything personal?"

"Nothing he shares with me. He seems sort of melancholy at times." Laura's face was drawn in, in concentration. She seemed unaware that she was now speaking of Rouse in the present tense. "He's spoken a few times this spring about Mrs. Ketchem, who started the clinic. I guess this year's the thirtieth anniversary of her death." She flipped her hands over. "And he turned sixty-five in February. He's very fit, you know. Bikes every day during the warmer months. But I think he's been experiencing one of those times when the reality of how old you are hits hard. You know?"

Russ smiled a little. "I'm turning fifty this November. Believe me, I know." He leaned forward. "Look, Laura, how long have you worked for Allan Rouse?"

"I practice with him, not work for him."

He nodded his head. "Sorry."

"It's been, jeez, twelve years now. Talk about the reality of getting old."

He pitched his voice lower. "One of the theories I'm working on is that there may be another woman involved."

Laura started laughing.

"No?" he said.

She couldn't speak for a moment. "If you knew Allan . . ." She took a deep breath, tried to wipe the grin off her face. "No. Absolutely not. Forget that he's one of the few husbands in the world who genuinely loves his wife. He didn't have the time to fool around on the side. His whole world was the clinic and home. I doubt he had half an hour a day unaccounted for." Her face sobered. "Until he disappeared."

"What about drugs?"

"What about them?" She tilted her head, causing her braid to fall over her shoulder. "You mean, like, did he write his own prescriptions too enthusiastically?"

"He wouldn't be the first doctor to wind up abusing."

She leaned back in her chair. "I don't think so. Like I said, he's a very healthy guy. The bike's out back in the carriage house for riding, the fridge is stocked with dark green cruciferous vegetables and low-fat dip, and he takes an aspirin every day. The only drug I've seen him use is Xanax. He has a bottle in his desk he dips into occasionally."

"Xanax. That's for . . . ?"

"Anxiety. I'm not saying it's not possible. All I can say is he's never appeared to be under the influence here at work."

"At home?"

"I've seen him drink too much at their annual Christmas party. That's about it." She stretched, cracking her back, and stood up.

"If you, as a medical professional, had a prescription-drug problem, how would you feed your habit? Can you get narcotics sent here?"

She shook her head. "We don't keep any controlled substances here at the clinic. It's just an invitation to get ripped off. If I were abusing, I'd write prescriptions for fake names and take them to as many different pharmacies as I could. Not here, in town, not where anyone would know me. I'd tell the pharmacist I was Jane Doe and get my goodies. And I'd make sure not to come back too soon or too often." She scooped up her clipboard. "Anything else? I hate to give you the bum's rush, but you saw what it's like out there."

Kevin bounced out of Rouse's office. "I got it, Chief." He held a letter out to Russ. It had been stamped on the back with a big red REC'D and dated March 17. He flipped it over, took just enough time to see it was addressed to the board of aldermen, and stuffed it into his jacket pocket. "Good work, Kevin."

The young officer glanced out the window. "Looks like you were right," he said. "It's started to rain. Will you be okay if I go get the car? I'll pull it forward by the entrance so you don't have to go so far."

Russ closed his eyes slowly and resisted the urge to break one of the crutches over the edge of the table. He was going to be one mean-tempered bastard when he got old and infirm, he could tell that already. "That's a great idea. Thanks."

Kevin said his good-byes to Laura and bobbed down the hallway. Russ bent down and retrieved his crutches.

"Here," she said, extending her hand. "Let me give you a good pull. It's a lot easier to get up that way." She smiled indulgently. "And I bet you won't let any of the guys at the police station do it for you."

He grunted. She tugged him upright and he drew the crutches in under his arms. "Okay, one last question. What do you think happened to Dr. Rouse?"

She rested the clipboard against her chest and folded her arms over it. "I think Debba Clow killed him."

"Why?"

"Because Al had the ability to fire up a person's temper, and Debba was a woman with a lot of temper to fire up. I couldn't imagine her going after him on purpose, but all alone out there, with him pushing her buttons?

Yeah, I can picture her bashing his head in and then dumping his body somewhere." She looked toward the hallway, where the patients were waiting. Her lively face was suddenly drained and tired. "What a waste. He was a fine physician." She glanced up at Russ. "He once told me the greatest compliment old Mrs. Ketchem ever paid him was when she told him no other doctor would ever love this clinic like he did. I suspect she was right."

CHAPTER 29

NOW

WEDNESDAY, MARCH 29

When the handicapped elevator dinged and Russ swung into the station hallway, he could hear some weird sounds coming from the squad room. He stumped down the hall and poked his head inside. Lyle MacAuley was on the phone, frowning and holding up one hand for quiet, while Kevin Flynn seemed to be doing an end-zone victory boogie.

"Uh-huh," he chanted. "Uh-huh. Uh-huh. Uh—whoops! Good morning, Chief." While he didn't exactly come to attention, the kid stood up straight and tugged his uniform blouse into position.

"What's up?" Russ asked. "Where is everybody?"

Kevin blinked. "It's after nine o'clock, Chief. Ed's on patrol and Noble took an accident call." Russ glanced up at the clock on the wall. The whole Linda-as-his-chauffeur-to-work thing was going to take some tweaking. It wasn't that she was unwilling. She just couldn't function without a morning cup of tea and a chance to put on her makeup. "We just got a call from the Farmers and Merchants Bank," Kevin continued. "Lyle's on with them now."

"Lyle's off with them," the man himself said, replacing the receiver in its cradle.

Russ pivoted to face his deputy chief. "What's the news?"

Lyle grinned. "Rouse's ATM card was used last night. At the ATM outside the Super Kmart in Fort Henry."

Yes. Russ clenched his fist, trapping the moment. "Was the video running?"

Lyle's grin grew even broader. "It was. They're sending a technician over to pull it even as we speak."

Kevin started his jive moves again, a skinny redheaded white boy channeling James Brown. "Uh-huh," he said. "Uh-huh."

"Thank you, Kevin." Russ stumped closer to Lyle's desk. "Where can we take a look?"

"At the downtown branch. That's where they run their security. They've got a computer set up that can enlarge the videos and make single-frame pictures. Just what we need."

"What are you waiting for? Let's go."

Kevin stopped in the middle of a joint-defying arm movement. "Hey. What about me? I'm supposed to be driving you."

"Tell you what, Kevin." Russ swung across the squad-room floor to Noble Entwhistle's desk. "I'll give you a chance to do some detective work." He balanced on his crutches and withdrew a sheaf of handwritten papers that had been shoved inside a phone book. "Noble started on the pharmacy project yesterday. He called every drugstore within a forty-five-minute drive, and he's drawn up a list here of places that have filled prescriptions written by Dr. Rouse." He handed the papers to Kevin. "I want you to get a photo of the doc from the file and hit the road. Flash it to everyone behind the counter: pharmacists, assistants, cashiers. See if Rouse was ever in there picking up stuff."

Kevin's eyes turned cartwheels at the prospect of running down information. "You want me to do the whole list?"

"Better split it up to leave something for Noble to do when he gets back. If he's still tied up after you've covered the first half, come on back and you can tackle the second."

As he and Lyle moved up the hall toward the elevator, Russ thought he heard the sounds again, coming from the squad room. *Uh-huh. Uh-huh.*

◆ ◆ ◆

The First Allegheny Farmers and Merchants bank had rechristened itself "AllBanc" a couple years ago, but only people from the city called it that. The grand old building on Main Street had suffered through an updating at the same time, with a glassed-in ATM replacing one of a pair of gracefully arched windows on either side of the front steps, and a brushed-steel nameplate not quite covering up the former name, chiseled out of New Hampshire granite 140 years before. The old front doors had been replaced, too, with automatically sliding bulletproof glass that made the entrance look like the outside of the Albany airport baggage claim. The whole effect was that of a dowager forced into hip-hop gear and Ray-Bans, suffering hideous embarrassment.

Russ ignored the wheelchair ramp at the side of the stairs and laboriously crutched his way up one step at a time.

"You're not impressing me, you know," Lyle said. "My definition of a fool is a man who works harder than he has to."

Russ loosened his grip on one crutch just enough to spare Lyle a finger. Lyle was still laughing when they passed through the smoked-glass doors into the bank.

A young woman in a tight skirt rose from a nearby desk when she caught sight of them. She trotted across the floor. "Deputy Chief MacAuley?" she said.

"That's me." Lyle smiled, showing many white teeth.

"Mr. Smith's expecting you." She glanced toward Russ and made a pouty face that Russ suspected had been well practiced in order for it to appear natural. "I guess we'd better take the elevator. Security's on the third floor."

"We could always send my friend here up while you and I walk," Lyle suggested. The young woman twinkled at him.

"Let's not keep Mr. Smith waiting, *Deputy* Chief." Russ swung over toward the elevator, a brass-doored relic that had mercifully missed out on modernization. He punched the call button.

"Aw, Dad. You never let me have any fun." Lyle winked at the girl. The elevator opened with a ping and they piled in, the door almost closing on Lyle and the girl because it took Russ too long to get himself and the crutches out of the way.

"I hate these things," he said under his breath as they rose to the third floor. Lyle shrugged.

"This way!" The young woman was first out of the elevator, which gave them a chance to admire exactly how tight her skirt was. She led them up the hall toward security, an unremarkable door with only a number to identify it. Lyle darted forward and opened it for her. She beamed at him. "Aren't you sweet? You remind me of my dad. He has these great old-fashioned manners, too."

Russ swung past Lyle into the office. "Thanks, old-timer."

He could make out only part of Lyle's rejoinder, and decided it was better to pretend he couldn't hear any of it.

The man who emerged from an inner room to greet then was tall, bald, and grim-faced. He had the rangy build of someone who had spent his whole life keeping in shape. "Hi," he said, thrusting out his hand. "John Smith, director of security."

Politeness kept Russ from checking out what Lyle made of the guy's name. *John Smith?* Instead, he shook Smith's hand. "Russ Van Alstyne, chief of police. I'm surprised we haven't met before."

"I'm pretty new here. I retired from my old job and we moved to these parts so my wife could be closer to her family. I signed on with AllBanc about eight months ago."

"Lyle MacAuley. We spoke on the phone." Lyle stepped forward and took Smith's hand. "You look too young to be retired. What was your former line of work?"

Smith looked at him. "I'd tell you, but then I'd have to kill you."

Russ waited for the punch-line grin. None came. "Okay," he said. "Can we take a look at this tape?"

"Right this way, gentlemen. Nicole, thank you. You're dismissed."

Lyle raised his bushy gray eyebrows at Russ, who shrugged. They followed Smith into a shadowy room of faceless metal file cabinets and a wide countertop workstation with three computers. One of them had what looked like a VCR player slaved to the CPU.

"I'm hoping to get the funding to convert the security cams to digital, but until then, we have to translate the actual tape into computer images." Smith rolled a chair in front of the augmented machine. "This enables us to lighten the images, get better resolution, blow things up—everything we need to better identify someone." He pointed to another wheeled work chair. "Chief, why don't you have a seat." He flicked on the monitor. "The ATM report indicated that the flagged card was used at nineteen-forty-seven hours."

Lyle caught Russ's eye and made a face.

"I've advanced the tape to nineteen-thirty. I'm putting it on fast forward until we get to the incident time." He opened a menu and clicked on a selection, and the monitor filled with a grainy black-and-white image of the floor, door, and part of the outer wall of the ATM kiosk. Numbers indicating the hour, minute, and second flickered by in the lower left-hand corner. As they watched, a woman with a toddler, an umbrella, and several large carrier bags entered, dropped the bags, folded the umbrella, took out cash, scolded the toddler, and left, all in the triple time of a Keystone Kop.

"You ever see any funny stuff on these?" Lyle asked.

Smith looked at him. "All the time."

The tape showed floor, partial wall, glass, edge of door. Russ watched the numbers hurtling toward 19:40. Then 19:42. Then 19:45.

"Slow it down!" He rolled closer to the screen.

Smith hit a key and the action slowed to normal speed. Someone entered the kiosk in a slicker and rain hat.

"That looks like a woman," Lyle said. "Look, she's got a purse."

"Yeah," Russ agreed. She was hefting two large Kmart bags. They watched as she put them down, dug through her purse, and after a search of two minutes, eighteen seconds, pulled out the ATM card. "Can't you get a better angle than this?" he asked Smith. "I can't see anything but her hat."

Smith hit another key and the action slowed further. "She'll have to reach up to punch in her PIN number. When she does, we'll get a better view."

He was right. As soon as she slid the card in, she tilted her head back to read the screen and they could see the face of—

"Shit!" Russ slammed his hand on the countertop. "That's his wife."

On the screen, Renee Rouse went on punching in the PIN number, selecting the amount of cash, and pulling sixty dollars from the machine.

"What is it you were looking for?" Smith asked.

Lyle opened his mouth, and Russ held up a hand to stop him before he said they could tell Smith, but then they'd have to kill him. "We've got a missing sixty-five-year-old doctor, disappeared twelve days ago. Search and rescue hasn't turned up any sign of him. I was hoping anyone found with his ATM card might be able to shed some light on where he is."

"Maybe his wife did him." Smith leaned back in his seat and folded his arms across his chest.

"I'll ask her when I see her," Russ said, pulling his crutches into position.

"When's that going to be?"

"As soon as we can get down to the car and get over to her place."

◆ ◆ ◆

Renee Rouse looked anguished. "I'm so, so sorry," she said, holding out the ATM card she had dug out of her handbag. "I didn't realize I had his. It was in the dish on my dresser, where I keep my change and things. I just grabbed it and stuck it in my bag."

Russ took the card. It had Allan Rouse's name along the bottom. "What about the PIN number?"

"We have the same one. Allan's birth month and year. It makes it easier."

Russ glanced at Lyle, then back to Mrs. Rouse. "Let me just go over this again," he said. "You and your husband have a joint account that you can access through his ATM card."

"That's right, that's where all the bills are paid from."

"And you have your own account, with your own ATM card, where you keep a smaller amount of money."

"Yes. Usually if I need cash I just write a little over at the supermarket. I was going to get cash back at the Kmart last night, but I forgot. That's why I used the card. I don't normally."

"Have you checked the balance in your account since your husband's been gone?"

"No. Usually Allan manages all that for me." She started to cry. "Oh, God, he's never coming home, is he? What am I going to do without him? What am I going to do?"

◆ ◆ ◆

Russ left a quick message with Clare's secretary, Lois, explaining he was going to be working and would have to take a rain check on their usual Wednesday lunch. It took a bit longer to extricate himself from Renee Rouse's living room. The doctor's wife whipsawed between begging for help, demanding police action, and crying. Russ guaranteed that he would check and see if anyone had withdrawn anything from her account, promised her that the Millers Kill Police Department was still treating this as a missing-persons case, and extracted her promise to call one of her friends to sit with her so she wouldn't be alone.

When he and Lyle were finally back in the car, Lyle had that vacant, dreamy look that meant he was thinking hard.

"How do you like Mrs. Rouse as a suspect?"

"Not much." Russ buckled his seat belt.

"Usually, the spouse is first call for the bad guy in these cases. We haven't even looked at her."

"We've confirmed that Renee Rouse placed numerous calls to friends from four o'clock onward, looking for her husband. Debba Clow was with Rouse between six and seven or seven-thirty the night he disappeared. We've got evidence that places him in her car. At eight-thirty, the wife is speaking with Harlene. At nine-thirty, Mark Durkee's already spotted Rouse's car, crashed into some trees off the road. How would you suggest we put Mrs. Rouse into this picture?"

"Maybe she was waiting in his car. Debba Clow never said she got a look inside."

"Okay, let's say she's sitting in the car, freezing her tail off while her husband chats about vaccinations with Clow. Clow drives off, leaving Mrs. Rouse with her husband."

"Who has a bashed-in head."

"What's she going to do with him? Even if she dumped him in the lake and crashed the car to cover her tracks, how does she get home in time to call Harlene looking for help?"

"She called on her cell phone."

Russ snorted. "Not out there."

"Maybe she and Clow are in on it together."

"Would you trust your neck to Debba Clow?"

"Maybe she hitchhiked out with someone."

Russ threw up his hands. "You're not going to give up, are you? Okay, look into it. See if she stands to inherit a bundle from insurance, if there's another man on the scene, the usual."

Lyle started the car. "I know it's a long shot. But there was something about the way she said she didn't know anything about the accounts. Creeped me out. My ex, if I took my checkbook out of my coat pocket, she knew about it."

"Yeah, I know what you mean. Linda handles most of our money." He stared out the window at the passing yards with their rapidly shrinking patches of ice and snow. A few more days up in the forties and it'd be gone. Unless they had an April storm, which wasn't out of the question.

"Do you know what the average date is for ice out on Stewart's Pond?" he asked Lyle.

"Third, fourth week in April, usually."

"You think there's patches of open water up there yet?"

"Sure. That's why everybody goes to Florida in March, you know. Because there's not enough ice for ice fishing, and there's not enough water for a boat."

"Let's get in touch with the staties' dive team, see if they're open for business yet."

Lyle glanced over at him. "What are you thinking?"

"I'm thinking that we're clutching at straws, with all this running around to pharmacies and trying to shoehorn his wife into the facts. I'm thinking it may be time to send someone down there, into Stewart's Pond. Because we need to find Rouse's body before all the evidence washes away."

CHAPTER 30

NOW

THURSDAY, MARCH 30

They had said the prayers together, and she had read Lauraine Johnson the Gospel and heard her confession. Now Clare spread the small linen square over the elderly woman's rolling bedside tray and arranged the round silver container and stoppered silver bottle on top. She unscrewed the pyx and removed the wafer, holding it up to Mrs. Johnson with both hands. "The body of our Lord Jesus Christ, which was given for thee, preserve thy body and soul unto everlasting life." On one of their first meetings, Mrs. Johnson had told her, a little embarrassed, that she was most comfortable with the old language from the 1928 prayer book. And why not? She had been in her sixties when the new prayer book became official. She tried to cup her hands to receive the host, but her body betrayed her, as it usually did these days, and she couldn't get them high enough.

"Let me." Clare leaned forward and placed the wafer on her tongue. "Take and eat this," she said, "in remembrance that Christ died for thee, and feed on him in thy heart by faith, with thanksgiving."

She said the offertory for the consecrated wine and held the bottle to Mrs. Johnson's lips. The old woman sank back onto her pillow, her eyes closed, while Clare folded the pyx and bottle into clean linen and replaced them in their small leather carrying case.

She laid a hand on Mrs. Johnson's forehead, pushing a weightless strand of silver hair back into place. "I don't think I need to tell you to go in peace, to love and serve the Lord."

Mrs. Johnson smiled, but did not open her eyes. "I'm going to do that soon enough, whether you tell me to or not."

"I need to do a shorter bedside service for you. This tires you all out. Last week your nurse chewed me out."

Mrs. Johnson looked at her. Her eyes were pale, as if too many days living had washed all their color away. "No. I love your visits." She lolled her head to one side. "You know what pleases me?" Clare shook her head. "That the last priest to tend to me on this earth is a woman." She let her eyes drift closed, and she smiled. "For most of my life, women couldn't serve on the vestry. Couldn't be in holy orders, couldn't sit in convention and vote with the men. I was in Philadelphia, you know, when the first eleven defied the bishops to be ordained. I was fifty-six years old." She opened her eyes again. "How old were you?"

"In 1974?" Clare smiled. "Nine."

"You're just a child yet." She managed to move her hand so that it fell on Clare's arm. Clare hadn't taken her alb off yet, and they both looked at the contrast between the ancient, ropy-veined hand and the fine white cloth. "I knew this," Mrs. Johnson breathed. Her eyes closed. "I knew we were good for more than ironing the altar cloths and holding bake sales."

When Clare slipped out of the room a few minutes later, the old woman was asleep. She had pulled her alb off and rolled it into a ball. It would mean wrinkles later, but she couldn't go flapping through the hospital corridors looking like a dean in a cathedral close. She didn't need to wear the long white gown when delivering the Eucharist, but the more things looked like a regular service, the more Mrs. Johnson liked it. The dying woman had precious few pleasures left in life. If it had been within Clare's power, she would have lined the walls with cut stone and set up a stained-glass window.

She stopped at the nurses' station. It was quiet in the early afternoon. Only the charge nurse, furiously typing her records into the computer, and a doctor buried in a file. "She's asleep," Clare told the charge nurse.

"Good," the nurse said. She looked up at Clare, her fingers still keystroking, as if they were more a part of the machine than of her body. "She needs to rest up for visiting hour tonight."

"I'll see you next week," Clare said. "Please call me if she wants me for anything."

The doctor straightened. "I thought I recognized your voice." He stepped forward. It took her a moment to place him; nondescript brown hair, a pleasant face, and the ubiquitous white jacket went a long way toward making him anonymous.

Then she remembered. "Dr. Stillman." She shifted her bundle under her arm and shook his hand. "How are you? What are you doing up here?"

"One of my older patients had a bad fall," he said. "Broke her hip." He gestured toward Clare's clericals. "Look at you. You can sure tell you're a minister now. You were a lot more casual when you brought your friend in. How's he doing?"

"I haven't seen him since then," she said. "He's been keeping pretty busy investigating Dr. Rouse's disappearance."

Dr. Stillman shook his head. "Bad business. You just don't expect something like that to happen in this area. Especially to a man as well respected as Allan Rouse. Lord only knows how they're going to staff the clinic with him gone."

"Not to sound like a Monty Python sketch, but he's not dead yet."

Dr. Stillman looked at her. "When people go missing in the Adirondacks for two weeks in winter, they don't walk out again." He gestured toward the elevator in the middle of the hall. "You headed out? I'll walk with you." He came around the work counter and fell into step beside her. "I've heard that there was a woman with him who was involved in his disappearance."

"There was a woman with him, but it's not what it sounds like. She was a former patient of his. Or rather, her children were. She'd been picketing the clinic. She thinks the preservative in their vaccinations caused her son's autism."

George Stillman's whole face opened up in understanding. "That woman. Oh, Lord, yes, she was over here at the hospital, too. Total nut job. What did she do, drag him out there to kill him?"

Clare looked at him, surprised. "I doubt it. He's the one who asked her to meet him. He wanted her to see the graves of some children who died of diphtheria in 1924."

Dr. Stillman stopped in front of the elevator and mashed the button. "Really? And the graves were around here? I wonder if they might have been my grandfather's patients. He lost quite a few to diphtheria in the early twenties. Couldn't persuade people to take the serum. They used to think gargling and nose sprays would get rid of it." He rolled his eyes.

"How do you know about it?"

He looked at her as if she were soft in the head. "Diphtheria? I studied it in med school."

"No, I mean about your grandfather. And his patients. Did he used to talk about them?"

Dr. Stillman shook his head. "He died in '48, before I was born. But he was a lifelong diarist. My dad kept every volume and passed them on to me." The elevator doors whooshed open and they stepped inside. "I've read them all at least twice. Incredible insight into life in the early years of the twentieth century and what it was like to be a country doctor. Someday I'm going to work them into a publishable form." He grinned. "Like when I'm retired."

Clare rested her balled-up alb and leather case against her hip. She tamped down the electrical surge that had flashed through her at the mention of the diaries. "Do you think I could take a look at them? The ones from 1924?"

The doors chimed and opened. Dr. Stillman gave her the soft-in-the-head look again. "Why?"

"It's complicated. Have you got a half hour?" They stepped out of the elevator into the first-floor admissions area. Before he could answer, she went on, "Short version is, the surviving child of that family is one of my congregation. And a hefty sum of her mother's money—the mother who lost the other four children to diphtheria—used to go to support the clinic and now is going to go to St. Alban's. I've been digging out bits and pieces of the Ketchems' family story ever since I learned we were going to be recipients of their money. If he was their physician, your grandfather's journals might be the only contemporary eyewitness account of what happened."

"That's the short version?"

"I told you it was complicated." She pressed her hand against her chest, not so subtly highlighting her clerical collar. "I promise I'll be very careful with them. I know how to work with old and valuable books." She had researched original sources occasionally in the seminary. Of course, that had been under the direct supervision of the rare-collections librarian, a man who had been known to turn the pages for seminarians whose skin-oil level he found fault with.

Dr. Stillman was waving his hand, demurring. "It's not that they're really old and valuable," he said.

"They are to you."

He looked at her. "Okay."

"Okay?"

"Okay, you can borrow them. The volumes you need." He glanced at his watch. "I've got another half hour before I'm done with rounds. How 'bout I meet you at my office after that? It's right next door, in Medical Building A."

"You keep them in your office?"

"I've got two teenagers and a back-to-the-nester in my house," he said, looking pained. "I keep everything I don't want torn apart in my office."

◆ ◆ ◆

Clare had time to swing over to St. Alban's, collect her messages, and get back to a few people before heading out to Dr. Stillman's office, Lois's admonition to "return that man's phone call!" ringing in her ears. Hugh Parteger had called again. Clare couldn't help but think that if he phoned her in the evening, from his apartment, instead of using the company line at his office, he'd be more likely to reach her.

Medical Buildings A, B, and C were as unique and graceful as their names promised. Large concrete shoeboxes two stories high, they housed most of the specialists who practiced at the Washington County Hospital. Stillman shared a receptionist and waiting room with three other doctors, and when Clare gave her name to the woman behind the glass divider, she was told to go right on in.

"You found me," Dr. Stillman said, rising from his desk.

"Well, you know. Medical Building A stands out. I hear it's the status address in town."

He laughed. "These places went up in the early sixties. I think it was one of those projects designed to wow the public with the creative uses of concrete." He stepped over to one of the bookcases lining three walls and ran his hand along a shelf of identical leather-bound books, untitled. "According to my grandfather, the land we're sitting on was the hospital farm in the thirties and forties. It supplied milk and fresh produce for the kitchens." He grinned. "The cafeteria would probably be a long sight better if they had kept it going."

"Are these the diaries?"

He pulled one off the shelf and handed it to her. AMSTERDAM STATIONERY SUPPLIES DIARY 1939 was stamped on the cover in gold. "They were freebies," Stillman said. "Grandfather got all his writing paper and ledgers and whatnot from them, and they threw in the diary every year as a thank-you."

"Like the old advertising calendars."

"Yes." He looked at the shelf again. "What years were you interested in?"

"Nineteen twenty-four. Probably ought to include 1923 as well." He removed two volumes and she swapped them for the 1939 diary. "And could I also look at 1930, too?" Maybe old Dr. Stillman had had something to say about Jonathon Ketchem's disappearance.

Stillman handed her a third book. "You know," she said, tucking them into the crook of her arm, "you should make some provision to leave these to the historical society. In case you don't get a chance to publish them."

"You're right," he said. "I shudder to think what might happen to them if my kids get their hands on them. My oldest is a so-called artist. She'd probably tear the pages out to use in one of her collages."

Clare thanked him and promised again to take good care of his grandfather's work. On her way back to St. Alban's for the five o'clock evening prayer, she dropped the three volumes at her house. She resisted the temptation to take a quick peek, knowing that if she did so, she'd wind up reading and probably be late for the service.

Evening prayer had a whopping seven attendees, but they were evidently as eager to get home as Clare, and after she concluded the service with a verse from Ephesians, they all scattered, and she was back in the rectory by dinnertime.

She figured that the rare-collections librarian would never have approved reading the diaries while scarfing down pasta, so she plunked her plate in front of the tube and ate with Jim Lehrer, who was never put off from discussing the day's events by the sight of her chewing rigatoni.

After she had washed up, she started a fire, stretched out on the sofa, and began reading.

Mar. 6th. V. Rainy & cold. Called to Mrs. B.G.'s house for delivery, got stuck in the mud as their creek had risen & had to walk the last mile. Mr. G. took his team & rescued my automobile. Mrs. G delivered of a boy, 6 lbs 5 oz at 6:00 pm, good color & sound lungs. Home early for supper—Hard rolls & sausages, chocolate cake.

Mar. 7th. Rainy & cold. Newspaper this morning filled with tales of flooding along the Sacandaga & the Hudson. I have observed much the same in my travels. Garaged the automobile & took the buggy today. In surgery: Saw Thomas F. for stitches, clean & debrided. Mrs. James McC. for removal of goiter, 12 oz & v. complete. Ralph Y., ag'd 4 for trench foot, powdered w/ alum & instructed Mrs. Y. to keep him out of water 1 week. Called to H. McAlistair's house, twins, ag'd 13.

Inflammation of throat, croupal cough, fever & difficulty breathing. Dx croup, Rx tincture of Aconite 1 tX20 minutes.

Mar. 8th. Clearing, cold. Called v. early to DeGroot house in the valley to see Jan DeG., ag'd 13. Sore throat & fever over the night, frequent urination & many bowel movements. Upon examination, white pseudomembrane. Dx diphtheria. Suggested hiring nurse, Rx gargle of potassium chlorate & saline drops. Lengthy talk w/ Mr. DeG., who resists idea of serum anti-toxin. V. disturbed to hear Mr. DeG. had several friends & neighbors to call Thursday, when his brother returned from Amsterdam. One family—McAlistairs. Strongly suggested he notify those attending the party of J's Dx. Promised to return to-morrow. Called again on MacAs, advised that catarrh may be diphtheria. Mrs. McA. more forward in her thinking & most eager to obtain serum for her twins. Returned to surgery, brought serum to McA. twins. Home v. late.

Mar. 9th. Clear & warming. Excellent sermon to-day by Dr. Lee on the evils of rum smuggling, which is much in the news for our area—compared those who "wink" the eye at it to the Citizens of Sodom who allowed vice to flourish. Dinner after w/ Mr. & Mrs. Collins, v. good crown roast & bread pudding. Called after on DeG. house, J. much worse, w/ foul-smelling white exudate & much coughing & sweating. Argued for using serum to Mr. DeG., who is much afraid of harming the boy w/ its use. Dx potassium chlorate as before, alternating w/ echinacea 1d/4 oz water. Called on McA. twins, breathing much better, throats continue v. inflamed. Rx gargle of potassium chlorate 1d, hydrastine 5 grains, water 4 oz.

Mar. 10th. Clear & cool, brisk winds. Roads still muddy & waterways overfull, so continued w/ buggy to-day. Much more secure in bad conditions, but I miss the speed of my automobile, as to-day had many calls. To Beermans' in the valley, neighbors of DeG., where Mrs. B. showing Sx of white diphtheria. Discussed use of serum. She was much concerned of vaccination-syphilis. I assured her all my anti-toxin was approved by the State & that each inoculation was sterile/ boiling needles, etc. After much debate she declined, feeling as an adult she was in less danger than a child. Rx potassium chlorate & echinacea gargle, w/ saline drops. Called on Jan DeG. Pseudomembrane sloughing off w/ much coughing, secretions. Throat v. sore, appetite nil. Rx steaming, nitrate of sanguinary 2x or 3x every hour, cold pack for throat. Called on McAs, twins showing much improvement. Rx continue palliative care for throats. Back to surgery, telephoned Dr. Whittinger in Ft. Henry, who confirmed four cases diphtheria under his care. We agreed to notify the State BOH & to request additional supplies of anti-toxin. Held surgery: McGeough boy sprained wrist. Mrs. S.H. (again!) whose many symptoms I trace to a lack of useful employment of her hours & an inattentive husband. Sent home w/ mild sedative. Mr. McFarland, with gastritis I suspect is inflamed by a habit of taking alcohol. Rx Aconite, 5 drops; Ipecac, 5 drops, into 4 oz water, 1t/hour. Advised on simple diet & no spirits. Home for supper—whitefish in sauce & sponge-cake.

Despite the unattractive recitations of secretions and foul smells, Dr. Stillman's ready list of meals and desserts set Clare's stomach rumbling. She put the diary down and went into the kitchen for something sweet. Since, unlike the doctor, she didn't have a wife at home cooking for her, all she could find was a tin of flaked coconut and a bag of chocolate chips. She ripped the bag open, tossed a handful into her mouth, and went back to the sofa.

March 11th. Clear and cold. Called on Mrs. B, Jan DeG., McA. twins. The latter show the only improvement, although I suspect J. will pass through the disease unharmed after he expectorates all exudate & hardened membrane. Kept Rx unchanged. Home for dinner. Told Ellen I was sending her & the children to her mother's house in Ft. Ann. While Charles & Elizabeth have been inoculated with the serum, I have no wish to put it to the test, & I fear there will be more cases of the diphtheria, not fewer. Put them on the 4:00 train. No surgical hours to-day. Telephoned Dr. Whittinger & Dr. McKernon to consult re: advising schools to close for the next few days. Dr. Whittinger volunteered to call the Superintendent with our concerns. At suppertime, was called to Mrs. Kenneth Clow's for her labor. As this was her eighth child, I scarcely had time to deliver her. Healthy, well-formed girl, 7 lbs 1 oz. I warned Mr. C. of the diphtheria & explained the danger of the contagion in a large family such as his.

March 12th. Clear & cold. Roads improved much so that I took out my automobile, which proved a mistake, as I was mistaken for a bootlegger traveling home from the Adamses, where I was called for at mid-night. Fearing the diphtheria I brought with me doses of the serum, & found two of the three girls ag'd 11 and 9 w/ poor color, imperfect respiration, occluded & throats & tonsils coated w/ brown exudate. Fever over 103 in both children. I explained the extreme gravity of their condition to the parents, & told them w/o the anti-toxin I would not expect the girls to live out the next 24 hrs. They consented. After inoculation, Rx aconite, 5 drops to 4 oz water and phytolacca, 15–20 drops to 4 oz Water. Also hydrochloric acid 20 to 2 oz simple syrup & 2 oz Water. Driving home I was much startled when confronted by armed men at Powell's Corners and ordered to stand out of my car. Police officer Harry McN. who knew me well as I have delivered all of his children, apologized at once they recognized me. Bootlegger activity is v. high w/ police on road as a result. Continued home where I slept late this morning. Breakfast Poached eggs and bacon and oatmeal.

Dr. Stillman's entries for March 12 and 13 were the shortest ones Clare had seen. They simply listed the current diphtheria patients and added two more, Maud Williamson, aged fifteen, and Roland Henke, aged eight. She tried to imagine how much time the doctor must have spent, driving around the countryside at, what, twenty-five miles an hour? And that was when he could use his car. Snow or mud or rain, he evidently went by horse-drawn buggy. No X rays, no penicillin, no anticoagulants or insulin or reliable blood transfusions. Did they even have aspirin back then? It seemed like a different world. And yet there were plenty of people around who had been born into that world. Mrs. Marshall. Mr. Madsen. Mrs. Johnson. Her own grandmother Fergusson had been fifteen when George Stillman wrote these entries. The same age as Maud Williamson.

March 14th. Light Rain & cold. Called on Mrs. B. Temp. above 102, breathing v. strained & sibilous. Dx bronchitis secondary to sloughing off of exudate into larynx. Rx Veratrum, 20–60 drops in 4 oz Water for fever; directed Mr. B. on use of steam and pounding her back to loosen secretions. Called on Jan DeG., improved, though v. weak. Impressed on Mrs. DeG. importance of complete rest as the toxin may have affected the muscles of his heart. Called on Adamses, where girls are much improved, temp. normal, throats v. sore but respiration eased. Mrs. A. v. emotional and wishing for some way to express gratitude; I asked her to tell her friends and neighbors the importance of timely inoculation. I have become convinced only a steady diet of personal testimony will lead many of my patients to accept the anti-toxin & other inoculants. Called on McA. twins, steady improvement, but warned mother of dangers of too early exertion. Called on Maud W. & Roland H., both unchanged, Rx unchanged. Spoke to Mr. W. and Mr. H. further on benefits of the serum. Mr. H. has heard stories that vaccination causes idiocy! It becomes hard to listen to such ignorance knowing science has the power to alleviate their children's distress. I am grateful Ellen and the children are gone away. No surgical hours, home early for supper, cold meat pie and chocolate pudding.

Mar. 15th. Clear and cold. Called around midnight by Jonathon Ketchem, of the valley, in great distress. Arriving before 2 am, to my great sorrow found two children had died. Sx as described by Mrs. K. diphtheria, in the boy the more malignant laryngeal form. Mary K. ag'd 2, gravely ill, lowered temp., palpitations, sibilous & inadequate respiration, extremities blue-tinged. Throat almost completely occluded by pseudomembrane. Mrs. K. reported the baby had been fighting hard for breath and seemed sleepy & eased now. It was my heavy duty to tell her the fatal termination was likely close. Peter K., ag'd 7, was post-acute stage, livid but clear throat, prostrate, weak & irregular pulse. I inoculated both children, though expect the baby will not survive the day. Explained the effects of the diphtheria toxin on the heart & warned Mr. & Mrs. K. of the dangers of exertion for Peter. Offered to reset Mr. K.'s fingers broken the day before in accident and set by himself. He refused tx. Not wishing me to sit for the death watch, I returned home & telephoned Mr. K.'s parents in Cossayuharie, who will join the Ks immediately. V. low in spirits & much discouraged by wastefulness since children might have been saved had I been called earlier this week. No appetite for breakfast and prayed the other households in my care will be Passed Over.

Clare shut the diary at that point. She felt as tired right then as George Stillman must have felt, hunched over a rolltop desk, writing carefully in his neat Palmer penmanship. She stacked the leather-bound books one atop the other on the coffee table. She closed the fireplace's glass screens and turned off each light one by one. On the stair landing, she paused for a moment, looking at the journals etched in the light of the dying fire. She went upstairs to bed. It took her a long time to fall asleep.

CHAPTER 31

NOW

FRIDAY, MARCH 31

Clare didn't tell Debba exactly why she wanted to see her when she
called after the seven o'clock Eucharist.

"Can we get together and talk? Today? I had an idea about the custody
case."

"Sure," Debba said. In the background, Clare could hear the sounds of
children shrieking and the watery grinding of a dishwasher. "Do you want
me to call Karen Burns and see if she can come, too?"

"No. Not yet." If she could use Dr. Stillman's journal to drive an emotional wedge between Debba and her antivaccination beliefs, maybe Kar-
en's cool logic could make the break clean by pointing out that vaccinating
Whitley would meet one of the major arguments in the ex-husband's
claim. But Clare was flying by instinct now, and her instinct was telling
her Karen would just get in the way. She flipped open her agenda. "I've
got a counseling session coming up and then a meeting with the church
musician. How about ten o'clock?"

"Okeydokey. See you then."

Clare reflected, as she was hanging up, that Debba was pretty upbeat
for a woman facing some serious questions by the police. But then again,
that was Debba. Upbeat and peaceable. Except when she wasn't.

◆ ◆ ◆

The purple buses were out. That was the first thing Clare saw as she
shifted into neutral and began rolling down the hill toward the Clow
house. Two figures—it looked like Debba and her mother, Lilly—were
hosing the behemoths down, and the kids were dancing around the spray,
leaping in and out of mud puddles. Clare coasted into the drive in front of
the house, inspiring Whitley to dash across the road from the barn, and
her mother, screeching, to run after her.

234

"Don't ever, ever run across the road!" Debba snatched the three-year-old up, squeezing her hard. "You didn't even look! You're going to get squashed flat as a pancake!"

Whitley wiggled out of her mother's grip and promptly lay down at Clare's feet in the gravel drive. "I'm a pancake," she announced.

Debba made a strangled noise of amusement and frustration.

"What's up?" Clare looked across the road, where Lilly Clow had put down her hose and was attacking the side of one bus with a soapy sponge. Skylar was walking around and around the barnyard, picking up rocks and dropping them into little hills. From the size of the piles, it looked as if he had been at the task for a long time.

"Those are for my mom's business, Hudson River Rafting. We're taking advantage of the nice weather to clean them off. They get dust and chaff and squirrel poop on 'em, wintering over in the barn." Debba had a bandanna tied over her kinky hair. She tugged it where it had slipped over her forehead. "You want to go in the kitchen and talk? I was going to get a cup of tea."

"Flip me, Mommy, flip me," Whitley said.

Clare opened her passenger door. Her parka was turning out to be too heavy, with the sun pouring out of the sky and the wind warm and southerly for the first time in memory. She tossed her coat into the front and took out Dr. Stillman's diary. "Tell you what." She handed the leather-bound book to Debba. "I'll flip the pancake here and take her back over to her grandmother. You read this."

Debba glanced at the imprint on the cover. "You want me to read a 1924 diary?"

"Not all of it. I stuck a bookmark into the section I want you to see. Go on in and have a cup of tea and then when you've read it, if you want to, we can talk about it."

Debba continued to look warily at the book, as if it were a gift-wrapped bomb, one that might go off in her hand, but one she didn't want to offend Clare by dropping.

Clare suddenly got it. "It's not a religious tract. I'm not trying to proselytize you."

Debba flushed. "It's not that I'm not a spiritual person," she said. "I'm just not into organized religion."

Clare bet Debba had several angel books and a copy of *The Celestine Prophecy.* "Don't worry. My religion's not all that organized itself." She stuck her hands in her pockets and hitched up her ankle-length skirt so she could crouch beside Whitley. "So what should I do with you, pancake?"

"Flip me!" Whitley stretched her arms wide. While Debba climbed the steps to the house, Clare rolled the child over on the gravel. Whitley made sizzling sounds.

"I think you're all cooked," Clare said. "I'm going to put you on the plate." She heaved the three-year-old off the drive and sat her on the hood of the Shelby. "Now I'm going to butter you." She pretended to smear something over Whitley's stomach. The girl giggled. "And pour syrup on you." She remembered her brothers' trick of lightly running their fingers through her hair, along her scalp, making it feel as if something slow and liquid was running down her head. She did it now to Whitley, who squealed and laughed and swatted at Clare's hands. "And now, since you're so big, I'm going to fold you up and see if your grandmother wants to share you with me."

She picked the girl up and crossed the road. Lilly Clow tossed her soapy sponge into a bucket. "Hey, Reverend Clare. Whatcha got there?"

"A pancake." Clare stood Whitley up on the muddy, hay-flecked ground. "Want some?"

Lilly lunged toward the girl's belly, making "yum-yum" noises. Whitley darted away, shrieking. "Grab your mom's hose and rinse off these bubbles for me," Lilly yelled after her.

"So you run Hudson River Rafting," Clare said. "I saw your buses go by last summer when I was visiting Margy Van Alstyne. She lives right by where Old Route 100 crosses the Hudson."

"I know Margy. She does good work for the environment." Lilly flipped one of her long gray braids over her shoulder. "When you're in the Adirondack tourism business, you owe a debt to folks like her. Too much development can wind up scaring visitors away." She grinned, her teeth white and fine in her tanned, lined face. "Of course, if it hadn't been for developers putting a bunch of dams on the wild waters in the first place, we wouldn't have the rafting business we do today. So I guess I like development so long as it happened a good long time ago."

There was a splatter of water, and Clare and Lilly jumped aside. Whitley, heavy-duty black hose clutched in her hands, sprayed at the side of the bus, rinsing off the soap, the windows, the tires, and, occasionally, the top of the bus. Skylar ignored her, steadily piling small stones in one hand

and then dropping them into puddles. "Isn't it a little early to be getting your things ready?" Clare asked.

Lilly shook her head. "The season starts in April. If it weren't so damn cold, we could take the punters out on the rivers next week. Even before the dams start releasing, there's some amazing water out there."

"What happens when the dams release?"

"Woo-he!" Lilly raised her hands and dropped them, raised and dropped them, like a person sketching a roller-coaster ride. "Class-four and -five rapids. Very challenging. There are places along the Sacandaga where I wouldn't make a run in April with a raft full of expert guides." She grinned. "I might have done it once, when I was younger, but now I gotta make sure I'm around to see my grandkids grow up. Hey, baby, stay away from that road, or you're going to have to have a time-out."

Whitley had dropped the hose and was inching toward the country road.

"Look!" Her grandmother strode forward and picked her up. "Here comes a car now, silly girl. No going on the road without a grown-up." She singsonged the last sentence, as if she had said it so many times it was mere rote by now.

The car was slowing down, perhaps responding to the sight of the little girl headed for the road. The Clows' front door banged, and Debba rattled down the porch stairs, the leather-bound diary in one hand. She crunched down the gravel drive. She looked at Clare, opened her mouth as if to say something, then addressed her mother, who was still holding Whitley in her arms. "Is she being unsafe again?" Debba paused at the edge of the road to let the car pass, but it slowed even further, then rolled to a stop between the house and the barn. Not pulling over, just stopped. In the road.

The weirdness of it made the back of Clare's neck prickle. Lilly glanced at her, glanced back at the car, shifted her granddaughter to her hip.

The driver was a woman, but hard to make out from their side of the road, with the morning sun bouncing straight off the driver's-side window. Then the door swung open and Renee Rouse stepped out, as impeccable as the last time Clare had seen her, her cashmere sweater and perfectly draped pants looking so out of place compared to the Clows' water-stained jeans and Wellies that for a moment, the gun she had in her hand seemed just another discrepancy, like the gold bangle and the leather pumps.

"Ho-ly Christ," Lilly said.

Renee stepped away from the car and swung the gun toward Debba, stiff armed, her movements jerky. "Where is my husband?" she said.

Clare could see it better now, a big .38, the sort of gun people bought when they went into a store and said, "Gimme something with stopping power." From the way she was holding it, Clare doubted Renee had ever done anything more with it than tell her husband to keep it locked up out of sight. She might not even have taken the safety off.

Debba's hands went up to waist height, as if she didn't know if she was supposed to raise them or not. "I don't know."

Renee took another step toward her. "You did something to him out there. I want to know what you did. I want to know where my husband is!" Her voice broke on the last word.

Lilly, her boots planted in the mud and her arms whipcorded around Whitley, swayed back and forth, as if torn between going to her daughter or retreating with her granddaughter. Skylar ambled within arm's reach, pebbles in hand, and his grandmother snagged him one-handed and drew him to her side.

"Mrs. Rouse." Clare was surprised at how calm she sounded, considering her heart was jackhammering in her chest and a tide of adrenaline was tripping every nerve ending she had.

Renee twisted toward her, keeping the gun pointed in Debba's direction. Clare could see her face now, pale white and blotchy red, her eyes swollen and stained with too much crying. Clare lifted her arms in the same welcoming gesture she used in church, unhurried, unthreatening. "I know your heart's breaking right now," she said, "but this isn't right. Look around you. There are children here. Are you really going to shoot a mother in front of her children?"

Renee looked at Whitley, who had stopped squirming on Lilly's hip and was now clinging to her grandmother, whimpering. Then the doctor's wife turned back to Debba. "If I have to," she said, her voice flat.

O-kay. That was the wrong question. How did she get involved in these things? She didn't know anything about negotiations. "Let Lilly take the children into the house," she said. "Then Debba and you and I can talk about this."

"No." She waved the gun toward Debba. "You don't think I'd do it. But I will. I want to know what you did with Allan!"

"I didn't do anything with him!" Debba shouted. Whitley started to cry, and Skylar, who had been staring at his mother, twisted out of his grandmother's hold and pressed himself to the purple bus.

Whang! The boy beat his hands against the bus. *Whang! Whang!* The hollow metallic sounds were like a whale assaulting a submarine.

"What is that?" Renee said, her head swiveling between Skylar and Debba. "What's he doing? What's wrong with him?"

"He's autistic, thanks to your husband!"

If Clare had had a gun, she would have shot Debba herself. Renee swung the gun straight at Debba's face. "I ought to shoot you right now, you witch!" Debba squawked and ducked, covering her head with her arms. Renee pivoted, and the gun was now pointed at Whitley. "Or maybe it should be her first!"

Lilly cried out and turned, moving forward, one step, two, before the gun went off with a sound that filled up the valley like God's handclap.

"Stop right there!" Renee ordered.

Clare clenched her teeth, forcing herself not to lunge forward. She realized the doctor's wife had shot high. Lilly stood in the barnyard, trembling, holding Whitley to her front so that her body was between her granddaughter and the gun. The echo of the shot rolled off. Debba was sobbing now, still bent over, her son beating away the outside world; *Whang! Whang! Whang!*

Clare considered the distance between herself and Mrs. Rouse. If she rushed fast enough and hard enough, she might be able to knock the older woman over even with a bullet in her. Then Debba could get the gun. If she could keep it together. If she even thought of it. Clare wasn't afraid. She was glad she wasn't afraid. Just worried that Debba wouldn't understand what to do, and that she'd die for nothing.

Hardball Wright stood behind her, draped his memory arms around her shoulders, and gave her a shake. *There's a better way. Misdirect. Feint. Delay. Reinforcements.*

And she saw it, the whole thing laid out, what she had to do.

There's hope for you yet, Fergusson. Hardball laughed in her ear.

"Mrs. Rouse," she said, this time letting her nerves show in her voice. "Let me go. I don't have anything to do with this. Please. Just let me go."

Debba and Lilly both looked at her in disbelief.

"Please," Clare said.

"You'll just call 911," Renee said.

"No. I swear to you, before God, on my priestly vows, I won't call 911."

"Clare!" Debba's voice was outraged. Renee Rouse glanced at her. Clare could have kissed her.

"Okay," the doctor's wife said. "You may go."

The walk across the road and up the gravel drive was one of the longest in her life. As soon as she slid into the Shelby, she yanked her bag off the floor and dumped its contents on the seat next to her. There it was. Her cell phone.

"Roll down your windows!" Renee had taken several steps closer to the drive. "I want you to roll down your windows so I can see you're not calling anyone."

People didn't even trust priests anymore. What was the world coming to? She leaned over and cranked down the passenger window with one hand, hitting the last-call-list button on her phone with the other. She scrolled down to Russ's cell phone number while unrolling her own window. She pressed the call button, dropped the phone in her lap, and shifted her car from park to first and back to park again. Then she turned the key and laid on the gas.

The screeching, coughing noise of the engine covered up the sound of Russ, saying "Hello?" She turned the key again. The car sounded as if it were dying. "Hello?" The tinny, unamplified voice sounded annoyed.

She leaned over toward the passenger window, making sure the phone's mike was unobstructed. "Mrs. Rouse," she shouted. "There's something wrong with my car! It won't start!"

Mrs. Rouse stood stock-still at that. Clare had pegged her as the sort of woman for whom any car emergency was man's business. And there were no men around to help out here.

The small voice in her lap was swearing now. Clare went on. "I want to come back out of the car, but I'm afraid you'll shoot me! Please lower your gun!"

Russ's voice had fallen silent. She risked a glance down. The call was still in session. He was listening.

"I haven't called 911," she yelled to Mrs. Rouse. "I kept my promise. Can I get out of the car and go stand by Debba?"

"Clare, tell me where you are." Russ's small voice was hushed, as if he was afraid of being overheard.

"Or if you want, I could go into the Clows' house!"

From her lap, she heard Russ telling someone to drive toward Powell's Corners.

Renee finally came to a decision. "Come back out here," she said. "Slowly. I don't want to see anything in your hands."

"I won't have anything in my hands. Please don't shoot me."

"Clare, can you hide your phone? Snap two times for yes."

She snapped twice.

"Keep the line open. I'm muting from my end, so no one will hear me saying anything. But I'll hear you. This is Renee Rouse? With a gun?"

She snapped twice.

"Jesus Christ," he said.

"What's keeping you?" Renee yelled. "I told you to get out of the car and get over here!"

Clare slipped the phone into one of her skirt pockets and opened the door. She walked slowly and carefully toward Debba. "Mrs. Rouse, you were going to let me go. Please, I beg you, let Debba's mother and two children go."

"I already told you no. That's far enough." She waved the gun at Clare, who stopped a few feet away from Debba. From across the roof of Mrs. Rouse's car, she could see Lilly's back, with Whitley's skinny legs wrapped around her waist. One of the girl's rain boots had fallen off. Renee's attention was on Clare, and Lilly was moving, step by step, closer toward her grandson. Debba saw her, too, and in a moment, Renee was going to realize what was happening.

Clare began to walk toward the doctor's wife. Renee frowned and trained the gun more decidedly on Clare. "Stop right there," she said. Clare took another step. "I said stop!"

Clare raised her arms dramatically. "Jesus!" she said. Across the barnyard, Lilly was almost to Skylar. Lord only knew what sort of sound the kids might make when their grandmother took off running. She'd better turn up the volume. "Jesus, call down Your healing power on these Your servants!" she bawled.

"Stop that," Renee said. Debba stopped staring at her mother and turned to look at Clare.

"Bring down the power of the Almighty and *save* these poor sinners!" She could do this. Her great-grandfather Avery had been a dirt-road preacher in Alabama a hundred years ago. "It is *sin* that fills our hearts with wrath and fear and pain! It is *sin* that separates us from our loved ones! It is *sin* that makes us turn our backs on Your loving aid!"

"Stop it! Stop it right now!" Renee advanced on Clare, her arm shaking.

Clare dropped to her knees, ignoring the gravel's bite. "Pray with me, Sister Rouse! Pray with me, Sister Clow!" She launched into the loudest hymn she knew. " 'Wha-at a friend we have in Je-sus! All our sins and grief to bear!' "

The car blocked her view of Lilly and the children, but she knew when it happened. Debba let out a strangled cry of fear and relief, and Renee spun around. She screeched, an inarticulate sound of rage, and turned on Debba and Clare. "Get up!" she shouted. "Get up!"

Clare shut up and climbed to her feet. She didn't see Lilly or the children. "Where are they?" she asked Debba.

"Behind the bus." Debba started to weep. "Behind the bus." She glared at Renee. "Shoot me if you want. You can't hurt my children now."

"Where is my husband?" Renee Rouse's voice dropped so that it was almost a whisper. She would do it, Clare thought. She would kill Debba. They had to tell her something. Anything. Keep her talking.

"I don't know," Debba said through her tears. "I told the police everything I knew. I told them. I don't know anything else."

Mrs. Rouse shook her head. "Turn around." Debba stared at her. "Turn around!" Debba did as she was told. Renee jammed the gun against the back of Debba's skull. "I'll give you one more chance. I don't care what happens to me. I won't go on without my husband."

Oh, holy God. This was going to be a murder-suicide. "Debba," Clare said.

Debba was crying harder now, her voice muffled and wet.

"Debba," Clare said. "You're going to have to tell her the truth."

Renee stared at her. "You know what happened?"

"I've been acting as Debba's spiritual adviser," she said. "She's made her confession to me."

"What?" Mrs. Rouse's eye lit up. "Tell me!"

What, indeed. If they said the doctor was still alive, Mrs. Rouse would demand that Debba take her to him. And going someplace with Mrs. Rouse would be a death sentence. They had to stay out of the car, out of the house, away from anyplace she could hole up in when the cops got here. They had to be right out here in the open when Russ arrived. What could they tell her? What?

"Go ahead, Debba," Clare said. "It's all right. Tell her about you and the doctor having an affair."

"What?"

"They were having an affair and Dr. Rouse wanted her to run away with him. So he took off first." *Why?* "So no one would know."

Debba, bless her heart, picked up the ball and ran with it. "Except I changed my mind. I decided to break it off. I couldn't uproot my kids."

Mrs. Rouse's eyes bugged out. "You're saying my husband had an affair with you? You slept with my husband?"

They heard the noise of an engine. A red pickup truck crested the hill, followed by a police car. Then another. No lights, no sirens, but they swooped down the hill almost faster than the eye could follow, faster than the time it took to decide what to do, faster than the heartbeats between waiting and hoping. Clare looked at the barrel of the gun, pressed into Debba's head, and she looked at Mrs. Rouse.

"Your husband does not want you to throw your life away," she said, knowing, of all the things she had said this horrible morning, it was the most true.

And then Russ's pickup and the squad cars were whipsawing over the yard and onto the drive, spinning up gravel and clots of mud and dead grass, and the doors were open and men tumbled out and there were one two three four five guns all pointed toward Mrs. Rouse. Debba buried her face in her hands and fell silent.

Renee Rouse looked at the officers, at Clare, at the sky, and she lowered her gun and let it drop to the ground.

Noble Entwhistle was the first to her, drawing her away, pulling her hands behind her back, reciting her Miranda rights.

Debba touched the back of her head, feeling the absence of the gun, and turned toward Clare. She opened and closed her mouth. "How?" she finally said.

Clare fished her phone out of her pocket. "What a friend we have in cell phones," she sang softly.

Debba started to laugh wetly, then jerked away as her mother and kids emerged from behind the bus. She ran blindly across the road, weeping and laughing, and crashed into her family.

Clare felt a hand on her shoulder and turned around.

"Are you all right?" Russ was looking at her. That was all, just his hand on her shoulder and his eyes. For a moment, she wanted to lean into him and let him hold her. Instead, she propped a smile on her face.

"It wasn't me with a gun to her head."

"Oh."

"What did you think of my preaching?"

He smiled. "Pretty good for an Episcopalian. Kevin Flynn was listening, too. I think he had a conversion experience on the way over here." He jiggled her shoulder, a small remonstrance. "What the hell were you thinking of?"

"Lilly Clow was trying to get the children out of sight. Mrs. Rouse got distracted when I was in the car, but when I got out, I was afraid she'd look back and stop Lilly. I figured if I acted strange but unthreatening, she'd keep her eyes on me for a few more seconds."

He glanced over to where Officer Entwhistle was guiding Mrs. Rouse into the back of the squad car. "I should have done something to stop this. Had someone with her. She really fell apart when Lyle and I spoke to her Wednesday."

"Do you honestly think anyone in Millers Kill could have foreseen she'd go around the bend?" She shook her head. "I guess this gives new meaning to the phrase 'crazy in love.'"

"It's not love. It's dependence. He was the oak, she was the vine, all that sort of garbage." He glanced down at the crutches he was balanced on. "You take away someone's crutch and what happens? They fall down."

"Poor lady." Clare watched as Officer Entwhistle closed the car door behind Mrs. Rouse. "She must have been building up to this every day since her husband disappeared."

"I don't think so," Russ said. His voice, dark and heavy, made her look at him. "I think I'm the one who tipped her over. Up until this morning, she was still hoping we were going to find her husband alive. All this"— the sweep of his arm took in the barnyard, the Clows huddled together talking with one of the officers, Renee sitting in the squad car—"all this is just a massive case of denial."

"What happened this morning?"

"I shouldn't have just told her—I should have prepped her more. But I was afraid she'd hear about it on the news first."

"What?"

"The divers started searching Stewart's Pond yesterday. This morning, I got the call. They found human remains."

CHAPTER 32

NOW

W e were on our way over there when I got your stealth call," Russ said. "Emil Dvorak should already be there." The county medical examiner. So Allan Rouse really was dead. Russ glanced across the street, to where Kevin Flynn and Lyle MacAuley were questioning the Clows. "As soon as Kevin's finished up, I'm headed for Stewart's Pond."

"I'll take you," Clare said.

Russ's mouth twitched. "Oh, you will, will you?"

She looked at the outline of Mrs. Rouse in the car. Clare sighed. "I suppose I ought to go sit with Mrs. Rouse and see if I can help her in any way."

"No," he said, "I don't suppose you ought to do that." When she looked sharply at him, he said, "Let her simmer down, Clare. I want her in the right state of mind when Lyle interrogates her."

"What's going to happen to her?"

He leaned forward into his crutches. "Pointing a gun at people and threatening them is a felony. We in the law enforcement field frown upon it."

"Oh, for heaven's sakes. You know what I mean. She's no criminal. She just went over the edge because of what happened to her husband."

He lifted his chin toward where the Clows stood, Debba rocking Skylar, Whitley hugging her grandmother tight. "What would you have said about her if she had hurt one of those kids, Clare?"

She looked down. The tips of his crutches were sinking into the wet soil, crushing the withered grass. Her own boots were splattered with mud drying into pale dirty streaks.

"Right," he said.

"I should see if there's anything I can do for them."

"Stop trying to help people for five minutes. What were you doing here, anyway?"

"Remember Dr. Stillman, who set your leg? The one who was the third-generation doctor?" He nodded. "He loaned me some of his grandfather's personal journals. There's all this stuff about the diphtheria outbreak in 1924, including an entry about the Ketchem children dying. I wanted Debba to read it. To get another perspective on vaccinations." She stuffed her hands into her skirt pockets. "Same thing that Allan Rouse was trying to do, I guess. I thought maybe words would have a bigger effect than the old tombstones." She looked at him looking at her. "What?"

"Nothin'," he said, his mouth crooked. A movement across the road caught his eye. "Let's get Kevin over here to take your statement. Kevin!"

She followed Russ back to his pickup, and she leaned against the bed giving her statement to Officer Flynn while his chief half sat, half stood against the passenger seat, resting his leg.

When she retrieved Dr. Stillman's journal from Debba, she gave her a quick, fierce hug and said, "We'll talk about this later, right?" Debba nodded, her lashes still wet with tears, Skylar still rocking and rocking in her arms. Clare dropped her voice, mock-confidential. "And I promise I won't tell anyone about your torrid affair with Dr. Rouse."

Debba gasped, blinked, and then started to laugh. She laughed and laughed until Lyle MacAuley and her mother both stared. She laughed until Skylar, serious faced, reached up and touched her cheek. "Funny Mama," he said. "Funny."

"What was that all about?" Russ asked her as she placed Dr. Stillman's diary in the front seat of her car.

"Laughing in the face of adversity," she said. She chucked the car door shut. "So, am I going to take you up to Stewart's Pond, or not?" Ignoring the voice of her grandmother, who was saying, *Nice girls don't extend invitations, they accept them.* Ignoring the voice of MSgt. Ashley "Hardball" Wright, who was reminding her, *A smart soldier does not deliberately put himself in harm's way.* A giddy fearlessness was fizzing through her veins, and at that moment she was perfectly willing to do something that would probably turn out to be a big mistake.

"Don't you have anything better to do?"

"Yes, which is why we need to get moving right now."

He glanced over at Kevin, who was dragging a ladder out of the barn. She couldn't figure out what he and Deputy Chief MacAuley were doing until she saw the jackknife and evidence bag in Lyle's hand. Apparently Mrs. Rouse's shot had gone into the barn's clapboard front. "Kevin," Russ shouted. The young officer stopped. "Reverend Fergusson is going to take me up to Stewart's Pond so I can catch up with the M.E. You drive her car up there and meet me as soon as you guys are done."

Kevin nodded. Lyle MacAuley gave them a long look before turning back to the ladder.

"Hope you don't mind driving my truck," Russ said, "because there's no way I'm going to try to wedge myself into that little skateboard of yours."

They jounced out of the Clows' drive, Clare climbing the gears as they drove up out of the valley until they were flying along a good fifteen miles an hour above the speed limit.

"Hello," Russ said. "Don't make me give you a ticket in my own truck."

"You can't," she said. "You don't have the little ticket book."

"Damn." He flipped open his glove compartment. "I knew there was something I forgot."

She laughed.

"Ah," he said. "I see my mistake now."

"What?"

"I thought I was getting into the truck with the Reverend Clare Fergusson. But no, it's actually Captain Fergusson, the terror of Fort Rucker."

She grinned at him. "It feels like that, yeah. Like I could get this machine airborne if I just hit . . ."

"Escape velocity?"

"Yeah."

He leaned back into his seat in a kind of studied nonchalance. "It's amazing how weightless you can feel once a gun's not pointed to your head anymore."

She laughed.

"You are, without a doubt, the damndest priest I've ever met."

"I worry about that." She slowed as they approached an intersection. "I'm not so sure I'm really cut out for parish life. Doing good is one thing. Being good is a lot harder."

"What would you be doing if you weren't rector of St. Alban's?" There was a tone to his voice she couldn't name, but she couldn't spare a glance at him as she swung onto Route 9.

"I don't know. I could re-up as a chaplain, but I think I'm too old for the army now. No, not too old. Too . . ." she thought about it. "I've lost a lot of my ability to fit in and follow orders."

He laughed. "I find it hard to imagine you ever had much of that ability."

"There ya go." She shifted up. "I'd probably go for some sort of missionary work. Feed the hungry, clothe the naked, that sort of thing. Doing something to ease somebody else's life—that's always seemed like the point, to me."

"What about flying? You know, quitting the priesthood entirely. There have to be a lot of opportunities for someone with your experience."

She laughed. "You can't quit the priesthood. I mean, yeah, you can not work as a priest. You can get kicked out of your bishop's diocese. But ordination is forever. Like baptism. You can't take it back." She glanced across the cab at him. "How about you?"

"How about me, what?"

"What would you be doing if you weren't nailing down that chair at the police station?"

He took his glasses off and fished a tissue out of his pocket. "When I retired from the army, I had a couple job offers to manage private security firms."

"I find it hard to imagine you running a rent-a-cop shop."

"Me, too." He cleaned his glasses, balled up the tissue. She glanced over again and found he was looking at her. "This is what I would be doing. This job. This is where I'm supposed to be."

She turned onto Old Route 100. "This way'll get us there, won't it?"

"It sure will."

They drove on in silence for a few minutes. "I think that's the real difference between us," she finally said. "You know you're in the right place. Doing the right thing. With the right person." He looked away from her. "I don't have that certainty. I thought my call would make me certain. But it hasn't."

"I've got fourteen years on you," he said, still looking out the window. "I've had a lot more time to figure things out." He pointed. "Don't miss the county road up there."

She slowed down and kept the speed moderate as she drove up to the reservoir. The road twisted and rolled, up and down.

"There." He pointed to a wide, cleared track through the trees. It was a good half mile before the site of the accident. "That's a boat put-in. That's where the diving team's working from."

She muscled the pickup down the trail, crunching over the last of the icy, hard-packed snow, the tires squelching and sucking through the water-saturated ground. The trees opened up to a clearing the size of a small parking lot, crowded with an ambulance, a state police dive truck, a trooper's squad car, and two unmarkeds. She could see three men, one in uniform and one braced with a walking cane, gathered around some sort of aluminum dock. She parked as close to them as she could, eyeing the heavy gray clouds that were collecting across the sky. The walk would be hard enough on Russ's leg without making him hike through rain. "Sit right there," she said, killing the engine. "Let me help you down."

"I can do it myself."

"I'm sure you can. But if your crutches get stuck in the mud and you pitch face forward while getting out, you're going to lose some of that cool law enforcement mystique."

He grunted when she opened his door, but he handed her his crutches and braced his hand on her shoulder while he lowered himself out of the truck cab. She returned the crutches when he was on the ground. "Thanks," he said. He caught her arm before she could move away. "That certainty thing," he said.

"What?"

"I'm not. Certain. About lots of things. I just know where I belong."

They walked down to where the men were standing, Clare shortening her usual stride so as not to outpace Russ. The man with the cane turned as they approached. He was short and squared off, his cropped graying hair almost the same shade as his expensive wool coat, and he might have been dapper if it weren't for the ropy white scar that split his forehead from eyebrow to hairline. "Reverend Clare," he said. "What are you doing here?"

"Hi, Dr. Dvorak." She hugged him. "I'm delivering Chief Van Alstyne."

Russ leaned on one crutch and shook hands with the medical examiner. "Hey, Emil. Anything yet from the dive team?"

The uniformed man had turned around as well. "Nothing yet. But I expect we'll hear from them soon. They're maxing out their time for this water temperature."

"Bob." Russ nodded.

"Russ."

"Still haven't made the BCI, I see."

"I'll get there." Bob's eyes flickered toward Clare. Russ followed his glance.

"Have you met Reverend Clare Fergusson?" he said. "She's the rector of St. Alban's in town. Clare, this is Sergeant Robert Mongue. He's with the state police."

Clare grinned at him. "Your uniform was the tip-off." He was as tall as Russ, but thinner, and his hair had long ago fled south. "Are you part of the dive team, Sergeant Mongue?"

"Nope. But they're assigned to our troop, so when they deploy, it becomes part of an NYSP investigation."

"Of course," Russ said pleasantly, "it's in our jurisdiction."

Sergeant Mongue nodded. "Absolutely. It's been two weeks, hasn't it? Tough, not developing any leads in all that time."

"Well, you know, when you take the time to actually investigate, as opposed to just picking a solution out of a hat . . ."

Clare thought she saw Sergeant Mongue's nostrils flare. He glanced down at Russ's cast. "I was sorry to hear about your leg. I heard you tripped and fell on your ass?"

Two pink spots stained Russ's cheeks. "It was an accident at a crime scene."

"Have you ever thought about establishing some minimum physical requirements for your department? You know, staying physically fit plays a major part in reducing accidents."

"I think the normal activity involved in community policing gives my men plenty of exercise. It's not like they spend all day sitting in a car with a speed gun."

"Do you hear something?" Clare said, happy to jump on any excuse to stop the pissing contest. The diesel-pumped roar of a boat motor echoed across the ice and water. They all turned toward the reservoir.

The boat swung around the edge of the shoreline. It was low and wide and traveling slowly to give the ice-crusted water plenty of time to ease around the prow. Clare could see three figures, bulky and anonymous in orange dive gear, sitting aft. Another two people, bundled against the cold, were in the cockpit.

"How do the divers manage in this kind of weather?" Clare said. "That water's still mostly covered in ice."

"They're wearing dry suits and neoprene liners," Sergeant Mongue told her. "They're probably more comfortable than we are right now. The real trick in extreme weather is keeping the tender and the pilot warm."

The boat steered toward the aluminum dock, and Mongue excused himself to step out onto the floating platform.

Russ's eyes narrowed. "The real trick in extreme weather.'" He parroted Mongue's voice very well. "Like he knows."

"What's with you two?" Clare pitched her voice low. "I thought I was going to pass out from the testosterone fumes."

He laughed. "Just a little intramural rivalry."

The boat slid into position next to the dock, and the tender—at least that's who Clare assumed it was, since the woman neither piloted nor dove—tossed a line to Mongue. They tied the boat into place and the divers stood up, lifting a webbed stretcher, and Clare had so steeled herself for the sight of Allan Rouse, pale and cold and waxy, that it took her a moment to process what lay on the stretcher.

"That's a skeleton," Russ said.

Dr. Dvorak glanced at him. "Very good." He turned to the divers, clambering over the side of the boat while balancing the remains. "Be careful."

The one who wasn't toting a skeleton removed her suit hood and climbed over the boat's bow. "Are you the M.E.?" she said.

Dr. Dvorak was beckoning the two divers closer. "Yes," he said, his eyes fixed on the remains. "Can you stop here for a moment?" he said when they reached his side. The remains were loosely wrapped in a fine net, and Clare could see that although the divers had been meticulous about keeping the pieces together, most of the bones were no longer connected to one another. Dr. Dvorak bent over the skeleton, examining it closely, touching it here and there with a single finger. The bones were long and brown, as if they had been steeped in tea for a decade or more. He straightened. "I think I can tell you with absolute confidence this is not Allan Rouse," he said to Russ.

"Ya think?" Russ glared at the bones as if they had been laid on the stretcher for the sole purpose of frustrating his investigation. "Who the hell is it?"

"Whoever it is, it . . ." Dvorak drew a thoughtful finger across the skeleton's pelvis, and another along the length of its thighbone. "He," he said, more emphatically, "has been in there for a long time."

The woman diver drew up to the stretcher, Bob Mongue close behind her. "We almost didn't spot it," she said. She had short, dark curls plastered against her scalp, and a cool, appraising look not unlike Dr. Dvorak's. Clare figured you'd have to be pretty unflappable to go diving through muck or dark water looking for dead people. "It was the car we noticed first."

The medical examiner went around to the other side of the stretcher, peering closely at the skull and neck bones. "Very well preserved," he said to himself.

"What car?" Russ said. He looked toward Bob Mongue. "You remember any missing person and car?"

The dark-haired diver shook her head. "This wasn't a car either of you guys would ever have heard about. From what I could see was left of it—the leather top and tires, some of the body—this was like a Model T or something. Old. Like, your-grandfather-drove-it-when-he-was-a-kid old." She peeled off a rubbery orange glove and ruffled her hair. "We can go in for it if you want. There aren't any single pieces left big enough to call for the winch. There's a leather roof, some wire-spoke wheels, stuff like that." She looked at Russ and Bob Mongue, who were staring at her. "Hey, we figured we were there for the body. Nobody said anything about a car."

Clare couldn't stand biting off her question one second longer. "Did he commit suicide, do you think? Drove into the water and drowned?"

The diver shook her head. "It was in the middle of the reservoir. His car never would have gotten that far."

Russ looked at Clare. She felt like she could read his mind. And he could read hers. "But he could have driven it in," he said, not looking away from her. "If he had come here a few days after the dam was finished and the river began piling up behind it. He could have driven right into the rising water—"

"At night," Clare said. "Into the condemned property, where nobody in his right mind would have gone."

"And parked the car. Waiting for the water to take him."

"I hate to toss a spanner into such a neat and tidy conclusion, but this man didn't drive himself anywhere," Emil Dvorak said. "Or if he did, he wasn't alone." He gently cradled the skull through the fine netting, lifting and rotating it so they could all see the back, where a network of fine cracks radiated out in a circle, like a fractured porthole. "See how depressed this is? This man may have been left in the water, but he didn't drown. He was killed by a massive blow to the head."

CHAPTER 33

NOW

MONDAY, APRIL 3

Clare and Norm Madsen accompanied Mrs. Marshall to the morgue. She hadn't wanted to go, despite a phone call from Dr. Dvorak late Friday afternoon, asking her if she could come in after the weekend and answer a few questions about her father.

"It couldn't be him," she said, turning around from the passenger seat of her car to address Clare. "What would his body have been doing there, anyway?"

"Remember the stories you used to spin when you were a kid?" Norm was a careful driver, hands at the two and ten positions, eyes on the road even while he was talking. "About your dad being ambushed by bootleggers?" He let the implication hang in the air.

In the backseat, Clare tried to think of a new way to answer the same question she had heard at least a dozen times since Russ had broken the news to Mrs. Marshall that the unidentified remains from the reservoir might be those of Jonathon Ketchem. There were only so many ways one could dance around the answer: Someone killed him and dumped his body there.

It had been a pretty miserable weekend all around. Friday's clouds had brought a steady spring rain that lasted, on and off, until Sunday night. Clare had spent a gray and solitary Saturday afternoon in the old nursery at the historical society, searching unsuccessfully for more records of the Sacandaga land sales and peering out through the curtains of rain toward the clinic, dark and closed. At St. Alban's, a leak worked its way through the roofer's tarp, rendering several pews in the north aisle uninhabitable for Sunday Eucharist. And much to her senior warden's dismay, she was in the newspaper. Again.

"Clare," Robert Corlew said, bearing down on her in the parish hall. "Did you see Saturday's *Post-Star*?"

She looked up from the table, where she was debating between the frosted brownies and the carrot cake. Coffee hour at St. Alban's was always a celebration of butter and sugar. Occasionally, someone with higher ideals would bring in grapes, or pineapple chunks on toothpicks, or apple slices. They usually went untouched.

"I sure did," she said, picking up a brownie.

"You're in it. In a news story. About a crazy woman holding people at gunpoint." He leaned in more closely. "I thought we agreed after last year that you weren't going to appear in print unless it was something nice and uplifting."

"An Easter message of hope, I believe you said."

Sterling Sumner had drifted over. "You know, the story went out over the wires. A friend in Albany called to ask me if my priest was the one mentioned in the 'State and Local' item."

She knew. There had been a message on her answering machine from the diocesan office. Someone on the bishop's staff wanted to Talk With Her. "It must have been a slow news day," she said.

"Clare! This isn't the kind of thing designed to attract new members—"

"New *pledge-paying* members," Sterling added.

"To St. Alban's! 'Local priest, artist held in armed standoff.'" He looked to Sterling for support. "Am I right? Would this make you want to try out St. Alban's?"

"I'm sorry!" Several heads turned in their direction, and she toned her voice down. "It's not like I set out that morning with the goal of having a gun stuck in my face."

"We've suggested before that you take a look at the people you're getting involved with," Sterling said. "You know what they say. If you lie down with dogs, you get up with fleas."

"I get involved with people who need me." She almost threw up her hands until she remembered the brownie.

"Notoriety isn't a desirable quality in a priest," Corlew said. "If we had wanted Daniel Berrigan, we'd have hired him."

"I'm not courting notoriety," she said. Corlew raised one eyebrow so high it nearly disappeared into the thicket of his hair. Or toupee.

"You must admit you've gotten involved in some pretty flamboyant incidents." Sterling tossed his boys-school scarf for emphasis.

She bit the inside of her cheek. Counted to ten. Quickly, but she made it. She could argue with these guys from now until Good Friday and she still wouldn't make them see things her way. It was time for a little dose of southern. She put one hand on Sterling's arm, and her other on Corlew's shoulder. "Gentlemen, you are absolutely right." They both looked at her suspiciously. "My grandmother always said a lady's name should appear in the paper only three times, and I can't say I disagree with her. I never spoke to any reporter about the unfortunate incident with Mrs. Rouse, and I promise you here and now I never will. In fact, I could live happy never speaking to another reporter again, except on church business."

"Like, about the white elephant sale," Corlew said.

"Or Easter messages of hope," she said.

The sight of the square brick facade of the county morgue yanked her back to the present. Mr. Madsen parked and they all got out. Mrs. Marshall looked up at the granite flight of stairs. "I won't have to . . . look at the body, will I?"

"I doubt it," Clare said, not adding, *There isn't much you would recognize.*

Inside, Mr. Madsen gave Mrs. Marshall's name to the attendant, who rang the medical examiner and then buzzed them through the door that separated the waiting room from the coroner's office and the mortuary. Dr. Dvorak met them in the hall. Clare introduced Mr. Madsen, who described himself as "a family friend," and Mrs. Marshall, who looked at the medical examiner's hand a beat too long before shaking it, perhaps envisioning where it had been.

"Chief Van Alstyne is already waiting for us," Dr. Dvorak said, limping down the short hallway to his office.

"Why?" Mrs. Marshall asked as the pathologist opened the door and ushered her through. Russ, seated at the far side of Dr. Dvorak's desk, rose when she entered. Mrs. Marshall, Clare had noticed, had that effect on men.

"The chief is always involved in a homicide," Dr. Dvorak said.

Mrs. Marshall turned on him. "Homicide?"

"Let's have you a seat, Lacey, and then we can hear what the doctor's got to say." Norm Madsen patted one of the straight-backed wooden chairs, government-issue circa 1957 and never changed since then.

"I'm sorry," Dr. Dvorak said. "I didn't know there would be so many." There were three chairs ranged between the bookcases and the plants in the small office. "Maybe we can nip down to the waiting room and get another."

"I'll stand," Clare said.

Russ, still standing, gestured to his chair. "Take this."

Clare looked pointedly at his cast. "I'm fine, thank you."

"I insist." His back was very straight. She wondered if it was Margy Van Alstyne or the army that had instilled his good posture.

"Sit down, Russ. Doctor's orders." Emil Dvorak glanced at him just long enough to see Russ lower himself back into the chair, then turned his attention to the folders neatly squared on his desk blotter. One of them was obviously modern, the kind of plastic-tabbed manila thing everyone bought by the boxful at Staples. The other had a different look to it. Older. It was muzzy green and shedding, like felt left too long outdoors. Clare realized it must be the seventy-year-old police file. The Millers Kill Police Department's oldest cold case had come alive again.

"Now, let me make sure I've got the relationship straight." Dr. Dvorak uncapped a fountain pen and flipped open the modern file. "You are Solace Ketchem Marshall, the daughter of Jonathon and Jane Ketchem."

"Yes."

"How old were you when your father disappeared?"

"Six."

"Mrs. Marshall, do you recall if your father ever broke two fingers? On his right hand? This would have been several years before he disappeared."

"I don't know," Mrs. Marshall said.

"Yes," Clare said.

Everyone turned to stare at her. "Dr. Stillman loaned me his grandfather's journals." She spoke to Mrs. Marshall and Mr. Madsen. "Old Dr. Stillman, the one you remember. He treated your siblings during the diphtheria epidemic. The ones that were alive when he was called." She was getting off point. "Anyway, in his journal, Dr. Stillman wrote that your father had two broken fingers he had set himself the night he came to fetch the doctor. The doctor offered to reset them, but your father refused."

Emil Dvorak nodded. "Good."

"Good?" Mrs. Marshall said.

Dr. Dvorak steepled his fingers. "The remains that were brought up out of Stewart's Pond were skeletonized. That means many of the normal markers a pathologist will use to establish identity are simply gone. In addition, this skeleton is old, certainly more than fifty years old, and there aren't any reliable dental records available." Dvorak opened the old green file and flipped through several pages. "We're fortunate in that the officer who investigated your father's disappearance was thorough. He sent off for Jonathon Ketchem's service records, from when he was in the army during World War I." Dvorak held up a page of brittle, browning paper between two fingers. "They don't have what we'd consider dental records per se, but there is a written account of the dental work your father had had done and the state of his health as of 1915."

"And?"

"Jonathon Ketchem was thirty-seven years old and in good health when he disappeared. He has no records of any broken bones, other than two fingers, which Reverend Fergusson has confirmed for us. According to his enlistment records, he had eight molar fillings." He tapped the modern folder. "The remains brought up from the reservoir are those of an adult male, between his mid-twenties and mid-forties. There is no sign of any premortem trauma other than two broken fingers on the right hand. The decedent had eight molar fillings made of a lead amalgam that fell out of use in the late 1920s."

Norm Madsen leaned forward. "So is this Jonathon Ketchem's body?"

Dr. Dvorak spread his hands. "That's what the evidence suggests."

"The body was found inside the remains of an old car," Russ said. "We had the divers bring up several pieces, but at this point, all we can say for sure is that it was some sort of old Ford."

"My father drove a Ford. That's what he was in when he went missing."

"I know. It's in the original report. Problem is, something like sixty percent of the cars sold in the county back then were Fords, according to Lee Harse over to Fort Henry Ford." Russ looked at the rest of them, looking at him. "Well, I don't know anything about old cars. The state crime lab has the recovered pieces and we've faxed their photos over to an expert Harse recommended. So hopefully, we'll be able to identify the exact model and year soon."

"But till then we don't know?" Mrs. Marshall twisted her fine-boned hands together, and Clare, from her vantage point near the door, was reminded of the long, elegant finger bones tangled in the divers' net.

Russ leaned forward, bracing one arm against Dr. Dvorak's desk. "Mrs. Marshall, the doctor here is going to tell you we can't really be sure. But I'll tell you what my gut says. There's no other missing person I know of who fits the bill. Now, I've put the info we have out on the wire. And maybe I'll get a report back from the Albany PD that they have a seventy-year-old unsolved missing-persons case, and their man has broken fingers and eight fillings and drove a Ford. But I don't think that's going to happen. I believe we've found the body of your father, Jonathon Ketchem."

Mrs. Marshall stiffened. After a moment she said, "How did he die?"

Russ looked to Dr. Dvorak.

"Did he drown? Was he shot?"

"If he was shot, there's no surviving evidence of it," Dvorak said. "I doubt, even if we had tissue to work with, that we'd find he'd been drowned." He glanced at Russ.

"What is it?" Mrs. Marshall was pale, composed but on the edge.

"It appears that the proximate cause of death was a blow to the back of the skull. Several blows." Dr. Dvorak paused for a moment, as if waiting for another question. When none was forthcoming, he went on. "From the extent of the damage, the cross-cranial impact zone, and the angle of de-clivity, I've concluded he was struck by a heavy, probably flat object with a surface area of at least eight to ten inches."

Mrs. Marshall looked at the pathologist. She turned to Norm Madsen, then to Russ. "I don't understand," she said finally. "What sort of weapon could that be?"

There was a silence. Clare wracked her brain for some idea. Tire iron . . . baseball bat . . . none of those were flat. "A frying pan," Russ said finally. "It has to be. Jonathon Ketchem was beaten to death with a frying pan."

CHAPTER 34

THEN

SATURDAY, MARCH 29, 1930

I s she asleep?"

Jane paused at the door to the kitchen. Jon hadn't lifted his head from the paper to ask the question. "Yes," she said. "She was all tired out from playing with the Reid boys today."

He grunted. She crossed to the sink and pumped more water into the basin before lifting her apron off its nail and pulling it over her head. She knotted it behind her and attacked the dinner dishes. She was all tired out as well, after walking Solace to and from the Reids, and doing the marketing, and seeing to the chickens and the house and three meals and a triple batch of cookies intended for St. Alban's bake sale tomorrow. As near as she could tell, Jon hadn't moved from the davenport all day, except to go out back to the necessary. She scooped through the basin and dragged up a couple forks. All day. More like all week. He hadn't been out of the house since Monday. She was the one who had brought him in the newspaper. The only reason he was in the kitchen right now was because the night was bidding cold, and the kitchen, with its woodstove, was the warmest spot in the house. He hadn't gone down cellar to shovel more coal into the furnace, and she'd be deviled if she was going to do it for him. As it was, she was going to have to step out to the woodpile on the back porch and chop kindling for tomorrow morning.

"You lookin' at the help-wanted notices?" She knew he wasn't.

He grunted again.

"Lula Reid was saying that Will has openings for a strong man on his crew. He needs reliable workers. He'd love to have a farmer like you, she said. Used to rising early and putting in a full day. The pay's real good."

He dropped the paper on the oilcloth-covered table. "You some sort of job broker now?"

She wiped one of her grandmother's blue willow plates dry and laid it on the counter. "Somebody's got to be. You haven't worked since February." She turned toward him, leaning against the sink. "You've got to find something, Jon. Why not work for Will's crew? At least it'd bring some money in."

He looked up at her from his chair. "Ketchems are farmers. We don't break rocks and pour asphalt so's rich men can drive up to the mountains without bumping their asses along the way."

"Jonathon Ketchem, I won't have that kind of language in my house!"

"Don't pester me and you won't have to hear it." He went back to his paper. She looked at him for a moment. He was still handsome, with his thick dark hair falling over his forehead and his dark eyes. Solace favored him. When they had made her, lying together in their marriage bed, had she loved him? One edge of his newspaper half fell over a painted iron trivet he had won for her, at a shooting gallery at the Sacandaga Amusement Park. He had been home on leave, full of stories about New York City and the South, looking like a million dollars in his uniform. Hadn't she loved him then?

She turned back to her dishes. She rested her reddened hands on the curved white edge of the sink and looked at her wedding band. He had wrestled it onto her finger in Justice Kendrick's parlor, with Mrs. Kendrick pumping out "Abide with Me" on their little organ and her best friend, Patsy, giggling with his brother David. She must have loved him then. She wished she could feel it now, feel something to go with the memories, instead of this blank incredulity that sent her searching for evidence that yes, once upon a time, she had loved the intimate stranger at her kitchen table.

"The dam's finished up," he said.

She was surprised he spoke. "I'd heard."

"Two days now, it's been filling up. Soon, it'll all be gone." The tone in his voice made her turn around. "The hayfield. The beanfield. Lord, I used to love that field in the spring, all the flowers peeping out. I wonder if the water rushes in fast or rises slow." He looked into some middle distance that only he could see. "I wonder if people's stuff comes floating by. You know, stuff that got left behind, not worth taking."

She turned back to the sink and grabbed another blue willow plate. "Anything in people's houses or barns got burnt down. You know that."

"Our barn could be knee deep in water right now."

"There's no barn left."

"Remember how the boys used to swing from that rope I hung on the crossbeam? Imagine 'em swinging back and forth and then letting go into the water."

She whirled, water splattering from the plate in her hand. "Don't talk about that! There isn't any barn there anymore!"

His eyes were spooky-empty, looking at things he had no business looking at. "A ghost barn," he said. "For ghost children." His voice broke on the last word.

She slammed the plate down so hard it rang. "Stop it! It's no good talking about it!"

"Why not?" He raised his head to her. "Why not?" He cracked the paper against the edge of the table. "Why can't we talk about it?" He stood up, racking his chair back. "It's all gone. Everything I ever worked for and wanted. Dead and gone, and all you can talk about is me joining up with some goddamned road crew."

"Because we've got to move on," she said. She turned back to the sink so he wouldn't see the hot blur in her eyes. She slid the skillet into the soapy water and scrubbed at it unseeing. "It doesn't do any good to talk about what was. It just makes us feel bad."

"I feel bad all the time, anyway," he said. "I used to be a father. I used to be a farmer. Maybe you don't want to remember. But I do. Remembering about it is all I've got."

She scrubbed the dish towel against her eyes and dashed it to the counter. "You're still a father, you jackass, unless you've forgotten that little girl upstairs." She turned to face him. "And you could be a farmer again. There's land around here going begging from the bank. Use some of the money and buy it!"

"No!" His voice felt like a blow to her stomach. "Not a penny of it. I'm not touching that money, and neither are you."

"Why not?" She jutted her chin forward, refusing to let him scare her. "You certainly earned it."

His hand jerked up and she flinched. They both looked at it, at the knotted bulges where his first two fingers had been broken and never set right. He lowered it to his side. "You blame me, don't you."

She shook her head.

"You do. I see you sometimes, looking at me. Thinking it's my fault."

"Then you're a fool. It's as much my fault as yours. Don't you think I don't lie awake nights, blaming myself? Going over and over everything? What I should have done, what I would have done?"

"You hate me."

"No."

"You hate me. Admit it."

"No."

He lunged forward and dug his fingers into her arms. "Say it! You hate me! Say it!"

"All right then!" she screamed. "I hate you! I hate you! I hate me!" She tore out of his grasp and clapped her hand over her mouth, her heart thudding, the echo of her words ringing through the kitchen.

He nodded, as if he had proved something to his satisfaction. "That night, when they were so sick. We should have been willing to die for them. If I had known, I would have given my life to save them. But we didn't know. That it was the end. Of all our lives."

"It wasn't the end." She was gasping now, her breath coming in high, hard pants. She thought she ought to bend over and put her head between her knees, but she was afraid. Afraid of what he'd do.

"It's like a curse." His eyes were gone again, his gaze somewhere over her head. "First the children, then the farm. There's nothing left of my life."

She sucked in another breath. "Well there's plenty left of my life. Solace."

"Solace," he said. "My poor baby girl. Having to take the place of all her brothers and sisters. What kind of life is that for a kid?"

She thought she had been afraid before. Now she felt frozen with fear, every nerve in her body strung tight and screaming, as if she had dropped without warning into an icy lake.

"You leave her out of this," she managed to say.

He turned to her, slowly, like he was working things out in his head. "What kind of life is this for any of us? You and me hating and aching and scared. And Solace. Even her name tells her she's just a makeup for the others. The third-place ribbon." He focused on her, really focused on her, for the first time since she had screamed at him. "Wouldn't you like a little peace, Janie? Just to lay down and not feel any pain anymore?"

"No." She was shaking. "Solace needs me."

He waved her answer off. "All of us."

She braced her hands against the sink and pushed herself forward. "I won't let you hurt her." She had failed before, in the call to lay down her life for her children, but she wouldn't fail this time. "I swear to God, I'll die before I'll let you hurt her."

He looked appalled. "I wouldn't hurt her." She felt a shock of relief rush through her, warm and liquid, until he said, "I don't want to hurt any of us. I want the hurting to stop."

"No!" She launched herself at him, punching and hitting, but he wrapped her in his big arms, strong from years of yoking and plowing and haying and baling, and for a moment, her body remembered what it had felt like, him holding her at the end of a long day.

"Think, Janie!" His voice was hot and hissing in her ears. "Who's to say it couldn't happen again? Do you want Solace to suffer like they suffered?"

"Get out," she said, her voice squeezed from where he was crushing her ribs. "Get out of this house."

"And if not by disease, how then? Run over by a car like the McGonnegal boy? Burnt alive like that little girl up Cossayuharie way? Or maybe she'll grow up to die having children, or eaten up inside by a cancer. Don't you see, Janie?" His voice grew very small, a tiny snake slithering into a dark hole. "We're all dead already."

Oh God, she thought. Oh God oh God oh God.

"I don't want to hurt you. Will you promise to be still?"

She nodded.

"Are you scared?"

She nodded.

"Don't be. I'll hold you. And we can stop hating each other. I'm so sick of it. Sick to death of it."

He released her slowly, keeping his hands up so he could grab her or knock her down. Her eyes darted to the kitchen doorway as she counted off everything that stood between her and Solace escaping out the front door. Through the front room. Up the stairs. Into Solace's room. Pick her up. Carry her downstairs. Out the door. The door. Had he already locked it for the night?

"Don't try it, Janie." He stepped close to her. She could feel the heat of his body. "If you run, I'll have to stop you. I've never laid a hand on you. Don't make me do it tonight."

"I don't want to die," she whispered.

"I do." He turned, then, away from the door to the front room, away from the stairs, and for a moment she watched without understanding as he laid his hand on the door to the back porch. Where the woodpile was.

The hatchet.

Then her hand closed around the skillet handle, wet and hot and slithering with soap, and she raised it and she swung it and she smashed it against the back of his beautiful dark hair with all the strength of her days of lifting feed and lugging wash and toting children. She smashed it, and smashed it, and smashed it, as he toppled to his knees and fell unstrung to the floor. Blood and soap froth and water splattered across the floor and over her apron and still she smashed the skillet down, over and over, pounding out her fear until she stopped suddenly and staggered back.

Everything was quiet.

She looked at him, sprawled on the linoleum tiles, and wondered if he was dead. She was afraid to move close enough to tell. The only things she had ever killed in her life—*except your children*—were chickens, and they liked to jump around after their heads were cut off.

She looked at the skillet in her hand and saw the blood and hairs sticking to it. It almost fell from her nerveless fingers. She plunged it in the sink.

Then she sat down and flopped over and put her head between her knees and breathed. She sat that way for a long time, until she registered the blood splatters on her apron, and then she sat bolt upright. She was going to go to jail. No. Jail was for thieving or running whiskey. She was going to go to the chair. She had murdered her husband. She was going to be taken away from her home and her daughter and strapped in the electric chair and fried. And Solace, her comfort, her joy, her only child, would grow up knowing that her father had been killed and her mother had done it.

"No," she said, and was surprised she had spoken out loud.

She had told Jon she wasn't ready to die. She had told him she wouldn't leave Solace. Her little girl needed her.

So. She looked at her hands. They were shaking. She grabbed them and squeezed them tight. Her little girl needed her. What she did in the next few hours would mean the difference between growing up with a mother who loved her or growing up under a stain of guilt and shame.

She looked at—her mind slid around the name "Jonathon"—the body on the floor. She would have to get rid of it. And any signs of violence in the kitchen. She thought. And thought. And thought some more.

She went upstairs to the linen closet and pulled out one of the old, stained sheets she used on the bed during her monthlies. She opened Solace's door and listened for a moment to her daughter's slow, even breathing. Then she carried the sheet downstairs and spread it next to Jo—the body. She squatted next to him and rolled him over. When she saw his open eyes, she almost lost her supper, but she closed her eyes, swallowed, and kept on. She rolled him again until he was smack-dab in the middle of the sheet, and then she twisted it around him, tying a thick knot at each end.

She stepped out onto the back porch. At its far side, it led to the privy, which led to the old tack room, which led to the stables, where they garaged the car. She went through the rooms, opening each door, and into the garage, where she swung the back door of the Ford wide. Jon had left the stable door open, and she considered closing it before she began, but figured that would look strange to any neighbors who might notice the car going out later. She would just have to brazen it out.

Back in the kitchen, she grabbed the sheet behind the fat knot at its head, and pulled. The homemade shroud bumped over the doorsill, out onto the porch. She hauled the body across the floor, through the narrow walkway in the privy, down three steps to the old tack room, and, taking a quick look around, into the shadows next to the car.

This, she guessed, would be the hardest part. She pulled on the knot until it—*he*—was in a sitting position. She squatted down and wrapped her arms around the waist. Like seeing his open eyes, the familiar feeling of embracing his middle came close to undoing her, and she had to clamp her teeth against a bubble of sound, half moan, half sob. She heaved him over her shoulder and staggered into a crouch, the best she could do against his weight. His dead weight, she thought, and then had to shut her mouth against a hysterical laugh. She slid and shoved him through the back door onto the floor.

She sponged up the splatters on the kitchen floor and door, scrubbing them until they were spotless. Then she finished the washing up: the plates, the pots, the glasses, and the skillet. She dried everything and put it away, just like always. She gathered several pieces of wood from the back porch and stoked the fire before untying her apron and tossing it into the stove. She almost dumped the dishwater down the drain, but thought better of it. Instead, she picked up the basin and lurched to the privy, where she dumped the water into the pit below. She pumped more water into the basin to make sure it was well rinsed, and sloshed that into the two-seater as well.

She went upstairs. Solace was still sleeping soundly. She was a good sleeper, never fussing after her story time, never rousing to demand a cuddle or a drink of water, unlike Lu—she stopped herself.

In her vanity mirror, she checked her appearance. She was looking for anything telltale: a bruise or a smudge of blood. There was nothing. It startled her, how normal she looked. No telltale lines of guilt. She wasn't even pale and washed out, as she might have expected. Well, not after all that hauling and cleaning.

She pulled a pair of Jon's pants right over her dress, tucking the skirt in around the too-large waist. Then she shrugged into one of his coats, clapped his hat on her head, and, at the last moment, took his wallet from the dresser top and slipped it into the coat pocket.

She paused at the bottom of the stairs. Took a deep breath. Pictured Solace in her bed, her round cheeks still babylike in sleep. Then she turned on the outside light and left the house.

She slammed the door. She jingled her keys and slammed the car door, too, doing everything she could to attract attention to her make-believe Jonathon. She started the car and backed it out of the garage, shifting it into first and rolling down Ferry Street, toward the river. She turned right, then right again, up Wharf Street. At the head of Wharf was the new cemetery. Its gates were closed and locked, as they were every night at sundown, but to her left, outside the cemetery proper, a stub of a driveway led up to and alongside the caretaker's one-room utility shed. She pulled the car in next to the shed and turned off the ignition.

This was the most dangerous part of her plan, the part she was leaving in the hands of God, who hadn't been noticeably kind to her.

She shucked off the hat, coat, and pants and dropped them in the back, atop the still, sheet-shrouded form. She slipped out of the car, closing the door just far enough to hear the snick of the latch. Prying off her shoes, she ran in stocking feet as fast as she could until she reached the head of Ferry Street. She flew down the cold, grainy sidewalk, and when she was within shouting distance of her own house, she shoved her feet back into the shoes and walked, panting for breath, to her next-door neighbor's.

Mrs. Creighton greeted the bell. "Why Mrs. Ketchem. Whatever are you doing here? Is everything all right?"

Jane pressed her hand against her chest. "I'm afraid Jonathon and I had a fight," she said. "He drove off in a pet and I ran out to try to persuade him to come back, but I haven't seen hide nor hair of him. You didn't by chance notice our car leave, did you?"

Since Mrs. Creighton was an elderly lady whose joy of an evening was sitting close to her radio, Jane wasn't surprised when she said, "No, dear, I didn't. Do you want to come in and sit for a moment? You look all out."

Jane heaved a sigh that might have been catching her breath. "What time is it?"

Mrs. Creighton stepped back from the door and peered at a large cuckoo clock looming on the wall. "It's just about nine o'clock."

"I'd better be getting back. My girl's at home alone. Maybe I'll bake some cookies for when he comes back."

"A peace offering." Mrs. Creighton smiled, wrinkling up her whole face. "That's a nice idea."

"Good night, Mrs. Creighton. I'm sorry to have bothered you."

"You're never a bother, dear. Send your little girl over tomorrow. I've made cross buns, and she can eat her fill."

Jane thanked her, went down the walk, along the sidewalk, and up her own walk to her front door, where the light still shone from "Jonathon"'s departure. She didn't have any time to waste.

She dashed upstairs and pulled one of her warm wool dresses right over her housedress. She rolled an extra pair of woolen stockings on and pulled her winter boots from the closet. Downstairs, she retrieved her hat and gloves from the box bench beside the front door and stuffed her hair under her beret. She paused at the kitchen stove, stirred up the fire, and laid three more logs in before turning down the damper. There should still be living embers there if she made it home before daybreak.

She went out onto the back porch, but instead of exiting through the privy, she went down the stairs into the yard. It was black and hushed. She gave her eyes a moment to adjust before trekking to the bottom of their yard, scrambling over the low fence, and making her way between two small stables almost identical to their own.

She stepped out onto Wharf Street with her heart choking off her throat. Her legs and back and arms shook with the urge to run pell-mell to the head of the street, but she forced herself to a pace resembling a woman, say, strolling home after an evening of cards with friends. Lights were on. People were home. At any moment, she expected to be accosted, expected to see a blaze of lights from around the corner as the police arrived to see what Jonathon's car was doing parked by the cemetery. There was nothing. She had, all without planning, hit the magic hour, after families had withdrawn into their houses, before dogs had been walked for the night.

The car was where she had left it. It took her two tries to open the door, her hand was shaking so. She started the ignition, backed into the street, and drove up Burgoyne, headed for Route 100, the road out of town. She was taking Jonathon home.

CHAPTER 35

NOW

MONDAY, APRIL 3

"You think my mother killed my father." It wasn't a question. Mrs. Marshall looked at Russ with all the dignity of her seventy-odd years. "That's impossible."

"There's no way we're going to be able to prove it to the satisfaction of the law," he said, his voice gentle. "But based on what physical evidence there is and the facts developed in the case file—"

"If she had been a suspect, the police would have investigated her. No one other than a few filthy-minded gossips ever suggested she had anything to do with my father's disappearance."

Russ tapped the old green police file. "She was investigated. To a degree. The police chief at the time, Harry McNeil, saw her house and talked to her neighbors. Her story was that her husband had left after a fight and she never saw him again, and there wasn't any evidence to contradict her."

"Well then." Norm Madsen spread his arm across the back of Mrs. Marshall's chair. "There you go."

Russ shook his head. "McNeil was laboring under some disadvantages, not the least of which was a mind-set that made it hard for him to imagine a woman murdering her husband and vanishing his body."

"Wait a minute. Wasn't this the era of Bonnie and Clyde and Ma Barker and all those female gangsters?" Clare crossed her arms over her chest.

"Sure. Women could be murderous. Bad women. But the general perception of females was still that of the gentler, finer sex. Jane Ketchem, a law-abiding, churchgoing mother, fit the bill."

Clare arched her eyebrows at him.

"McNeil questioned her once, in her own home, two days after Jonathon vanished. She could have cleaned up all signs of an altercation by then." He

269

twisted slightly, facing Mrs. Marshall. "If this had happened today, we'd have taken the wife down to the station and interrogated her. We'd search the house with the assumption that the wife had done it, dusting for fingerprints, scraping for fibers, looking for traces of blood and bone. We'd spray with Luminol to look for cleaned-up bloodstains. Technology that wasn't dreamed of in 1930."

Clare opened her mouth to speak but closed it again.

"What you're saying is that my mother got away with it because she got kid-glove treatment from the police." For the first time, Mrs. Marshall's voice held something other than stiff indignation.

He nodded.

She sat for a moment. "My mother was the most moral woman I knew," she said finally.

"None of us can know what happened that night," Russ said. "Your mother may have been an abused wife who snapped. She may have been defending herself. It may all have been a tragic accident that she felt she had to cover up." He leaned forward until he caught her eyes with his. "I'm so sorry. I only hope you'll find some comfort in finally knowing what became of your father."

"My father," she said. She turned to Clare. Her scarlet lipstick was the only slash of color in her pale face. "Will we be able to—can we have a funeral service for him?"

"Of course," Clare said.

"How long until I can have his body back?" Mrs. Marshall asked Dr. Dvorak. He glanced at Russ.

"I'd like to wait a few days," Russ said. "There are a few police departments going through their old records, just in case. Once I hear from them, Emil can release the remains to you."

"Do you have any other questions I can answer?" Dr. Dvorak said.

Mrs. Marshall looked down to where her handbag sat in her lap. "I think . . . I'd just like to go home now. If I have any further questions—"

"Call me at any time. Please."

Everyone got to their feet as Mrs. Marshall did, Russ yanking on his crutches, Dr. Dvorak pushing himself up with his cane. Clare had time to twist behind Mr. Madsen's back and mouth, "I'll call you later," at Russ before joining the general exodus up the hallway and out of the morgue.

In the Lincoln, in the backseat as wide and comfortable as a sofa, Clare edged forward until her shoulders were jammed between the front seats.

"How are you doing?" she asked Mrs. Marshall. "You've just been handed an awful lot to deal with."

Mrs. Marshall shook her head. "I feel like I've been looking at an Escher picture. You know him? Etchings of people walking along impossible stairs?"

Clare nodded.

"You think you're looking at birds, and all at once you realize you've been looking at fish. That's what it feels like." She looked over at Norm Madsen. "You knew my mother. You were her attorney, for heaven's sake. Could you ever have imagined her murdering anyone? Let alone her husband?"

Mr. Madsen took his time before answering. "People can do surprising things, Lacey."

Clare thought of what he had said to her after the emergency vestry meeting that started her whole involvement with Jane Ketchem. *She was the only woman who could ever scare me. And the fact that she's dead doesn't make me any less scared.*

"She never . . ." Mrs. Marshall peered more closely at her old friend. "She never said anything to you about it?"

Mr. Madsen actually tore his gaze from the road and looked at her. "Good Lord! Of course not."

She sagged back into her seat for a second and then stiffened again. She twisted to face Clare. "Do you remember what Allan said, that day we went to tell him? About my mother?"

"He said you had no idea what the clinic had meant to your mother."

"Do you think he knew? Do you think she told him?" She pressed her spindle-fingered hands against her sunken cheeks. "Oh my God, what if he knew what happened to my father all these years and he never told me!"

Clare rubbed her knuckles against Mrs. Marshall's arm. "Even if he had some sort of knowledge of your father's death, I'm sure the only reason he would have kept quiet was to protect your feelings. He must have known how much you loved your mother. He wouldn't have wanted to do anything to tarnish her memory for you."

Mrs. Marshall closed her eyes for a moment. "All these years, I thought he had left me. I thought my father abandoned me." She opened her washed-blue eyes, and Clare was struck by how much the pain of the very old looked like the pain of the very young. Vulnerability, and disbelief, and nowhere to hide from it.

"But he didn't. He was taken away, but he didn't leave me. All this time, I thought . . ." She blinked, and the tears spilled down her cheeks and collected in the soft folds of her skin. "He used to tell me he loved me, when I was a little girl. And for years now, years, I didn't believe him. But he was telling the truth. All those years." She pressed her hand against her mouth. "He didn't leave me."

◆ ◆ ◆

When Clare reached her office, it was to find Lois with a handful of pink WHILE YOU WERE OUT slips. "If anyone sends you clippings, make sure I get a copy for the parish scrapbook," Lois said, handing them over.

"Sure," Clare said. "It'll make good reading for the next priest. Kind of a what-not-to-do list." There was one from a *Post-Star* reporter and another from a columnist at the *Albany Times Union.* There were two new messages from the diocesan office, one from the bishop's secretary and the other from the editor of the newsletter. Three were blessedly normal, someone with a question about Easter Eve baptisms, a couple wanting to reschedule a premarital counseling session, a dinner invitation from Dr. Anne. One was from Hugh Parteger.

She ought to get right back to the bishop's office. She could ask them what to do about the reporters. And of course she needed to return her parishioners' calls. She picked up the phone and dialed Hugh's number.

"Vicar!"

"Is this a bad time?"

"I'm just going over a proposal from a pair of twentysomethings who feel now is just the right time to break into the dot-com market with a luxury-car directory and delivery service. All they need from us is a half mil for start-up and a big, encouraging hug."

"Are they going to get it?"

"Indeed not. I'm going to smack them upside the head, as the natives say, and tell them to go get real jobs. The Internet is dead. Silly buggers."

"So, you called me."

"Vicar, I've called you four times the past month. You're hard to get hold of. Listen, there was an article in the *Times* yesterday."

"The *New York Times?*"

"No, the *Kankamunga Times.* Of course, the *New York Times.* It's all about how this lady whose husband went missing showed up at the home of his alleged mistress—"

"Oh God, it doesn't say mistress, does it?"

"—and said lady proceeded to hold the mistress, her mother, her two children, and the town's Episcopal priest at gunpoint until the police arrived. Dateline, Millers Kill, New York."

"It doesn't give out my name, does it?"

"Hah! I knew it must have been you. No, it only named the wife and girlfriend. The article said it was the priest who phoned the cops."

"Yeah, that was me."

"Good God, you're a regular Xena, Warrior Priestess, aren't you? I've got to get you down here so I can show you off to my friends. You poor baby. Were you frightened?"

She smiled at the conjunction of Warrior Priestess and poor baby. "It was scary. But I was pretty sure Mrs. Rouse didn't really want to hurt anyone. She just cracked under the strain of her husband's disappearance." Unlike Jane Ketchem. "I knew if we could just keep her talking, the police would get there and everything would be okay."

"Did that surly chief of police show up? Rip Van Winkle?"

"Russ Van Alstyne. And he's not surly."

"Hah. At that dinner we went to last summer, he practically patted me down and administered a field sobriety test before he let me drive you home." His voice shifted, went warmer. "Look, I really do mean it about you coming to the city to visit me. And not just because you're a fifteen-minute celebrity."

"Please tell me no one else has seen the article."

"It was on the third page of the Region section. Must have been a slow news day."

She groaned.

"What do you say?"

She didn't pretend to misunderstand him. "It's not a good time. Three Sundays from now is Easter. Things are going to get frantic."

"And after Easter?"

She hesitated. "If I came down to see you, I'd need someplace to stay. Not with you."

"My animal sexual magnetism is simply too much in close quarters. I know. I get that all the time."

One of the things she liked best about him was the way nothing was ever serious. Nothing ever counted for too much or weighed too heavily. "When I get caught up in the middle of things, I'm not always as careful as I ought to be about what people will think of my actions. So when I can spot a problem in advance, like my congregation's reaction if I overnight in New

York with a handsome single man, I like to take steps to cut it off at the knees."

"Handsome single man, eh?"

"With a British accent. Known to be devastating in the U.S."

"You do realize, don't you, that you're the only girl I've ever dated that I didn't have sex with. I feel like the reformed rake in one of those Barbara Cartland romances."

"So shineth a good deed in a naughty world."

He laughed. "Okay. If I get a female friend to issue an invite, will you come for a visit after Easter?"

"This wouldn't be one of those innumerable girls you've had sex with, would it?"

"Despite what you see on HBO, New York isn't entirely overrun with single women desperate to sleep with a heterosexual investment banker. Alas. So no, I think I can find someone whose favors I haven't shared."

"Maybe you know a nun?"

"A lesbian nun."

"A blind, senile lesbian nun. With a flatulent dog." She smiled into the phone.

"All right. I'll get you a berth with a blind, senile lesbian nun and you'll let me take you out to dinner. Sounds fair."

"It's a deal."

She said good-bye smiling. She always felt better, talking with Hugh. Lois was right, she ought to keep in touch with him more regularly. Her mother would love him.

Her intercom buzzed and Lois's voice came into the office, the Ghost of Phone Calls Yet to Be Returned. "While you were on, Karen Burns called. She wants to talk to you about this Debba Clow person. Also, Roxanne Lunt called from the historical society. She has some research packet the librarian there left for you."

She didn't know exactly what Karen wanted, but it was bound to take longer and be less pleasant than Roxanne's research packet. She rang the historical society director.

"I'm so glad you called!" Roxanne's energy level hadn't dimmed since their last conversation. "Look, Sonny Barnes told me you had been asking about the Hudson River Regulating Board and the Sacandaga land buyouts."

"Sonny Barnes?"

"Our librarian. I bet he didn't introduce himself, did he? Sonny's a little challenged on the social-adeptness front." That was an understatement. "Anyway, about your research?"

"I was interested in what had happened to a local family. The Ketchems. But as it is, I've just recently found out—"

Roxanne steamed forward. "I have, right here in my hands, the financial records of the long-defunct Adirondack Land Development Partnership."

"Say what?"

"They were one of the groups that popped up like mushrooms when the HRRB was formed. They were land speculators who had friends on the board. They bought up properties that were going to go underwater and resold them to the board for a nice profit, and they also snatched up land near areas that were undergoing development."

"Sounds like a recipe for success, if not for sleeping soundly at night. How come they went under?"

"It was a huge, racy scandal. In 1932, the three partners and a bunch of friends were whooping it up at one of their twenty-five-room cottages. There were lots of scantily clad girls at the party, none of whom were their wives, and at the end of the night, two women were dead. There were rumors of orgies, the whole nine yards. Nowadays, they would have just gone on *Live with Regis and Kelly* and tearfully apologized, but in those days it wasn't so easy. One of the partners killed himself, and the Adirondack Land Development Partnership went bankrupt."

"How did the historical society wind up with their financial records? Wouldn't they have been confidential?"

"We don't actually have the original documents. That's probably why Sonny didn't think of it. He loathes copies. In the early eighties, a true-crime writer who summers around here researched the case for a book. She got copies of the partnership's records, and when she was done, she donated them to us. Wasn't that thoughtful?"

"Yeah." The question of what had happened to Jonathon Ketchem was over. She wasn't going to find anything in a bunch of financial documents about why his wife killed him, then spent the rest of her life insisting he was dead and building up a living memorial to his name. Unless it was the question of where the money for the clinic came from. Had the Ketchems made a bundle when their farm was sold? Or had there been some sort of insurance on Jonathon Ketchem that no one except his wife knew about? "I'd like to take a look," Clare said. "Can I come by tomorrow?"

"Nobody's going to be around tomorrow. I'm here this afternoon."

"I'm tied up for the rest of the afternoon and then five o'clock evening prayer."

There was a pause. Clare thought she heard the tap-tap-tap of Roxanne's manicured nail against the phone. "How long does that last?"

"I'll be free by six."

"Okay, you nip over here right afterward and I'll let you in. I won't be staying, but I'll set the alarm for you so that all you have to do is trigger it when you leave. How does that sound?"

"Terrific. Thank you."

She hung up feeling as if she'd accomplished something, recognizing, even as she let herself warm to the feeling, that it was really just busy-work, no different from when she had been a teen and had prided herself on working on one of her dad's engines while she should have been writing a paper or cleaning her room. It was always easy to escape into work that didn't matter. The hard part was settling down to the unpleasant tasks of life. She picked up her sheaf of pink papers, shuffled them, and then picked up the phone again. It was time to explain to the bishop's office how the rector of St. Alban's had gotten herself into the newspapers. Again.

CHAPTER 36

NOW

She was sitting at the worktable, gazing out the window in the historical society's old nursery, when she realized she hadn't ever called Russ.
She had wanted to talk with him out of earshot of Mrs. Marshall, but in
the rush of the day, the intention had slipped away from her. She reached
into the pocket of her oversized trench coat and pulled out her phone. At
least she could count on it to work in town. Usually.

She hesitated, considered where he might be at 6:30 on a Monday night,
and dialed his cell phone. She was avoiding calling him at home because
of who might answer. Could there possibly be a clearer indication that her
relationship was inappropriate? *If you want to be good, don't put yourself in
places where you're tempted to be bad,* her grandmother Fergusson would
say. *When your gut says to retreat, listen to it!* Hardball Wright would say.

And yet, she wasn't hanging up, was she?

"Van Alstyne here."

"Hey. It's Clare. Is this a bad time?"

"Hey." She could hear some sort of machine noise in the background,
a rhythmic chittering. "I'm still at work. Getting in some faxes. Trying to
cross off some possibilities for either of our missing men. Where are you?"

Pellets of rain, reconnaissance for the coming storm, strafed the window. "I'm sequestered in the top floor of the historical society."

"Look, when I suggested you try a volunteer stint there, I didn't mean
you had to move in."

She laughed. "I'm not cataloging. I'd been asking questions about
when the dam went in on the Sacandaga and what happened to the people
who were displaced. Roxanne called me with this cache of documents
that have lots of the records of the financial transactions. You know, who
bought the land, how much they paid for it."

"Sounds deadly. The only time I go through financial records is when I'm forced into it."

"Like in Dr. Rouse's case?"

"Yep. Although Lyle pitched in and did a fair share of the scut work, especially with the Rouses' personal finances."

"Anything that gives you a lead?"

"Nothing that looks any different from every other professional who has to buy a new SUV every third year to impress the neighbors. Three cards carrying big balances, but no signs that they ever went over the limit or couldn't pay on time. Line of equity, car loans—again, nothing that stands out."

"So your theory that Allan Rouse might have been dealing prescription drugs . . . ?"

"Doesn't look like it holds water. Or my idea that maybe he was abusing. Kevin Flynn hit every pharmacy between here and Gloversville, and no one could remember ever seeing him. We've run down his phone log in case we could spot an accomplice, but no luck."

Clare removed a stack of pages from the box in front of her and flopped them on the table. The copied documents were just that, loose-leaf copies stored three inches deep in a manuscript box. "What about the clinic's records?"

"They're more complicated, so we're not through with them yet. So far, it looks like all the funding from the town is accounted for."

"What about the money from the trust?"

"I'm still trying to track everything down that doesn't come from the town. He only had to account to the board for their money, so everything else—donations, sliding-scale fees, the trust—is all stuck in around the edges, as it were."

"What?" she said.

"What do you mean, 'what'?"

"You had a funny note in your voice."

He laughed quietly. "Busted. Until I pin down every penny, I'm still not giving up on the idea that there might have been some financial shell game going on."

"What about Mrs. Rouse? That was what I wanted to talk to you about earlier today." She flipped through a few pages. It looked as if the entries were in chronological order. She tipped the whole box over until the papers flopped into an upside-down pile and picked up the last several documents. No index. Shoot.

"What about her?"

"Remember what you said to Mrs. Marshall, about how the police would treat a suspected spouse nowadays? How come you haven't grilled Mrs. Rouse?"

"Because she can account for her whereabouts. She was already making phone calls all over town, trying to track down her husband, while he was alive and well at Stewart's Pond with Debba Clow. We've interviewed people who spoke with her, and her phone records confirm those calls were made from her home phone. Lyle suggested she and Debba might have been in cahoots, but I find that hard to believe."

She flipped over pages until she started seeing "1929." She began working her way forward from the last of the Adirondack Land Development Partnership's documents in that year. "If they were, it'd certainly put a different complexion on Mrs. Rouse's visit to the Clows, wouldn't it?"

He laughed. "You make a great conspiracy theorist. Have you figured out who killed JFK yet?" She heard someone calling out a good-bye in the background.

"I ought to let you go," she said.

"I'm fixing to head out right now. Tell you what, give me a minute to hobble downstairs and find my hands free and I'll call you from my car."

"You drove yourself in to work? How can you manage the clutch?"

"I swapped with my mom. She has a Toyota Camry. Plenty of room for my leg, and no shifting."

"I thought Linda was taking you in."

"That wasn't working out as well."

As well as what? she thought, but kept her mouth shut. "Okay, give me a call when you get settled."

She glanced out the window again after he hung up. The threatening rain clouds had closed off the sky, darkening the soggy back garden and the tree-shrouded alley beyond. She could see her own face in the glass, its lines soft, her eyes dreamy. She looked as if she ought to be singing the chorus of "Hello Young Lovers." She rolled her eyes and went back to the partnership's accounts.

McThis and McThat, with the occasional MacWhosit and Someones-son thrown in for light relief. The location of the land, the structures thereon—she supposed that was so they would know what would have to go before the flooding started—the agent who handled the purchase. Date of transaction and price. Date of possession, which she guessed meant when the prior owners beat it. She had an uneducated eye, but it seemed as if most of the farmers were getting a raw deal. Even in the 1920s, $7,000 couldn't have been much for forty acres, a house, and a barn.

And there they were, in the 1928s. Jonathon and Jane Ketchem. Fifty-five riverfront acres: $7,455. Date of possession, October 16, 1928. They hadn't held on to the bitter end, but they had gotten close. Maybe they had brought in one last crop.

They didn't get any more money than anyone else. Yet with it they had bought a house in town, and Jane Ketchem went through the depression without having to work. Admittedly, it was a modest house and a frugal life. But she had still managed to send her daughter to college, start a clinic, and leave an endowment of over one hundred thousand dollars. Could the Ketchem farm have generated so much income that they had had a goodly chunk of change put away? Clare doubted it. All the farmers she knew around here wound up sinking too much into their operations to build up any significant reserve. It might have been easier for the family farmer in the 1920s, but she'd bet it wasn't *that* much different from now. And anyway, if they had had money in the bank or the stock market, what happened in 1929 when the market crashed and the banks went bust?

Her phone began playing the first notes of a Bach fugue. "Hello," she answered.

"It's me."

"Hi, you. Let me know if driving with a broken leg and talking get too complicated, okay?"

"You bet," he said. "Headed down the highway," he sang in a passable baritone, "in my mother's Camry, lookin' for adventure. . . ."

"I've just realized that if you're in Margy's Camry, she must have your pickup. That's a scary thought."

"After the way she lectured me on its wasteful consumption of fossil fuels, I'll be surprised if she ever gets into it."

"Remember those land-sale records I was researching? I found the Ketchems' farm. Listen to this." She read him the information off the paper. It had been a large ledger sheet, reduced when the copies were made, and she had to squint at it, even with the desk lamp on. Time to turn on the overhead light. "Now, does that sound to you like enough to buy a new house, send your kid to college, live on for forty years, and endow a trust fund?"

"Maybe she used S & H green stamps."

"Seriously."

"I dunno. Her in-laws were pretty well set up. Maybe they supported her. Thinking their son had run out on her and all. Little did they know. Why is this such a big deal with you, anyway?"

She propped her chin in her hand and stared through her reflection into the gathering night. "It's this money. It's in my hands now, and I want to know where it came from. It certainly didn't make anyone else associated with it very happy, did it? I'm beginning to think it's like the Hope diamond or something."

"Your Mrs. Marshall's had it for years, and it doesn't seem to have doomed her to a life of woe. In fact, she seems to have done pretty darn well for herself."

"Except that for her whole life she thought her father had walked out on her. And she never gave herself the chance to be a mother. Although, to be fair, she told me that was because of what happened to her siblings. Which is a completely different issue." A gust of wind splattered the window with a handful of rain. It was dim enough now that the shadows were blurring into the pavement, and the winter-dead grass and the carriage house and the alley pavement beyond were all shades of gray and grayer.

In the carriage house behind the clinic, a light went on.

She bolted up in her seat. "Russ," she said. "There's somebody in the clinic. In the old garage out back." She stood to get a better view, realized she would be outlined to anyone emerging into the alley, and snapped off her lamp. The old nursery sprang to life in shadows.

"What do you see?"

"Nothing yet. A light just came on. There's a window on the side, just the same as the historical society's carriage house. I don't see anyone moving or anything."

"The clinic attaches to the carriage house in the back, doesn't it?" he said. "Could be somebody's trying to break in, thinks he can rip them off for some prescription drugs. Hang tight, I'm turning the car around."

"I don't see any other lights on at the clinic. What should I do?"

"You shouldn't do anything. Stay put. I'm on my way. We've had this discussion before, remember? Me cop, you priest."

"Holy crow."

"What?"

"The light's gone off." She searched for some sign of movement through the rain-streaked window. She had good eyes. Pilot's eyes. She could see this. "Somebody's coming out."

"Where? The front? The back?"

"The back. Out of the carriage house."

"How many? Male or female?"

"One. Looks sort of like a man, but it's hard to tell. Whoever it is, he's pushing a bike." She watched the figure pause at the corner of the carriage house. It seemed to be oddly proportioned, bulky, long and flapping, a huge hat tied down around its head.

"Rouse kept his bike in the carriage house," Russ said.

"I think he or she's a street person. Oh Lord, I hope it's not someone who comes to our soup kitchen." Another possibility struck her and she sucked in her breath. "Russ, maybe this is your missing link to Dr. Rouse."

"The thought had occurred to me." His voice was dry.

"Uh-oh."

"What?"

"He's walking the bike up the alley."

"Which way?"

"Um, left. Toward Washington Street." She snatched up her coat and headed toward the hall. "I'm going to follow him."

"Clare, no. Stay put."

She took the stairs two at a time. "I'm not going to get near him. I'm just going to tail him."

"Oh, for Christ's sake!"

"Well you're not about to get out of the Camry and run him down on foot if he vanishes between some houses, are you?" She snapped the switches on the brass-plated light fixtures. "I'll tell you where he is and then you get the car in front of him and cut him off."

"Clare, this guy could be an addict. That means dangerous, desperate, and unpredictable."

Roxanne had left a Post-it note over the alarm. "Trigger here, then 60 seconds," it read. Clare turned on the alarm. "Too late," she said. "I've just armed the building security. I have to get out in one minute or sirens go off."

"Great! Let the sirens go off. I'd prefer it. It'll trigger a call to the station and we'll have a squad car there in ten minutes."

She shrugged into her coat, buttoned it to the neck, and yanked the door open. The wind almost tore the knob from her hand. "You call the station if you think we need backup."

She could hear him chomping off obscenities before they could tinge her delicate ears. She clattered down the steps and crunched over a shell-and-gravel path to the garden gate, set in the middle of a tall iron fence.

"Listen to you," he said. "*We* do not need backup because *we* are not trained law enforcement officers."

The gate groaned open. Clare dashed across the garden, her boot steps squish-squish-slapping against the soggy ground. She tried the door to the carriage house. Locked. The iron fence that divided the historical society from the clinic and alley was bolted into the side of the carriage house. "Crap," she said.

"What?"

"I can't get out the back of the garden. Unless . . ." She ran to the other side of the carriage house, where a brick wall bristling with dead ivy took the place of the fence. In the summertime, it must look like an impenetrable barrier, but now—"Yes," she said. "Hang on, I have to drop you in my pocket." She flattened herself against the carriage house and squeezed through the claustrophobic gap, the ivy tugging and snapping the back of her raincoat. She could hear Russ's voice in her pocket, demanding that she talk to him.

She burst out of the opening and stumbled into the alley. She retrieved the phone from her pocket. "Got out of the garden," she said. "I'm after him." The rain splattered over the stone, and she splashed through widening puddles that were already runneling down the center of the alley.

The narrow street emptied out between a Dumpster and a plastic garden shed. She stopped on the sidewalk, looked left, right, and found her target, a dark shape pedaling up Washington Street, bent against the rain that had already plastered her hair against her head and run beneath the collar of her coat. "He's headed up Washington Street. Toward, um, Elm."

"I'll be there in just a few minutes. Clare, hang back. Getting this guy isn't worth risking your getting hurt."

"I am hanging back. I'll be fine." She crossed the road and strode toward the street person, keeping him in sight but not breaking into a run.

She kept hard to the edge of the sidewalk, where she could duck into a front walk or driveway in order to avoid being spotted. On a street empty of everything except darkness and the rain, she was going to stick out like a lighthouse. A car sped down the street from the opposite direction, throwing up sheets of water, and for a moment she thought it might be Russ and said, "Is that you? Can you see me?" but it was a Camaro that went past, picking her out in its headlights, almost drenching her. She jumped out of the way, and when she looked up, the figure had stopped on the corner. Watching her.

"Oh, crap, he's seen me."

"Where are you?"

Then the shape bent over the handlebars and was gone, almost before she could register the movement. "He's taken off!" She loped after the vanished form.

"Where?" Russ's voice was all patience, cut with strangled worry.

"He went left at the intersection. Don't know the street name. Away from where the Rouses and the Burnses live." It was hard to run clutching the phone to her ear. "I'm gonna drop you in my pocket for a sec." She did so as she rounded the corner. The clinic intruder was at least a block ahead of her, coat flapping past the rear wheel of the bike, hat jouncing. For a moment, she saw the white blur of a face, seeking her out, and then the bulky form was gone again. Where? She lengthened her stride, her boots pounding against the pavement, her breath rasping in her ears. The rain lashed her face, forcing her to screw up her eyes and look sideways. She splashed across one roadway and skidded to a halt at the second.

She grabbed her phone. "I think he's ducked down Fisher Street."

"There's a whole warren of short streets down there. I'm driving toward the riverfront, so I'll be ahead of you."

"'Kay." She dropped the phone in her pocket and jogged down Fisher Street, swinging her head from left to right, praying for that one telltale glimpse out of the corner of her eye. And she got it. Just a flicker of movement, a faint gleam on metal, a rosy wink from the rear reflector.

She cut across the street, cleared the sidewalk with one leap, and dodged a pair of waterlogged yew bushes to shortcut through someone's yard. She almost skidded out of control on the soggy remains of last year's lawn, but stumbled through to the cross street, the intruder's long coat skirling ahead of her, leading her on.

She held her phone up like a mike. "He's going through the cemetery."

She dropped it again and charged ahead, the water splashing up her coat with every stride, so that she was more wet than dry. She ducked through the cemetery's low brick entrance, dashing rain out of her eyes to keep the fleeing figure in sight. Please don't let him hide in the mortuary, she thought. The winter dead of Millers Kill had to wait for their burials until April; the long semisubterranean mortuary would be full right now.

But whoever it was showed no signs of stopping. The pinwheel rain hat bobbed in and out of Clare's view, pedaling headlong toward the cemetery's side entrance. She pelted over walkways turned to stony brooks and graves where the spongy earth sagged under her bootfalls. She zigged and zagged past fenced-in family plots and curved stone benches. The figure vanished through a screen of trees. Sprinting to catch up, Clare dodged a Civil War–era oak and found herself one footfall away from James and Nancy McKeller, husband and wife. She hurdled their stone with a wild launch into the air and came down hard, stumbled, recovered, and dashed through the side entrance.

A muffled voice was coming from her pocket. It took two tries to grab the phone, her wet fingers slipping over its plastic case. "Where are you?" Russ was asking.

She glanced up at the dripping street sign. "Second Avenue." A grandiose name for a single block of one-and-a-half-story houses. She jogged down the sidewalk, the phone pressed against her ear. "Where are you?"

"On Lower First Avenue. I figure he's headed for the old chandleries."

"The what?"

"I'll tell you later. Is he still in sight?"

She glanced between the houses as she jogged past. "No. I think he went to the end of the street, but I don't know which way he turned."

"He couldn't have gone to the right." She reached the end of Second Avenue and saw what Russ meant. The street petered out into a marshy tangle of elephant grass and cattails. "All these streets dump into First Avenue, and that's—"

She swiveled and ran to the left. One house, two houses, three, and there she was, at the intersection with Upper First Avenue and Lower First Avenue. She heard a shout, muffled and distant from down the street, echoed over the phone.

She pounded down Lower First, a street as much a mausoleum as that in the cemetery. Low, shuttered buildings with spray-painted doors and rusting hulks of unidentifiable origin in their yards. A two-story inn untouched so long that its paint had peeled totally away, leaving it raw, gray, and warping. A series of storefronts, roofs rotting, porches leaning, windows boarded with plywood turned silver with age. And there, crutching toward the last building in the row, Russ.

His mother's car, windows steamed, lights off, was parked at the street's terminal point, where the pavement ended and a tumble of boulders sloped down into the Millers Kill. It looked as if a pair of lovers had driven down to enjoy some privacy and a view of the fast-moving, snow-charged river. The bike was overturned in the middle of the street, its rear wheel still spinning.

"What happened?" She skidded to a halt in front of him, sucking breath to speak.

He balanced between his crutches, one hand awkwardly pinching his gun to the palm rest. "I was talking to you on the phone and I saw the guy." Rain was rolling down his hair, dripping off the ends. "I opened the car door and swung my gun out and ordered him to stop. He dumped the bike and ran in there." He pointed to the decrepit wooden building squared between the street and the river. Rotting stumps of pilings ran along its waterfront side. "Here, take this," he went on, handing her his gun. She took it stock down and automatically checked the cartridge and the safety.

"I'm not going to use this on anyone." She wiped her forehead in a useless attempt to keep the rain out of her eyes.

"I'm not planning on using it on anyone, either. It's too damn hard to move while holding on to it, and if I stick it back into my belt holster it'll take me too long to get it out. Goddamn broken leg. Pardon my French."

He crutched toward the door. "Stay behind me, and when I say gun, put it in my right hand."

She fell in behind him. "You're not ordering me to stay in the car?"

"Would you listen if I did?"

"No."

"Okay then. May as well take advantage of you."

There was no porch fronting the building, only two granite steps leading up to a gaping doorway. Clare looked up to the second story, where shattered windows stared endlessly into the past. "What is this place?" She pitched her voice low.

"It was a chandlery about a hundred and eighty years ago. A ship's provisioner. This is the oldest part of the town, from back in the seventeen hundreds when everything moved in and out by boat." She heard his crutch tips thunk wetly on wood, and then she stepped through the doorway, careful to stay at his back.

"Good God." She had to fight not to gag. The dark empty space reeked of urine and human waste.

"I know." He shifted forward into the darkness, thump-step, thump-step. The wooden planks beneath them were uneven, swollen with age and soaking up things Clare didn't want to imagine. "This is one of the hidey-holes for the hard-core homeless in the area. Every six months or so, we come in here, roust everybody out, and cart them off to shelters or the hospital. It's useless, of course. There aren't enough beds in the addiction unit or the mental-health facility for people asking for help, let alone for these guys, who don't want anything to do with it. We only round 'em up because the aldermen are scared someone's going to wreck himself up here and sue the town."

There was a creak ahead of them and Russ froze. Clare stood still behind him, letting the rain drip off her. "C'mon," he said.

"There doesn't seem to be anyone here now," she whispered.

"We were down here in early March. There'd been a fight, and one guy cut another one up real bad. We had the ambulance, a fire truck, the works. Usually they stay away awhile after something like that. They don't want to get caught if we show up again."

"What happened to the man?"

"Which one?"

"The one who was hurt."

"He got patched up in the ER and then hung around town for a while. He had some sort of chronic illness. TB? He hung around the clinic for a while, getting treatment. Yeah, it must have been TB. Of course, as soon as he was well enough, he vanished."

They came to an open doorway. The waterfront wall to their right was pierced with glassless windows, but the rain and the hour seemed to slow the gray light, so that it sluggarded across the floor and died before it reached the middle of the room.

"I'm going to go through that door and back up against the wall on the right-hand side." He pitched his voice just above a whisper. "I want you to point the gun in front of you right after I'm out of the way, then step in beside me. Got it?"

"Yeah."

The handle of the gun was slippery in her hands, from rain and nervous sweat. Russ thudded through the doorway and sideways, the rubber crutch-tips squeaking in protest, and she braced the gun and stepped forward, sweeping it in front of her, lurched to the side, and slammed against the wall, jarring loose a powdery shower of dried birdshit on both of them.

"I bet you watched *Starsky and Hutch* when you were a kid." His voice was dry. "C'mon, there's no one in here."

They crossed the warped, bulging floor to the next doorway. Russ peered around its edge. "End of the line," he said. He held his right hand out. Clare gave him the gun. Russ crutched through first, Clare tight behind him. Where the other rooms had soared high into the musty darkness, this ceiling was barely high enough for Russ to pass without ducking. Open-case stairs pierced the low ceiling on the left- and right-hand walls. Below each stairway, trap doorways yawned, revealing two other stairs, leading to the cellar. From the amount of mouse droppings and dirt encrusting the doors, Clare suspected they had lain open a long time.

"Police," Russ said, in a voice that cracked with authority. "Put your hands up in the air and walk out into the open."

Silence.

"He has to be here, right?" Clare whispered. The glass was broken out of the windows tucked near the stairs, but the narrow wooden crossbars, the lights, were intact. The wall opposite them was solid, featureless.

"No other way out." He pointed toward the room overhead. "A couple of vents under the eaves up there. Too small for a human. Cellar down there's beneath the stone foundations."

"What are we going to do?" She looked at Russ's cast.

"Don't worry, I'm not going to go dashing up after him." He glanced at the dark rectangle swallowing the cellar stairs. "Or down."

There was a splash. Clare swiveled toward the right-hand stairs. "What was that?"

"Sounded like something in the cellar." He crutched closer, until he stood next to the long side of the open trap door, like a graveside mourner. "It's well below the waterline. Probably pretty wet down there."

Another noise. Sloshing. Movement.

"You there in the cellar," Russ shouted. "Come to the foot of the stairs with your hands up. There's no way out." His voice warmed a shade. "I can promise you it's a hell of a lot warmer and drier at the station than it is here."

Clare went around him and squatted at the head of the stairs. She could see them descending straight down into the gloom of the cellar. Like the other stairs in the building, these were open case, simple boards nailed to risers, no railing. "You can tell they constructed this before OSHA was around," she said. In the single patch of gray light that made it to the bottom, she could see a flash of black water and the skeletal remains of a barrel. "Do you want me to go down? There's no way you can maneuver those stairs."

He stared at her. "You're kidding, right?" He shook his head. "You've read too damn many Nancy Drew mysteries. No, you don't get to go down into the creepy cellar where the bad guy lurks. Alone, unarmed, and without a light. Don't be an idiot."

More splashing. Rhythmic. Not like someone walking through water. The sound of something slapping against the water. Dropping into it.

"This is the nonidiot way to get the bad guy." Russ kept his voice casual, but he moved closer to the edge of the opening, his crutch tips bracing against the hinges of the trapdoor. He watched the darkness below as he spoke. "I'm going to stand in the door to this room with my gun out and ready. You're going to go back to the car, call the station, and have them send a couple units out here. Then you'll stay in the car until they arrive." She opened her mouth, but he cut her off. "It's not just to keep you safe. If anything happens to me, or if the suspect gets past me, you'll be able to see where he goes and call for help."

She reached into her pocket and pulled out her cell phone. "I forgot all about it." She grinned up at him. "I've still got your phone on the line. I'll be using up my minutes—"

The sound was like the ceiling falling in, rumble, pound, bash, and she swung her head and saw the man, already halfway across the room, hat tumbled off in the rush, hard-soled shoes slicing the floor, and Russ twisting around, tangled in his crutches, raising his gun, and she was rising from her crouch shouting, "No!" and the man leaped, he bounded, his arms crossed before him, smashing into Russ, the crutches clattering away and Russ was falling into the tomb-shaped opening, and she dove forward without thinking, to block his fall, to catch him, her fingers closing on his arm and she was yanked off balance and it was too late. Let. Go. her brain said, but in the time it took to flash the message to her hand she had smashed shoulder and hip against the stairs and hit the floor with the force of a car wreck, icy cold water parting beneath the slap of her body, then clapping over her, soaking her to the bone in an instant. The blow knocked the breath out of her, and she inhaled too quickly, panicking, swallowing more of the scummy water, choking and sputtering. She jerked upright, hacked, and gasped. Above her, the rectangle of gray narrowed. She looked up. The trapdoor was ready to drop, propped up by the man's stiff and trembling arm. It was too dim to make out his expression. Only the pale whiteness of his face.

"No!" she cried. "Don't!"

"I'm sorry," Allan Rouse said. Then he dropped the door.

CHAPTER 37

NOW

The darkness clapped shut over them like the lid on a coffin. There was a thunk as the bolt slid home, locking them in. The raw horror-story sound of it pulled an involuntary whimper out of her throat. Then Rouse's footsteps crossed the floor overhead.

The other stairway. She exploded out of the water, seeing, now, with precious seconds wasted gaping at the dark, the pale rectangle that was the other overhead door. She ran for the other stairs as if running in a nightmare, legs dragging through shin-deep water, damp cobwebs curling across her face, barely outlined brick support columns looming in her way. She was halfway to the stairs, splashing and gasping, when she heard the complaint of rust-eaten hinges.

"Dr. Rouse!" she screamed. "Don't do this! Don't leave us down here!"

"I'll send someone," he said, his voice hollow. "When it's safe."

"For God's sake!" The door kachunked closed, and the pressure wave flattened the air around her, thinning her voice, pushing it into the far, unseen corners of the cellar.

For the love of God, Montresor!

She shivered violently, hot and cold all at the same time.

"Clare?" Russ's voice, rough and waterlogged, brought her back to herself. He coughed and retched, and stirred in the water.

She slogged toward the sound. "Keep talking," she said. "I can't see anything."

"Are you all right?" His words induced another round of coughing.

"I think so." She slammed into a brick column and reeled backward. "Or I will be if I don't knock myself out," she wheezed. She slowed down and let her outstretched hands take the lead. "You sound terrible. How's your leg?"

"I just swallowed some water when I fell." He coughed. "So much for avoiding showers to keep my cast dry."

Her hand touched his hair. She knelt in the water beside him, wincing at its bite, and touched his face, his chest, his arms. He was soaking. "You're okay? What else did you hit?"

He was touching her, as well, the pat-pat-patting of fingers asking, Are you here? Are you whole? He folded one of his hands over hers. His fingers were cold. "I twisted when I fell. I knocked my arm pretty good, but at least I didn't break my head open. How about you?"

She rotated her arm, and a steady throb in her shoulder sizzled into a cramp of pain. She sucked in her breath. "I think I banged up my shoulder a little. Everything else is working fine." She stood up, holding on to his hand. "Let's get out of this water." She found his other hand, clasped it, and hauled. He was taller than she, and heavier, and she had to lean backward to get the leverage. When he was upright, she wrapped her arm around his waist, he slung his arm over her shoulder, and they hobbled toward the stairs.

She could hear him every time he had to step on his broken leg. He breathed in through his nose, hard, and held it. "I'm sorry," she said. "This hurts, doesn't it?"

"I'll be fine." He clipped his words.

The back of her outstretched hand banged against wood. "Ouch," she said. "Okay, let's get on the stairs."

She waited until Russ had sat on one of the steps and pulled himself up out of the water. Then she crept up the stairs, bent over, one hand touching the edge of the wooden planks so she wouldn't fall off, the other held over her head. Her fingers hit something solid. The trapdoor. "I'm going to try to open it," she said. For a second, she thought of the stuff she had seen on it, the mouse pellets and the dirt and God knew what else. *It'll shower off.* She braced her shoulders and upper back against the door and pushed. Nothing.

She went up another step so that she was folded tight beneath the door, and pushed again. This time she felt something giving way, the ripping sound of wood splitting. Her feet slid inward. She heard a crack.

"Holy crow!" She scrambled to a lower rung just in time to avoid breaking through the step. She reached down. She had splintered it into two pieces.

"What happened?" Russ said.

"I've discovered the stairs are weaker than the door." She made her way hand and foot back down the steps. He took up most of one rung, so she sat above him. "I suppose I should try the other one."

"Bolted shut?"

"Yeah."

"Then the other one probably is as well. Give it a rest before you try it." They sat for a moment. "Was that who I thought it was?" he asked.

"Allan Rouse." She was seized with another spasm of shivering. "Showing some flexibility on that 'First, do no harm' thing. At least he promised to send help back for us."

"Oh yeah?" "She could tell from his voice that he was shivering, too. "He didn't provide a timeline for our rescue, by any chance?"

"No."

"'Cause whether it's before or after we die of hypothermia will make a difference."

She hunched over, trying to find some core of warmth in her sopping clothes. "Yeah."

"What do you have on under that coat?"

She rasped a laugh. "Are we back to that again?"

His voice was patient. "Just answer the question."

"One of my clerical blouses."

"Take off your coat and move down here next to me. Keep hold of it." She could hear the zipper on his jacket, and the plank creaking and bumping as he repositioned himself. She struggled out of her clinging coat before carefully feeling her way to the next lower rung, touching wood and then a damp jeans-covered thigh.

"Excuse me," she said. She swept her hand back and forth and realized he had straddled the step, jamming his good leg between this rung and the next, resting his cast on the step below them.

"Sit with your back toward me." He had taken his arms out of his parka, leaving it hanging from his shoulders. She did as directed, drawing her knees up, draping her coat over them like the proverbial wet blanket. He wrapped his arms around her. "Better?"

"A little, yeah."

"It won't keep us in the long run. It'd take our clothes three days to dry out in this humidity, and the temperature can't be much above forty degrees. But I've always found it's easier to think when you're warm."

"This isn't exactly warm."

"Give it some time."

She let her head tip back. He rested his cheek against her hair. She could feel the rise and fall of his chest as he sighed. "I should have made you stay in the car," he said.

"Darn right, you should have."

He laughed, and she joined him, laughing helplessly and shivering and clutching at her coat so it didn't fall.

Eventually, they fell silent. Where their bodies met, wet shirts crumpling between them, she began to feel warm. Even the damp underside of her coat didn't seem as frigid as it had a few minutes ago. "I think we're throwing off heat," she said.

"It wouldn't surprise me." His voice was dry.

She opened her mouth to make a joke and was amazed to hear herself say, "I've thought about this." He was quiet. The darkness, the anonymity of it let her go on. "About you holding me, I mean. Not about being stuck in a wet, freezing cellar. In fact, when I imagine it, it's usually in a much warmer place. With fewer clothes on. And, of course, none of those inconvenient moral issues hanging over us. So it's pretty much a fantasy. Free-floating. Please stop me before I make more of an ass of myself than I already have." Her cheeks were so hot she could have steamed her coat dry with them. "Sorry. I tend to babble when I'm nervous."

He tightened his arms around her. "I know," he said, his voice low in her ear. Then she felt his lips on her cheek, and she turned her head, and his mouth slid over hers and they were kissing. It was sweet, so sweet, and as his mouth moved over hers she felt a string she hadn't known was tied tug free inside her chest, and everything that made her who she was fell open to him. She made a noise, encouragement, maybe, or applause, and he slanted against her harder, his hands tangling in her hair. His mouth, his hands, the moan trapped in his throat made her mindless. She licked, kissed, stroked, clutched, utterly lost in him until a twist of her hips sent her coat slithering down across her knees, heading for the water below. She yanked free of him and grabbed it before it fell.

They both froze. The cold, damp air chilled her blouse, raising gooseflesh all along her arms. She could hear him, rasping for breath.

"I'm—," he started to say, and she cut him off.

"Don't say you're sorry."

"God, no." In the pause, she could hear him trying to catch his breath. "Are you?"

She ought to be. She knew that. "No," she said.

Another sharp breath. She thought she could feel him, leaning toward her. Then he said, "This isn't the time. Or the place." His voice was thick and harsh.

There isn't any time or place, she wanted to cry, but she kept it to herself. Instead she said, "Hold my coat. I'm going to try the other door." A jolly wade through icy shin-deep water should cool her ardor. She thrust the coat at him and went down the stairs by hand and foot. They weren't as far above the water as she had thought, and when she stepped off the stairs into the icy murk she knew why.

"The water's rising." She tried to keep her voice calm. "It's up past my knees now."

He swore. "The river," he said. "It's rising."

"What?"

"Every year, we get some flooding with the snowmelt. Add in a few hard rains, and presto. Flash flood. Goddamnit."

His muffled swearing followed her as she sloshed across the floor, hands outstretched. She cast about for the other stairs, and had a moment of disoriented panic before whacking into a semisubmerged step. She crawled out of the water to the top and pushed against the trapdoor. She shoved and rattled it for form's sake, but she knew she wasn't going anywhere.

"Any luck?" he called. His voice spread through the darkness, lapped against the outermost walls. She realized the cellar was bigger than she had thought, probably encompassing the entire footprint of the building.

"It's not budging." She gritted her teeth and descended into the water again. "Any idea how deep it's likely to get?"

"Deep. The Millers Kill has been known to rise ten feet above normal, and we're well below water level right now. There must be a weak spot in the foundation."

"It'd have to be more than a weak spot. It's got to be coming in by the gallon to rise this quickly." She waved her hands in front of her and struck a brick column. She paused. "I don't hear any water rushing."

"Probably a chunk missing near the cellar floor. Could be this place is partially underwater most of the year, except maybe midsummer when the river is at its lowest. The good news is, the ceiling is definitely above water level, even when the river's high, like it is today." His voice was much closer. She sloshed forward, gritting her teeth against the cold slicing into her legs.

"And the bad news?"

"It's not much higher. If the water rises to level with the Millers Kill, we'll be sitting in it up to our necks."

In water a few degrees above freezing. He didn't have to spell it out for her. As the heat leached from their limbs, they would go numb. Then, as their bodies started to shut down, they would get sleepy. Finally, when their core temperatures cooled to seventy degrees, they would die. She had seen a special on the Discovery Channel that had said fishermen in the North Atlantic could survive ten minutes in the water without survival gear. She and Russ wouldn't last much longer.

She collided with the stairs. "I think there may be a way out," Russ said as she hauled herself, dripping, up the steps. "I think there may be a bulkhead here somewhere."

"You mean a door in the cellar? With steps coming down from the street?" She sat on the rung below him.

"C'mere," he said, wrapping his hands around her arms and lifting her into the cradle of his legs. He drew her close and tossed her coat over her. "There's nothing on the street side. But I'm pretty sure I remember seeing one facing the river. I used to fish all along the kill back when I was a kid. It was a long time ago, but it'll still be here. Somewhere."

"But if it's facing the river, wouldn't it be underwater, too?"

"Maybe. But even so, we'd be out of here. At the worst, we'd be carried downriver some until we could swim for the shore."

"No, at the worst, we'd be swept away in the freezing water and drown."

"Yeah. Well." He tightened his hold on her. "I'm going to try it. I want you to sit tight on these stairs."

"So I can be the girl from *Titanic* who stays high and dry while you, the guy, vanish beneath the icy waves? I don't think so."

"Didn't we just agree you should have stayed in the car?"

"I was joking."

"Clare." Maybe it was the total darkness that made his voice so intimate. "If anything were to happen to you, I'd . . ."

"You'd what?"

The darkness, and the sense that they were the only inhabitants of a world bound by the unseen walls stretching out around them.

"I'd walk into my brother-in-law's field and lie down and let the corn grow up around me."

No one else in their world. No costs, no considerations, only two voices in the dark. And honesty.

"Okay. Same here." She twined her arms over his, hugging him closer. "Remember the helicopter?" She had taken him for a disastrous ride last summer.

"I promise you, I will never, ever forget the helicopter. So long as we both shall live." She could hear the smile in his voice. "You told me to hold on."

"So now we're both holding on. No you going and me staying behind. We sink or swim together."

He pressed a kiss into her hair. "Even if I said please?"

"No."

He made a noise deep in his throat.

They sat in silence for a while. Clare was damp where she wasn't wet, aching with the chill, and both of them reeked. She felt as if she could stay right where she was forever. But the realization of it roused her. They didn't have forever.

"I may as well get down there and see if I can find this bulkhead before it gets any deeper." She leaned forward, folding her coat and draping it over one of the steps. She climbed down the stairs and waded into the water.

"Hang on." She could hear a bumping sound as Russ went down the steps on his rear. He gasped when he hit the water. "I'm coming with you." He jostled her arm, trailed down and took her hand. "Let's see. The stairs are parallel to the river side of the building, so the wall should be right—" They struck an uneven patch of stone. "Here," Russ said. "You go left, I'll go right." He gave her hand a squeeze before letting go.

She spread her hands over the dank stone and began her search. Step, sweep. Step, sweep. Cobwebs stroked her face and clung to her hair. She tried not to think of the creepy-crawlies that might be living there. At least nothing was squeaking. The only sounds were the lapping of water against stone, Russ's periodic huffs of pain as he bore down on his broken leg, and her own chattering teeth. She reached the corner of the building.

"I'm at a corner. Do you want me to continue? This wall runs away from the river, parallel to the street."

"No, come on back toward me."

He didn't have to ask twice. She waded through the water, trailing one hand over the stone to keep her bearings. "Where are you?"

"Right here."

"How's your leg?"

"Better. Of course, that's because it's gone numb."

"Mine, too." Touching his back to orient herself, she moved past him and pressed both hands against the foundation wall. The moldy, old, something-died-in-here smell was worse. She tried not to breathe too deeply. Step, sweep. Step, sweep. "Is it my imagination, or do you feel the water rising?"

"It's your imagination."

Imagination or no, the faster they found the bulkhead—if there was one—the sooner they'd be out of this death trap. She increased her pace. So she had no one to blame but herself when she tripped over a knee-high obstacle and tumbled into the water. The shock of the cold took her breath away, and she flailed and scrambled her way back onto her feet.

"Clare? What is it? What happened?"

She forced words from her tightly clenched jaw. "There's something here. I tripped."

He bumped into her, and brushed her as he bent over, feeling out the obstacle. She wrapped her arms around herself and shook. *I will never be warm again.*

"You found it, darlin'." He straightened, pulled her into a tight embrace, chafed her back. "Steps. It's a high bulkhead door, which means it may not be underwater. You ready to check it out?"

She nodded. "Okay."

"Good girl." He released her.

She shuffled forward until her boots struck something hard beneath the water. She stepped up. "Take my hand," she said. He interlaced his fingers with hers, and she steadied him as he mounted the first step. Stretching out one arm in front of her, she took a second step. The third was above the water. "It's right here," she said, thumping a wooden door with her knee. Russ stepped up beside her and she let go of his hand. Stretching up and down, she made out two crossbeams, bracing the vertical planks. "It must go right up to the ceiling."

She heard his fingers tapping several inches above her reach. "It does," he said.

The wood was soft and pulpy. Reaching left, she found out why. Water was rolling through the crack between the door and the jamb, running in swift rivulets down to the stone step below. "This thing is leaking," she said. "There's water backed up on the other side."

"Not at the top. Lets see how high it goes."

She traced the edge of the door upward, past one set of hinges, until her fingers moved past the running water onto damp, flaky wood. "It's about as high as my neck," she said.

"I figure there are two possibilities," he said. "It could be water's collected in the well created by the outside stairs. In that case, when we open the door, we'll be hit with a gush. But we'll be able to walk out once it's drained."

"And the second possibility?"

"The river's risen above its banks here."

"So when we open the door—"

"It floods the cellar. Right up to your neck."

She didn't point out that she was standing on steps that raised her a foot and a half above the floor. If the cellar flooded, it would be well above her neck.

"If that's the case," he went on, "the best thing we can do is hang on to the door until the water levels have equalized. Then we can pull ourselves out and hopefully hang on to the building. Once we've got our footing, we'll just walk out of the water to the end of the street."

"Sure thing. No sweat."

"Look, I'll be more than happy if you want to get back up on the top of the stairs and wait. You'll be above the water there."

"We've already been through that." She reached to her right and hit his arm. "How do we open the door?"

"There are two wooden bars resting in brackets. Maybe eight inches long, two inches high. One above the door handle, one below." He shifted. "They're swollen with all the water. So they're going to be hard to move." He stood, silent. She let him think it through. "This is how we'll do it. I'm going to kick the lower one out of its bracket."

"How are you going to do that with a broken leg? Maybe that should be my job."

"Your job is going to be standing behind me and hanging on as tight as you can. The only place we can get a grip and not be washed away to the back wall is the door handle here. I'm going to hold that and you're going to hold me. Okay?"

"Okay."

"All right, get underneath my arm here and help me balance myself."

She ducked beneath his shoulder and took as much of his weight as she could, while he drew his uninjured foot off the floor. His breath hissed between his teeth, and she winced for what he must be feeling.

Thunk! Thunk! Thunk! He tilted forward and stood on his good leg again.

"Did you get it?"

"I think so." He bent over, feeling for the bar. "Yeah. The door is bowing out down here. Whatever's behind it, it's got plenty of force. So hang on."

She wrapped her arms around his waist and clasped her hands over her wrists. "I'm ready."

He sidled closer to the door, until his chest was against the planks and she could feel the spongy wood against the backs of her hands. He bent his arm.

Whump! Whump! Whump!

"Shit," he hissed.

"Stuck?"

He blew his breath out in frustration. "I wish I had my work gloves."

She could feel his muscles tensing, his whole body weighing in behind the palm of his hand as he beat against the stubborn bar. Whump! Whump! He grunted.

"Anything?"

"Yeah. It gave some. Hang on tight, this next one may do it."

He brought his arm down a final time, clipping her shoulder, then struck the bar. She felt a shudder, and the door exploded open.

Clare and Russ were flung backward and to the side as the pent-up water crashed through the bulkhead doorway into the cellar. The freezing water battered her, yanking her away from Russ, who was swinging one-handed in the torrent, clawing for the door handle. She dug her fingers into her wrists, locking herself around his waist. A wave slapped her face, leaving her blind and choking, and before she had the chance to hack the water from her mouth another one broke around her, and her head was underwater. She scrabbled at Russ's shirt, dragging herself up his body. She broke through to the air and gasped.

"—around my neck," Russ was shouting, and she flung one arm, then the other, around his neck and pushed herself up until her head was level with his. She wrapped her legs around his waist and hung on as they tossed in the torrent hurtling through the confines of the doorway. They pitched from side to side, water sluicing over their faces, floating higher and higher as the river sought its level. She felt Russ's arms straining downward against the flood tide, clinging to the door handle that had been their lifeline, but now threatened to anchor them under the rising water.

"It's too low!" she shouted in his ear. "You have to let go!"

"Hang on!" he shouted. She tightened her arms and legs and felt a jolt as he let go one hand and the water tried to sweep them away. He whacked his free hand against the door, fingers scratching for some purchase. His back shifted, he heaved his other hand forward, and they were head and shoulders above the water again. His arms were trembling with the effort of tethering them to the door.

She blinked the water out of her eyes and looked through the doorway, where a patch of steel-wool sky threw off just enough light to limn the bricks of the outer wall and the white froth of the river gushing over the rocky embankment and whirlpooling through the doorway. Russ held them fast through the suck and slop of the water crescendoing in dark currents between the stone walls. They bobbed higher. The cascade eased, from a dam spill to a millrace to a stream. The flow from the river outside eddied around them.

"Hold on," Russ said. "I'm gonna try to get us out of here." He released his hold and pulled them, hand over hand, along the upper edge of the door. They were floating so close to the ceiling that Clare bumped her head when Russ hauled forward.

They reached the edge of the bulkhead door. Russ jammed his fingers between the door and its frame. "I'm not going to try to swim across this. The cold. It's making it hard to move."

She jerked her head in a nod. From here, the bulkhead opening looked to be a mile wide. Her arms and legs felt heavy, detached. Her hands, clasped around her wrists, seemed to belong to another person. She had stopped shivering, stopped hurting. Instead, she felt numb. Numb and exhausted. And she hadn't even been working, like Russ had. She had just clung on like a limpet.

"I'm going overhand along the top of the door frame," he said. "Once we're out of the bulkhead, I think we'll be able to walk through the water toward the higher ground."

She nodded again.

"You okay?"

"Cold."

He rolled over, facing upward, and reached for the frame. Clare clung to his back, her hair trailing in the water, her face tipped high so she could breathe. Hand by hand, he carried them across the current. Her head bumped against something solid.

"Wall," she said.

He turned, plunging his hands in the water, feeling for the top of the bulkhead's outer wall. "Got it," he said. His voice was thin. Tired. "I'm holding on to it. Climb over my back up onto the bank. It's only about a foot underwater there. Keep to the building."

Clare had to flex her hands to get them to unlock. Her muscles were cramped and unwieldy. She could barely control her arms and legs as she splashed and floundered over Russ. For a second, reaching down past his head and feeling only more water, she panicked, until she struck the rubble that made up the narrow strip of land between the riverbed and the chandlery. She crawled onto it, turned to face Russ, and collapsed. The water came to her chest. "Give me your hands," she said. "I'll pull you over."

His flesh had all the warmth of a dead fish. She tightened her grip on his hands, braced her unfeeling feet against the edge of the bulkhead's stone wall, and, pushing and pulling, hauled him out of the pool that was the entrance to the cellar.

He flailed his way onto the submerged embankment and sagged against her, panting. "We gotta get out of here," he said when he had caught his breath.

Leaning on each other, they lurched to their feet. Standing, the water was up to her shins. Russ steered her toward the side of the building, and pressed to the wet bricks for balance, they staggered over the uneven, moss-slick stones of the embankment. Her clothes were so sodden, and her legs so deadened, that she didn't realize they were walking out of the river's overflow until she noticed that the slosh-slap of her steps had changed to a squish-squelch of boots on rock. She moved away from the wall. "Let me help you," she said, shouldering beneath his arm to act as his crutch. They stumbled over garbage and up the eroded slope to the road, and she could see Margy Van Alstyne's car, and it was the most welcome sight in the world.

They crossed the road like zombies. Russ popped open the driver's door, and Clare staggered around to the other side. They fell in at the same time, clunking the doors shut behind them. It took Russ three tries to get the keys out of his pants pocket, and when he finally started the engine and they were hit with the first blast of hot air from the vents, Clare went boneless. They sat in silence.

After a minute, she noticed his cell phone, dangling from the car charger. She tugged on the curly cord, fishing the phone off the floor. "Look," she said. "You're still connected to my phone." Which was lying somewhere at the bottom of the submarine cellar.

Russ didn't open his eyes. "Hear anything?"

She pressed the phone to her ear. "Glug, glug," she said. He rolled his head to look at her. She started to laugh. He blinked, then started to laugh as well. They laughed and laughed until their bodies shook and the Camry rocked and tears rolled down their cheeks.

Eventually, they wound down to gasps and sighs. She pressed the off button, hanging up on the river, and handed him the phone. He stared at it as if he was having a problem remembering what it was for. He looked at her. "If you were Allan Rouse, where would you be right now?"

"Home with my wife."

"That's my guess, too." He punched in a number.

"What are you going to do?" she asked.

"I'm going to send two cars over there. I'm going to have one of 'em stop at the station for some dry clothes. And I'm going to drive to Rouse's house and nail that son of a bitch to the wall."

CHAPTER 38

NOW

They pulled up behind a black-and-white already parked outside the Rouses' home. Butted up against Russ, supporting him as he limped to the door, Clare felt like a half-drowned cat returning home to the man who had stuffed her in a sack and tossed her in the river. The cold rain was a misery on her just-thawing skin. She thought the evening had inured her to further shock, but she blinked in surprise when the door was opened by Mrs. Marshall.

"Good God." Mrs. Marshall stepped aside, wrinkling her nose at the smell. They limped into the entrance hall. "What on earth happened to you?"

Clare could hear a drone of voices from the living room. "It's a long story," she said. "What are you doing here?"

Through the archway, she could see Renee Rouse, hovering over Officer Mark Durkee, who was reading the Miranda warning from a laminated card to a crumpled, raggedy figure curled up in the recliner. "Do you understand these rights as I have told them to you?" Durkee said.

"I . . ." Allan Rouse looked past him to Russ and Clare. He gaped. "I . . ."

"You tell him what the charges are yet?" Russ asked.

"We're starting with breaking and entering, resisting arrest, false imprisonment and attempted homicide." Durkee said.

"No!" Mrs. Rouse said.

Russ looked at her. "The good doctor here locked me and Reverend Fergusson into a flooding cellar. If we hadn't managed to break out, officer Durkee would be fishing for our corpses tomorrow."

"But—I didn't—" Rouse's face crumpled in on itself. "I never meant to hurt anybody!" He burst into sloppy sobs, burying his face in his hands.

Russ squelched into the barrel chair that Clare had so delicately perched on about a million years ago. He looked around the tastefully decorated room, stopping when his eyes fell on Mrs. Marshall. "Ma'am, what are you doing here? Did you know about Dr. Rouse's reappearance?"

Mrs. Marshall stood as far away from the rest of them as she could while still being in the room. "I did not. I arrived here a few minutes ago and was as surprised as you to see Allan back home."

"What brought you here in such lousy weather?"

"Renee called. She sounded distraught. She asked me to please come over." She looked at Clare, dripping onto the Aubusson carpet, at Dr. Rouse in his homeless-man disguise, and at Officer Durkee, snapping cuffs on the doctor. Her spine stiffened. "So far, this whole day has been an extraordinary and unpleasant novelty."

Clare caught Russ's glance and once again had the sensation of knowing exactly what he was thinking. *Not all of it.* Her cheeks flushed. He turned toward the Rouses. "And you two." His voice whipped across the room. "In addition to the criminal charges you're facing, you can expect bills from the volunteer fire department, the mountain rescue squad, and the state police diving team for services rendered during your faked disappearance. And I will personally urge Debba Clow and her mother to lodge civil complaints against the both of you." His mouth worked, as if he had bitten into something disgusting. He glared up at Mrs. Rouse, who was standing behind her husband's chair, her arms around his shoulders. "Was that all an act?" he asked her. "Waving the gun around? To cover up his footsteps? Throw us off?"

The expression on Renee Rouse's face was enough to convince Clare that her behavior hadn't been part of a plan. Mrs. Rouse opened her mouth, but her husband cut her off before she had the chance to speak.

"She didn't know anything. It was entirely my fault. Everything's been my fault."

Russ didn't take his eyes off Rouse. "Mark, take notes. I think Dr. Rouse wants to tell us what the hell's been going on."

Mark Durkee flipped a pad open and clicked his pen.

"If you have information that will exonerate your wife, now's the time to spill it. The DA's going to have some sympathy for a woman who's been driven to distraction because her husband's disappeared. She's going to be less kind to a co-conspirator."

Allan Rouse looked up at his wife. His face sagged in new folds. He seemed immeasurably older than he had when Clare had first seen him, only a month ago. "I'm sorry, sweetheart. I know it doesn't help, but I did it for you. To protect you." He twisted to face Russ. "I ran away. Because."

The room was silent except for Clare drip-drip-dripping onto the carpet. "Because," Russ prompted.

"Because I've been using the Ketchem endowment money for personal expenses." He glanced up at Mrs. Marshall. "I'm sorry, Lacey."

She stared at him. "For how long?"

He looked at his shoes. "Since your mother died." He lifted his head. "I needed it, Lacey. I had a growing family, and I was bleeding away my prime earning years in the clinic. Even with the extra cash, I was still making thousands less than my peers."

Mrs. Marshall held herself stiff, but her hands were shaking. She clasped them together. "Allan. My mother died thirty years ago. Are you telling me you've been embezzling from her trust all these years?"

"I needed it," he said. He twisted around, looking toward his wife again. "I wanted us to be able to afford a decent house. And to put money away for the kids' college tuition." He reached for her, the handcuffs clinking against each other. "I didn't blow it on crazy stuff. I just wanted to provide a good living for us."

Renee took his hands. Her brown eyes swam. "Sweetie, don't you know you didn't need to give me things?" Her voice was thready, choked out of a tight throat. "All I ever wanted was you, and our children, and a quiet life here at home."

"It wasn't that much," he said. "Just enough to give us some breathing room."

"It was three hundred thousand dollars," Mrs. Marshall said. Her tangerine-colored lips tightened. "That my mother intended to serve the poor and the sick."

Rouse whirled. "Your mother owed me," he said, all trace of apology gone from his tone.

Russ held up his hands leaving wet stains behind on the chair's arms. "Stop right there. Before we go any further, Dr. Rouse, I want your statement as to what happened the night of March nineteenth. Debba Clow, in a sworn statement, claims you called her, asked her to meet at the Ketchem family cemetery at Stewart's Pond, and, during your discussion, fell, injuring your head."

Rouse nodded. "I had been thinking a lot about Mrs. Ketchem. And Mr. Ketchem. Since I got the news about losing the trust money." He glanced at his wife. "I didn't really do any work when I went to the clinic that afternoon. I just needed time to think. There was a letter, from Lacey, to the board of aldermen, and when I read it, I knew that they'd be looking at the records of what I had done with the Ketchem funds. All I could picture was the scandal. Public disgrace. Prison. I decided to kill myself."

Mrs. Rouse let out a strangled moan. Her husband went on. "But I got to thinking about that Clow woman. And I thought, if I could just persuade her about the immunizations, that would make up a bit for what I'd done. Mrs. Ketchem would like it. So I did just like she said. I asked her to meet me, and we went, and we talked." His mouth twisted, and all at once he was the old Allan Rouse again. "The stupid woman couldn't get it into her head that infectious diseases can kill you no matter how many homeopathic remedies you dose yourself with. You just can't teach some people."

"Did you fall accidentally?" Russ said.

"Oh, yes." Rouse touched his head. "Worried me. I thought I might have concussed myself. But my vision was good, and I was alert. I didn't want that idiot Clow woman driving me back home. I intended to return to the clinic, leave Renee a note, and then use my gun." Mrs. Rouse made the noise again. "I'm so sorry, sweetheart." The doctor patted her hands as well as his cuffs allowed. "I just didn't want any of this to touch you."

"So what happened?"

"I guess the blow to my head was worse than I thought. I got into my car, started it up, and promptly drove myself into a tree." His gaze drifted to some middle distance. "I remember sitting there, in the dark and the cold, and thinking this was it. I had reached the absolute lowest point of my entire life." He shivered. "And then another car stopped to help me." His voice took on a note of wonder. "Skiers, going home to New York City. And it came to me, just like that, that I could go with them. That I didn't have to die. I could just . . . disappear." He looked up at Mrs. Marshall. "Like Jonathon Ketchem did." He glanced at Russ. "It was like I had been weighed down with heavy chains, and suddenly, I was free. I took my wallet and the cash I had taken out for our trip. I left everything else behind. I told them I lived in the city and they drove me the whole way. Once I was there . . ." He spread his elbows, showing off his scavenged-from-the-Dumpster attire. "It's very easy for a sixty-five-year-old man to vanish in New York City."

"So what brought you back?"

Clare thought of Hugh's phone call and knew before Dr. Rouse opened his mouth. "I read a story in the paper yesterday morning," he said. "About Renee." He looked up at her. She clapped her hands over her reddened cheeks. "I couldn't let her go on wondering what had happened to me. I knew I had to come back and explain everything."

"We appreciate that," Russ said.

"Sweetie, why didn't you tell me in the first place? I would have helped you."

Rouse shook his head. "I don't know. First it's one thing, then another, and another, and by the time you realize what's happening, the trouble's grown like a tumor and taken over your brain." He looked at Clare. "I'm sorry about locking you in that cellar. I just wanted to see Renee. I was still thinking that somehow I could get away from all this."

"I want to know why you had Renee call me," Mrs. Marshall said. Her usually pale cheeks were pinpointed with bright pink, and her voice was charged. "Was I to get an apology as well? Before you vanished for a second time?"

"I owe you an explanation," Rouse said.

"I should think so."

"Your mother would have understood. We grew very close those last months before she died. Near the end, she confided in me. So I'd understand what the clinic truly meant to her. It was a work of . . ." He looked to Clare. "What's it called when you do something to make up for a sin you've committed?"

"Expiation. Atonement. Redress."

"That's it. Lacey, for your mother, the clinic was a way to atone—"

"If you're going to tell me my mother killed my father, save your breath." Mrs. Marshall crossed her arms. "I already know."

Dr. Rouse stared.

"We sent a dive team into Stewart's Pond looking for your body," Russ said. "They brought up remains tentatively identified as Jonathon Ketchem's. The M.E. ruled cause of death was blunt-force trauma with a wide, flat instrument."

"A frying pan," Rouse said under his breath.

"Ahh," Mrs. Marshall sighed. "So Chief Van Alstyne was right." Clare looked at the older woman for any signs of distress or grief, but she seemed to have gained strength from Rouse's confirmation. Maybe having her father restored in memory outweighed the knowledge of what her mother had done.

"But you don't know why." Dr. Rouse's voice grew more certain.

"There are only a few reasons why people kill their spouses, and we see the same sad stories over and over again." Russ shifted forward in the barrel chair, as if he were about to rise. "Repeating one of 'em isn't going to help Mrs. Marshall. And it certainly can't make a difference to either of her parents at this point."

Dr. Rouse continued to look at Mrs. Marshall. "I know why," he said. "Do you want to know? Do you want to know what I've been carrying around ever since your mother made me her secret accomplice? God only knows, I'm tired of hauling it around."

Clare glanced around the room. Everyone, including Officer Durkee, was looking at the slim woman at the far edge of the archway.

"Yes," Solace Ketchem Marshall said. "Tell me."

CHAPTER 39

THEN

She saw them arrive in the pale silver light before dawn. She was up early, after the first good night's sleep she had had in three days, to check on Peter and Lucy. They were both sleeping, exhausted to the bone by the relentless coughing that had finally gotten all of the clinging phlegm out of their throats yesterday. They were cool to the touch when she laid hands on them, and as she walked soundlessly out of the back bedroom, where she had quarantined them, she thought about sending Jon over to the Norridges'. Mrs. Norridge bottled up lemon juice, and honey and lemon tea would help soothe the children's raw throats.

She paused at the kitchen window and there they were, three trucks this time—three!—barely visible against the ground fog rising from the water field. They turned up the barn lane and disappeared into the huge hay barn.

The scrape of boots on the floor turned her away from the window. Jon entered the kitchen, dropping a kiss on her cheek before opening the bread box and pulling out a half loaf. "How are they?"

For a moment, she thought he meant the men in the trucks. Then she recollected herself. "Better. They both slept through the night, and I expect sleep will be what they need for the next few days. I was hoping you could run to the Norridges' and pick up some of her lemon juice." She went to the icebox and grabbed a crock of butter. She dropped it onto the table next to him and watched while he sliced off a thick piece and buttered it. He liked something in his stomach before morning milking.

"Sure. I can take Jack along. Get one of them out of your hair."

She hugged him. "Would you? Thanks." She stepped back, her eyes falling on the window again. "They're here again. Three trucks this time."

"Huh. They must be hauling enough booze to float the fleet down in New York City." He patted her fanny, which always made her jump to make sure no one could see. "Don't worry about it, honey. They'll stay out of our way and we'll stay out of theirs."

"Have you gotten the money for this month yet?"

He tipped back his head and laughed. "You're the practical one, aren't you?" He grinned at her and she couldn't help smiling. "It's already swelling our bank account to unheard-of proportions. Demon Rum is going to make you a rich woman, Janie girl."

She slapped at his arm. "Rich or poor, those cows aren't going to wait. Get on with you."

◆ ◆ ◆

She had breakfast ready and Jack and Mary up by the time he returned from milking the herd and turning them out to water. Jack was a handful, cranky one moment and tearful the next. She clapped her hand to his forehead but didn't feel any fever coming on, thank God. She poured an extra lick of maple syrup into his oatmeal to keep him quiet while she buckled Mary into the high chair. She heard the splash of water at the pump outside where Jon cleaned up, and handed the baby her spoon.

He came through the back door, his normally cheerful face somber.

"What is it?" She laid his oatmeal bowl at his place and crossed to the stove to turn the eggs. "Something wrong with one of the cows?"

He glanced at Jack, busy scooping oatmeal into a pile and stirring syrup around it. "Seems the police have had extra patrols out. There was a close call. Some gunfire."

She turned toward him. "Good Lord. Anyone . . ." She didn't want to finish the sentence.

He shook his head. "No. But it's best if there isn't any activity tonight."

She spread her hands. *What?*

"No traveling tonight," he said, checking Jack again to see if he showed any signs of interest in the adult conversation. "Maybe tomorrow night."

"Oh, no." She flipped the eggs off the skillet onto a plate and slapped the cover on. "That wasn't the agreement. One night per visit, that's what they pay for."

Jon stood up from the table and crossed to the stove. He took her into his arms. "Janie, girl," he whispered in her ear, "these are desperate men with guns. If they want to extend their stay, they're going to do it." He released her and sat back down to his breakfast. "After all, what are we going to do?" He took a bite of oatmeal. "Call the cops?"

◆ ◆ ◆

She cleaned off the breakfast dishes and helped Peter and Lucy to the privy, since they were both so weak they could scarcely stand. Peter made her wait outside, but she sat with Lucy, singing and smoothing her hair while she did her business, and then propped them up on pillows and gave each of them a tray. Sweet tea and milk bread. She had just cracked open *The Blue Book of Fairy Tales* for a read when she heard Mary wailing from the nursery. Jane had gated the two littles in with enough blocks to make an entire city and the toy farm and Lucy's doll things—which were normally off-limits to Mary and therefore very enticing—and she had counted on at least a half hour before any crises. She was wound up to light into Jack, since she figured he had whacked Mary a good one to make her cry, so she was shocked beyond speech when she stepped over the gate to see her four-year-old sprawled unmoving among the tiny farm animals.

She snatched him up. Mary sobbed and sobbed, reaching for her mother for comfort. Jane sat on the floor Indian-style and rested her son in her lap while wrapping one arm around her frightened toddler. Jack was hot to the touch, but pale, his lips and the edges of his ears and nostrils tinged almost dusky blue. His little chest shuddered beneath his shirt, heaving with the effort to breathe. Jane pried his mouth open and recoiled when she saw the gray and white blotches coating his tongue and throat as far as she could see.

Dear Lord, she thought. The black diphtheria.

◆ ◆ ◆

There was no choice for it. She abandoned Mary, howling, in the nursery, where at least the gate would keep her out of harm's way. She wrapped Jack in a baby quilt and clutched him against her shoulder, hoping the upright position would help his breathing. Then she set out across the barnyard to find Jon.

The wind was raw in her face, the bite of it bringing tears to her eyes, and she half walked, half ran along the fence until she saw him. He was manuring the cornfield, and he pulled Gig and Haley up when he saw her. He was off the seat and halfway across the field when she reached him. "Jack's sick," she said, before he had a chance to ask what she was doing wading through the mucky soil in her house shoes.

He wrapped his arms around them and kissed Jack. "Hey, little man," he said. "You're not feeling good?" His voice was easy, but when he turned to her, his face was drawn.

"I think it's the black diphtheria," she whispered.

"How could it be?" He lowered his voice as well, although the only creatures within earshot were the horses, standing stolid and disinterested in their harness. "The other kids—"

"Maybe they had something else. Or maybe they had it easy. Or maybe I'm wrong." Her voice broke. She took a deep breath to calm herself. She had to stay calm. "We need the doctor to see him. Hitch Gig and Haley up and go fetch him." Jon looked over to the silage barn. "Now," she said.

She returned to the house while Jon took the horses to the barn. She propped Jack into the padded chair in the parlor, covered him with a quilt, and wheeled the butler's table, one side extended like a tray, next to him. Upstairs, Mary had collapsed onto a quilt and fallen asleep, her fat cheeks red and streaked with the salt trail of tears. Jane eased her and her quilt off the rug and laid her in her crib, giving her a guilty kiss for leaving her alone to cry herself to sleep.

She set the kettle on to steam Jack and looked in on the olders. Peter was reading to himself from the fairy tales, and Lucy had fallen asleep. Peter looked up when she came in. "Mama, where were you?" His voice was a hoarse whisper. "I heard you run out of the house, and Mary was crying and crying. It was really annoying." At that moment, Jane could have kissed him for his seven-year-old's inability to see past his own nose.

"Jack's sick, and I had to get your daddy to go fetch Dr. Stillman. I'm back now. Let me know if you need me, but do it quiet. Lucy needs her sleep."

In the parlor, Jack roused enough to protest when she draped him with a pillowcase and slipped a pan of steaming hot water beneath him. Beneath the clock chiming noon, she could hear Jon entering the kitchen. She hurried in. He was standing there, not reaching for his good coat, not taking a cup of milk before the road, not doing anything. Just standing there.

"For heaven's sake," she said. "Get a move on. And when you're at the doctor's, ask to use their telephone and call your parents. I'm going to need your mother to help me with nursing and taking care of the baby." Still he didn't move. "Jon?" He looked at her. "Jon, what is it?"

"I can't go."

She stared at him. She knew what the words meant, but they made no sense, any more than if he had said, "I can't fly" or "I can't leap over the barn." He reached for her hands. "The bootleggers. They won't let me go. They said they're afraid the police will question me about have I seen 'em." He looked out the window. "I guess maybe they're afraid I'm chickening out."

She pulled her hands from his. "That's ridiculous. You're not going to the police. You're going for the doctor. Why on earth would we turn them in? We've made more money from sheltering them over the past twelvemonth than this farm's earned in the last five years." She looked up at him. "Oh, for heaven's sakes. Are the horses hitched to the buggy?"

He nodded.

"I'll go talk to them. You stay with Jack and make sure he doesn't burn himself on the hot water. There's more on the stove when his pan cools down." She whipped off her apron, tossed it on the back of a chair, and strode out the door before Jon could answer.

Bright sunshine dazzled the whitewash on the barns and chicken coop but gave off no warmth. When she plunged through the door of the hay barn, the contrast between the light and the dark blinded her. She couldn't hear anyone, although she could smell tobacco smoke and briefly wondered if any of the rumrunners was countryman enough to know that you don't let sparks among the hay. "Who's in charge here?" she said.

A man appeared at the edge of the loft above. She couldn't make out his features, but he wore a fancy city hat that was as out of place as she would have been in a Broadway speakeasy. "You must be the missus," he said.

"My husband's harnessed up our team to go to town and fetch the doctor. He's going to leave now. He'll be back as soon as he reaches Dr. Stillman. He's not going anywhere but Dr. Stillman's and he's certainly not about to go yapping to the police."

"No one's going anywhere."

She looked up through the gloom. "I'm not going to get a crick in my neck arguing with you. Come down here and talk to me."

The man laughed, but descended the ladder, taking care not to brush his suit against the rungs. She was surprised when he faced her. He was younger than she was, and looked as sober and respectable as Dr. Fillmore, the Presbyterian minister. His voice was the only thing that gave him away. "Here I am, lady. You can get me to move, but your husband ain't going anywhere."

"One of my children is very sick. He needs a doctor's care. There's no more or less to it than that."

"The roads are swarming with cops on patrol. No one leaves this hay rack until I say so."

"My son needs a doctor!"

"So does he." He glanced toward the back of the barn. "Hey, Ted, bring Etienne out here." Two more men walked from behind an ancient phaeton, dragging a third between them. The young man—scarcely more than a boy—was open-shirted, and his chest and shoulder were bound in a bloodstained bandage. The men holding him wore shoulder holsters stuffed with wicked-looking black-barreled handguns.

"Good Lord." She covered her mouth.

"We're not getting any help for Etienne, and you're not getting help for your kid." He grinned at her, the choirboy smile of someone whose worst sin was skipping school to catch frogs. "Don't worry. Kids get sick all the time. And we'll be gone tomorrow night."

"Tomorrow!" His words jerked her attention from the wounded boy. "We can't wait that long." She tugged on her dress, pulling herself together. They were, after all, in business together. After a fashion. And she could conduct business. "Even if my husband ran into the police on the road, there's no reason for them to suspect him of anything more than what he is—a farmer going to town for the doctor. We'd be crazy to turn any of you in. We're outside of the law ourselves, giving your people shelter all these months. Do you think we'd risk putting ourselves in jail?"

"Lady, maybe you're not aware that Judge Jacob DeWeese is the fellow we'd come before if we was caught up here in Podunk County. DeWeese doesn't like us gentlemen bandits, don'tcha know. Just last month he gave three guys from Avenue B ten years hard labor in Clinton." He grinned at her again. This time, she saw the edge of his teeth. "My boys and me ain't planning on sweating out the next ten years of our lives building roads and shoveling snow. We're staying put. And you're staying put." He grasped her upper arm, a light and unthreatening touch that sent her skin crawling. "You been good hosts for our guys. I'd hate to have to hurt you or your husband." He steered her toward the door. "Now, you run along. And as soon as we're out of your hair, you can get the doc for your little fellow."

He released her, and she stumbled out the door into the cold sunshine. She blinked. She swung around, but the door shut in her face. She didn't know what to do. She took a few steps toward the cow barn. Gig and Haley waited in harness near the wide front doors. Could she snatch them and ride off? No, that was ridiculous. Those two couldn't outrun a bullet. Maybe Jon could hike up the back forty to the woods? There were trails there that led through the mountains toward Millers Kill. Of course, Jon was no woodsman. She looked past the open fields and fences to the distant tree line. He'd be spotted long before he reached the shelter of the forest. She circled slowly where she stood. Everything was familiar to her, the house, the coop, the barns. The chickens pecking in their run, the horses waiting in their harness. It was as if she had never seen any of it before. She was a stranger here herself.

CHAPTER 40

THEN

FRIDAY, MARCH 14, 1924

Mary fell sick around midnight. Jane was asleep, but wakened to the baby's faint whimpering sound as if a gunshot had gone off in her ear. She sat up, disoriented for a moment by the darkness and the lack of Jon in the bed. No, that was all right. He was sitting up with Jack. So she could sleep. She paused, halfway down to the bed again, but the sound came again. Not Mary's usual squawk-then-resettle. Jane swung out of bed and padded to the nursery.

Pale. Feverish. Dusky blue. Jane clamped her teeth together to keep from crying out. She lifted the baby from her crib and settled her on her shoulder. Mary's breath rasped and rattled in her ear all the way downstairs.

Jon was sitting in one of the parlor chairs, Jack asleep on his chest. A lantern burned beside them, casting shadows over the cups and liniment bottles and rags littering the table. "What are you—" He broke off when he saw Mary.

"The baby's got it." Jane crouched down next to the chair. "We have to do something."

"What?" Jon's voice was as hoarse and choked as Peter's. "Tell me what to do and I'll do it. Tell me how to get past those men without getting a gunshot to the back. Tell me."

She drew another chair near and picked up the glass of salt and goldenseal gargle she had prepared earlier. She poured some one-handed into a child's cup and, seating Mary on her lap, forced some of the liquid into her mouth. The baby spluttered and gagged. Jane clamped a rag over her mouth and let her cough it out. Then she looked at Jon.

"You'll have to go through the woods."

"They'll hear me if I take one of the horses out of the barn."

"On foot. Go through the woods on foot until you reach the telegraph line. You can follow that down to town."

"That'll take all night!"

"And you could have Dr. Stillman here by the morning. Once he's here, there won't be anything they can do about it."

"What if they try to hurt the doctor? What if they try to hurt you or the children after he's gone?"

"They're not going to show themselves to the doctor. And . . . and . . ." She cast about for a way to ensure the bootleggers wouldn't hurt them out of spite.

"I could collect some of the neighbors on my way back. Have 'em show up here with their guns."

"Good Lord, no. That's all we need. A shoot-out in our barnyard. No, you stay in town after you fetch the doctor. I'll tell them that you're returning after they leave, and if we aren't all okay, you're going to the police with their names and descriptions and license plate numbers and what all."

"I don't like it."

"I don't care." Her voice cracked on the last word. "Look at them." She brushed Mary's fine blond hair away from her forehead. The two-year-old's chest heaved as the air whistled in and out of her throat. Jack was asleep, barely breathing, deep plum-colored circles beneath his eyes and every freckle standing out against his pale cheeks like ink scattered across a page.

"Okay. I'll go." Jon stood, settling their son against a pillow in the chair and drawing the quilt back over him.

"Change into something dark. And warm."

He nodded and disappeared upstairs. Mary on her shoulder, she went into the kitchen and threw a few splits of wood into the stove. She pumped water into the kettle and set it on to boil. Jon returned, wearing his green twill pants and brown barn coat. "How's this?"

"Good," she said. "Don't forget your hat and gloves."

He looked as if he wanted to smile for her, but couldn't. Instead, he wrapped her and the baby in a bear hug. "I love you," he said.

"I love you, too. Be careful."

Then he was gone. Hushing the baby, she circled around the stairs and went into the darkened dining room. Through its window, she could just make out Jon's outline as he crossed beneath her wash line, heading for the fields. She wanted to plaster herself to the glass and watch him until he was safe out of sight, but she made herself turn and retrace her steps back to the kitchen. Normal. In control. She had children to look after.

She peeped in on the olders. She was worried about Lucy, as well, who had slept almost all of the day and had no appetite when awake. In the light from the kitchen, she could see where heavy, rust-tinged phlegm had run from her daughter's nose and mouth to stain the pillowcase. *Oh, Lord, that doesn't look good.* She was on her way to get a rag to clean it up when she heard the shot.

Oh sweet Jesus no. Her body urged her to race out the door and find her husband. Her body told her to flee to the back bedroom and hide in the dark. Caught between impossible demands, she trembled, frozen, in the hallway. There was no other noise. There were no more shots. And then she heard it, the sound of footsteps and a man's complaining, and, thank God, thank God, Jon's voice, demanding to be let go.

The door burst open and the fancy suit came in, followed by two men she hadn't seen before, controlling Jon with his arm twisted up to the middle of his back.

She clutched Mary to her. Her nightgown covered her more than many dresses, but it was still her nightgown, and no man other than her father and husband had ever seen her in one. She jerked her chin up. "Let my husband go."

The man in the fancy suit laughed. "You got a spunky one there, mister. You ever have to wallop her one to make her mind?" He gestured toward the kitchen. "Take him in there."

Jane scurried ahead of them. She shut the bedroom door and backed against it.

"What's in there?" one of the men asked. He had a droopy mustache that could have belonged to a dime-novel cowboy.

"Two sick children," she said. She was amazed her voice didn't shake. "Who need to see the doctor."

The fancy suit indicated his men should sit Jon at the table. They released his arm, and he rubbed his wrist, watching them all the while with wide, white-rimmed eyes.

"That's what I mean. We've already been through this, but you didn't listen. You've got kids. What do you do if they don't listen to you?" He stared at her. "You wallop 'em."

She hugged Mary so tightly the baby started to cry, a thin, mewling version of her usual full-lunged bawl. "Don't you touch my children," Jane said. "Don't you dare touch them."

The young man touched his chest. "What kind of a person do you think I am? I don't hurt kids." He nodded to the man with the droopy mustache, who grabbed Jon's wrist and prized his hand flat. The fancy-suited man pulled a gun from beneath his jacket. Jane opened her mouth to plead, to shriek, when he reversed the gun in his hand and smashed the butt end against Jon's index finger.

Jon screamed. The third man leaned against his shoulders, forcing him into the chair, while the droopy mustache pushed his hand open. Jane saw the young man's arm rise, the carbon gleam of the gun's handle, like a ball-peen hammer, and then he smashed it down again, shattering Jon's middle finger.

Her husband screamed and wept and howled. Mary wailed breathlessly, and from behind the bedroom door, Jane heard Lucy cry out and Peter stumble from his bed. The man in the fancy suit looked at her, eyebrows raised. "Well? Go settle 'em down."

She sidled through the door, closing it behind her. "Shh. Sssh."

"Mama, I can't see!"

"Get back into bed, Peter."

Lucy's voice was weak and clogged with phlegm. "Mama?"

"Daddy's had an accident. He hurt his hand, but he'll be all right. He didn't mean to wake you up. Everything's fine. Go back to sleep now." She stepped through the door and latched it behind her.

Jon was rocking in the kitchen chair, hunched over his hand, moaning again and again. "Since we're all friends, I'll consider this a lesson learned." The man in the fancy suit slid his gun back into its holster. "You've been good hosts over these past months, and this is a real good stop along the trail. I'd hate to have to kill one of you." He looked at Jane. Smiled a choirboy smile beneath dead eyes. "So I trust this is the last time we'll have to have this conversation."

Jane nodded.

"Good. Let's go, boys. Ted's got the next watch, so we can catch some shut-eye." He smiled at Jane. "I suggest you do the same, missus."

◆ ◆ ◆

Jack died at ten o'clock in the morning.

◆ ◆ ◆

After that she stopped thinking, stopped feeling. She trundled around, a mechanical mother wheeling on a track; wipe off Lucy's nose, coax Peter to eat something, balance Mary over the steaming pan, take one child to the privy, take another, clean up Lucy's lunch after she vomited it all over the floor, bathe the baby to cool her fever, bring Peter paper and pencils.

She didn't tell the other children about their brother. She lost track of Jon. He was insubstantial, somehow, a ghost flitting through the rooms. They were all ghosts, waiting for darkness to come and set them free.

The men left half an hour before midnight. Three trucks, lights out, rumbling over the lane and away down the road. As soon as they were gone, she and Jon went to the barn and harnessed the horses. They worked quickly, silently. She didn't want to talk with him, and she didn't want to think why. It was important, the most important thing in the world, that he be gone, that he fetch the doctor, and once that happened, everything would be all right. Everything would fall into place again.

"Janie," he said, perched on the buggy seat. There was that in his voice that would shatter her like the bones in his fingers. If she let it.

"Hurry," she said, and turned to the house. Inside, she stoked the stove, put the kettle on, opened another can of liniment to rub into Mary's chest. She was up in the nursery, and even from the kitchen Jane could hear her, rattling and choking, fighting for each breath.

She checked in on the olders before heading upstairs. Peter was sleeping. His breathing was easy, and except for his pallor and his listlessness, she thought him well on the mend. More rheum had run from Lucy's mouth and nose onto her pillow. Jane swiped it off—she had changed the pillowcase three times during the day—and laid a hand on Lucy's forehead.

She was cool. Jane crouched down beside her daughter's bed. She put her other hand on Lucy's chest. Which was silly. Cool flesh was a good sign. No fever. She waited. She waited for Lucy's chest to rise and fall. Nothing happened.

"Lucy." She shook the girl. "Lucy, wake up." She shook her harder. "Lucy." She sat on the bed, scooped her daughter into a sitting position. Lucy's arms and head flopped. "Lucy." She shook her, hard, and pressed her ear to her daughter's mouth. Nothing. She pushed Lucy's hair, sticky from the phlegm and greasy from days in bed, away from her face. Her sweet face. The girl was so proud of her thick brown hair. She would have to wash it, Lucy would hate to—but she couldn't see anymore, not the dirty hair, not the still face, as the tears blinded her eyes and she curled around her little girl and sobbed.

◆ ◆ ◆

Sometime later, she came to herself again. The kettle was singing on the stove. She tucked Lucy into bed, flipping the pillow around so her head rested on the clean side. She took the liniment from the kitchen table and went upstairs. Mary was lying in her crib, her eyes open but unfocused, the way she looked some mornings right after she had awoken. Beneath her gown, her chest and belly flexed. Dragging a breath in. Forcing a breath out. Jane opened the gown, rubbed the liniment in with firm strokes, and lifted her from the crib. She wrapped her in a light quilt and settled into the rocking chair, cradling her baby girl. She had nursed her in this very chair. Not so many months ago. She looked down. In the shadowed light, Mary's eyes met hers. Her little body eased as she relaxed into her mother's arms. Soon, the doctor would be here. Soon, everything would be all right. Jane cuddled her baby close. The weight, the heft of her. The life of her. She began to rock.

CHAPTER 41

NOW

TUESDAY, APRIL 4, AND WEDNESDAY, APRIL 5

After Officer Durkee had removed Allan Rouse to the station for book-ing, Clare, backed up by the just-arrived Lyle MacAuley, insisted Russ get checked out at the hospital. He left, under protest, in his deputy chief's care.

She wanted Mrs. Marshall to go, too. "I don't think you should be alone," she said. "And I certainly don't think you ought to be driving home this late at night all by yourself."

The older woman patted her arm. She had actually hugged Allan and Renee as they left, a shining example of Christian forbearance Clare wasn't certain she could have emulated. "I'll be fine, dear."

"You've had a pretty big shock. Please, at least just let me call Mr. Mad-sen and have him take you home. You can wait here until he comes." She looked around at the Rouses' well-made furniture, their family pictures, the books and magazines in the glass-fronted cases. She wondered what had been earned, and what had been stolen from Jane Ketchem's money.

Mrs. Marshall did that mind-reading thing again. "What am I going to do with the trust money?"

Clare didn't pretend to misunderstand. "Money isn't good or bad in and of itself. It's what you do with it."

Mrs. Marshall bit her lip, scraping a spot in her lipstick. "It might as well have been a blood payment for my brothers' and sisters' lives. For my parents' lives."

"However they earned that money, whatever your mother did, surely she sacrificed enough to make it clean."

"You'd think so." The older woman's voice regained some of its tart-ness. "Unfortunately, for thirty years it's benefited the Rouse family in-stead of the clinic. That's not what she wanted. I feel . . ." She took Clare's hands. "I feel as if I owe it to her to do something with it. Owe it to all of them."

"Something . . . that's not the church roof?"

"Not all of it. Would you think it terrible of me if I only put in enough for the immediate work? If we had to rely on fund-raising to make up the rest?"

Clare shook her head. "I was never wild about the idea of taking the money away from the clinic. Do you want to set the trust back up again? Make payments to the board of aldermen this time, to keep it all out in the open?"

"I don't know. The clinic's gotten along without it perfectly well all these years. I believe I'd like to find something more personal."

Clare smiled slowly. "Let me introduce you to Debba Clow."

"The one who won't vaccinate her child?"

"We're working on that. Maybe hearing your parents' story might help. I have her number in my—" Clare slapped her pockets, reflexively patting for her cell phone, until she remembered where it was. Her clothes were half dried by now, and smelled of mildew. "Never mind. She has a son, Skylar, who could benefit from someone with deep pockets taking an interest in him. She wants to teach him at home, and they could use aides, autism specialists, extra speech and occupational therapy—you could make a difference. And it would be"—she smiled a little—"personal."

With a little more pressing, Mrs. Marshall agreed that they should call Mr. Madsen, and the elderly attorney seemed happy enough to be of service. "When you're my age," he said, "you don't sleep all that much anyway."

By the time they dropped Clare off in front of the historical society to retrieve her car, she was pretty well dried off. She sat behind the wheel for several minutes. Debating: Rectory? Or the hospital? She didn't surprise herself when she went for the hospital. If Russ had been released, she'd be on her way without much time lost. If he was still there, and awake, they could talk. She could picture herself, sitting on the edge of his bed. Maybe holding his hand. And they would talk.

Her clericals did the trick again, getting her past admissions after hours. Although the security guard in charge did look strangely at her. Walking past the dark plate-glass window of the gift shop, she saw why. In addition to the reek and the damp wrinkles, her black blouse and pants were streaked with dried mud, and her hair was—well, better not to think of it. Russ didn't care.

She took the elevator up to the third floor. "I'm here to see Russ Van Alstyne," she said to the charge nurse. "Downstairs, they told me he had been admitted?"

"That's right." The nurse, a twenty-something man with curling hair, flipped open a chart. "He had to have his leg recast. And he had some signs of fluid in his lungs, so he's being kept overnight for observation. But I'm afraid he's asleep now." He looked at her clerical collar. "Are you his . . . ?"

She smiled over her disappointment. "Just let him know that Clare Fergusson stopped by to see him. Thanks." She pushed away from the nursing station's counter.

"Excuse me?" A voice hailed from down the hall. "Are you Clare Fergusson?" Clare turned. A pocket goddess—there was no other word for her—was walking toward her. She smiled and waved. "I was just coming out to grab another cup of tea and I heard your name." She was tiny, curvy, with a tousle of Marilyn Monroe hair and a flawless complexion. She reached for Clare's hand. "I just had to say thank you." Up close, she had soft-edged lines around her eyes and overlapping front teeth that made her smile charming instead of perfect. "I'm Linda Van Alstyne."

Clare moved her hand up and down, propped a smile on her face, said something.

"Mother Van Alstyne told me you were the one who got Russ out of the woods and to the hospital when he broke his leg. I'm so grateful. He just goes out and does these crazy things, you know." She laughed. Musically, of course. "So I'm glad he has friends looking out for him."

Clare said something else. She thought she might melt into the floor, like the Wicked Witch of the West. She was the Wicked Witch. She deserved melting.

"Were you visiting someone from your church?"

Clare's mouth worked.

"Well, it's great to finally meet you. I'll tell Russ you said hi, okay?" She gave Clare's hand a final squeeze and glided back up the hall to the kitchenette like the woman in the Roethke poem. Describing circles as she moved.

Clare felt her way to the elevator. Sometime later, she found herself in the chapel room. She sat for a long time in the half-light, staring at the nondenominational wall hanging at the front of the room. Just sitting. Then she thought. Then she prayed. After a while, she rose from her seat and went into the family lounge next door, which had vending machines, a coffeemaker, long sofas—and a writing desk, stocked with hospital stationery. A sixtyish couple slept on one of the sofas, he stretched out with his head in her lap, she sitting, her head tipped, snoring. Clare pulled the desk chair out as quietly as possible. She sat, head bowed, over the tablet of writing paper. Then she wrote. It wasn't a long letter. It fit on a single sheet of paper. When she was done, she folded the sheet into an envelope and printed Russ's name on it.

She took the elevator back up to the third floor. The charge nurse tilted back in his chair and scruffed his curls when he saw her. "Didn't expect you back."

She slid the letter across the counter. "Could you see that Mr. Van Alstyne gets this? When he's awake?"

"Okay."

She hesitated. "It's for him. Nobody else."

He searched her face. "I understand."

She turned her back on the ward and its inhabitants, took the elevator down, and left the hospital without looking behind her. But in her car, she thought about it. The dark space and the rising water and his hands tangling in her hair. Then she shifted into gear and drove home.

CHAPTER 42

NOW

APRIL 22, THE GREAT VIGIL OF EASTER

He was sitting in the dark in the rearmost pew of St. Alban's Church holding a candle and he didn't know why.

No, that was a lie. He had done what she asked him to in that damn letter. He had stayed away and he hadn't called her. He had shown up at the Kreemy Kakes Diner and sat alone for the past two Wednesdays, impatient and pissed off, wondering when she was going to snap out of it and call him.

At some point between Wednesday lunch and this Saturday evening, he had realized she wasn't. Which should have been hunky-dory with him, except that he had found himself crammed into a corner of his office, the edge of his hand in his mouth, trying not to let Harlene hear him. Crying, for Chrissakes, like a baby.

He just wanted to talk with her. If she was going to cut him off, he wanted to hear it from her, not from some piece of paper. She had asked him not to contact her. Fine. She hadn't written anything about not showing up in church. He had seen the service listed in the paper. How could he have guessed the church was going to be full at ten o'clock on Saturday night?

There was a rustling, and everyone went quiet, and then Clare was at the door, surrounded by a bunch of other people, all of them in white robes. A skinny, balding guy was holding a candle nearly as big as he was. Clare was cupping some sort of bowl, and he was startled when something inside it flashed into flame. It was the only light in the building, and it made her look like a priestess from a time before anybody had even dreamed of Christianity.

"Dear friends in Christ," Clare said, in a voice that rang over the stone and carried to every corner. "On this most holy night, in which our Lord

Jesus passed over from death to life . . ." She went on with the invocation and then invited everyone to pray. He ducked his head. Everyone else seemed to know the words. Then the skinny guy backed away and brought the tip of the huge candle down to the bowl, lighting it. The white-robed people, all of whom had plain white tapers stuck in cardboard disks just like his, lit their candles from the big one. Then they touched candles with the folks sitting nearby, and next thing he knew, the guy sitting next to Russ was lighting his candle and gesturing for him to pass it on. The fire flowed forward, a wave of tiny lights surging to the front of the church until the whole space was illuminated.

Pretty impressive. He turned to look at the fire that had started it all and caught Clare just as she glanced toward his pew. Her eyes widened, but then she and the others were all marching up the aisle and there was a lot of fiddling with the big candle and the skinny guy singing about rejoicing. He went on and on about the candle and the light and the night being a Passover.

Then Clare said, "Let us hear the record of God's saving deeds in history," and the congregation got to sit down. After that, there was an endless string of Bible readings, the choir singing a psalm, and a prayer, one right after another. Russ felt like a kid again, trapped in the Methodist church with his mom pinching him whenever he squirmed. He amused himself by tipping his candle from one side to the next, laying out the melted wax in patterns, until Clare walked to the pulpit and began her sermon.

"And so the Day dawns," she said. "You cannot stop it, no matter how much you might want to cling to the ordinary and the mundane. The day breaks, the mourners come, the stone is rolled away. 'Why do you seek him here, among the dead? Go, he is living.' And everything is changed."

He knew he was imagining it, that there was no way she could see through the darkness and the light all the way to the back row, but it felt as if she were talking to him. Only to him.

"How frightening to embrace life, when one expected cold stillness. Scary. But none of us can stop it, and we're wrong to try. We become used to deadening who we are and what we feel, but now the stone is rolled away. We cannot wrap the linens around ourselves again. No one ever promised that transformation was easy, but we are called to have courage. And faith." She smiled, radiating light, and he could feel his heart cracking. "I want to walk the road with you, equally amazed, and see what we can make out of a world so new and so different."

There was more, much more, three people baptized, and everyone vowing to renounce evil, and then the white-robed assistants pulled down black cloths that had been covering the cross at the front of the church and everyone shouted "Alleluia!" like it was a big party. The lady to his right took pity on him and handed him an open book, pointing out where they were in the service, and he realized it wasn't that they all had memorized the words, it was that everyone read from the same book.

He didn't go up for communion. He sat while the rest of his pew shuffled by, and he knelt when they did for the prayers, and he stood when Clare shouted, "Go in peace! To love and serve the Lord! Alleluia!" Then he waited, while the people around him hugged one another and rattled on about their Easter Sunday plans and left by twos and threes.

Eventually, there were only two left. He sat while she pulled off the heavy satin drape she had donned before celebrating the Eucharist, folded it, and laid it crossways over the altar rail. He sat, and she walked down the aisle, taking her time, and slid into the pew, next to him, as if meeting him in her church after midnight was a usual part of her routine.

Then he noticed her hands, half covered by her white linen robe. Shaking. "So. What did you think of the great vigil?" she said.

"It was beautiful. Long, but beautiful."

They sat for a moment. Then she said, "You're interested in developing your faith life?"

"That sounds like something they teach you to say in *Ministers Monthly* magazine."

"Yeah. Well. It's not the done thing to ask someone what they're doing in your church."

"I came to see you. To talk."

"I thought I covered everything in that note."

"You know what really killed me about that Dear John letter? You signed it 'Love, Clare.'"

She looked down at her lap. "That's a common way of ending a letter."

"Yeah. Right."

She glared at him. "You're a man in love with his wife, Russ."

He pointed toward the altar. "And you're a woman in love with her boss."

She looked at him blankly, then hiccuped up a laugh. "I guess you're right."

He turned to face her. "Clare, I love you."

Her laughter vanished. Her eyes widened. "I can't believe you said that."

He pushed on. "And you love me, too." She pressed her hands over her mouth. She shook her head. "You can't make that disappear by writing me a letter. Were you listening to your sermon? I was. You can't make yourself dead again when you've come alive. So you're scared. Christ knows, I am, too. But like you said. We have to have courage."

She bent over, breathing deeply.

"Clare?" He tried to see her face. "Clare? You're not going to faint, are you?"

She let out another short laugh. "No." She sat up, took a breath, then stood. "Come here."

He grabbed the cane he used to help him get around in his walking cast and followed her up the aisle, across, to a place where the pews had been cleared away. He could see from the water damage that this was where the roof had given in.

"This is the window that Mrs. Marshall gave in her mother's memory. It's hard to see at nighttime, but you can make the details out."

He looked at it.

"I've been thinking a lot about the Ketchems. About what went wrong for them, and for Allan Rouse. I think they all saw something they wanted, something they were tempted by, and they said, 'I deserve this.'" She looked up at him. "I don't want to make the same mistake."

He reached out and took her hand in his. "I'm not trying to talk you into an . . . an affair. I don't want to be unfaithful to my vows."

She smiled, a shaky, crooked smile. "Me, neither."

"There's something in me that recognized you. Right from the start. The parts of me that always felt alone, the parts of me that I always kept hidden away, out of sight—I could see that you had them, too." He smiled a little. "Sorry. I'm not saying this very smoothly."

She stepped closer. "I never asked you to be smooth. Just to be yourself."

He had to close his eyes for a moment, to get himself under control. "That's just it. I know I can tell you, 'This is who I am.' And your answer will always be—"

"Yes."

"Yes."

"I didn't want to fall in love with you," she said. He tightened his grip on her hand. "I'm sorry." Her voice was on the edge of crying.

"Oh, love." He let his cane clatter to the stone floor and pulled her to him. "Why?"

She tipped her head back to meet his eyes. "Because we're going to break our hearts."

He wanted to reassure her, but what could he say? She was right. So he rocked her back and forth and they clung to each other, while the candles burned down and the sad-faced angels held out their glass promises. *For he doth not afflict willingly, nor grieve the children of men.*

1. In an interview, Julia Spencer-Fleming said, "In *Out of the Deep I Cry*, Clare Fergusson talks a couple of times with the historical society's librarian. Unbeknownst to her (or to any reader, because the fact isn't spelled out anywhere) he is dying from cancer. Does this affect the plot? Not in the least. But I could picture his lank, wasted frame, his curt, don't-waste-any-time way of speaking, and the way he was sinking into his devotion for his collection—the thing that would outlive him. He became a fully realized person to me, and so I was able to make him a more fully realized character in the book, despite the fact that his entire appearance is limited to a few pages." Do you have a sense that other characters also have an unspoken backstory? Which ones? What do you think theirs might be?

2. Much of *Out of the Deep I Cry* takes place in the 1920s and 1930s. What about those years, as revealed in the book, seemed most alien to a modern sensibility? What seemed most familiar?

3. Listening to Renee Rouse, Clare muses that in all love stories, the couple seems "destined to fall in love." Is this true about Clare and Russ?

4. What do you think about Linda Van Alstyne? Is she the kind of woman you expected? What do her interactions with her husband—over the phone—and with Clare tell you about her marriage?

5. Did Russ and Clare go too far over the line when they were trapped in the flooded cellar? Should Russ have accepted Clare's "Dear John" letter?

6. The mystery in *Out of the Deep I Cry* is entangled with the issue of vaccination, past and present. What do you think of Debba Clow's reasons for not vaccinating her daughter? Is the risk of the return of epidemics worth the right of parents to decide for their children?

7. We get to see a lot of Clare's ministry in this book: performing liturgies, counseling, dealing with the nuts and bolts of running a church. What do you think of her as a priest? Would you want her as your minister?

St. Martin's
Griffin

8. At the end of *Out of the Deep I Cry*, Clare says, "We're going to break our hearts." Is she right? What could she and Russ have done to avoid getting to this place?

9. The book has a complicated framework—the present-day story straightforward, the historical tale scooping backward through the 70s, the 50s, the 30s, and into the 1920s. Did this make it difficult to follow the plot? How did "reading backward" affect your sense of the characters in the past?

10. Does the eighteen-year-old Russ we meet at the beginning of the story seem like he could grow up to be the forty-nine-year-old man we see in the rest of the book?

11. The weather and the landscape around Miller's Kill play an almost characterlike role in the book. Why does the author rely on nature so much? Can you think of other novels where the setting is so intrinsic to the story?

12. What do you think of Jane Ketchem? Is she a murderer? What do you think might have happened to her if she had confessed to Chief McNeil?

13. Young Allan Rouse's reasons for becoming a doctor have more to do with security and status than a desire to heal the sick. Yet he stays as the clinic's physician for a lifetime. Is he a bad doctor? Is he an immoral man?

For more reading group suggestions, visit
www.readinggroupgold.com.

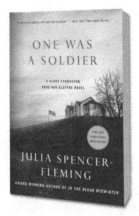

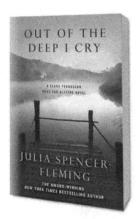